image comics presents

THE WALKING DEAD™

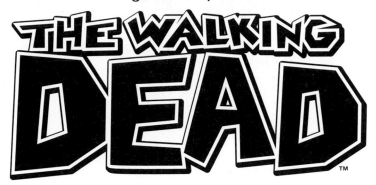

ROBERT KIRKMAN
CREATOR, WRITER

CHARLIE ADLARD
PENCILER

STEFANO GAUDIANO
INKER

CLIFF RATHBURN
GRAY TONES

RUS WOOTON
LETTERER

CHARLIE ADLARD
& DAVE STEWART
COVER

SEAN MACKIEWICZ
EDITOR

For SKYBOUND ENTERTAINMENT

Robert Kirkman - Chairman
David Alpert - CEO
Sean Mackiewicz - SVP Editor-in-Chief
Shawn Kirkham - SVP Business Development
Brian Huntington - VP, Online Content
June Alian - Publicity Director
Andres Juarez - Art Director
Jon Moisan - Editor
Arielle Basich - Associate Editor
Carina Taylor - Production Artist
Paul Shin - Business Development Coordinator
Johnny O'Dell - Social Media Manager
Sally Jacka - Skybound Retailer Relations
Dan Petersen - Director of Operations & Events

International inquiries: ag@sequentialrights.com
Licensing inquiries: contact@skybound.com

WWW.SKYBOUND.COM

IMAGE COMICS, INC.

Robert Kirkman—Chief Operating Officer
Erik Larsen—Chief Financial Officer
Todd McFarlane—President
Marc Silvestri—Chief Executive Officer
Jim Valentino—Vice President

Eric Stephenson—Publisher / Chief Creative Officer
Corey Hart—Director of Sales
Jeff Boison—Director of Publishing Planning & Book Trade Sales
Chris Ross—Director of Digital Sales
Jeff Stang—Director of Specialty Sales
Kat Salazar—Director of PR & Marketing
Drew Gill—Art Director
Heather Doornink—Production Director
Nicole Lapalme—Controller

IMAGECOMICS.COM

THE WALKING DEAD, VOL. 30: NEW WORLD ORDER. First Printing. ISBN: 978-1-5343-0884-8. Published by Image Comics, Inc. Office of publication: 2701 NW Vaughn St., Ste. 780, Portland, OR 97210.

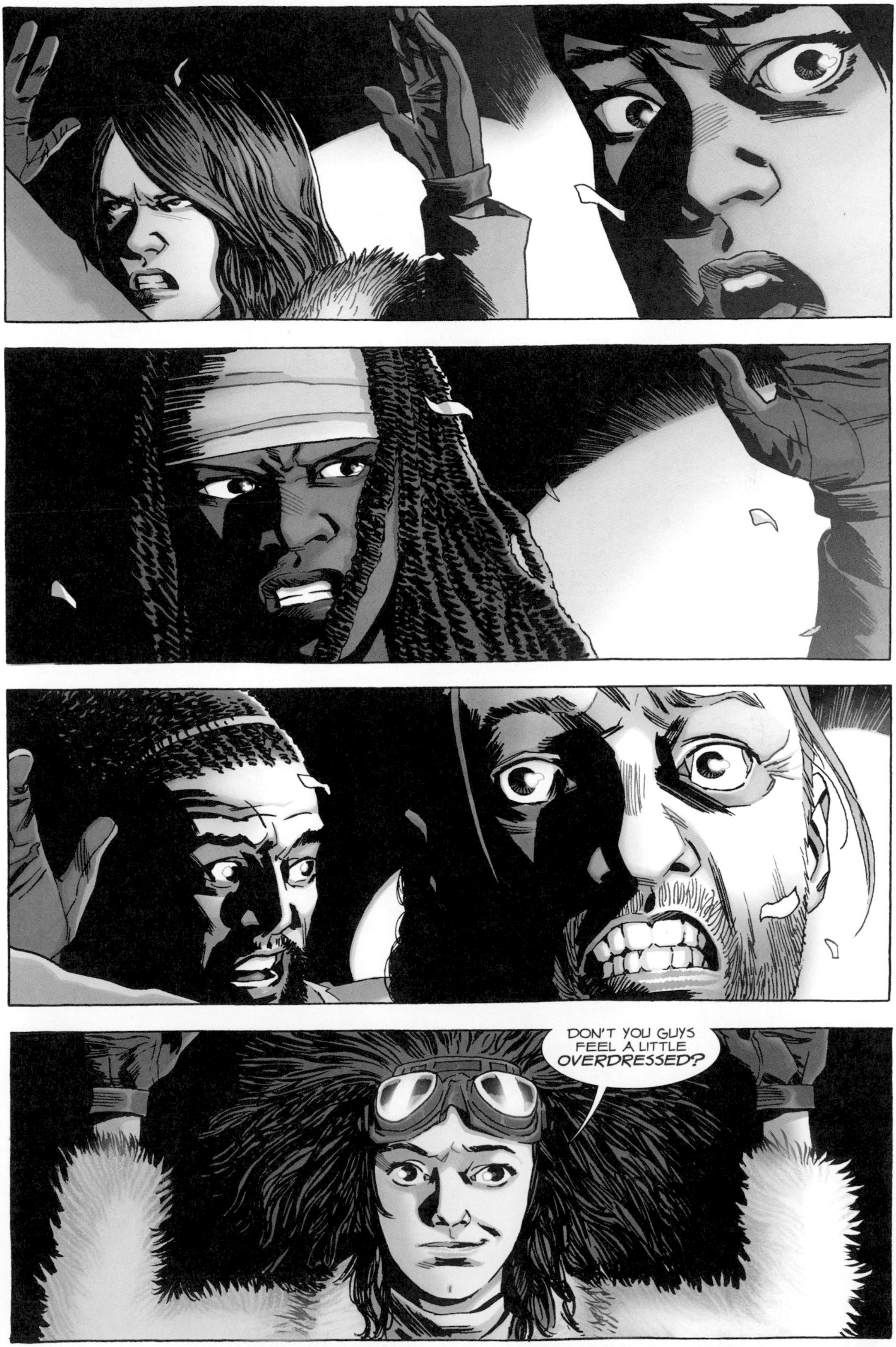
DON'T YOU GUYS FEEL A LITTLE OVERDRESSED?

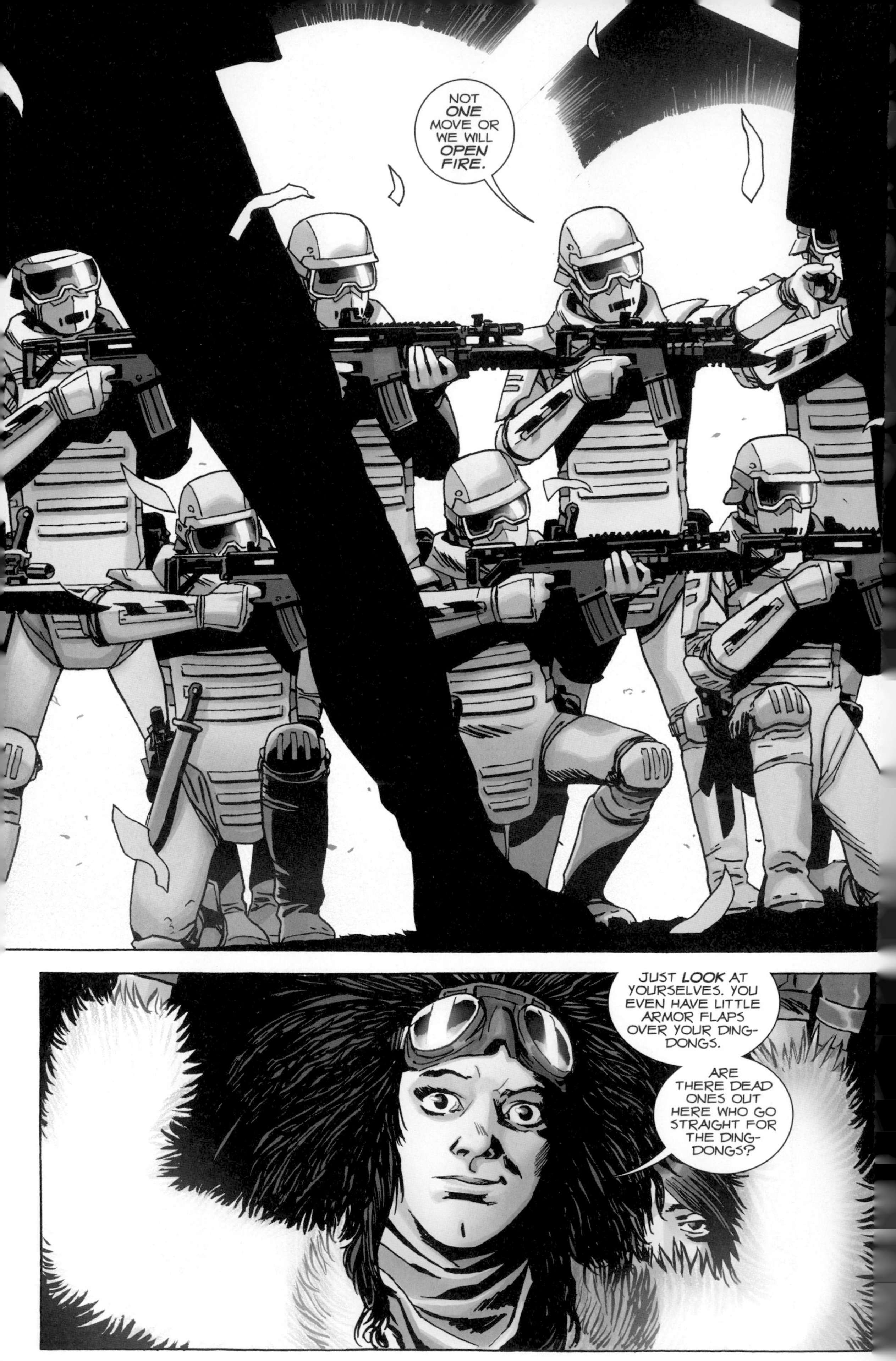
NOT ONE MOVE OR WE WILL OPEN FIRE.
JUST LOOK AT YOURSELVES. YOU EVEN HAVE LITTLE ARMOR FLAPS OVER YOUR DING-DONGS.
ARE THERE DEAD ONES OUT HERE WHO GO STRAIGHT FOR THE DING-DONGS?

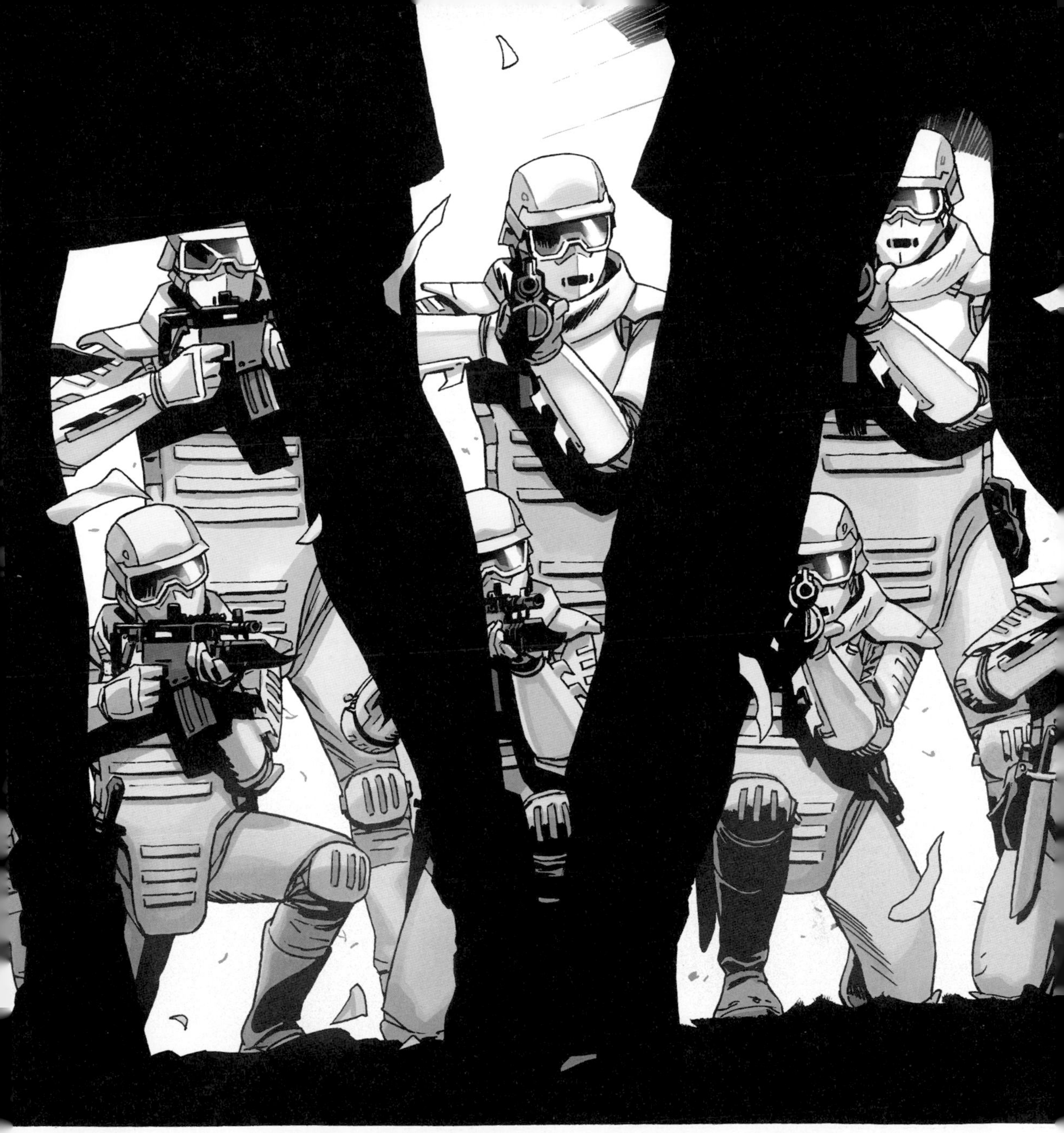
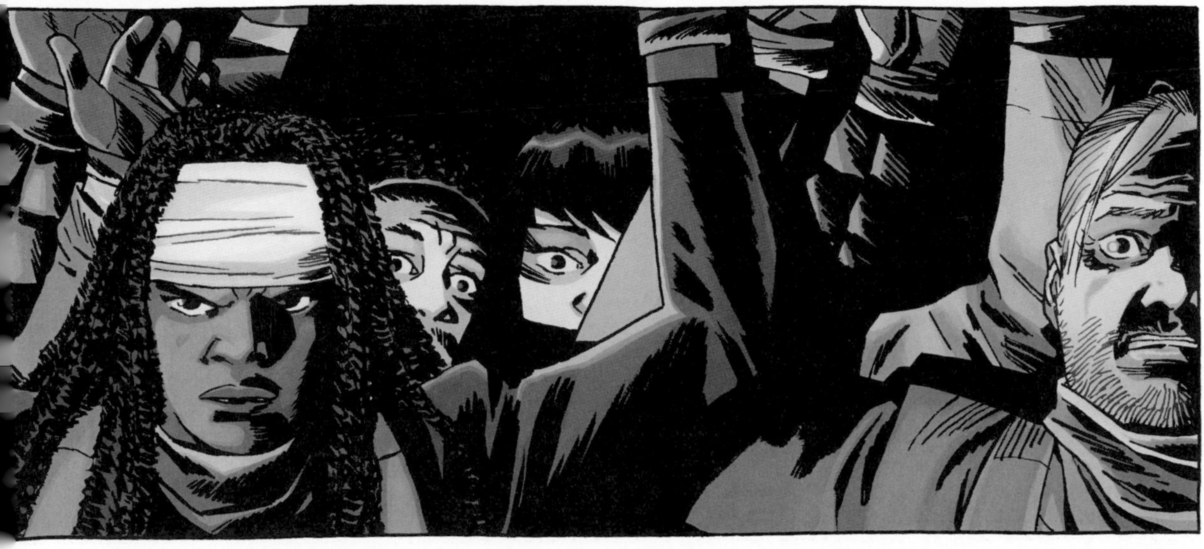

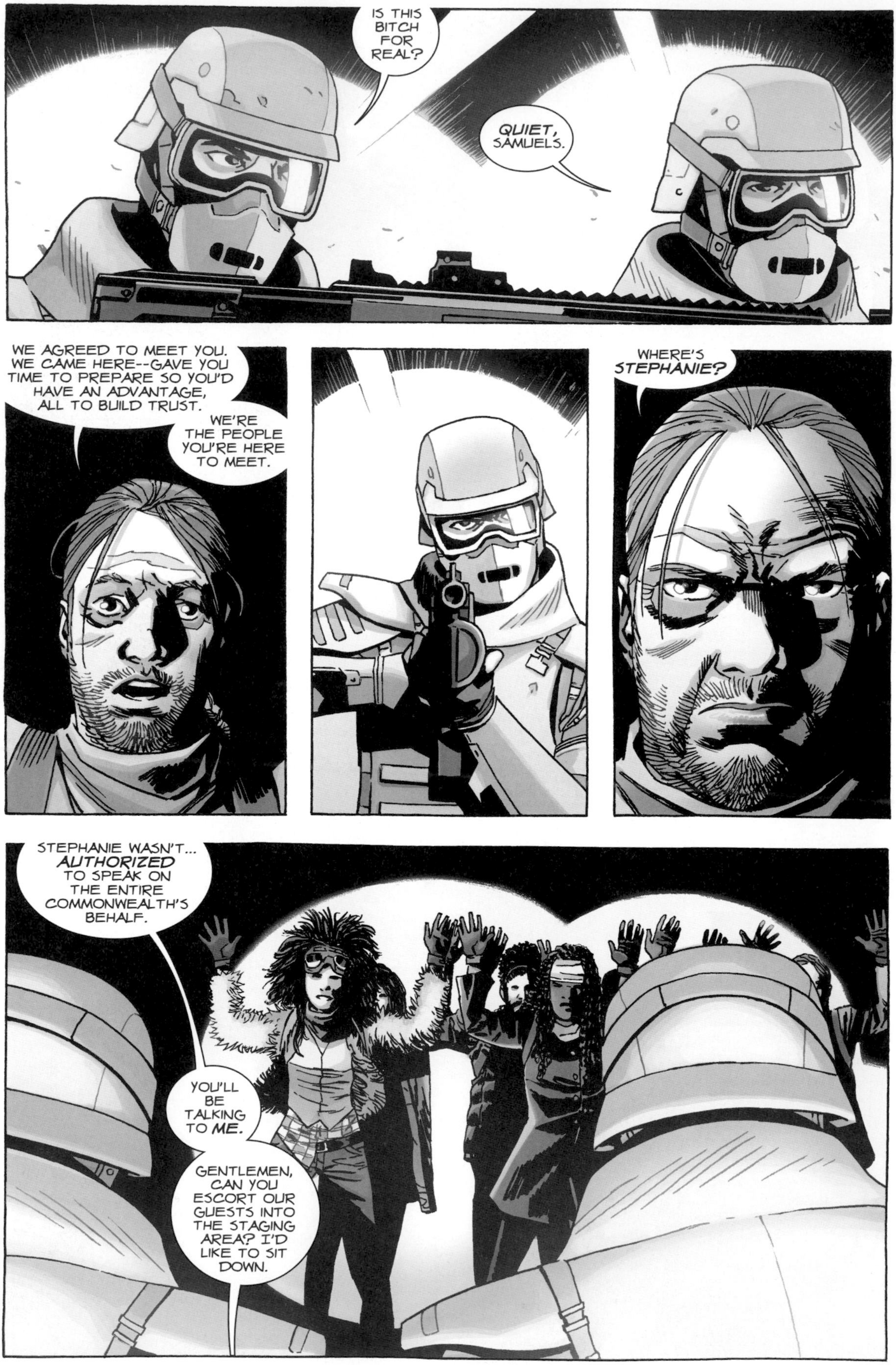
IS THIS BITCH FOR REAL?
QUIET, SAMUELS.
WE AGREED TO MEET YOU. WE CAME HERE--GAVE YOU TIME TO PREPARE SO YOU'D HAVE AN ADVANTAGE, ALL TO BUILD TRUST.
WE'RE THE PEOPLE YOU'RE HERE TO MEET.
WHERE'S STEPHANIE?
STEPHANIE WASN'T... AUTHORIZED TO SPEAK ON THE ENTIRE COMMONWEALTH'S BEHALF.
YOU'LL BE TALKING TO ME.
GENTLEMEN, CAN YOU ESCORT OUR GUESTS INTO THE STAGING AREA? I'D LIKE TO SIT DOWN.

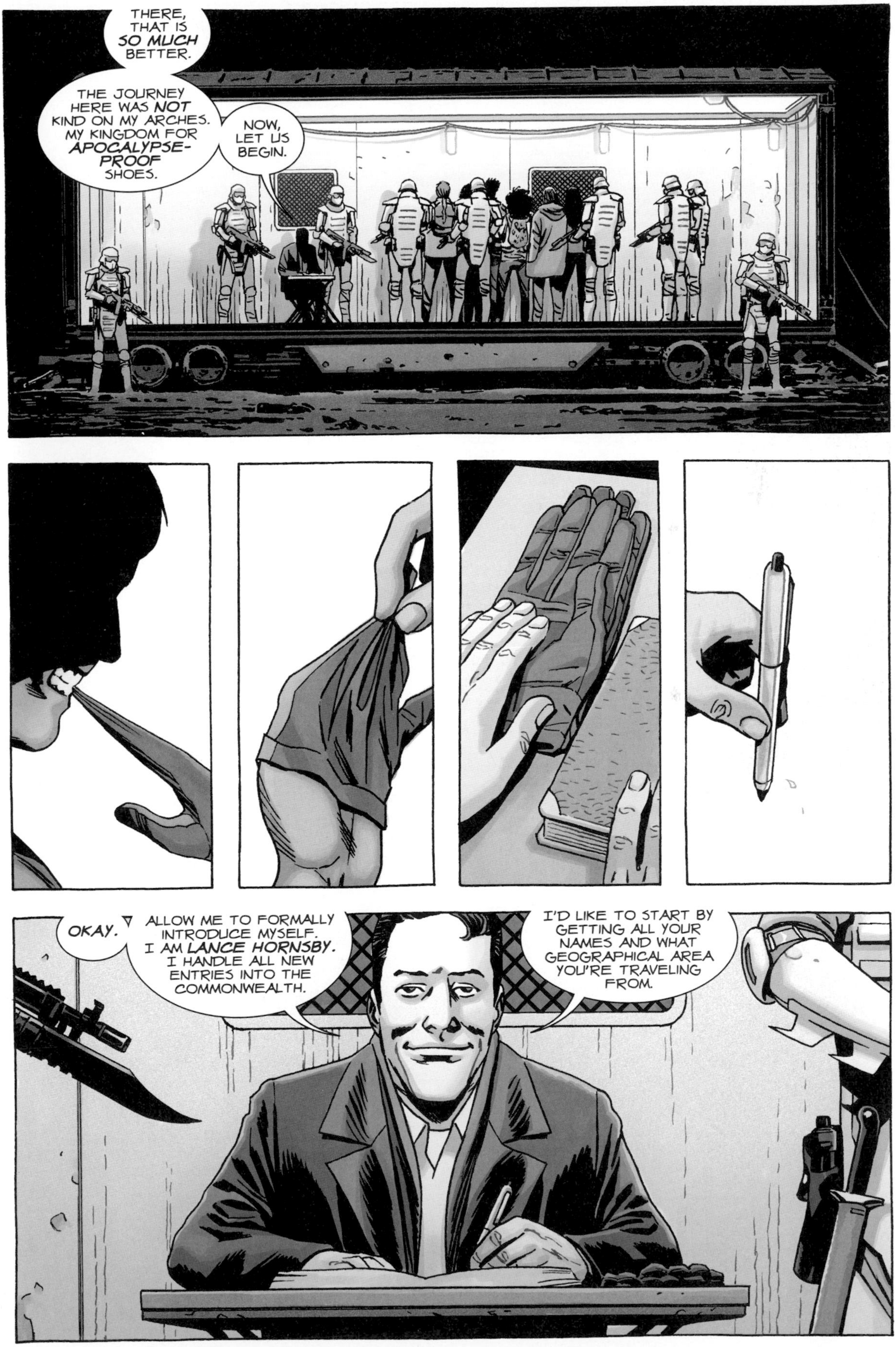
THERE, THAT IS SO MUCH BETTER.
THE JOURNEY HERE WAS NOT KIND ON MY ARCHES. MY KINGDOM FOR APOCALYPSE-PROOF SHOES.
NOW, LET US BEGIN.
OKAY.
ALLOW ME TO FORMALLY INTRODUCE MYSELF. I AM LANCE HORNSBY. I HANDLE ALL NEW ENTRIES INTO THE COMMONWEALTH.
I'D LIKE TO START BY GETTING ALL YOUR NAMES AND WHAT GEOGRAPHICAL AREA YOU'RE TRAVELING FROM.

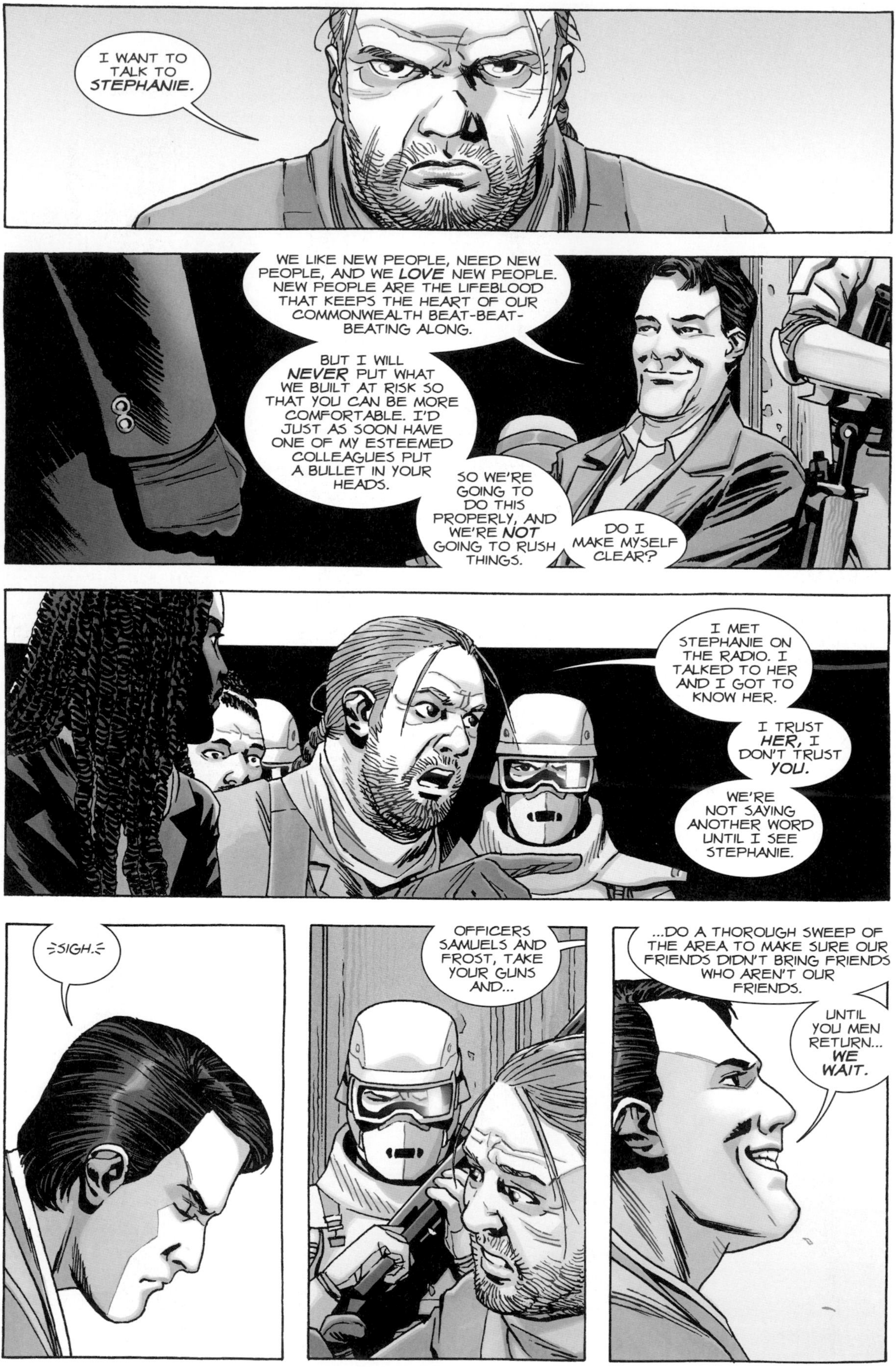
I WANT TO TALK TO STEPHANIE.
WE LIKE NEW PEOPLE, NEED NEW PEOPLE, AND WE LOVE NEW PEOPLE. NEW PEOPLE ARE THE LIFEBLOOD THAT KEEPS THE HEART OF OUR COMMONWEALTH BEAT-BEAT-BEATING ALONG.
BUT I WILL NEVER PUT WHAT WE BUILT AT RISK SO THAT YOU CAN BE MORE COMFORTABLE. I'D JUST AS SOON HAVE ONE OF MY ESTEEMED COLLEAGUES PUT A BULLET IN YOUR HEADS.
SO WE'RE GOING TO DO THIS PROPERLY, AND WE'RE NOT GOING TO RUSH THINGS.
DO I MAKE MYSELF CLEAR?
I MET STEPHANIE ON THE RADIO. I TALKED TO HER AND I GOT TO KNOW HER.
I TRUST HER, I DON'T TRUST YOU.
WE'RE NOT SAYING ANOTHER WORD UNTIL I SEE STEPHANIE.
=SIGH.=
OFFICERS SAMUELS AND FROST, TAKE YOUR GUNS AND...
...DO A THOROUGH SWEEP OF THE AREA TO MAKE SURE OUR FRIENDS DIDN'T BRING FRIENDS WHO AREN'T OUR FRIENDS.
UNTIL YOU MEN RETURN... WE WAIT.

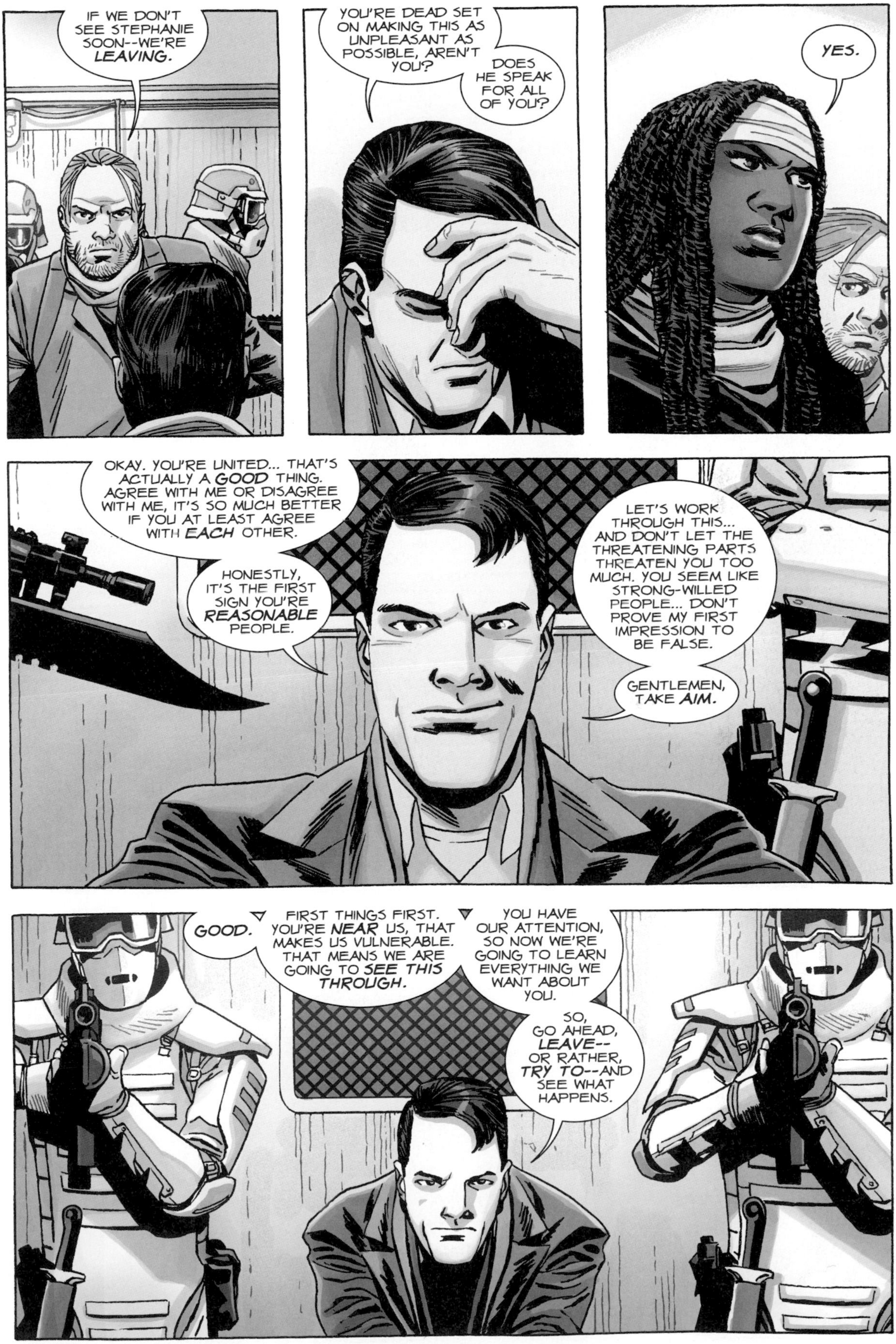
IF WE DON'T SEE STEPHANIE SOON--WE'RE LEAVING.
YOU'RE DEAD SET ON MAKING THIS AS UNPLEASANT AS POSSIBLE, AREN'T YOU?
DOES HE SPEAK FOR ALL OF YOU?
YES.
OKAY. YOU'RE UNITED... THAT'S ACTUALLY A GOOD THING. AGREE WITH ME OR DISAGREE WITH ME, IT'S SO MUCH BETTER IF YOU AT LEAST AGREE WITH EACH OTHER.
HONESTLY, IT'S THE FIRST SIGN YOU'RE REASONABLE PEOPLE.
LET'S WORK THROUGH THIS... AND DON'T LET THE THREATENING PARTS THREATEN YOU TOO MUCH. YOU SEEM LIKE STRONG-WILLED PEOPLE... DON'T PROVE MY FIRST IMPRESSION TO BE FALSE.
GENTLEMEN, TAKE AIM.
GOOD.
FIRST THINGS FIRST. YOU'RE NEAR US, THAT MAKES US VULNERABLE. THAT MEANS WE ARE GOING TO SEE THIS THROUGH.
YOU HAVE OUR ATTENTION, SO NOW WE'RE GOING TO LEARN EVERYTHING WE WANT ABOUT YOU.
SO, GO AHEAD, LEAVE--OR RATHER, TRY TO--AND SEE WHAT HAPPENS.

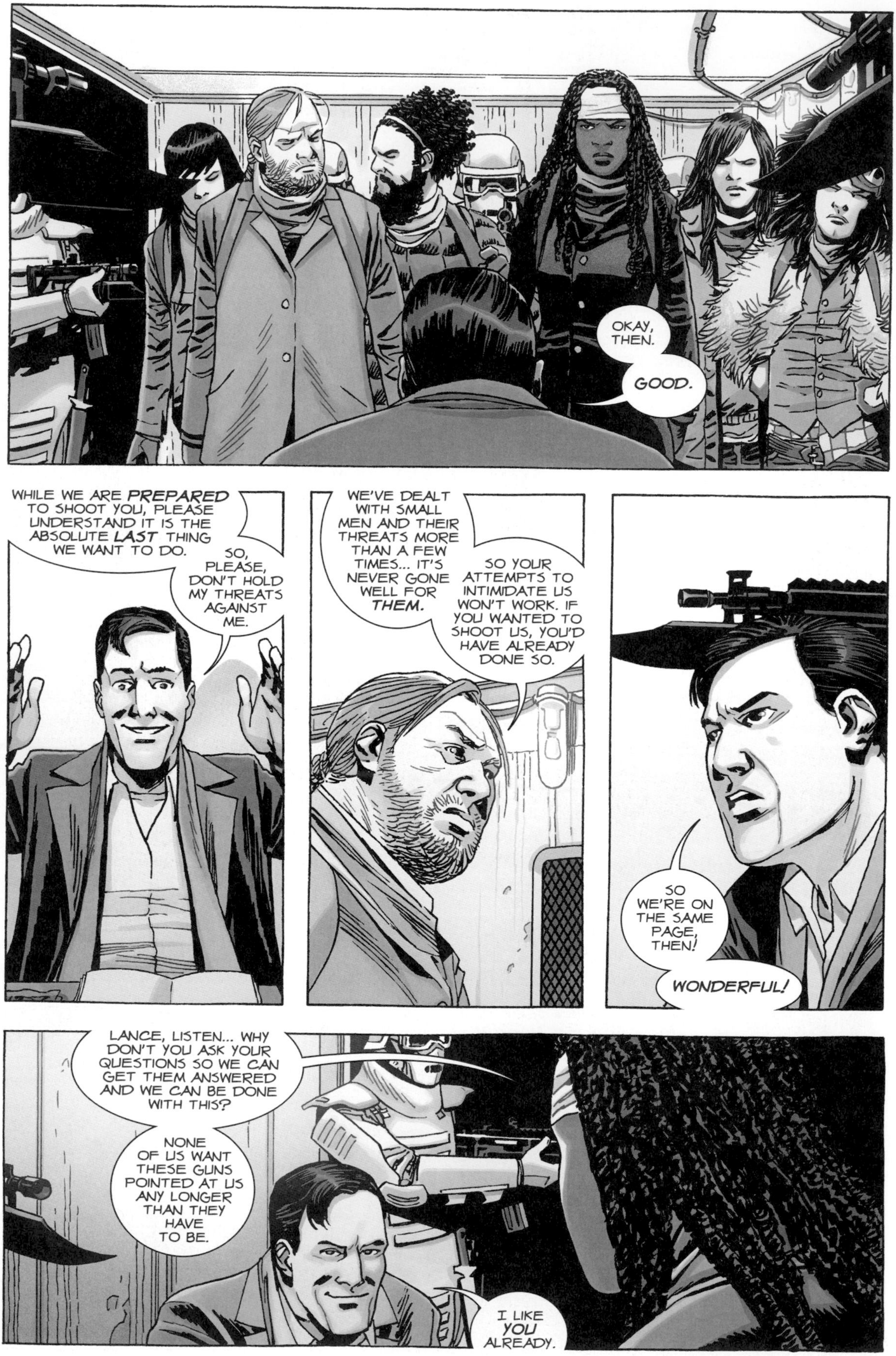
OKAY, THEN.
GOOD.
WHILE WE ARE PREPARED TO SHOOT YOU, PLEASE UNDERSTAND IT IS THE ABSOLUTE LAST THING WE WANT TO DO.
SO, PLEASE, DON'T HOLD MY THREATS AGAINST ME.
WE'VE DEALT WITH SMALL MEN AND THEIR THREATS MORE THAN A FEW TIMES... IT'S NEVER GONE WELL FOR THEM.
SO YOUR ATTEMPTS TO INTIMIDATE US WON'T WORK. IF YOU WANTED TO SHOOT US, YOU'D HAVE ALREADY DONE SO.
SO WE'RE ON THE SAME PAGE, THEN!
WONDERFUL!
LANCE, LISTEN... WHY DON'T YOU ASK YOUR QUESTIONS SO WE CAN GET THEM ANSWERED AND WE CAN BE DONE WITH THIS?
NONE OF US WANT THESE GUNS POINTED AT US ANY LONGER THAN THEY HAVE TO BE.
I LIKE YOU ALREADY.

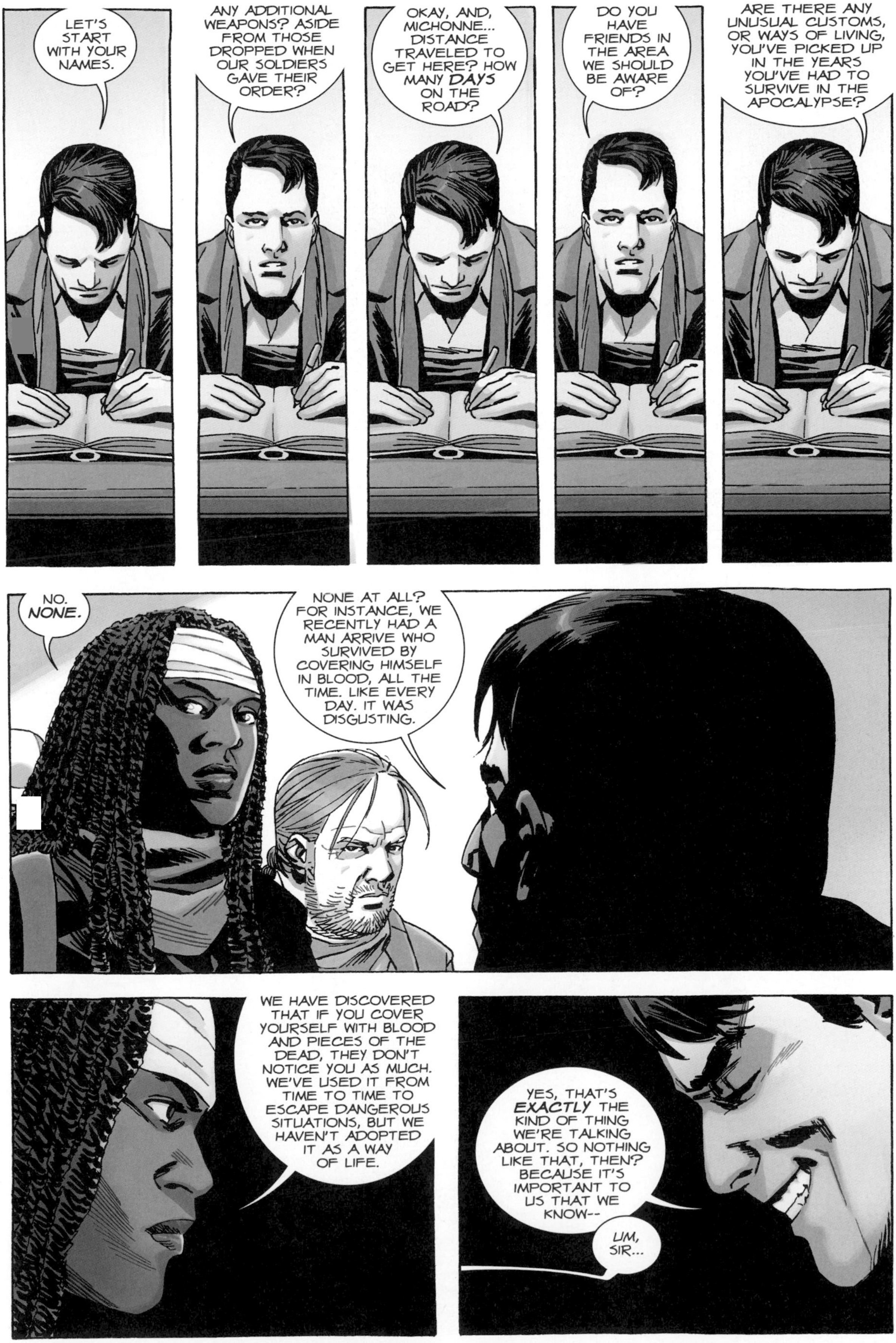
LET'S START WITH YOUR NAMES.
ANY ADDITIONAL WEAPONS? ASIDE FROM THOSE DROPPED WHEN OUR SOLDIERS GAVE THEIR ORDER?
OKAY, AND, MICHONNE... DISTANCE TRAVELED TO GET HERE? HOW MANY DAYS ON THE ROAD?
DO YOU HAVE FRIENDS IN THE AREA WE SHOULD BE AWARE OF?
ARE THERE ANY UNUSUAL CUSTOMS, OR WAYS OF LIVING, YOU'VE PICKED UP IN THE YEARS YOU'VE HAD TO SURVIVE IN THE APOCALYPSE?
NO. NONE.
NONE AT ALL? FOR INSTANCE, WE RECENTLY HAD A MAN ARRIVE WHO SURVIVED BY COVERING HIMSELF IN BLOOD, ALL THE TIME. LIKE EVERY DAY. IT WAS DISGUSTING.
WE HAVE DISCOVERED THAT IF YOU COVER YOURSELF WITH BLOOD AND PIECES OF THE DEAD, THEY DON'T NOTICE YOU AS MUCH. WE'VE USED IT FROM TIME TO TIME TO ESCAPE DANGEROUS SITUATIONS, BUT WE HAVEN'T ADOPTED IT AS A WAY OF LIFE.
YES, THAT'S EXACTLY THE KIND OF THING WE'RE TALKING ABOUT. SO NOTHING LIKE THAT, THEN? BECAUSE IT'S IMPORTANT TO US THAT WE KNOW--
UM, SIR...

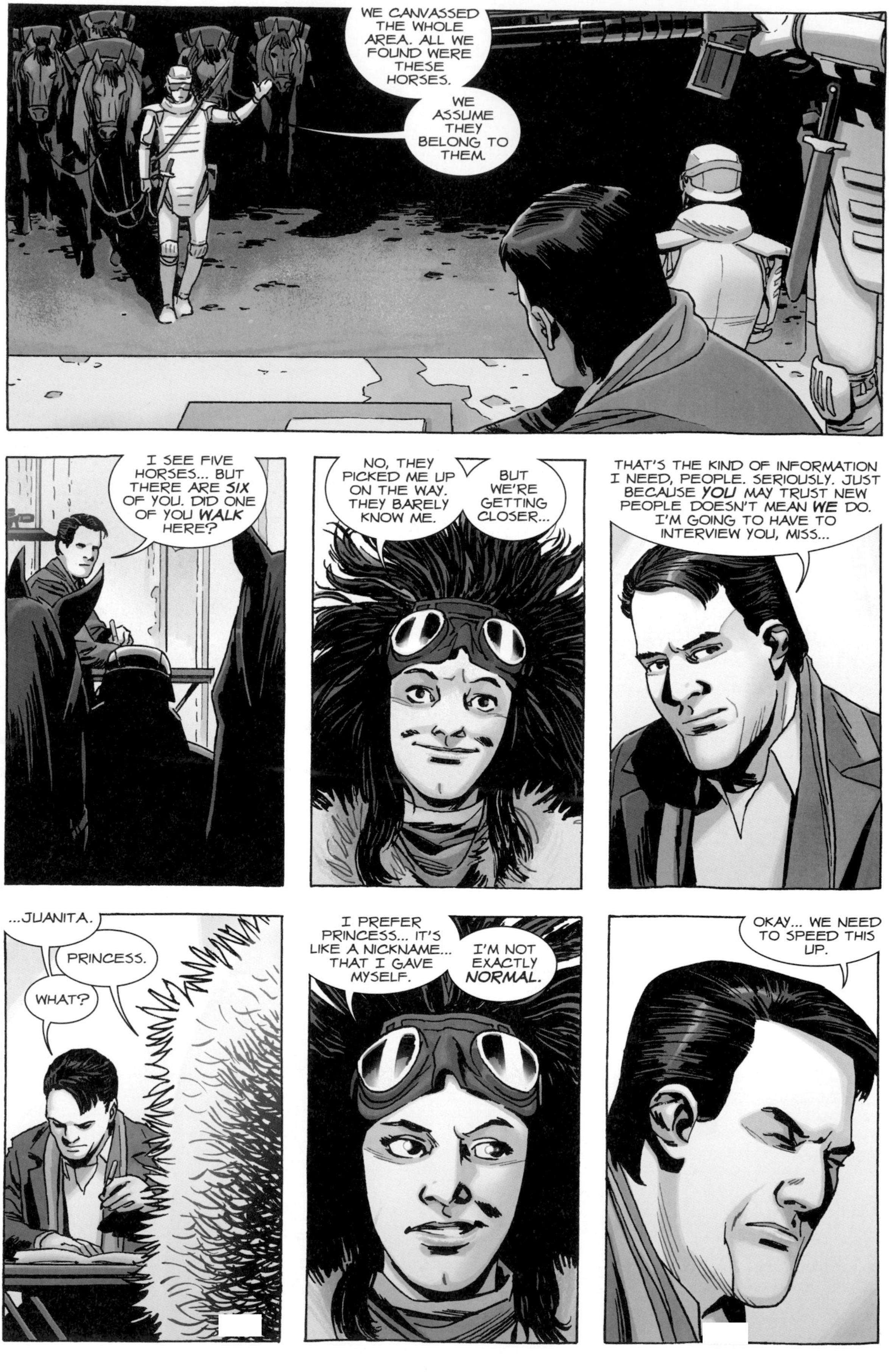
WE CANVASSED THE WHOLE AREA. ALL WE FOUND WERE THESE HORSES.
WE ASSUME THEY BELONG TO THEM.
I SEE FIVE HORSES... BUT THERE ARE SIX OF YOU. DID ONE OF YOU WALK HERE?
NO, THEY PICKED ME UP ON THE WAY. THEY BARELY KNOW ME.
BUT WE'RE GETTING CLOSER...
THAT'S THE KIND OF INFORMATION I NEED, PEOPLE. SERIOUSLY. JUST BECAUSE YOU MAY TRUST NEW PEOPLE DOESN'T MEAN WE DO. I'M GOING TO HAVE TO INTERVIEW YOU, MISS...
...JUANITA.
PRINCESS.
WHAT?
I PREFER PRINCESS... IT'S LIKE A NICKNAME... THAT I GAVE MYSELF.
I'M NOT EXACTLY NORMAL.
OKAY... WE NEED TO SPEED THIS UP.

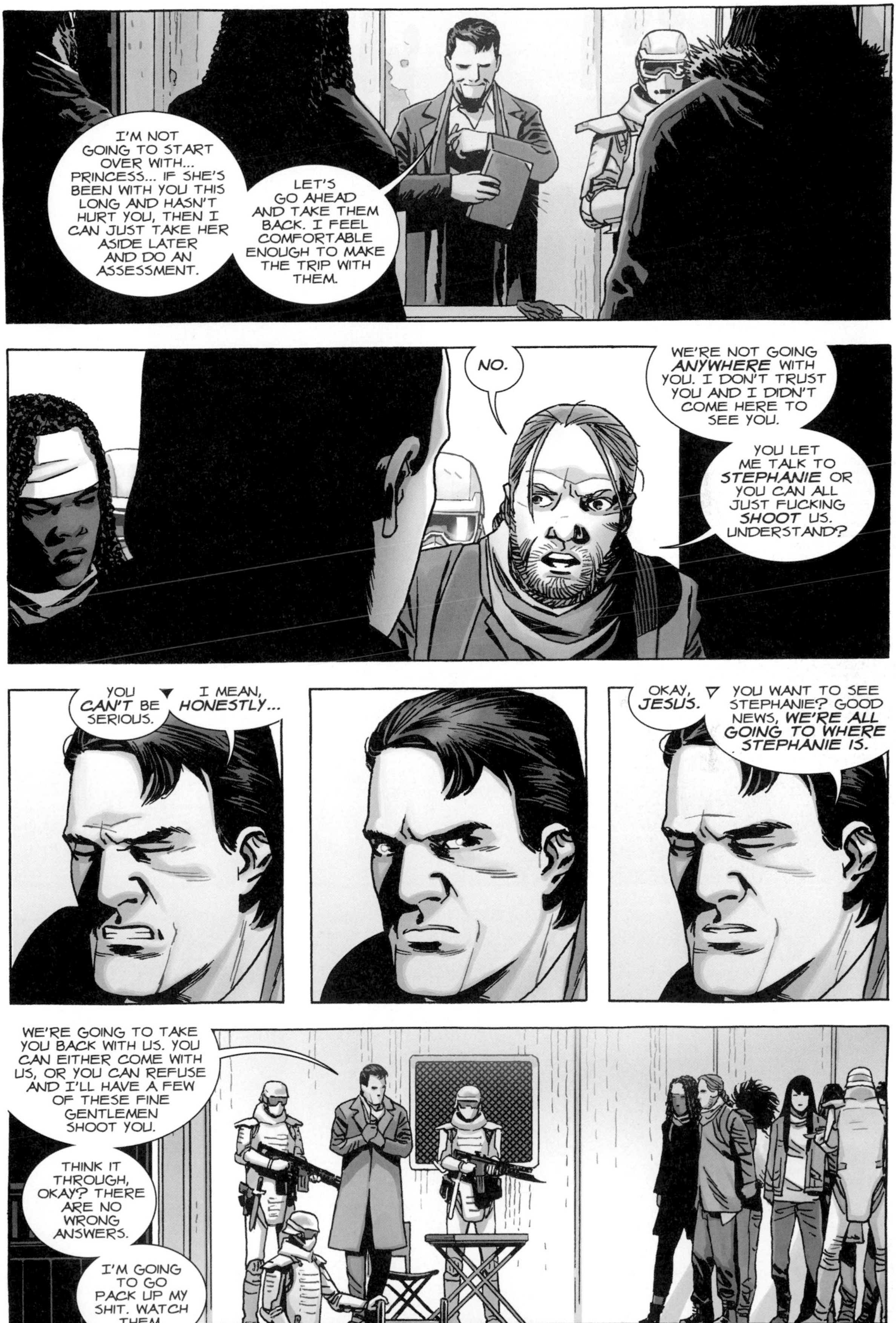
I'M NOT GOING TO START OVER WITH... PRINCESS... IF SHE'S BEEN WITH YOU THIS LONG AND HASN'T HURT YOU, THEN I CAN JUST TAKE HER ASIDE LATER AND DO AN ASSESSMENT.
LET'S GO AHEAD AND TAKE THEM BACK. I FEEL COMFORTABLE ENOUGH TO MAKE THE TRIP WITH THEM.
NO.
WE'RE NOT GOING ANYWHERE WITH YOU. I DON'T TRUST YOU AND I DIDN'T COME HERE TO SEE YOU.
YOU LET ME TALK TO STEPHANIE OR YOU CAN ALL JUST FUCKING SHOOT US. UNDERSTAND?
YOU CAN'T BE SERIOUS.
I MEAN, HONESTLY...
OKAY, JESUS.
YOU WANT TO SEE STEPHANIE? GOOD NEWS, WE'RE ALL GOING TO WHERE STEPHANIE IS.
WE'RE GOING TO TAKE YOU BACK WITH US. YOU CAN EITHER COME WITH US, OR YOU CAN REFUSE AND I'LL HAVE A FEW OF THESE FINE GENTLEMEN SHOOT YOU.
THINK IT THROUGH, OKAY? THERE ARE NO WRONG ANSWERS.
I'M GOING TO GO PACK UP MY SHIT. WATCH THEM.

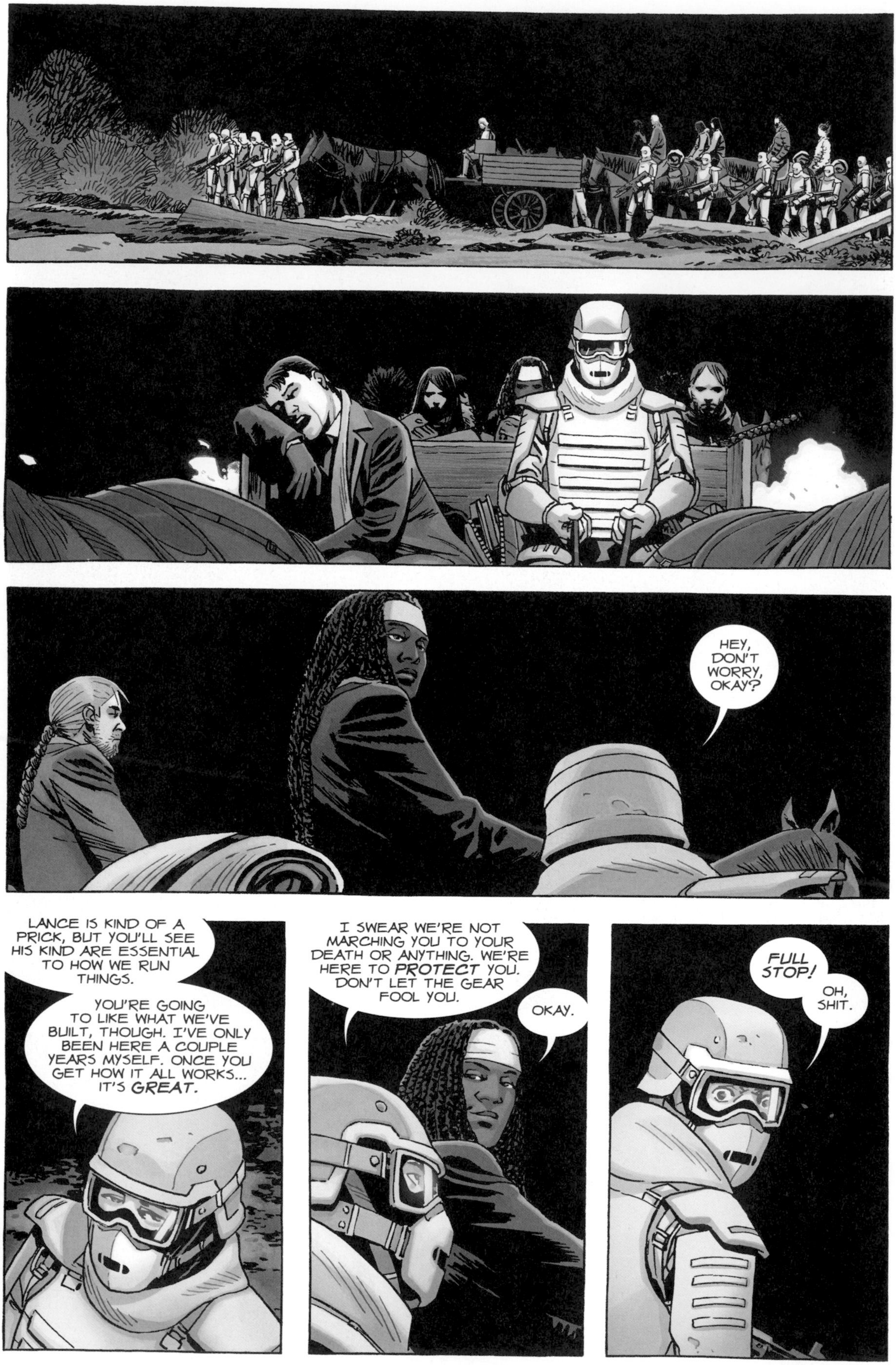
HEY, DON'T WORRY, OKAY?
LANCE IS KIND OF A PRICK, BUT YOU'LL SEE HIS KIND ARE ESSENTIAL TO HOW WE RUN THINGS.
YOU'RE GOING TO LIKE WHAT WE'VE BUILT, THOUGH. I'VE ONLY BEEN HERE A COUPLE YEARS MYSELF. ONCE YOU GET HOW IT ALL WORKS... IT'S GREAT.
I SWEAR WE'RE NOT MARCHING YOU TO YOUR DEATH OR ANYTHING. WE'RE HERE TO PROTECT YOU. DON'T LET THE GEAR FOOL YOU.
OKAY.
FULL STOP!
OH, SHIT.

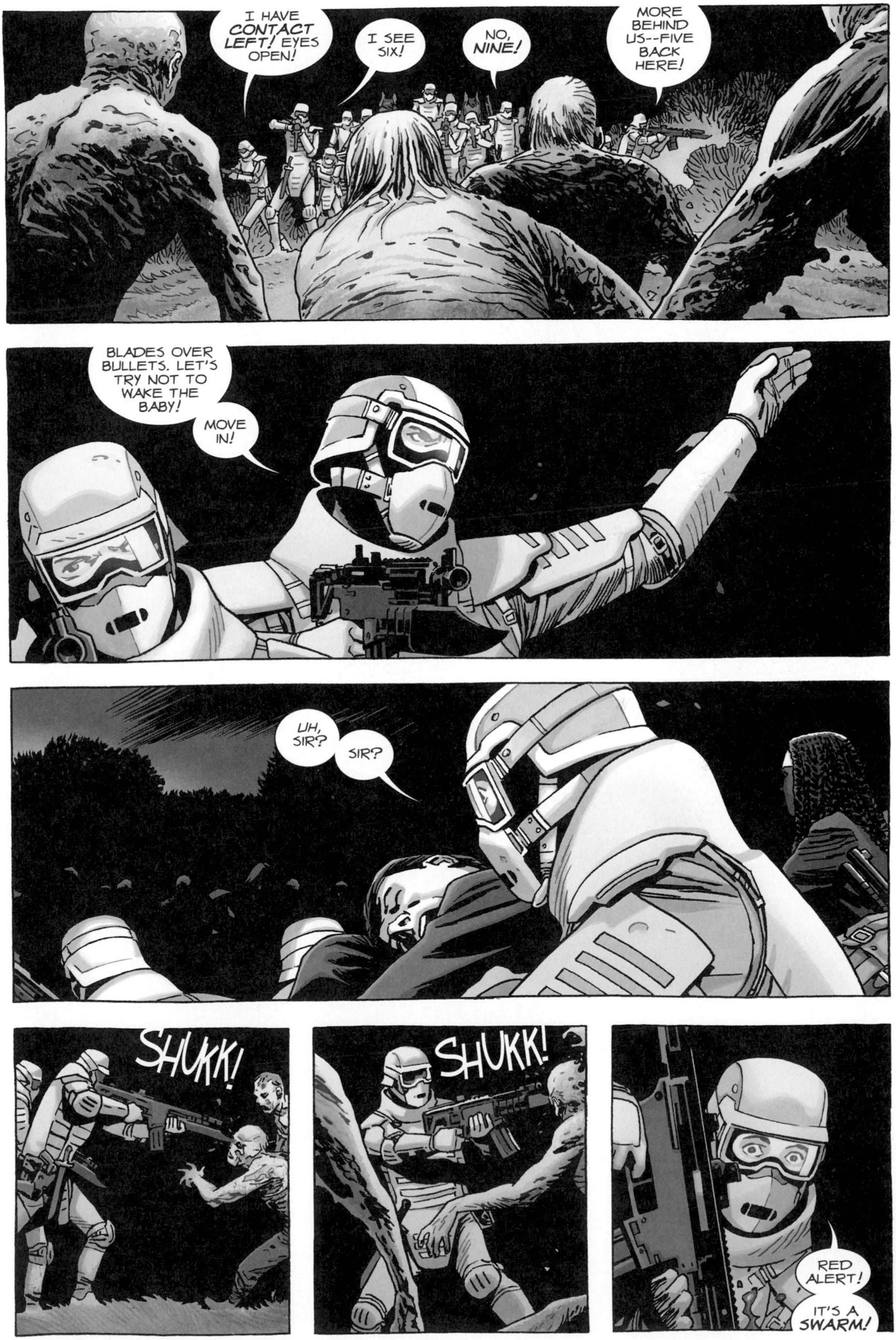
I HAVE CONTACT LEFT! EYES OPEN!
I SEE SIX!
NO, NINE!
MORE BEHIND US--FIVE BACK HERE!
BLADES OVER BULLETS. LET'S TRY NOT TO WAKE THE BABY!
MOVE IN!
UH, SIR?
SIR?
SHUKK!
SHUKK!
RED ALERT!
IT'S A SWARM!

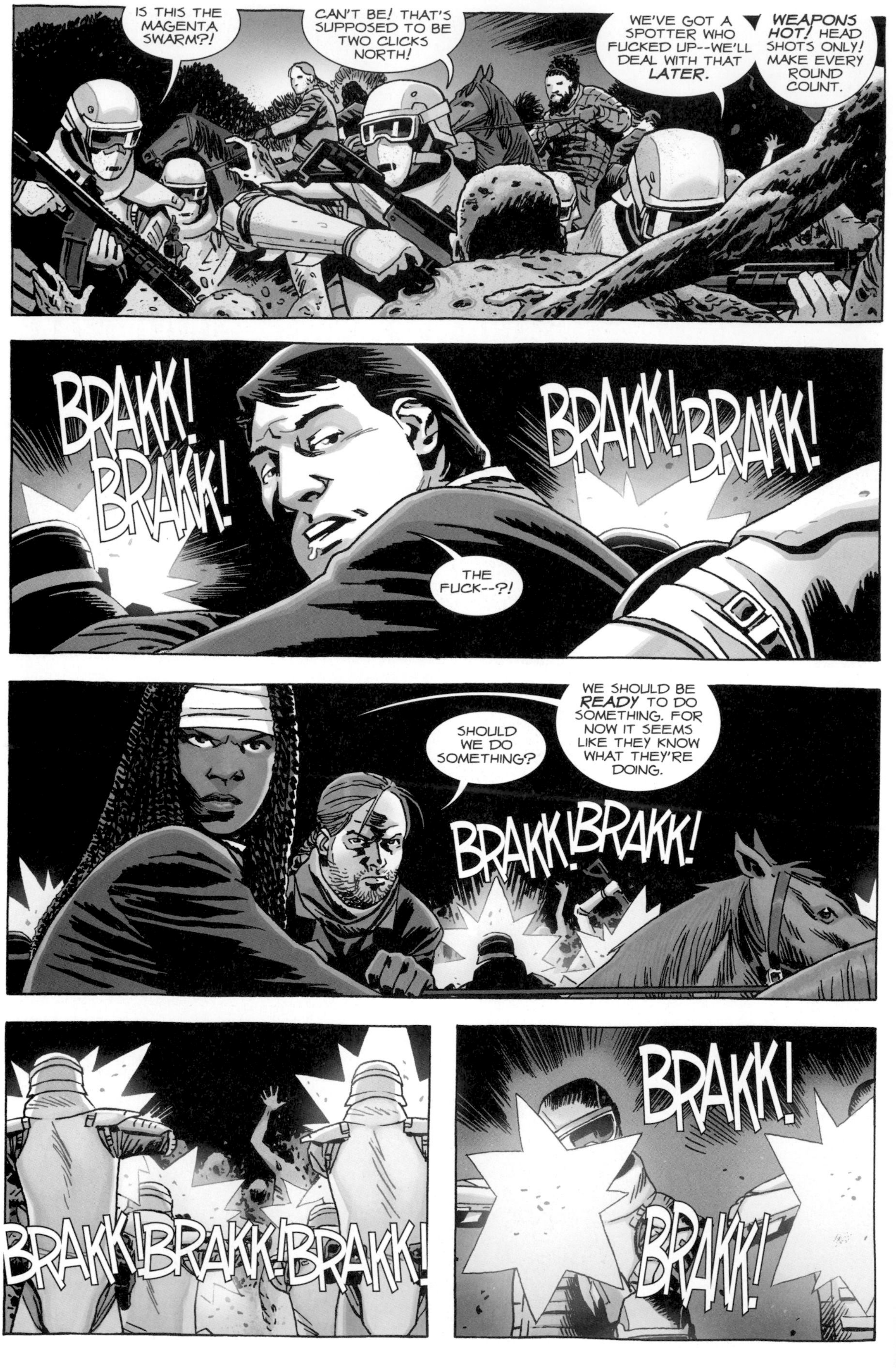
IS THIS THE MAGENTA SWARM?!
CAN'T BE! THAT'S SUPPOSED TO BE TWO CLICKS NORTH!
WE'VE GOT A SPOTTER WHO FUCKED UP--WE'LL DEAL WITH THAT LATER.
WEAPONS HOT! HEAD SHOTS ONLY! MAKE EVERY ROUND COUNT.
BRAKK! BRAKK!
BRAKK! BRAKK!
THE FUCK--?!
SHOULD WE DO SOMETHING?
WE SHOULD BE READY TO DO SOMETHING. FOR NOW IT SEEMS LIKE THEY KNOW WHAT THEY'RE DOING.
BRAKK! BRAKK!
BRAKK! BRAKK! BRAKK!
BRAKK!
BRAKK!

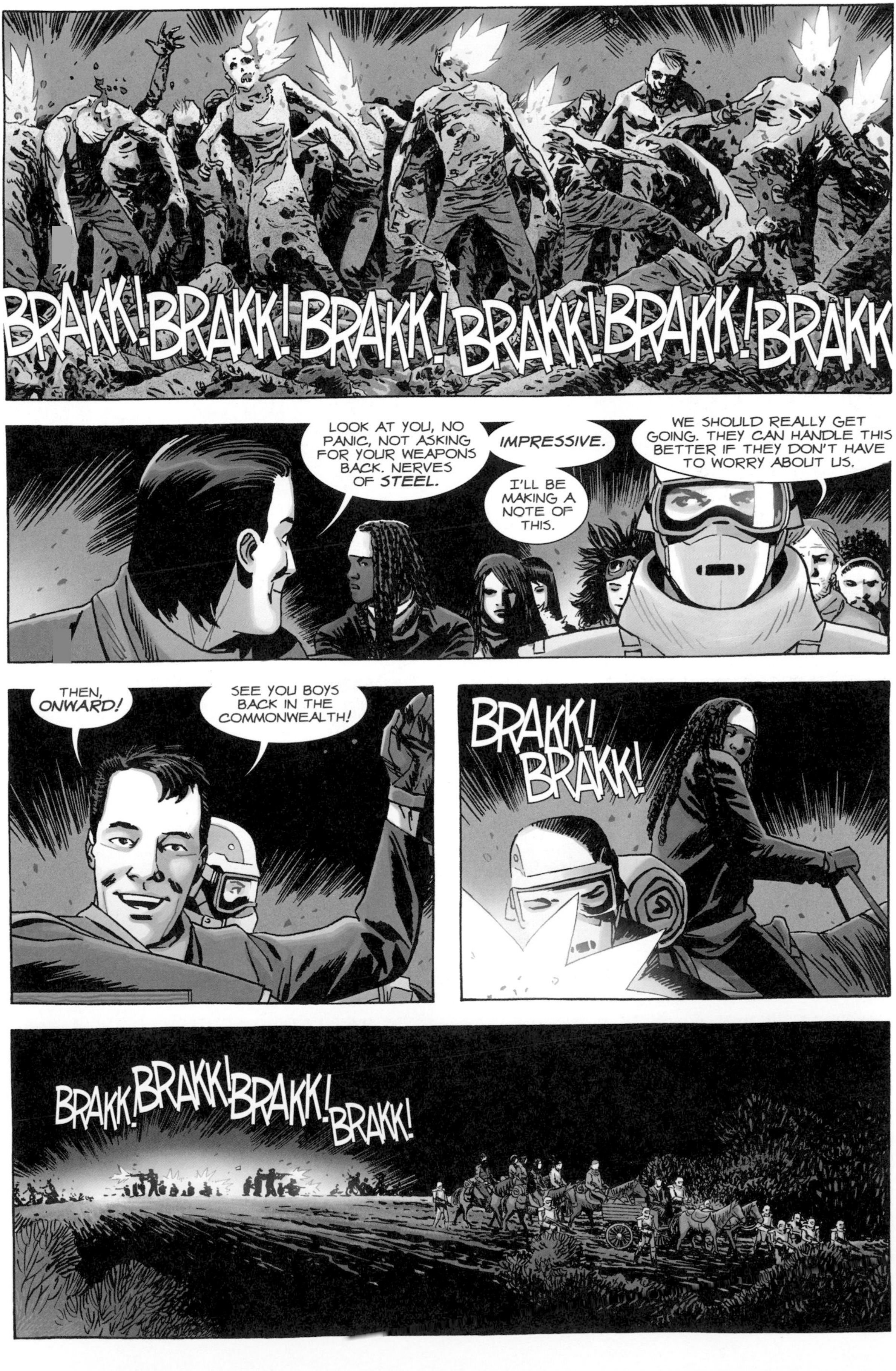
BRAKK! BRAKK! BRAKK! BRAKK! BRAKK! BRAKK! BRAKK
LOOK AT YOU, NO PANIC, NOT ASKING FOR YOUR WEAPONS BACK. NERVES OF STEEL.
IMPRESSIVE.
I'LL BE MAKING A NOTE OF THIS.
WE SHOULD REALLY GET GOING. THEY CAN HANDLE THIS BETTER IF THEY DON'T HAVE TO WORRY ABOUT US.
THEN, ONWARD!
SEE YOU BOYS BACK IN THE COMMONWEALTH!
BRAKK! BRAKK!
BRAKK! BRAKK! BRAKK! BRAKK!

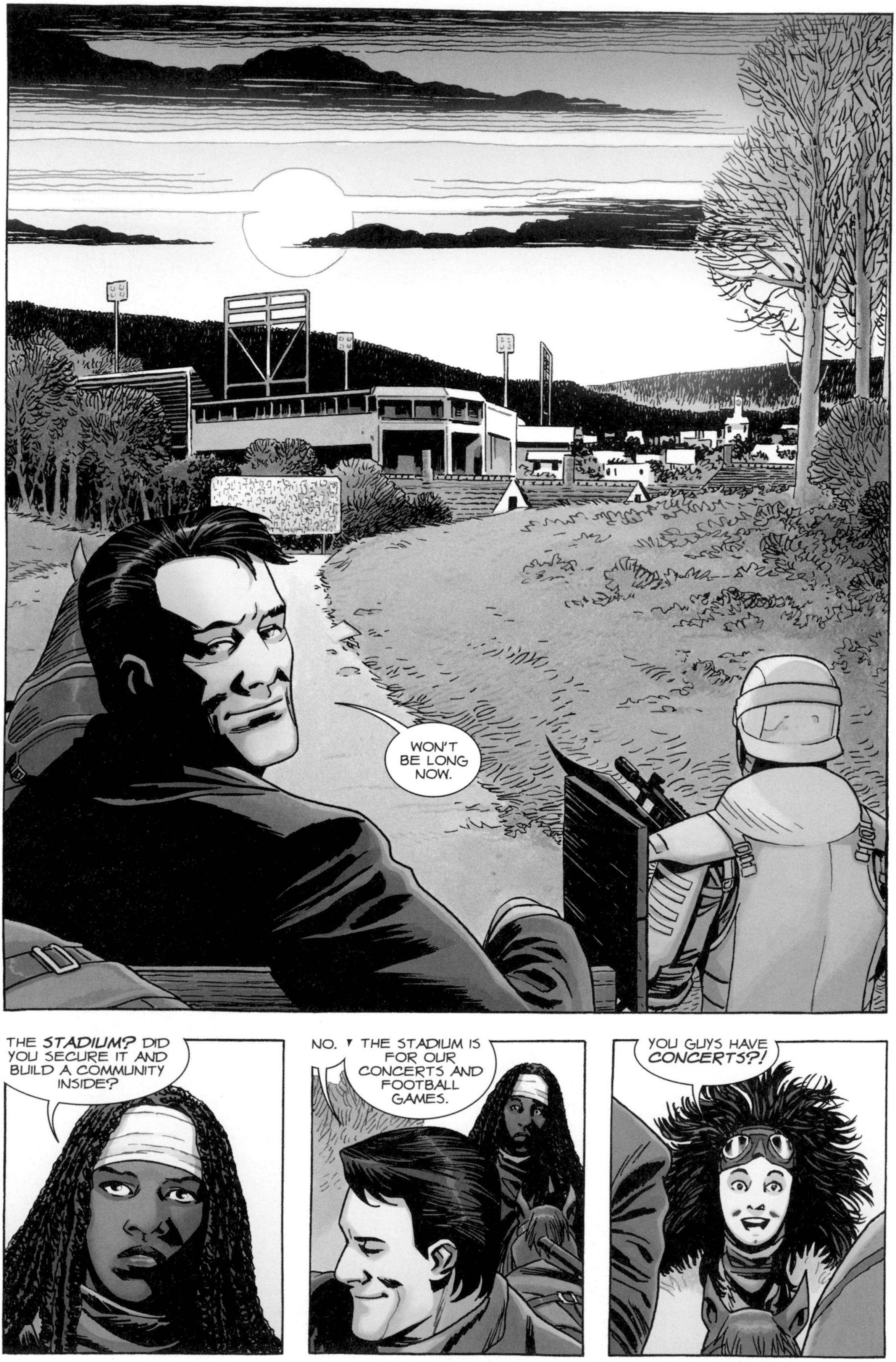
WON'T BE LONG NOW.
THE STADIUM? DID YOU SECURE IT AND BUILD A COMMUNITY INSIDE?
NO.
THE STADIUM IS FOR OUR CONCERTS AND FOOTBALL GAMES.
YOU GUYS HAVE CONCERTS?!

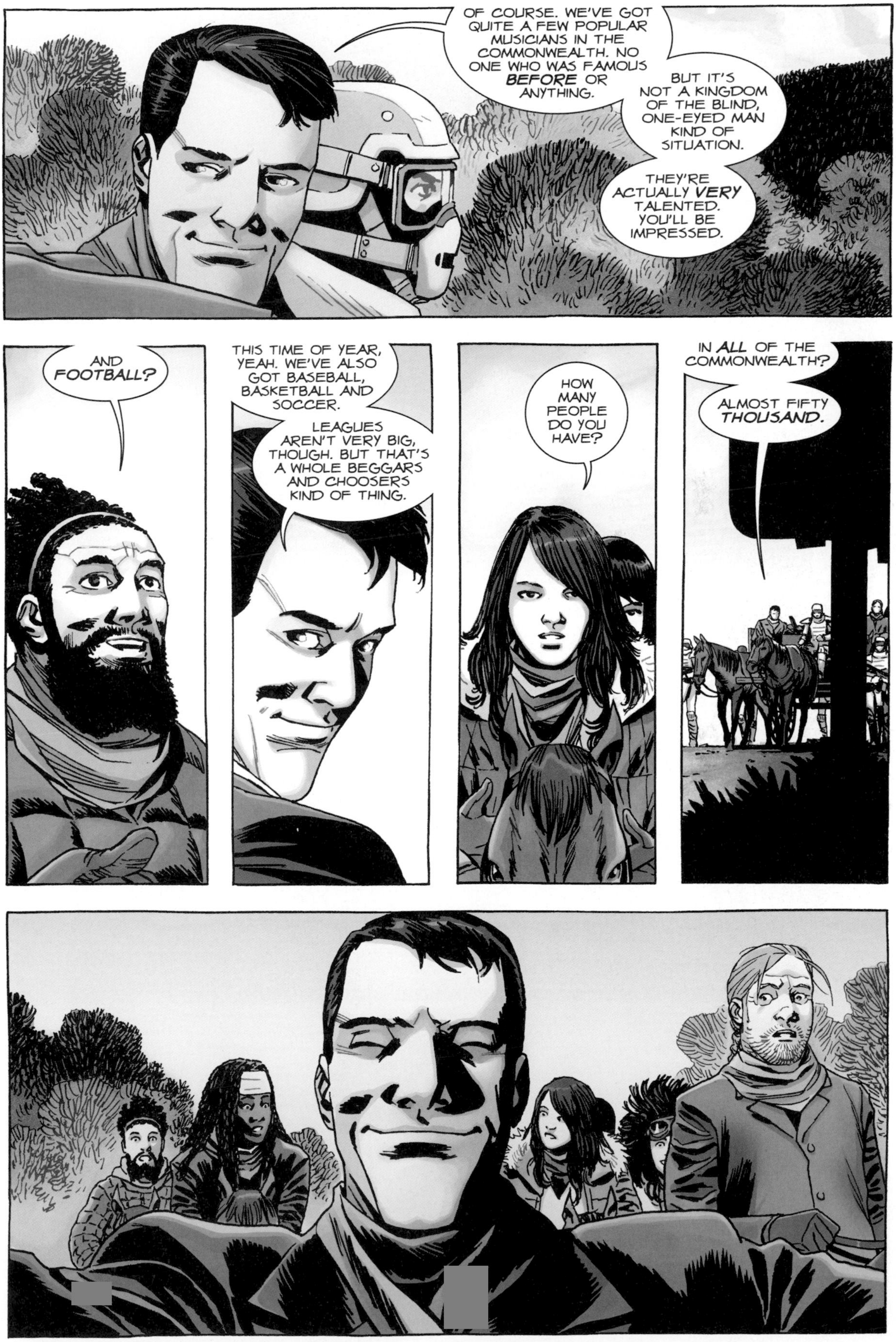
OF COURSE. WE'VE GOT QUITE A FEW POPULAR MUSICIANS IN THE COMMONWEALTH. NO ONE WHO WAS FAMOUS *BEFORE* OR ANYTHING.
BUT IT'S NOT A KINGDOM OF THE BLIND, ONE-EYED MAN KIND OF SITUATION.
THEY'RE ACTUALLY *VERY* TALENTED. YOU'LL BE IMPRESSED.
AND *FOOTBALL?*
THIS TIME OF YEAR, YEAH. WE'VE ALSO GOT BASEBALL, BASKETBALL AND SOCCER.
LEAGUES AREN'T VERY BIG, THOUGH. BUT THAT'S A WHOLE BEGGARS AND CHOOSERS KIND OF THING.
HOW MANY PEOPLE DO YOU HAVE?
IN *ALL* OF THE COMMONWEALTH?
ALMOST FIFTY *THOUSAND.*

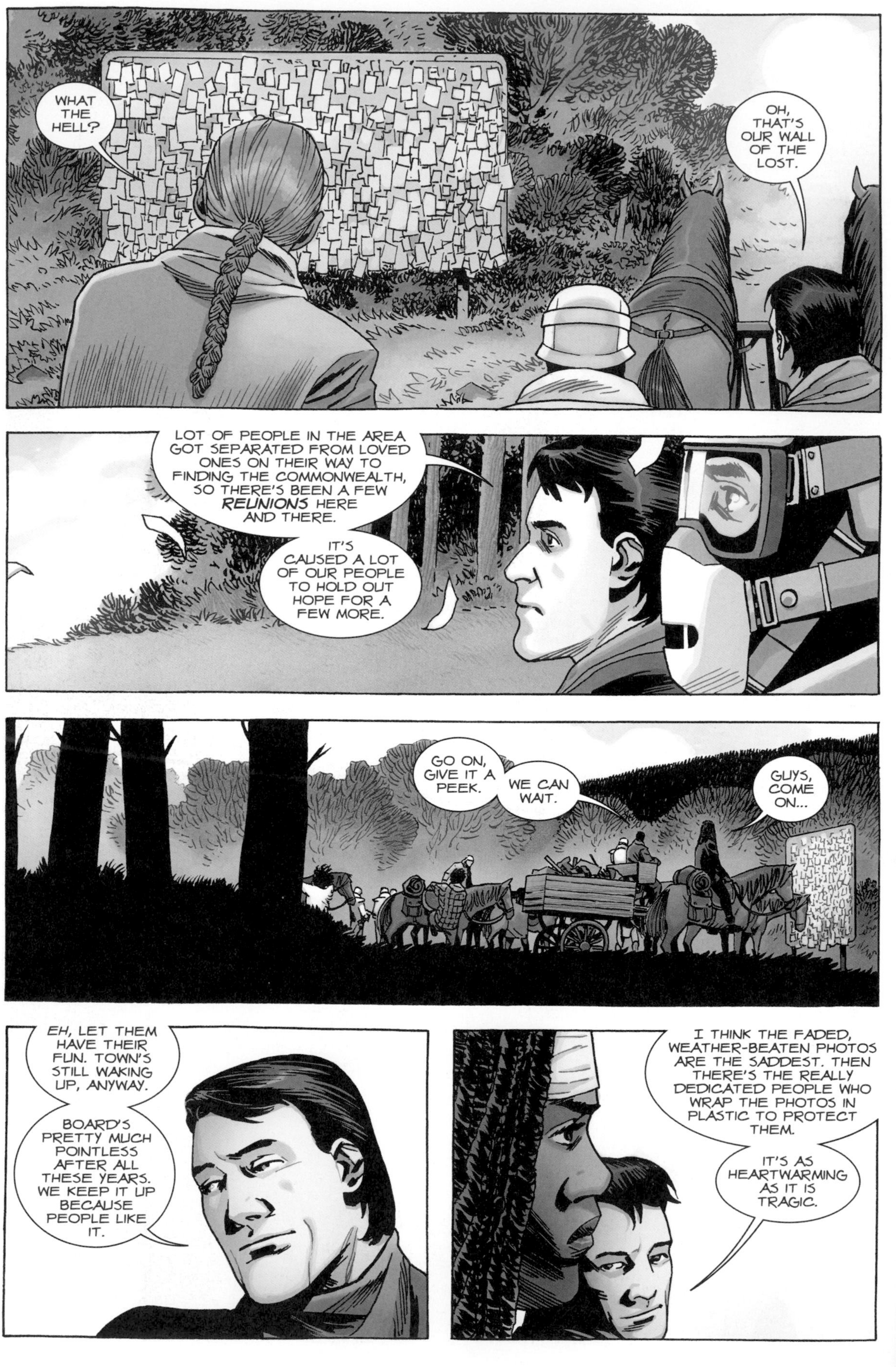
WHAT THE HELL?
OH, THAT'S OUR WALL OF THE LOST.
LOT OF PEOPLE IN THE AREA GOT SEPARATED FROM LOVED ONES ON THEIR WAY TO FINDING THE COMMONWEALTH, SO THERE'S BEEN A FEW REUNIONS HERE AND THERE.
IT'S CAUSED A LOT OF OUR PEOPLE TO HOLD OUT HOPE FOR A FEW MORE.
GO ON, GIVE IT A PEEK.
WE CAN WAIT.
GUYS, COME ON...
EH, LET THEM HAVE THEIR FUN. TOWN'S STILL WAKING UP, ANYWAY.
BOARD'S PRETTY MUCH POINTLESS AFTER ALL THESE YEARS. WE KEEP IT UP BECAUSE PEOPLE LIKE IT.
I THINK THE FADED, WEATHER-BEATEN PHOTOS ARE THE SADDEST. THEN THERE'S THE REALLY DEDICATED PEOPLE WHO WRAP THE PHOTOS IN PLASTIC TO PROTECT THEM.
IT'S AS HEARTWARMING AS IT IS TRAGIC.

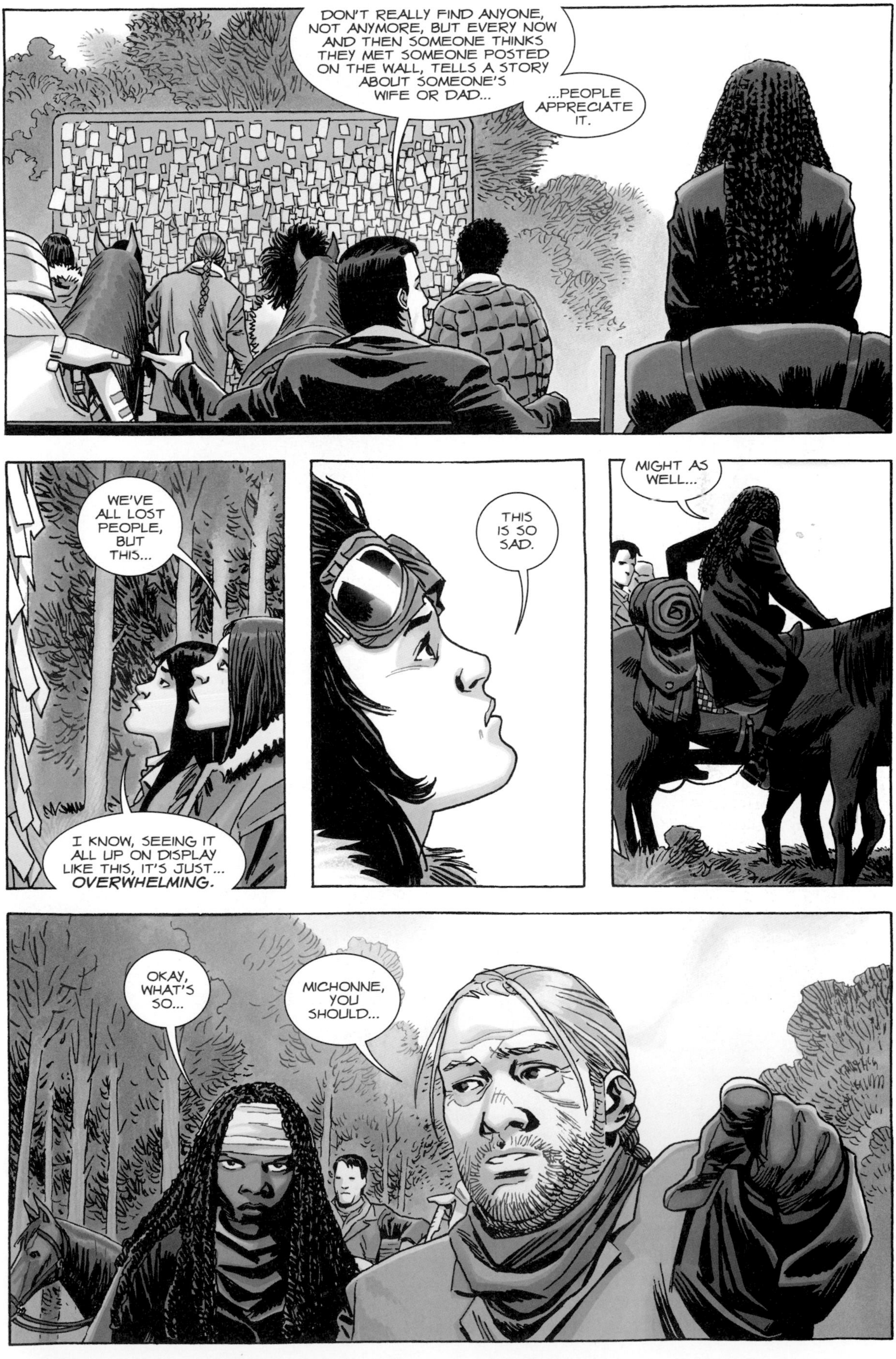
DON'T REALLY FIND ANYONE, NOT ANYMORE, BUT EVERY NOW AND THEN SOMEONE THINKS THEY MET SOMEONE POSTED ON THE WALL, TELLS A STORY ABOUT SOMEONE'S WIFE OR DAD...
...PEOPLE APPRECIATE IT.
WE'VE ALL LOST PEOPLE, BUT THIS...
I KNOW, SEEING IT ALL UP ON DISPLAY LIKE THIS, IT'S JUST... OVERWHELMING.
THIS IS SO SAD.
MIGHT AS WELL...
OKAY, WHAT'S SO...
MICHONNE, YOU SHOULD...

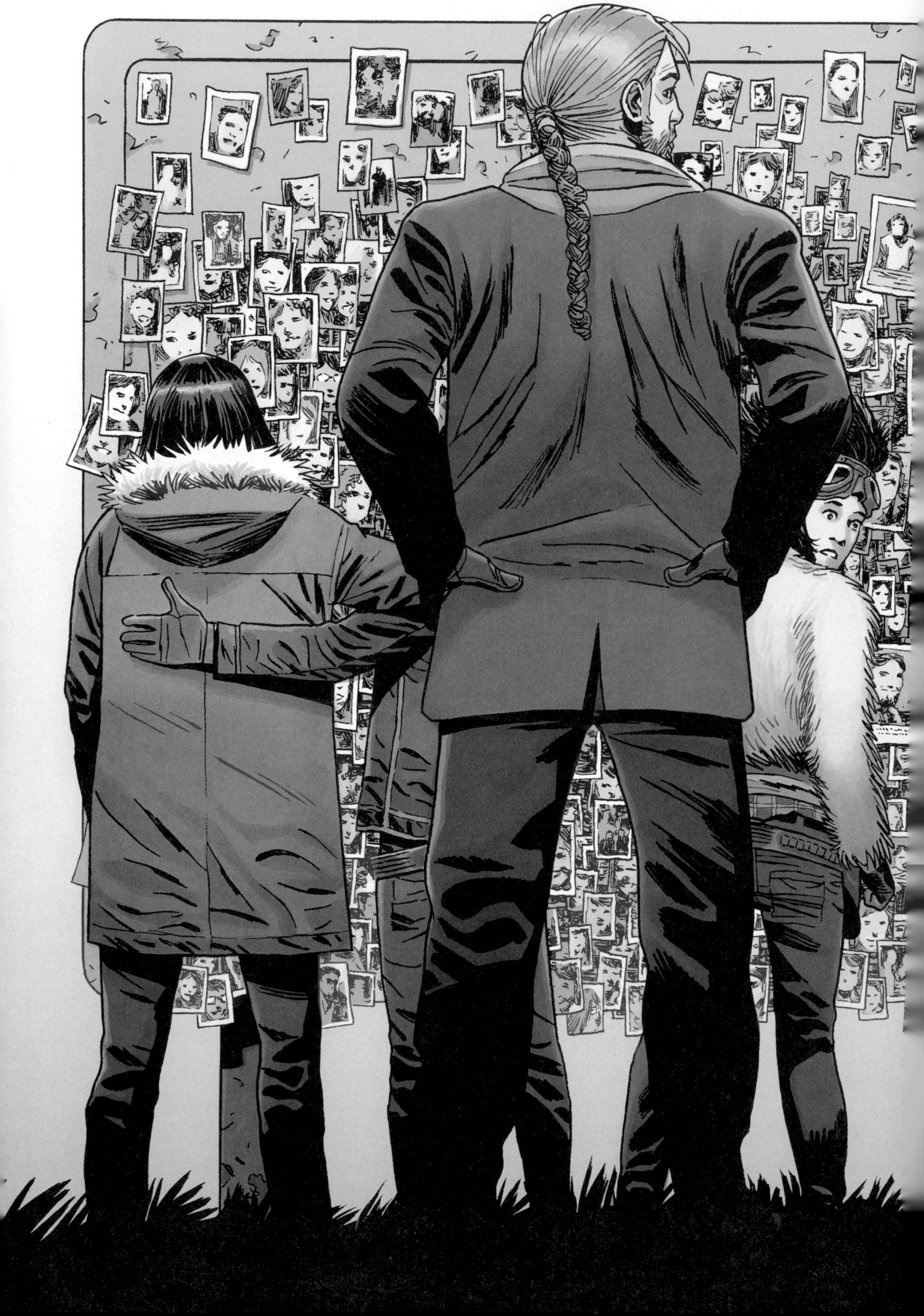

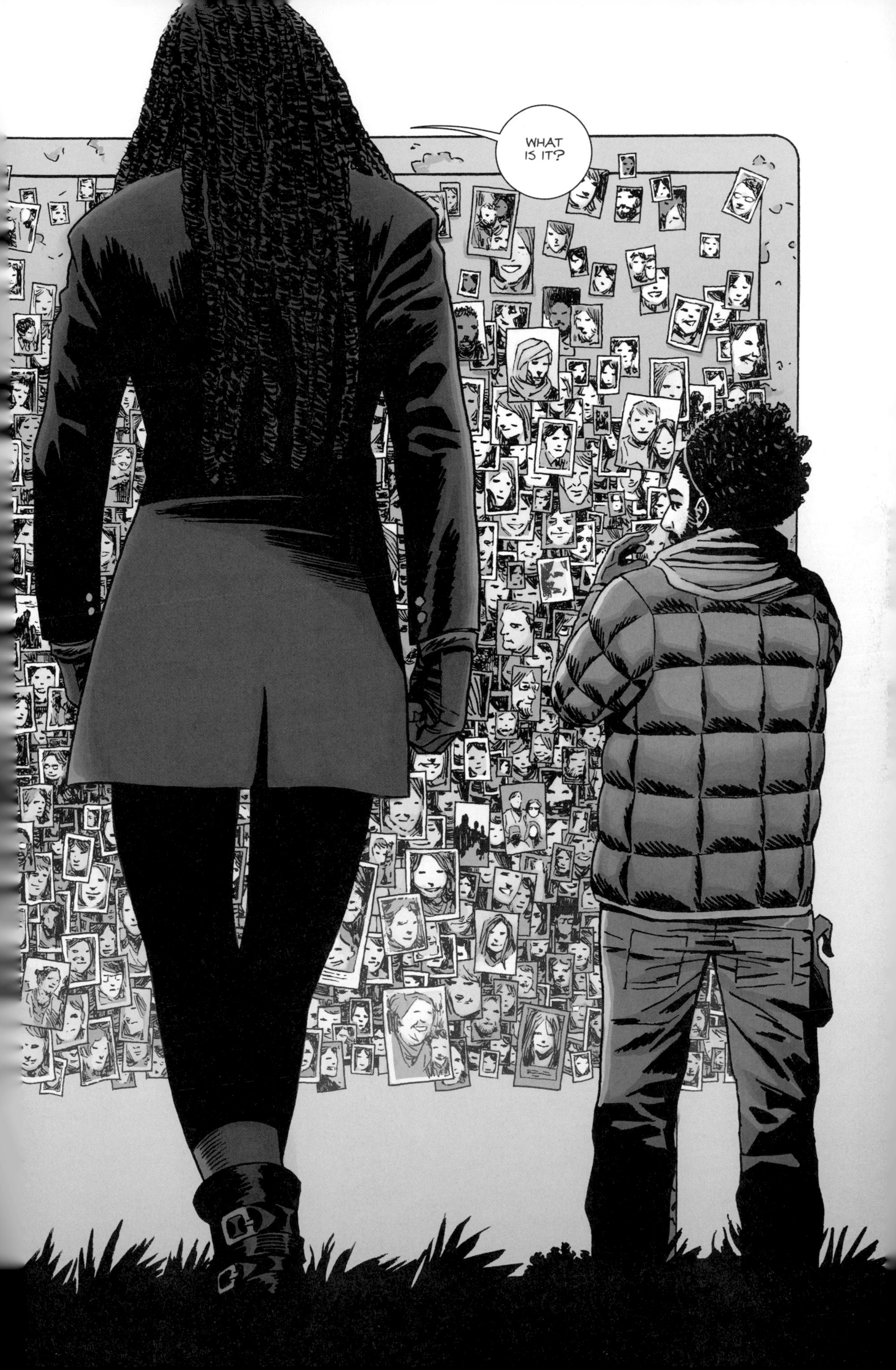
WHAT IS IT?

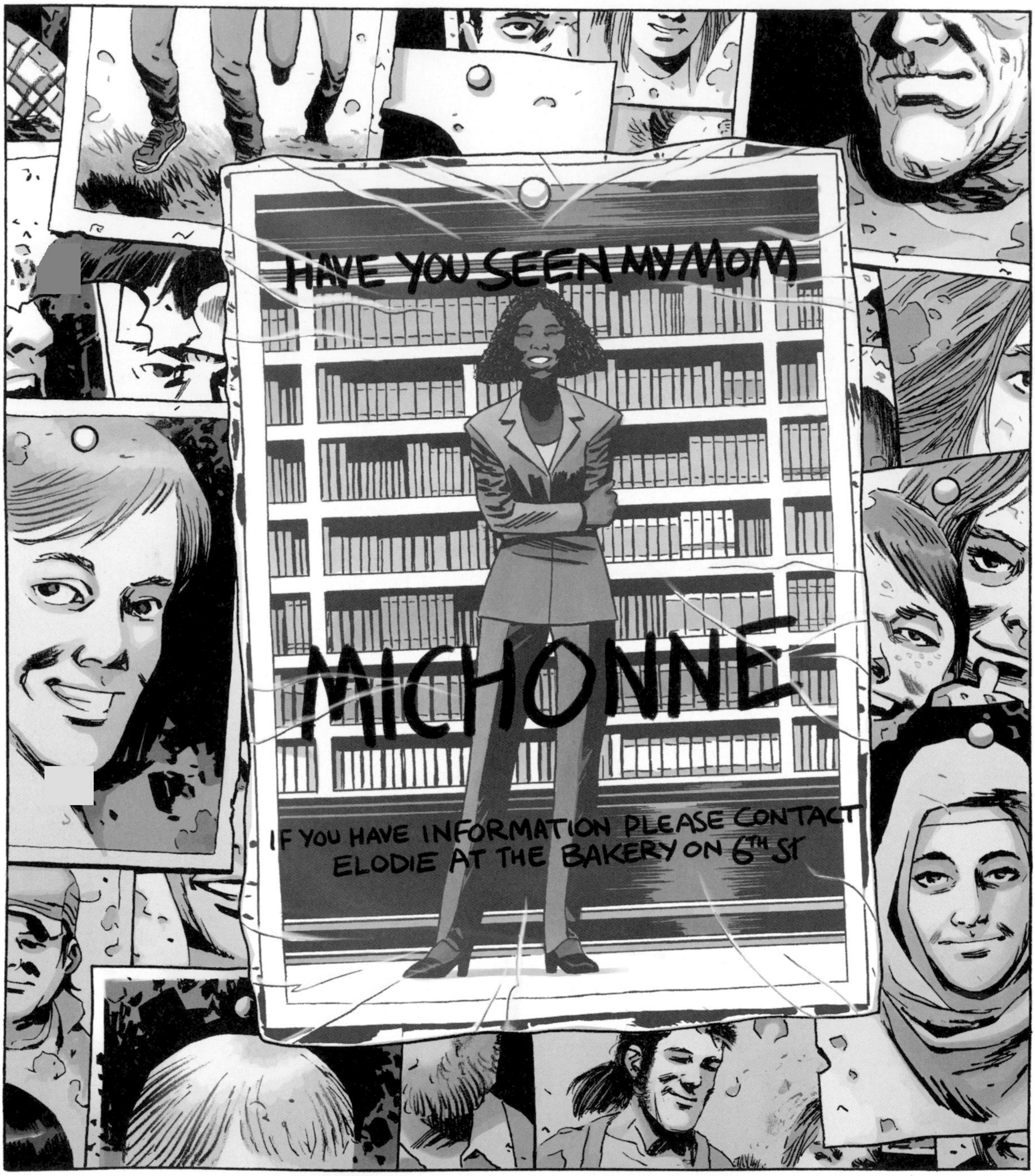
HAVE YOU SEEN MY MOM
MICHONNE
IF YOU HAVE INFORMATION PLEASE CONTACT ELODIE AT THE BAKERY ON 6TH ST

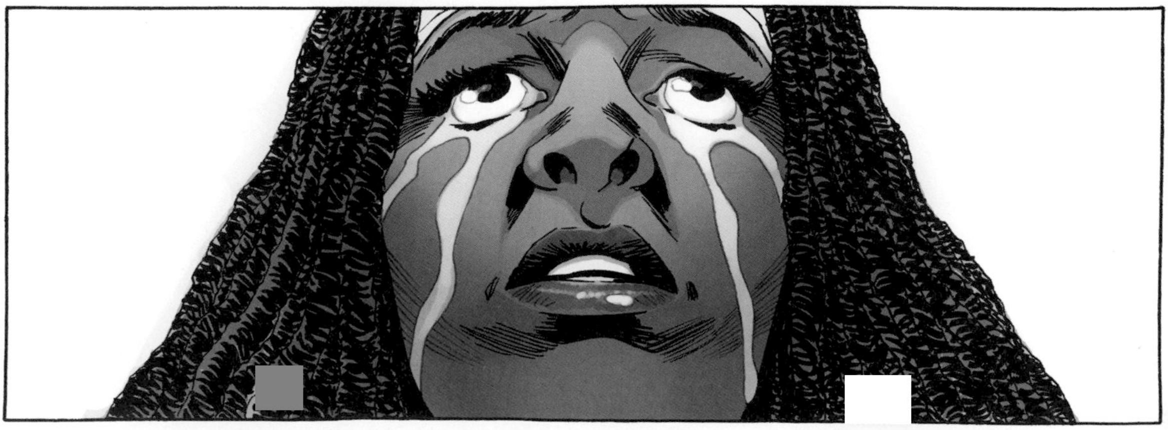

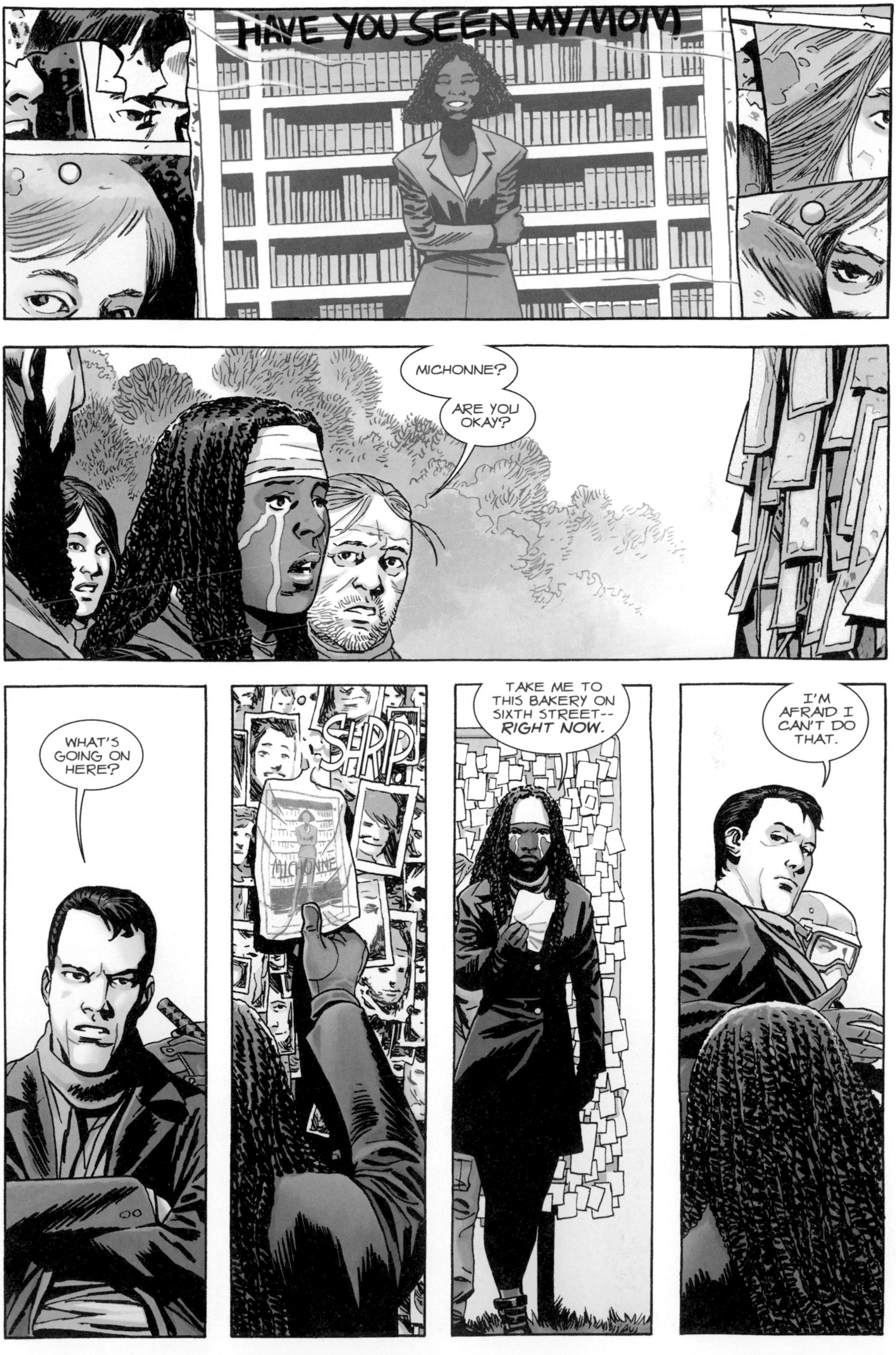
HAVE YOU SEEN MY MOM
MICHONNE?
ARE YOU OKAY?
WHAT'S GOING ON HERE?
SHRIP
MICHONNE
TAKE ME TO THIS BAKERY ON SIXTH STREET-- RIGHT NOW.
I'M AFRAID I CAN'T DO THAT.

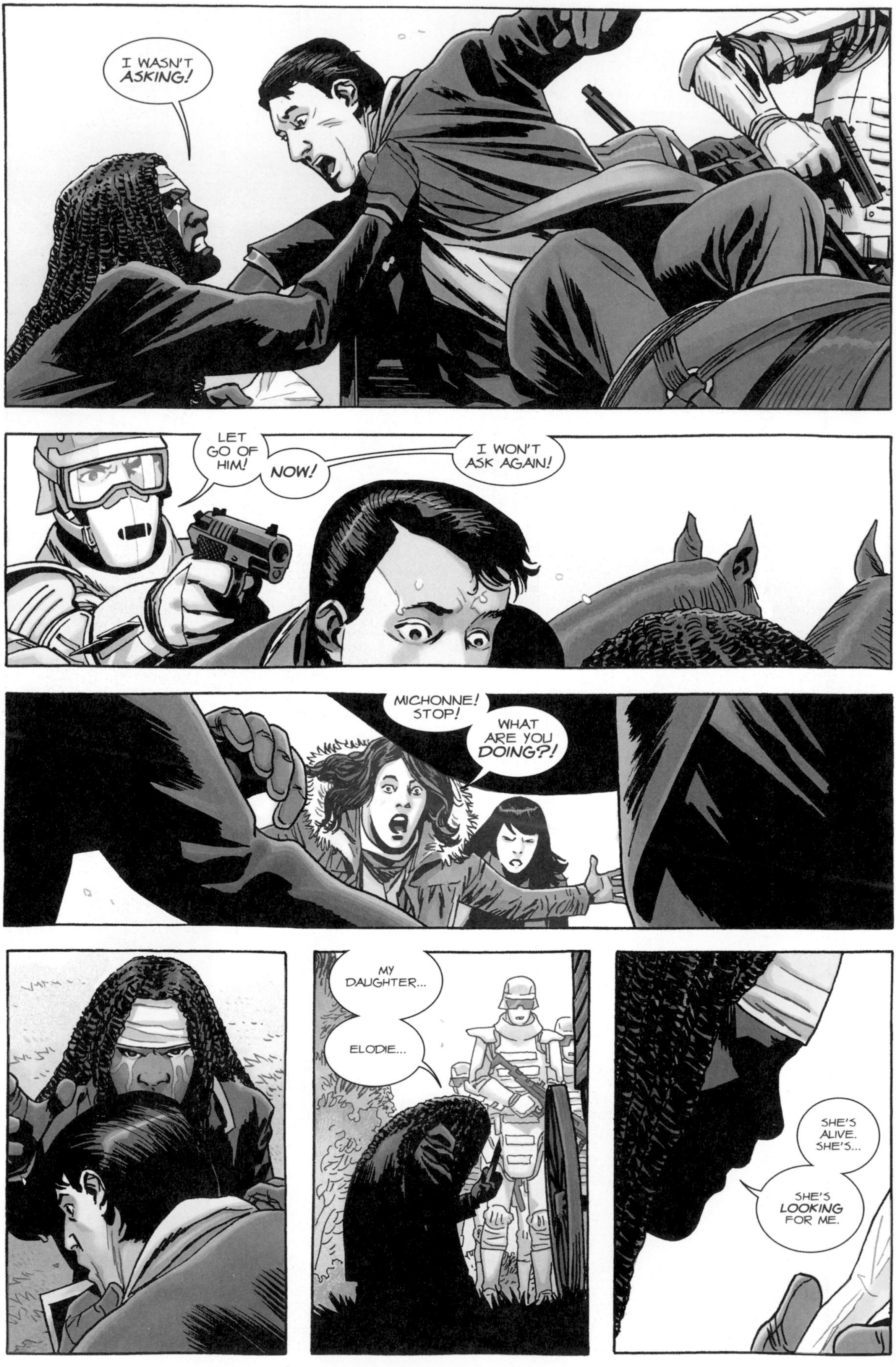
I WASN'T ASKING!
LET GO OF HIM!
NOW!
I WON'T ASK AGAIN!
MICHONNE! STOP!
WHAT ARE YOU DOING?!
MY DAUGHTER...
ELODIE...
SHE'S ALIVE. SHE'S...
SHE'S LOOKING FOR ME.

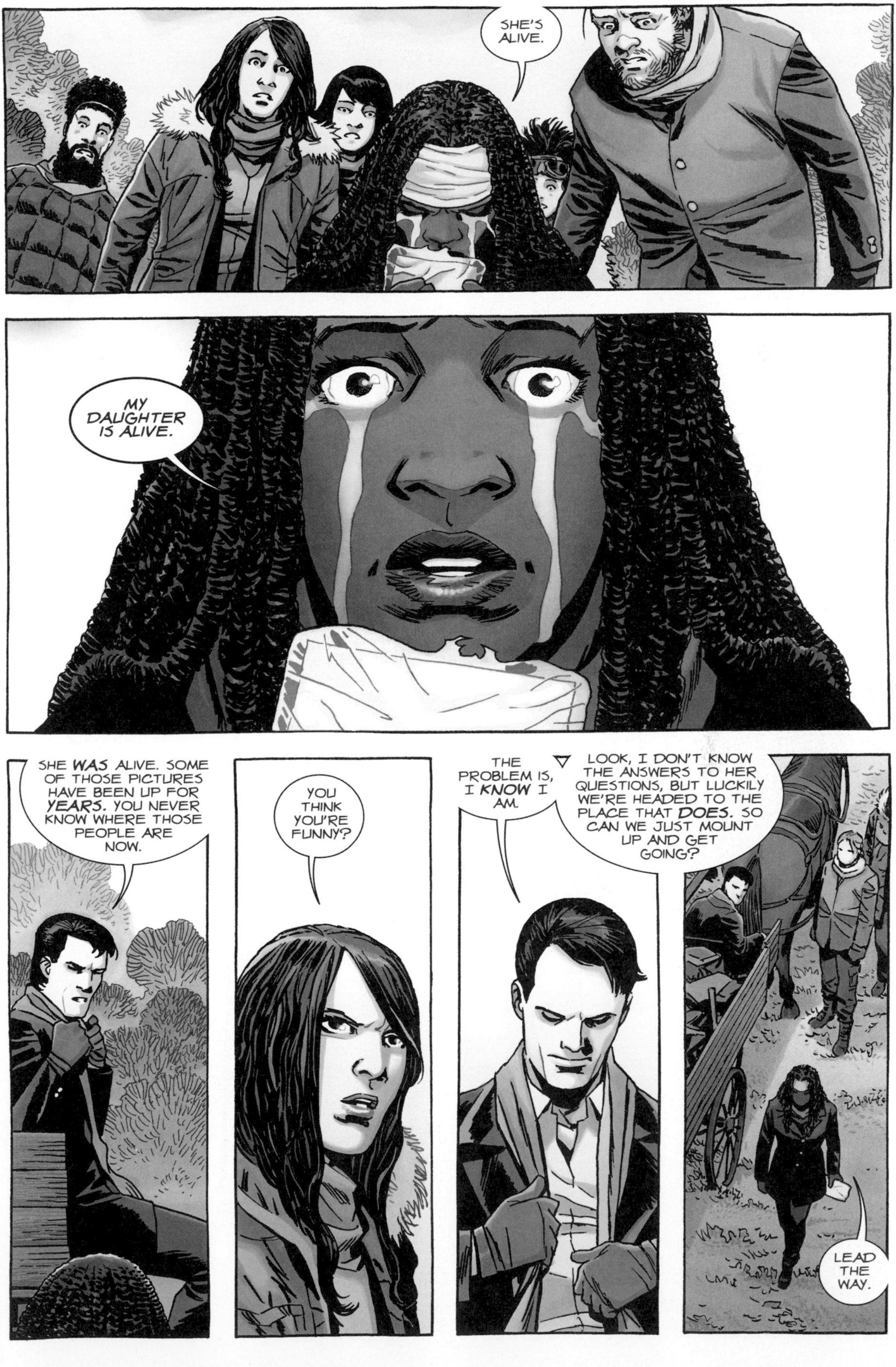
SHE'S ALIVE.
MY DAUGHTER IS ALIVE.
SHE WAS ALIVE. SOME OF THOSE PICTURES HAVE BEEN UP FOR YEARS. YOU NEVER KNOW WHERE THOSE PEOPLE ARE NOW.
YOU THINK YOU'RE FUNNY?
THE PROBLEM IS, I KNOW I AM.
LOOK, I DON'T KNOW THE ANSWERS TO HER QUESTIONS, BUT LUCKILY WE'RE HEADED TO THE PLACE THAT DOES. SO CAN WE JUST MOUNT UP AND GET GOING?
LEAD THE WAY.

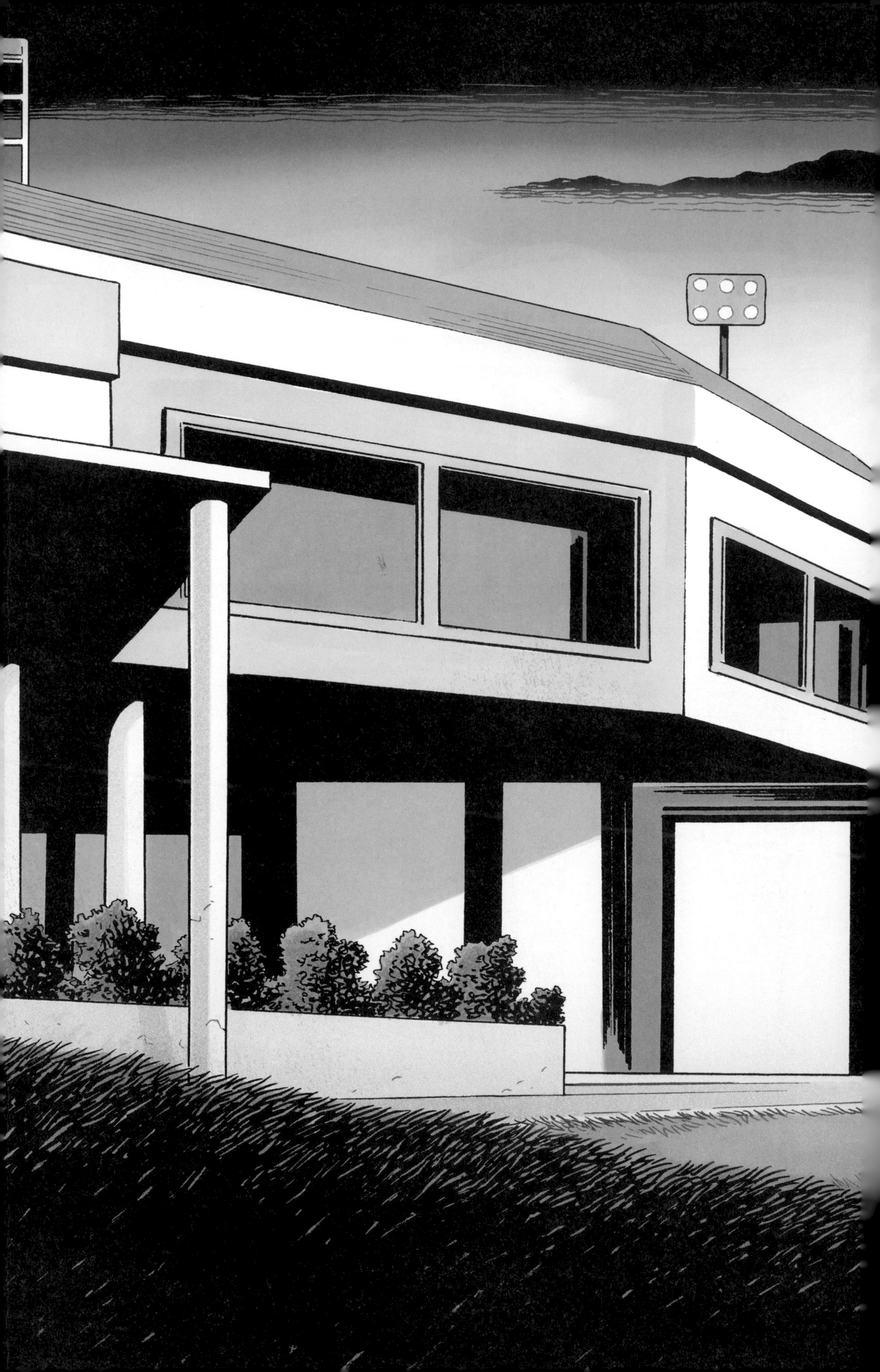

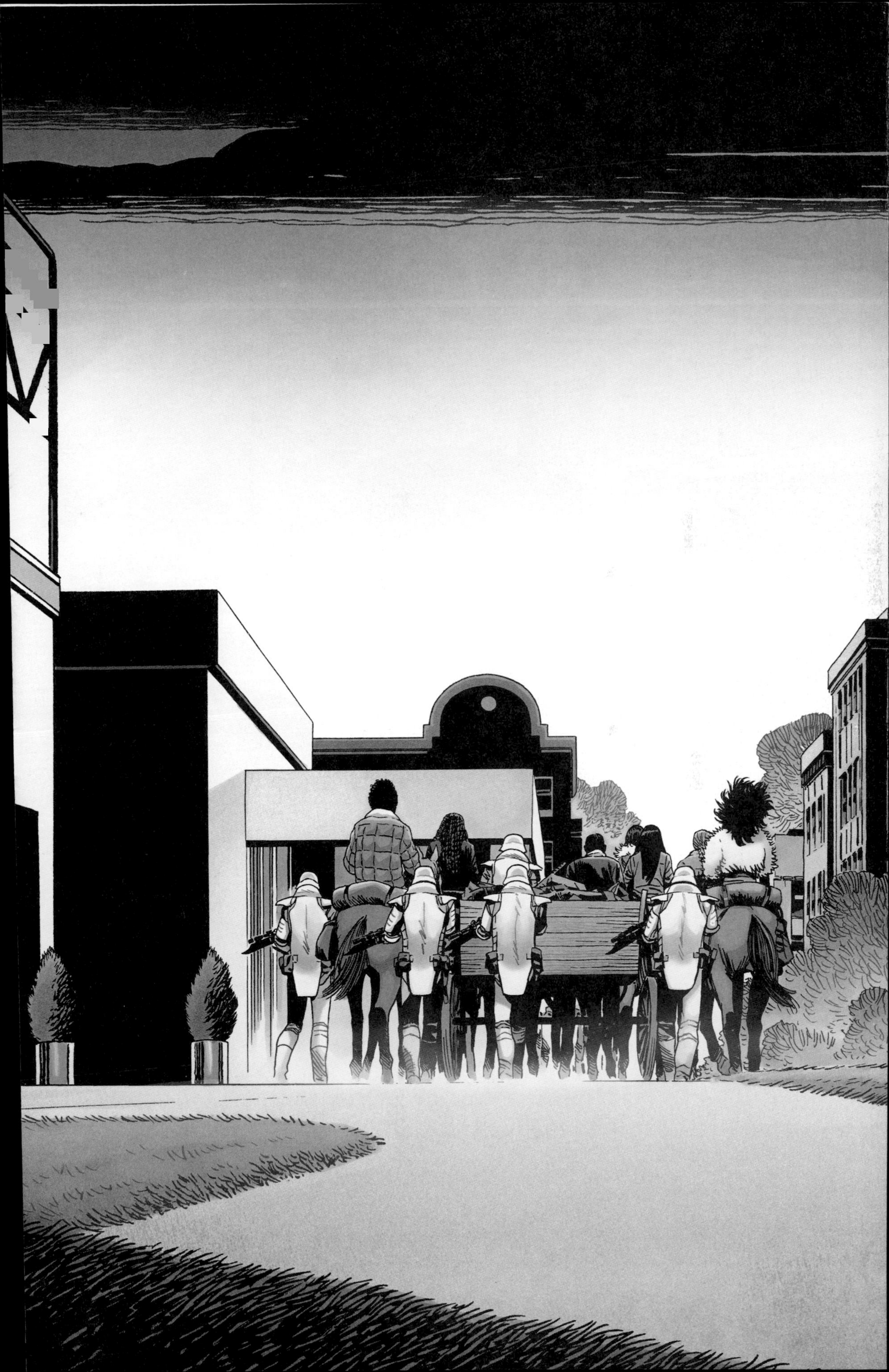

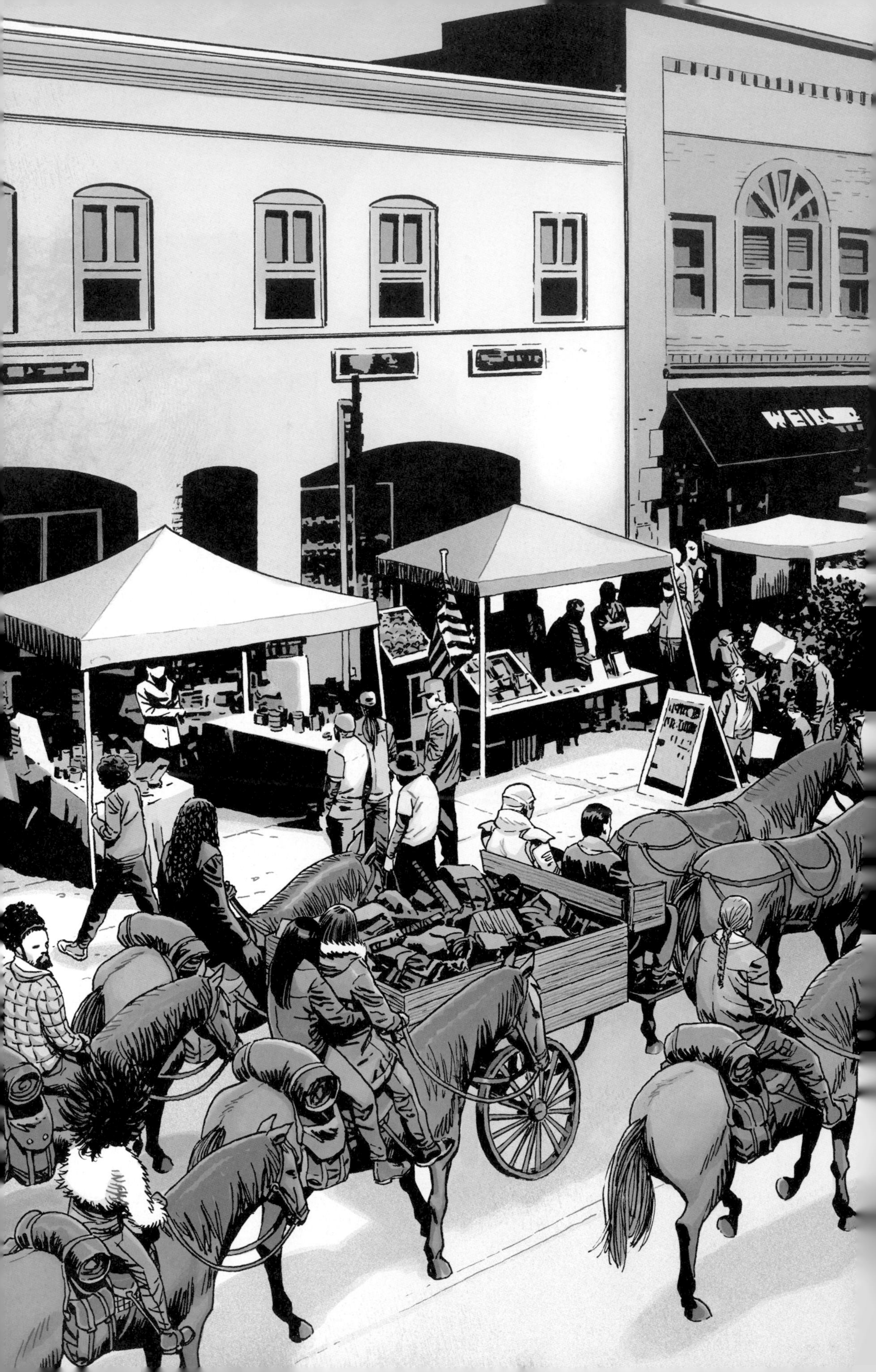

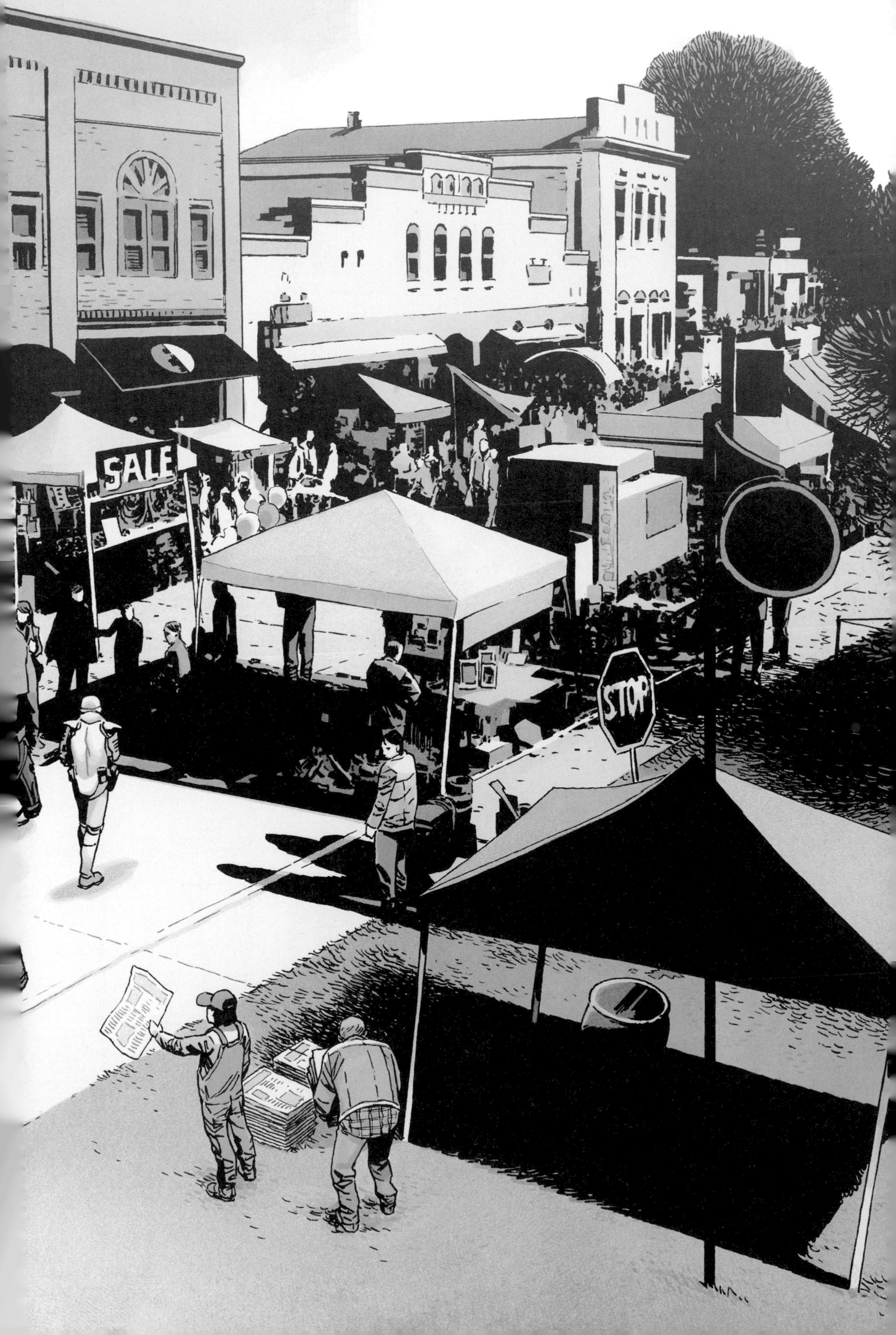
SALE
STOP

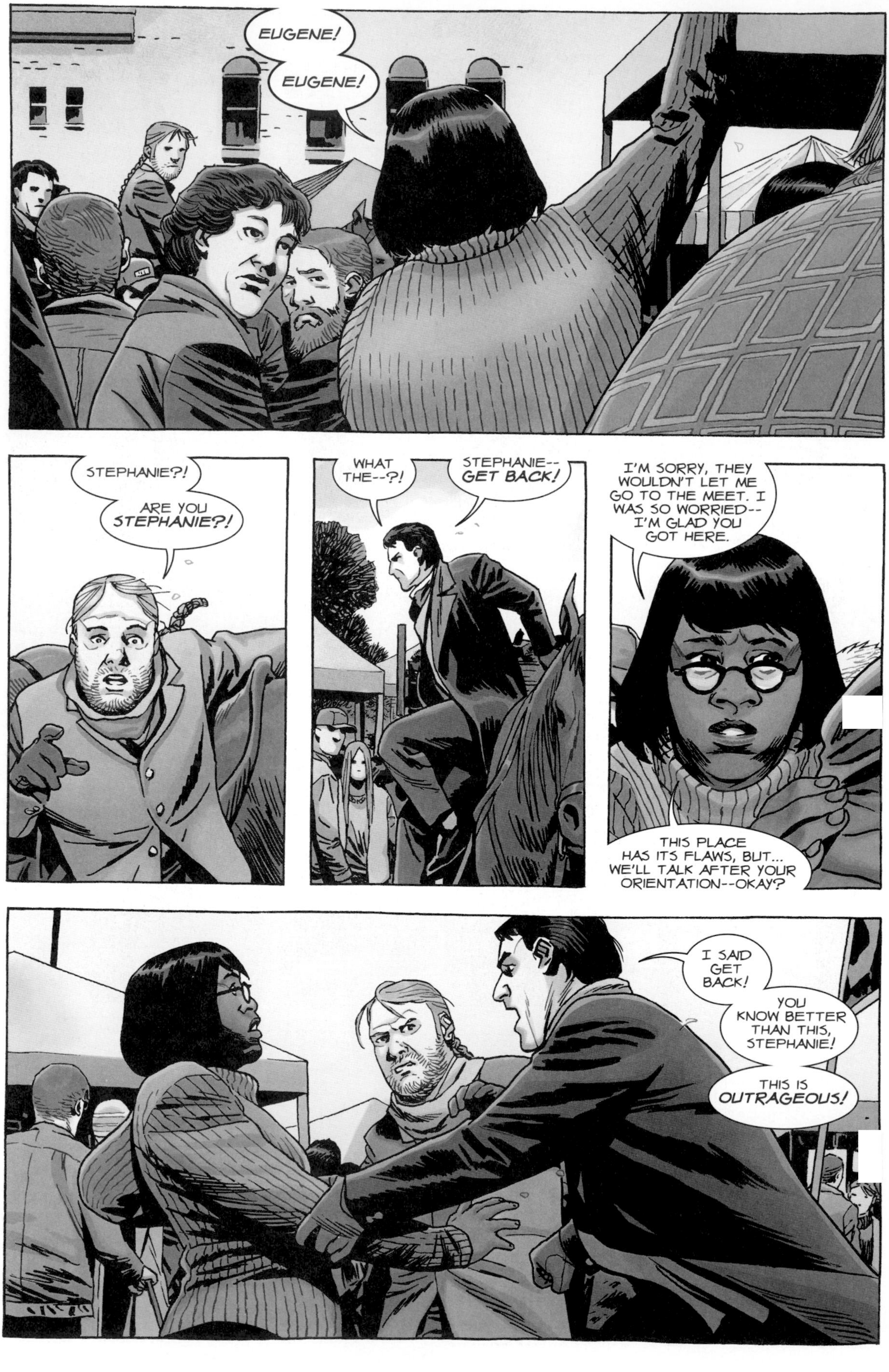
EUGENE!
EUGENE!
STEPHANIE?!
ARE YOU STEPHANIE?!
WHAT THE--?!
STEPHANIE-- GET BACK!
I'M SORRY, THEY WOULDN'T LET ME GO TO THE MEET. I WAS SO WORRIED-- I'M GLAD YOU GOT HERE.
THIS PLACE HAS ITS FLAWS, BUT... WE'LL TALK AFTER YOUR ORIENTATION--OKAY?
I SAID GET BACK!
YOU KNOW BETTER THAN THIS, STEPHANIE!
THIS IS OUTRAGEOUS!

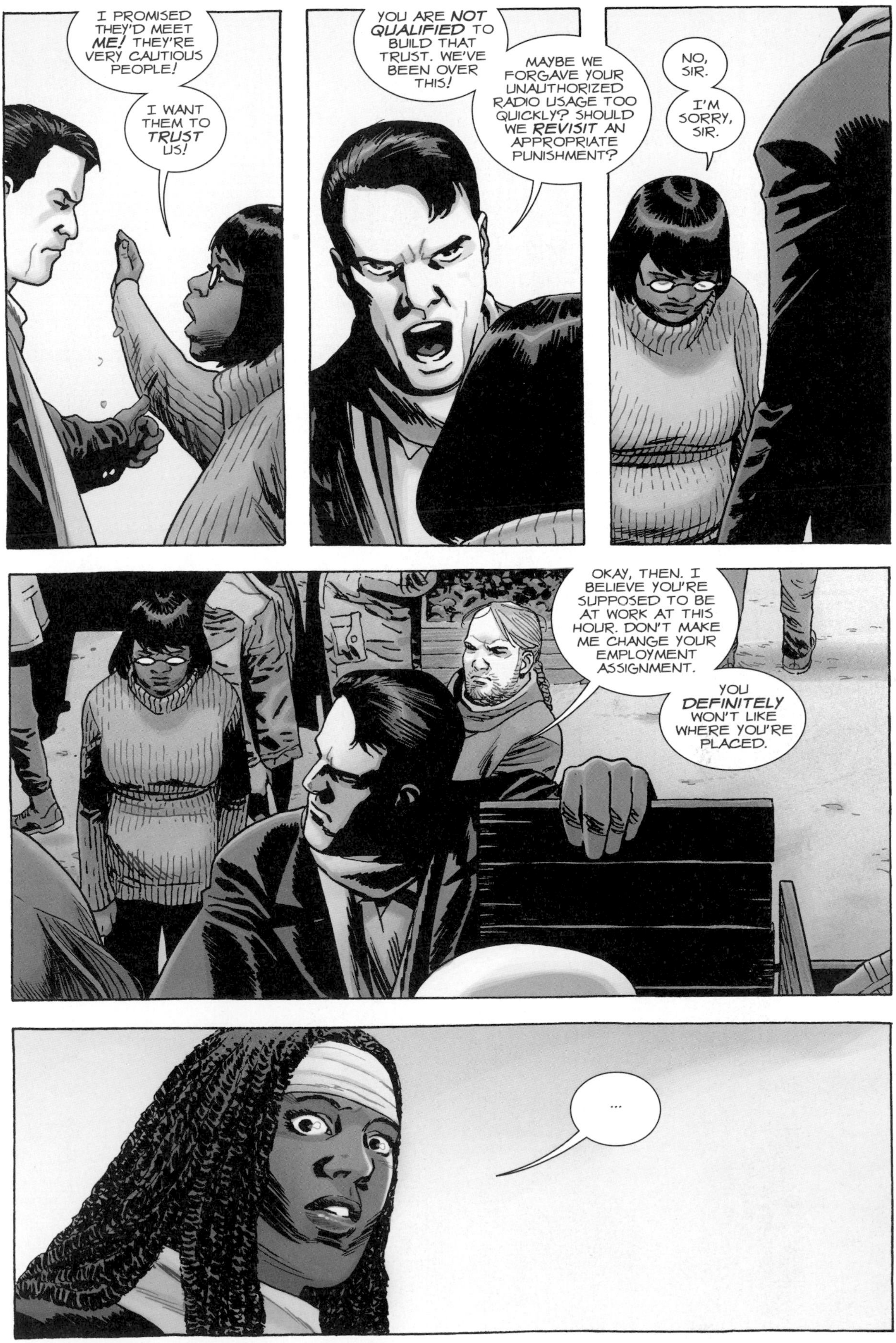
I PROMISED THEY'D MEET ME! THEY'RE VERY CAUTIOUS PEOPLE!
I WANT THEM TO TRUST US!
YOU ARE NOT QUALIFIED TO BUILD THAT TRUST. WE'VE BEEN OVER THIS!
MAYBE WE FORGAVE YOUR UNAUTHORIZED RADIO USAGE TOO QUICKLY? SHOULD WE REVISIT AN APPROPRIATE PUNISHMENT?
NO, SIR.
I'M SORRY, SIR.
OKAY, THEN. I BELIEVE YOU'RE SUPPOSED TO BE AT WORK AT THIS HOUR. DON'T MAKE ME CHANGE YOUR EMPLOYMENT ASSIGNMENT.
YOU DEFINITELY WON'T LIKE WHERE YOU'RE PLACED.
...

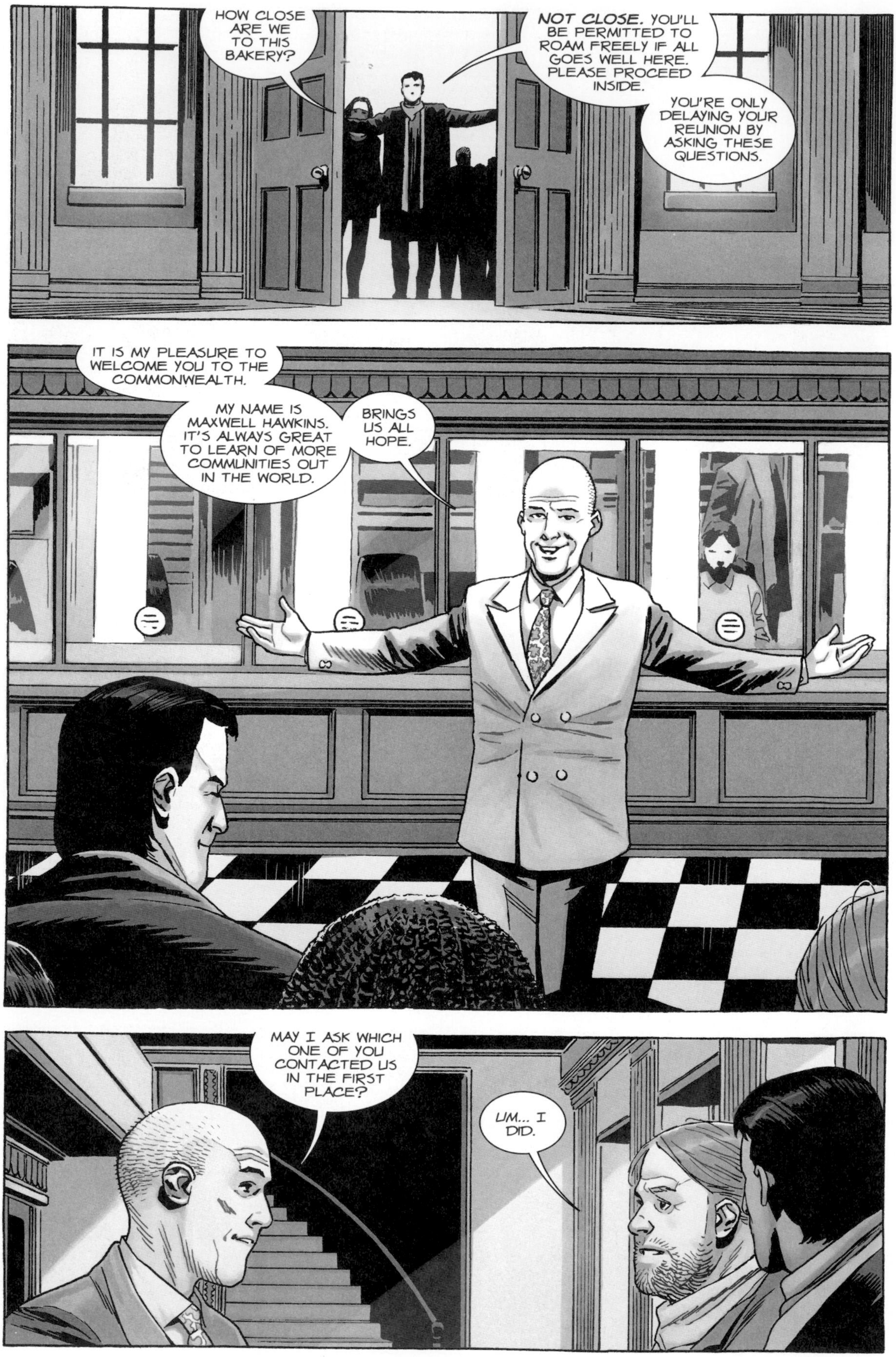
HOW CLOSE ARE WE TO THIS BAKERY?
NOT CLOSE. YOU'LL BE PERMITTED TO ROAM FREELY IF ALL GOES WELL HERE. PLEASE PROCEED INSIDE.
YOU'RE ONLY DELAYING YOUR REUNION BY ASKING THESE QUESTIONS.
IT IS MY PLEASURE TO WELCOME YOU TO THE COMMONWEALTH.
MY NAME IS MAXWELL HAWKINS. IT'S ALWAYS GREAT TO LEARN OF MORE COMMUNITIES OUT IN THE WORLD.
BRINGS US ALL HOPE.
MAY I ASK WHICH ONE OF YOU CONTACTED US IN THE FIRST PLACE?
UM... I DID.

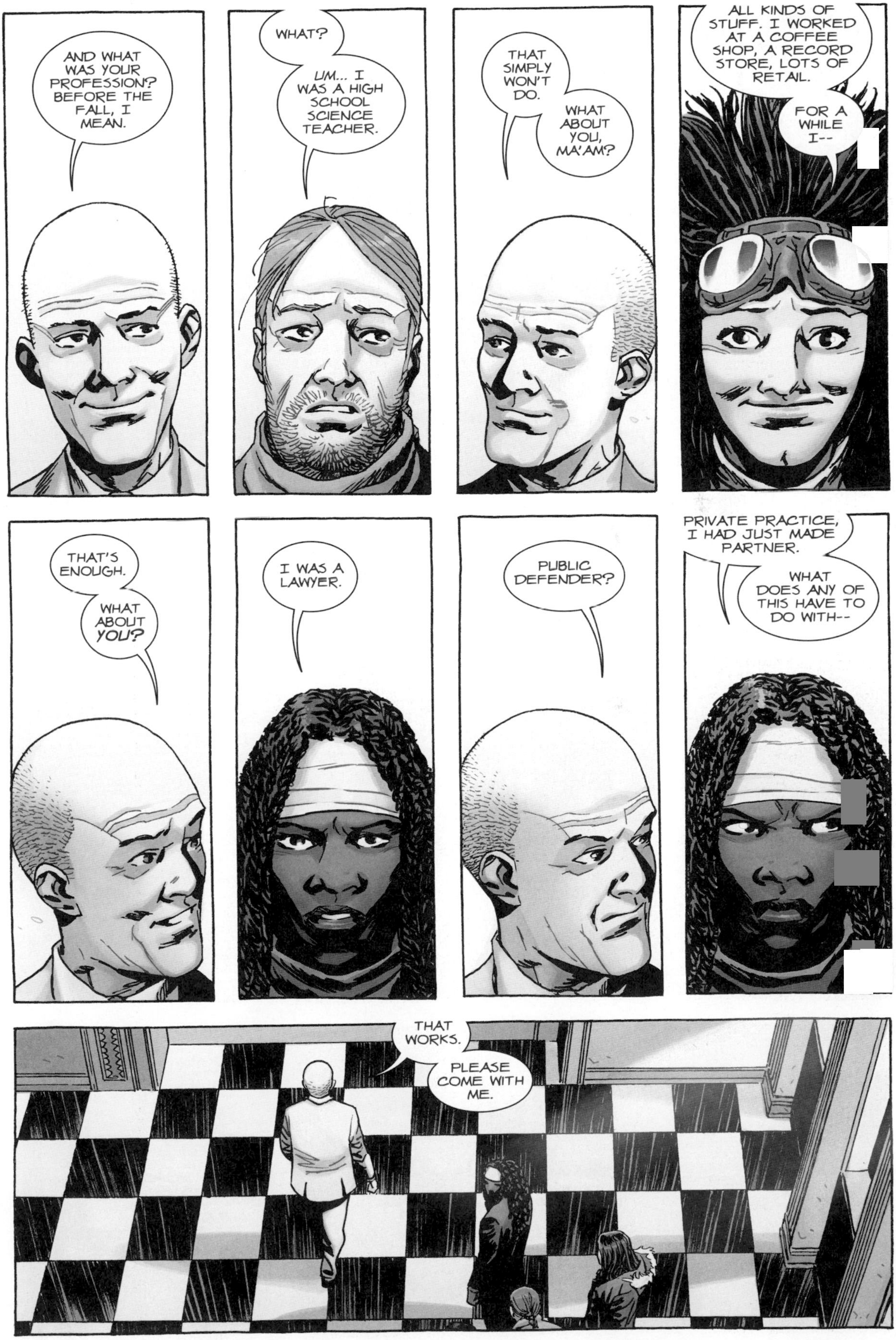
AND WHAT WAS YOUR PROFESSION? BEFORE THE FALL, I MEAN.
WHAT?
UM... I WAS A HIGH SCHOOL SCIENCE TEACHER.
THAT SIMPLY WON'T DO.
WHAT ABOUT YOU, MA'AM?
ALL KINDS OF STUFF. I WORKED AT A COFFEE SHOP, A RECORD STORE, LOTS OF RETAIL.
FOR A WHILE I--
THAT'S ENOUGH.
WHAT ABOUT YOU?
I WAS A LAWYER.
PUBLIC DEFENDER?
PRIVATE PRACTICE, I HAD JUST MADE PARTNER.
WHAT DOES ANY OF THIS HAVE TO DO WITH--
THAT WORKS.
PLEASE COME WITH ME.

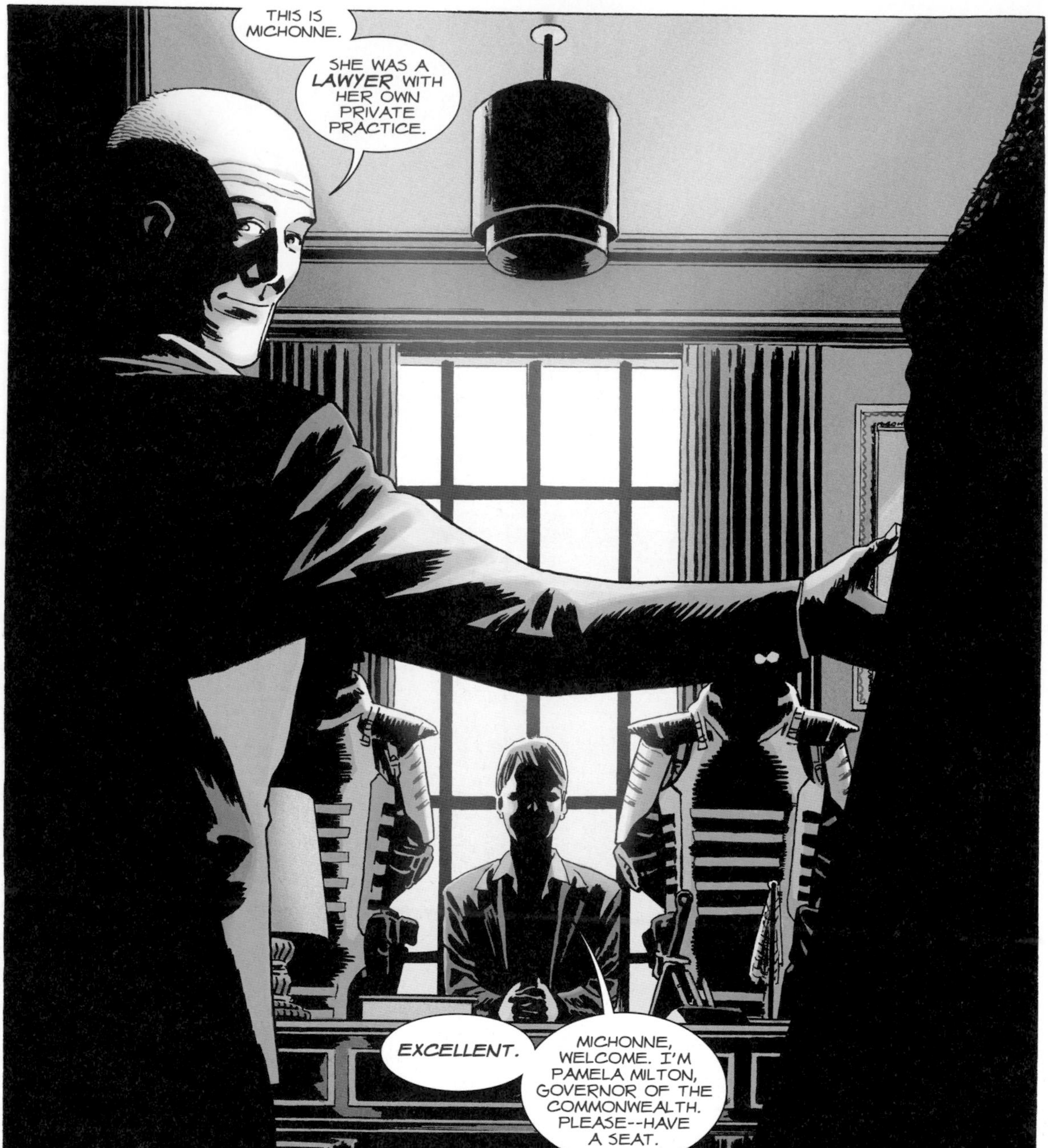
THIS IS MICHONNE.
SHE WAS A LAWYER WITH HER OWN PRIVATE PRACTICE.
EXCELLENT.
MICHONNE, WELCOME. I'M PAMELA MILTON, GOVERNOR OF THE COMMONWEALTH. PLEASE--HAVE A SEAT.

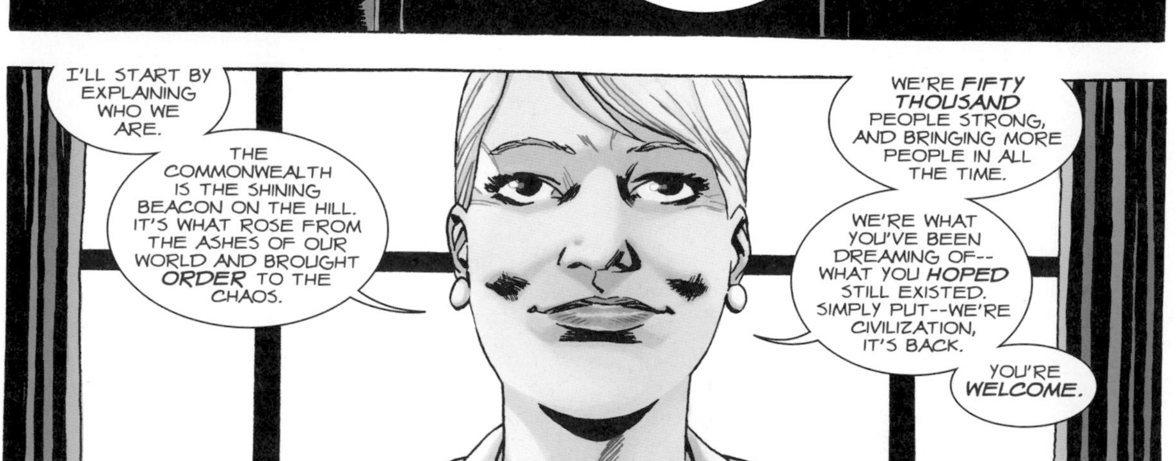
I'LL START BY EXPLAINING WHO WE ARE.
THE COMMONWEALTH IS THE SHINING BEACON ON THE HILL. IT'S WHAT ROSE FROM THE ASHES OF OUR WORLD AND BROUGHT ORDER TO THE CHAOS.
WE'RE FIFTY THOUSAND PEOPLE STRONG, AND BRINGING MORE PEOPLE IN ALL THE TIME.
WE'RE WHAT YOU'VE BEEN DREAMING OF--WHAT YOU HOPED STILL EXISTED. SIMPLY PUT--WE'RE CIVILIZATION, IT'S BACK.
YOU'RE WELCOME.

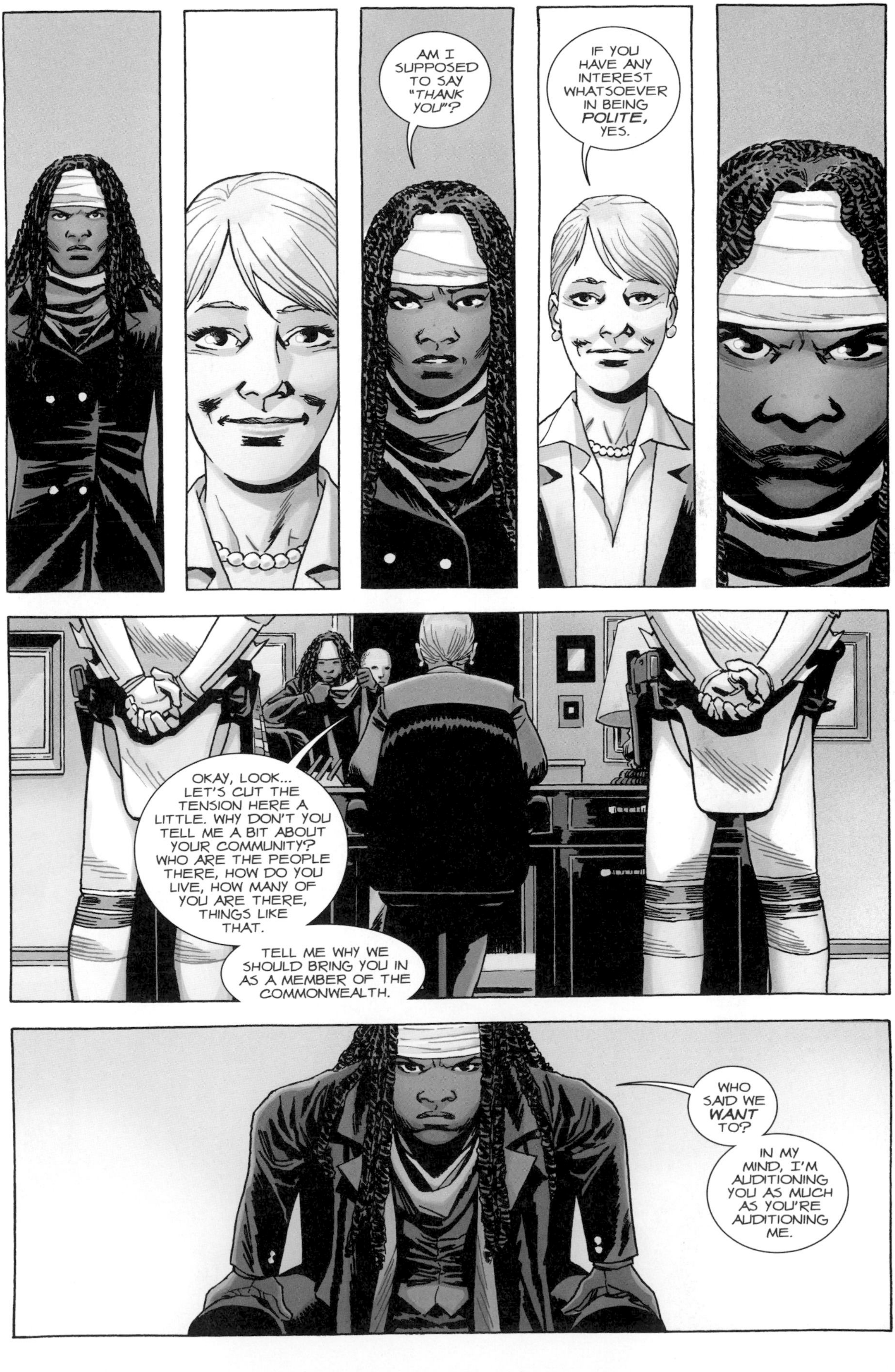
AM I SUPPOSED TO SAY "*THANK YOU*"?
IF YOU HAVE ANY INTEREST WHATSOEVER IN BEING **POLITE,** YES.
OKAY, LOOK... LET'S CUT THE TENSION HERE A LITTLE. WHY DON'T YOU TELL ME A BIT ABOUT YOUR COMMUNITY? WHO ARE THE PEOPLE THERE, HOW DO YOU LIVE, HOW MANY OF YOU ARE THERE, THINGS LIKE THAT.
TELL ME WHY WE SHOULD BRING YOU IN AS A MEMBER OF THE COMMONWEALTH.
WHO SAID WE ***WANT*** TO?
IN MY MIND, I'M AUDITIONING YOU AS MUCH AS YOU'RE AUDITIONING ME.

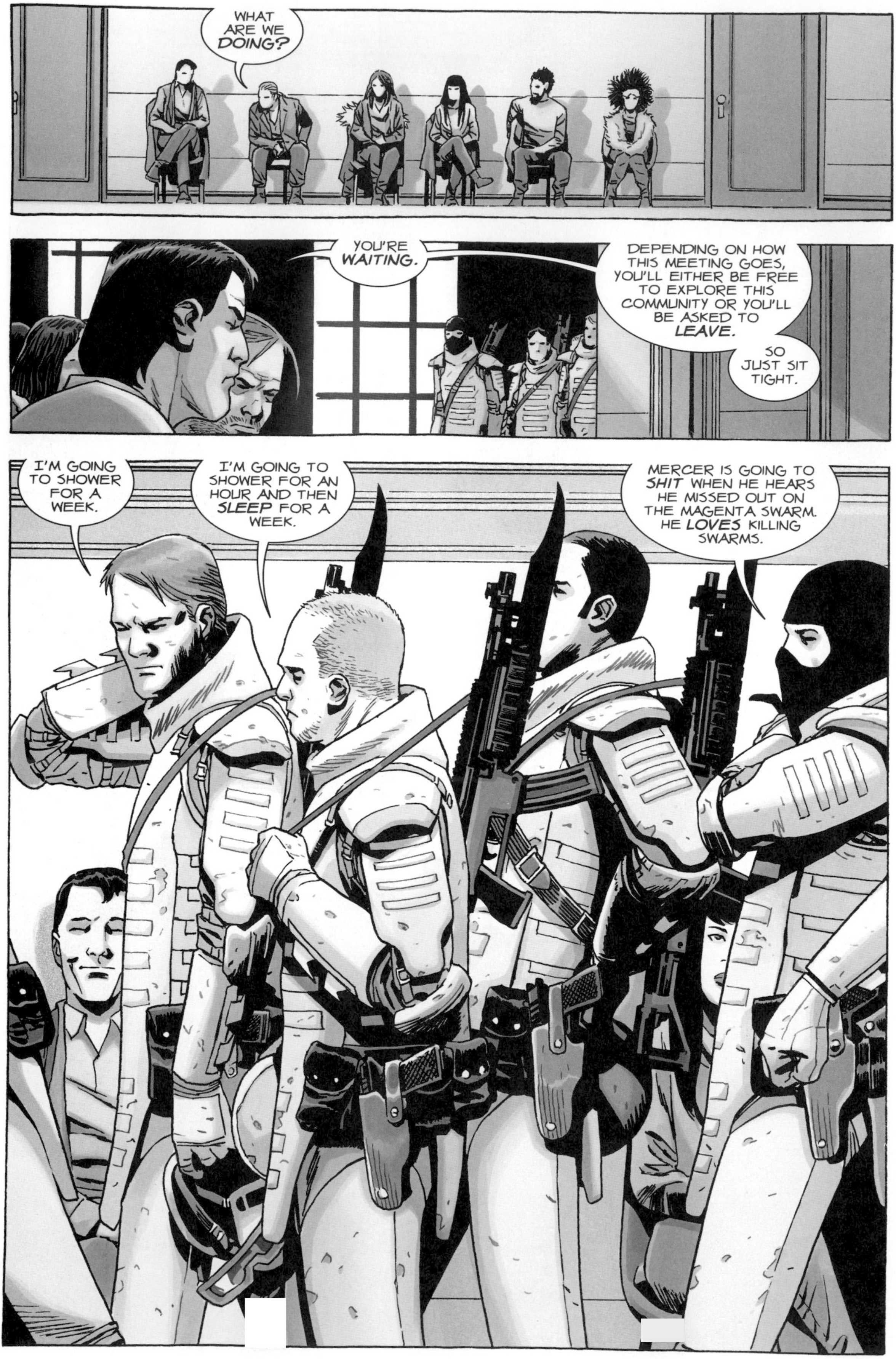
WHAT ARE WE DOING?
YOU'RE WAITING.
DEPENDING ON HOW THIS MEETING GOES, YOU'LL EITHER BE FREE TO EXPLORE THIS COMMUNITY OR YOU'LL BE ASKED TO LEAVE.
SO JUST SIT TIGHT.
I'M GOING TO SHOWER FOR A WEEK.
I'M GOING TO SHOWER FOR AN HOUR AND THEN SLEEP FOR A WEEK.
MERCER IS GOING TO SHIT WHEN HE HEARS HE MISSED OUT ON THE MAGENTA SWARM. HE LOVES KILLING SWARMS.

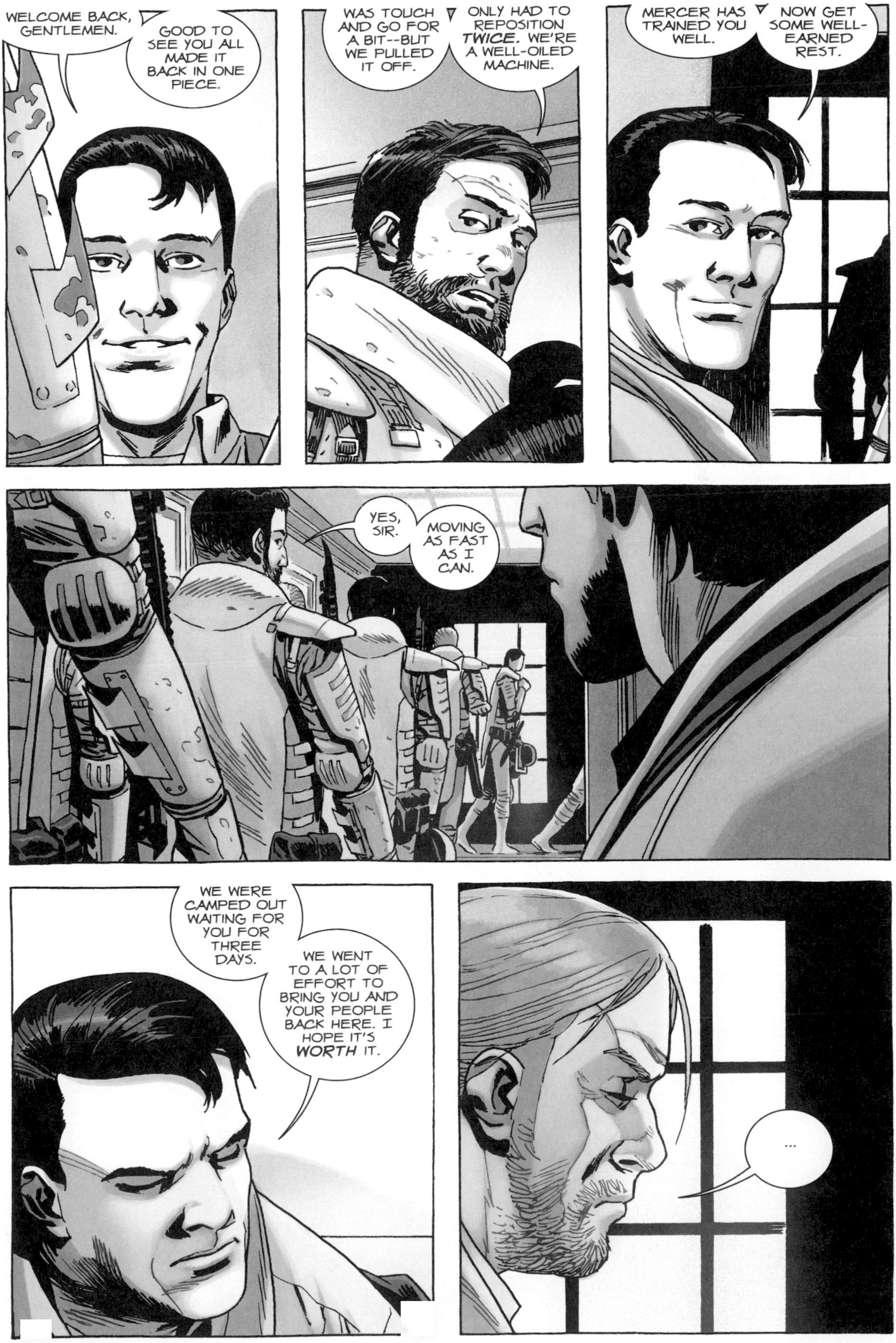
WELCOME BACK, GENTLEMEN.
GOOD TO SEE YOU ALL MADE IT BACK IN ONE PIECE.
WAS TOUCH AND GO FOR A BIT--BUT WE PULLED IT OFF.
ONLY HAD TO REPOSITION TWICE. WE'RE A WELL-OILED MACHINE.
MERCER HAS TRAINED YOU WELL.
NOW GET SOME WELL-EARNED REST.
YES, SIR.
MOVING AS FAST AS I CAN.
WE WERE CAMPED OUT WAITING FOR YOU FOR THREE DAYS.
WE WENT TO A LOT OF EFFORT TO BRING YOU AND YOUR PEOPLE BACK HERE. I HOPE IT'S WORTH IT.
...

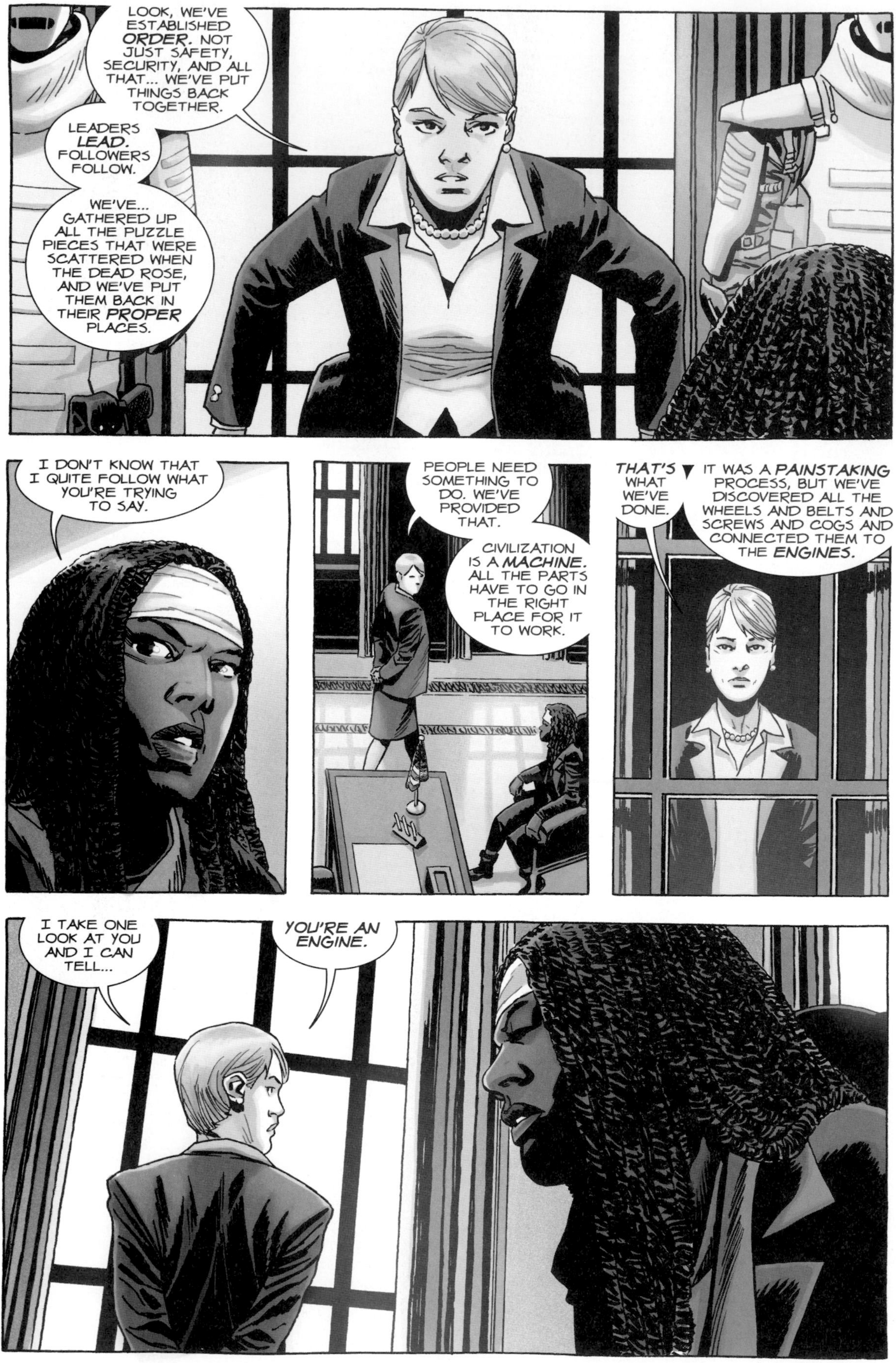
LOOK, WE'VE ESTABLISHED ORDER. NOT JUST SAFETY, SECURITY, AND ALL THAT... WE'VE PUT THINGS BACK TOGETHER.
LEADERS LEAD. FOLLOWERS FOLLOW.
WE'VE... GATHERED UP ALL THE PUZZLE PIECES THAT WERE SCATTERED WHEN THE DEAD ROSE, AND WE'VE PUT THEM BACK IN THEIR PROPER PLACES.
I DON'T KNOW THAT I QUITE FOLLOW WHAT YOU'RE TRYING TO SAY.
PEOPLE NEED SOMETHING TO DO. WE'VE PROVIDED THAT.
CIVILIZATION IS A MACHINE. ALL THE PARTS HAVE TO GO IN THE RIGHT PLACE FOR IT TO WORK.
THAT'S WHAT WE'VE DONE.
IT WAS A PAINSTAKING PROCESS, BUT WE'VE DISCOVERED ALL THE WHEELS AND BELTS AND SCREWS AND COGS AND CONNECTED THEM TO THE ENGINES.
I TAKE ONE LOOK AT YOU AND I CAN TELL...
YOU'RE AN ENGINE.

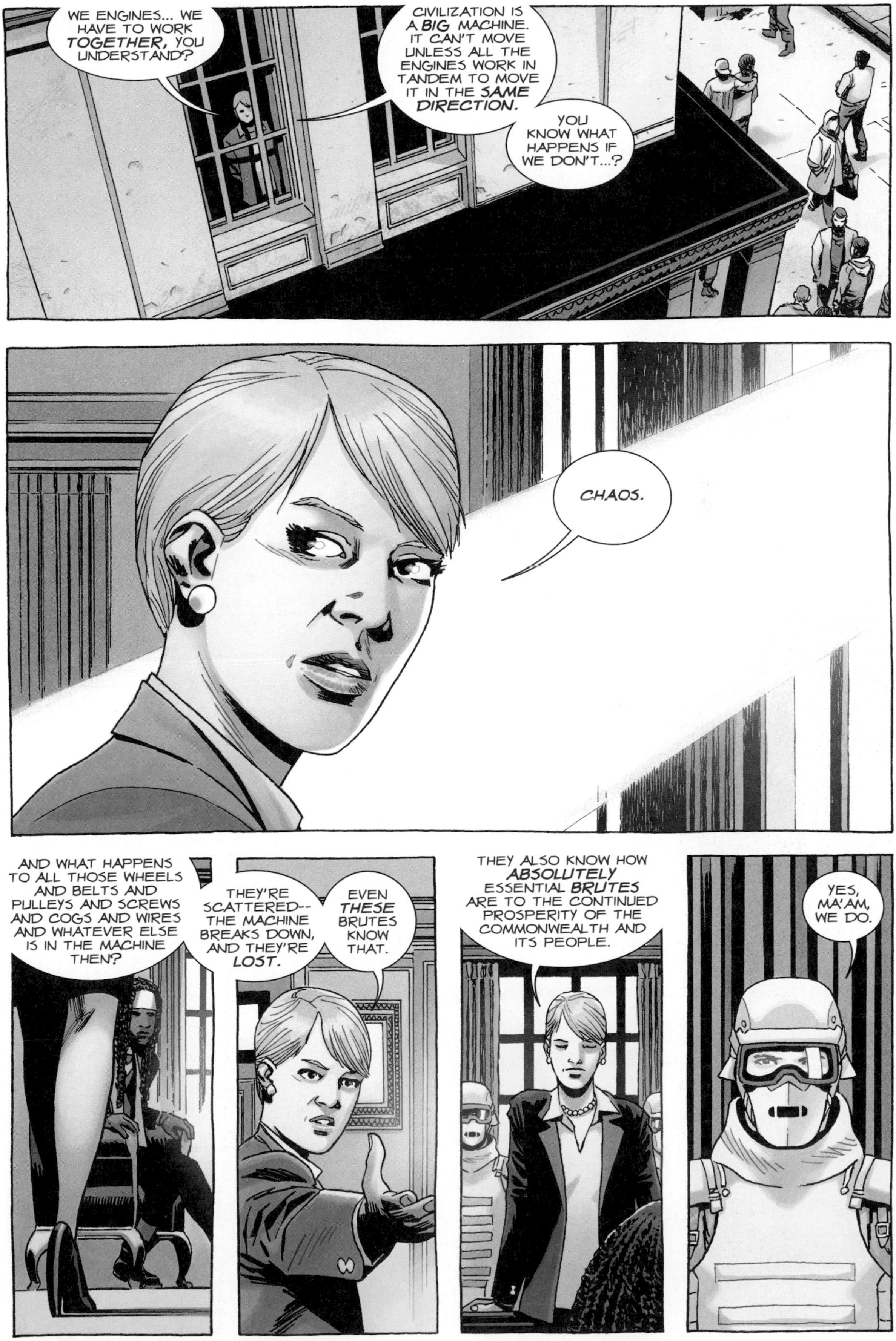
WE ENGINES... WE HAVE TO WORK TOGETHER, YOU UNDERSTAND?
CIVILIZATION IS A BIG MACHINE. IT CAN'T MOVE UNLESS ALL THE ENGINES WORK IN TANDEM TO MOVE IT IN THE SAME DIRECTION.
YOU KNOW WHAT HAPPENS IF WE DON'T...?
CHAOS.
AND WHAT HAPPENS TO ALL THOSE WHEELS AND BELTS AND PULLEYS AND SCREWS AND COGS AND WIRES AND WHATEVER ELSE IS IN THE MACHINE THEN?
THEY'RE SCATTERED-- THE MACHINE BREAKS DOWN, AND THEY'RE LOST.
EVEN THESE BRUTES KNOW THAT.
THEY ALSO KNOW HOW ABSOLUTELY ESSENTIAL BRUTES ARE TO THE CONTINUED PROSPERITY OF THE COMMONWEALTH AND ITS PEOPLE.
YES, MA'AM, WE DO.

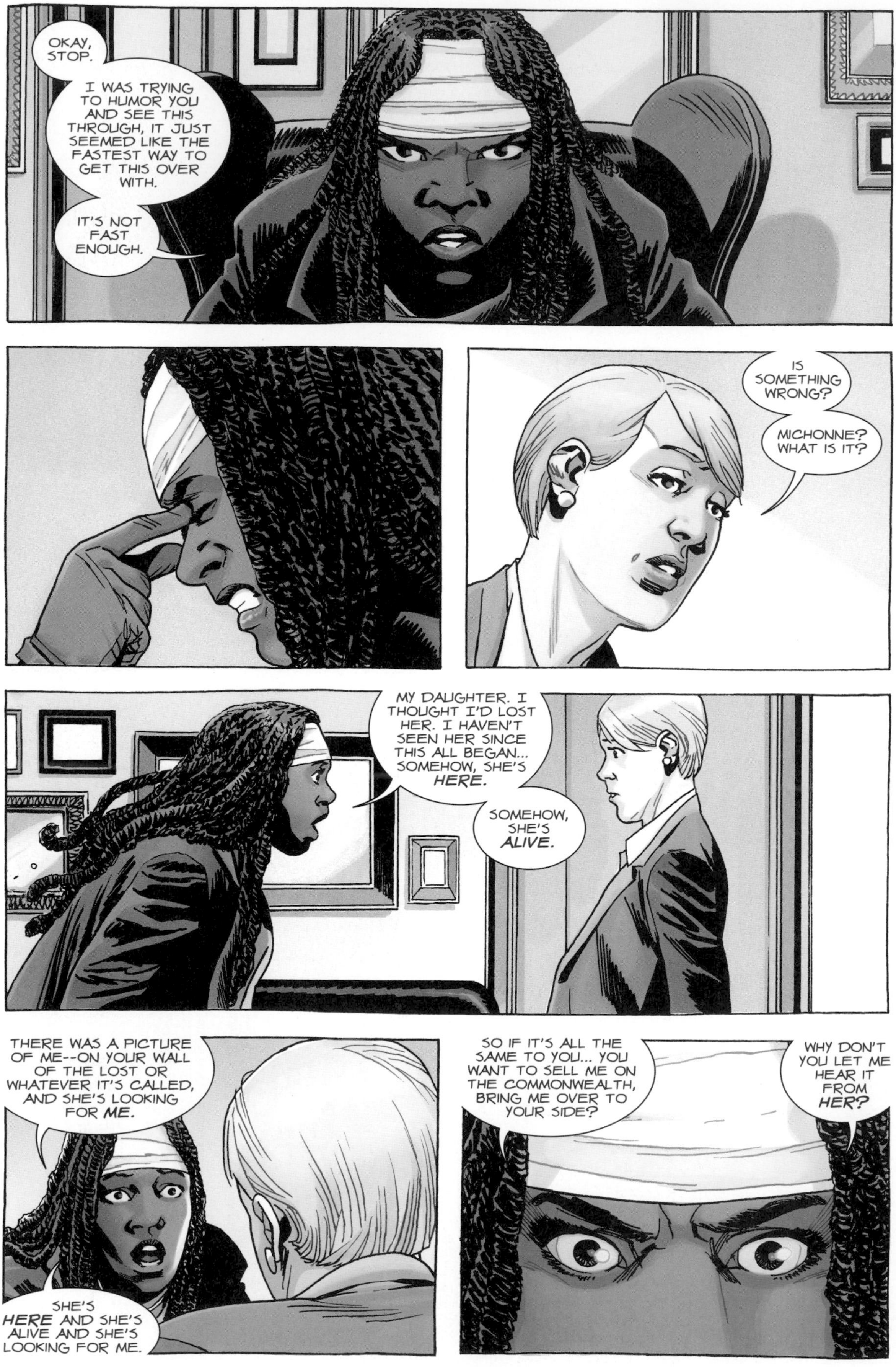
OKAY, STOP.
I WAS TRYING TO HUMOR YOU AND SEE THIS THROUGH, IT JUST SEEMED LIKE THE FASTEST WAY TO GET THIS OVER WITH.
IT'S NOT FAST ENOUGH.
IS SOMETHING WRONG?
MICHONNE? WHAT IS IT?
MY DAUGHTER. I THOUGHT I'D LOST HER. I HAVEN'T SEEN HER SINCE THIS ALL BEGAN... SOMEHOW, SHE'S *HERE.*
SOMEHOW, SHE'S *ALIVE.*
THERE WAS A PICTURE OF ME--ON YOUR WALL OF THE LOST OR WHATEVER IT'S CALLED, AND SHE'S LOOKING FOR *ME.*
SHE'S *HERE* AND SHE'S ALIVE AND SHE'S LOOKING FOR ME.
SO IF IT'S ALL THE SAME TO YOU... YOU WANT TO SELL ME ON THE COMMONWEALTH, BRING ME OVER TO YOUR SIDE?
WHY DON'T YOU LET ME HEAR IT FROM *HER?*

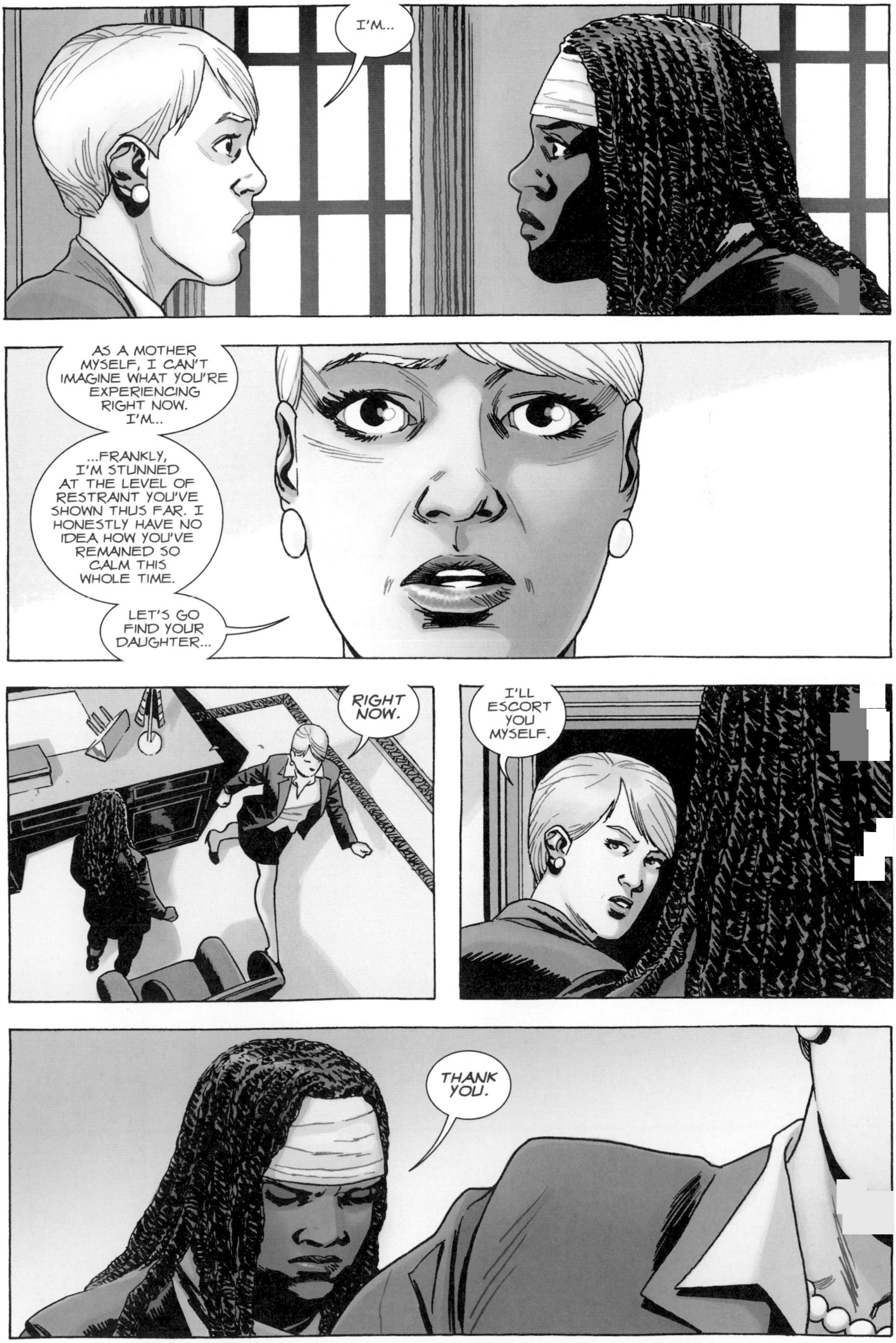
I'M...
AS A MOTHER MYSELF, I CAN'T IMAGINE WHAT YOU'RE EXPERIENCING RIGHT NOW. I'M...
...FRANKLY, I'M STUNNED AT THE LEVEL OF RESTRAINT YOU'VE SHOWN THUS FAR. I HONESTLY HAVE NO IDEA HOW YOU'VE REMAINED SO CALM THIS WHOLE TIME.
LET'S GO FIND YOUR DAUGHTER...
RIGHT NOW.
I'LL ESCORT YOU MYSELF.
THANK YOU.

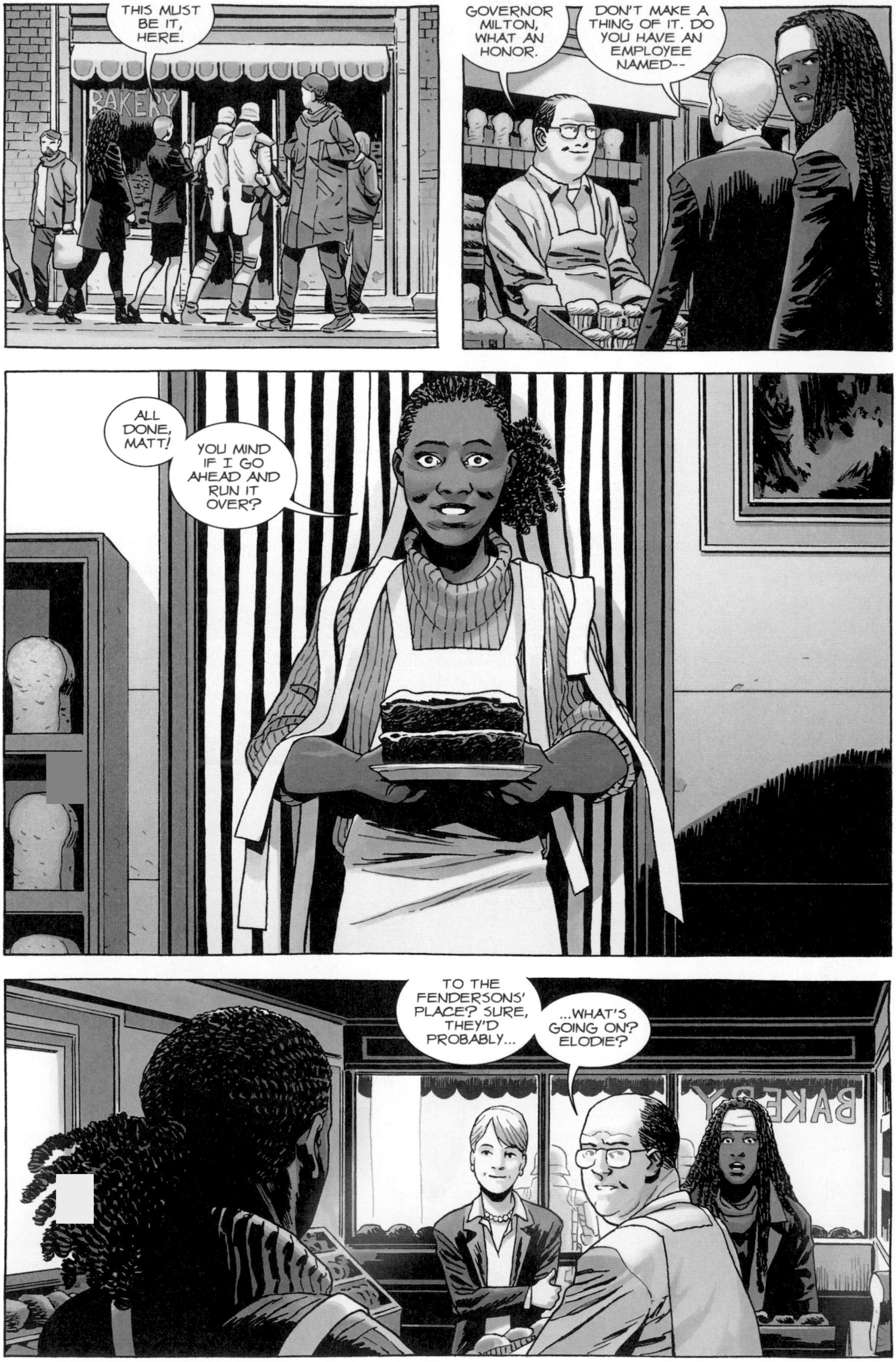
THIS MUST BE IT, HERE.
BAKERY
GOVERNOR MILTON, WHAT AN HONOR.
DON'T MAKE A THING OF IT. DO YOU HAVE AN EMPLOYEE NAMED--
ALL DONE, MATT!
YOU MIND IF I GO AHEAD AND RUN IT OVER?
TO THE FENDERSONS' PLACE? SURE, THEY'D PROBABLY...
...WHAT'S GOING ON? ELODIE?

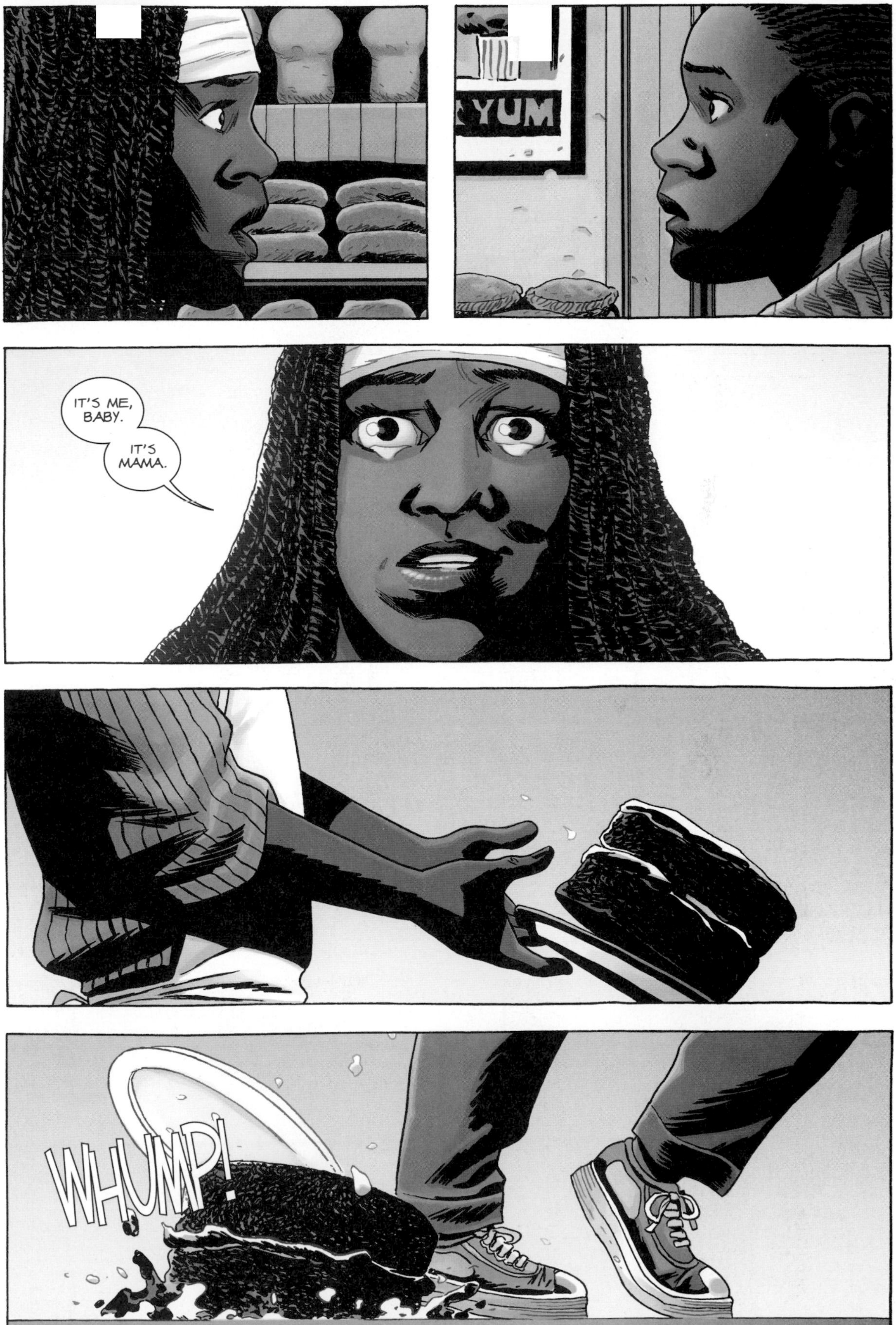
IT'S ME, BABY.
IT'S MAMA.
WHUMP!

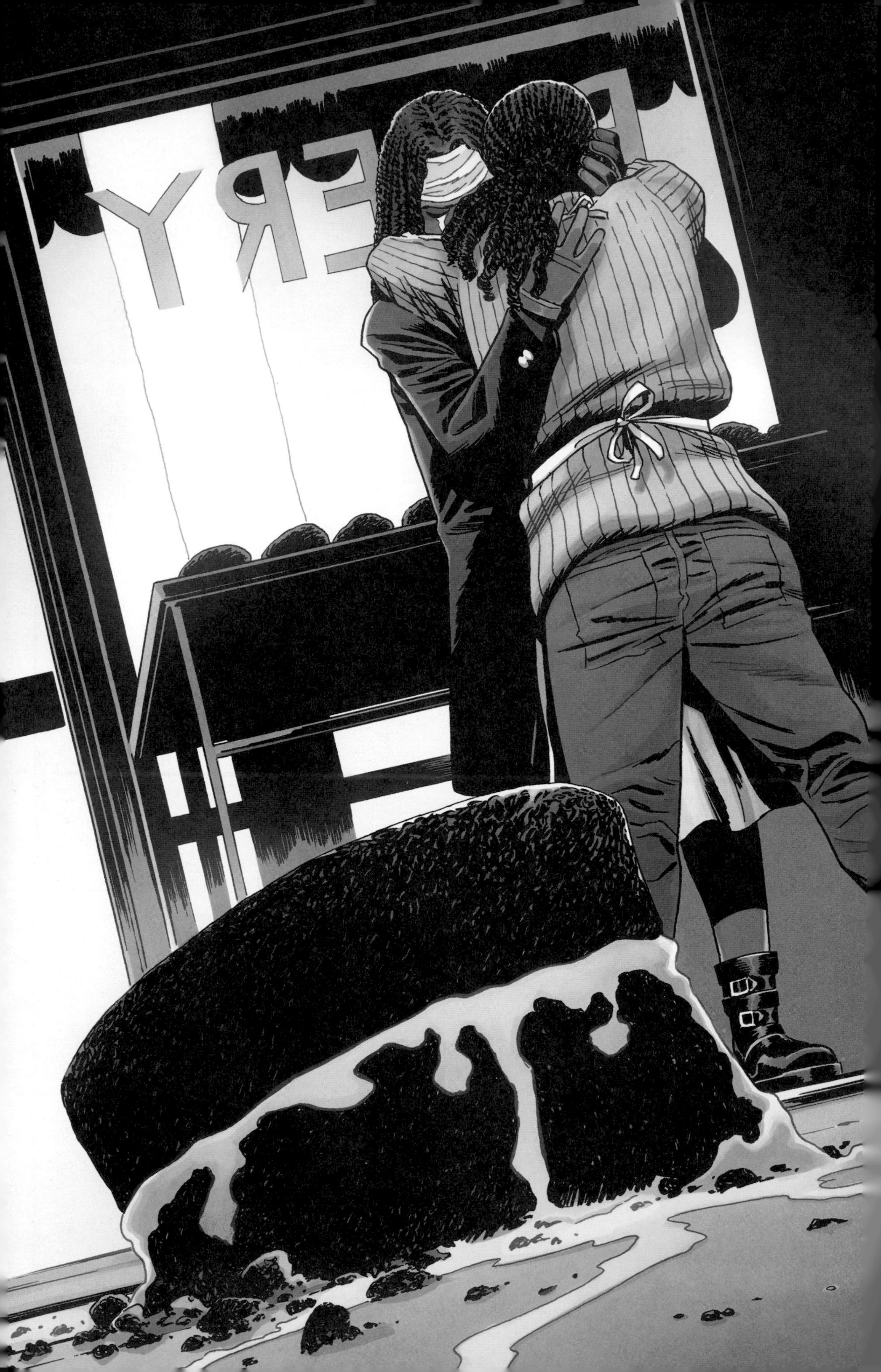

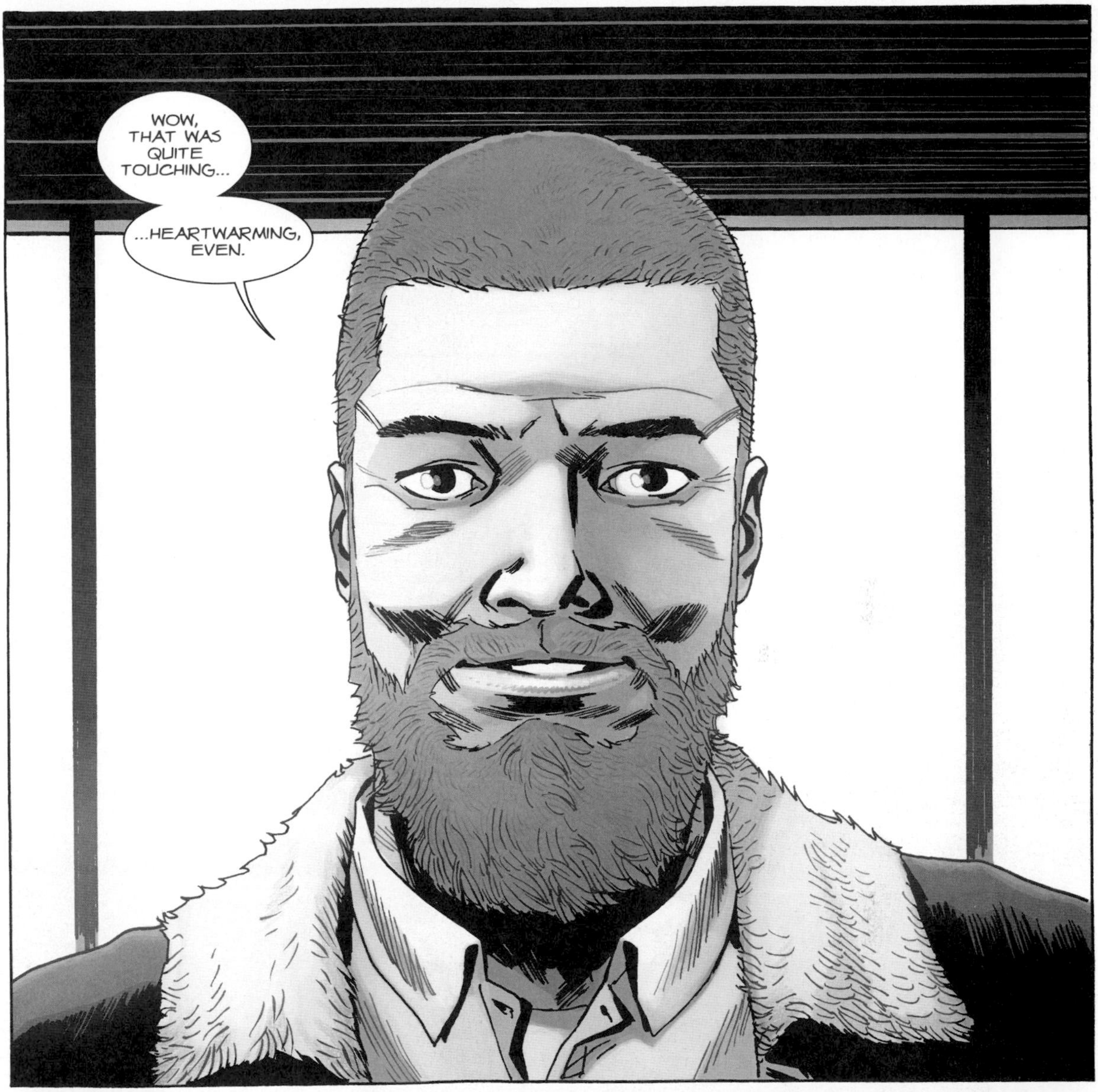
WOW, THAT WAS QUITE TOUCHING...
...HEARTWARMING, EVEN.
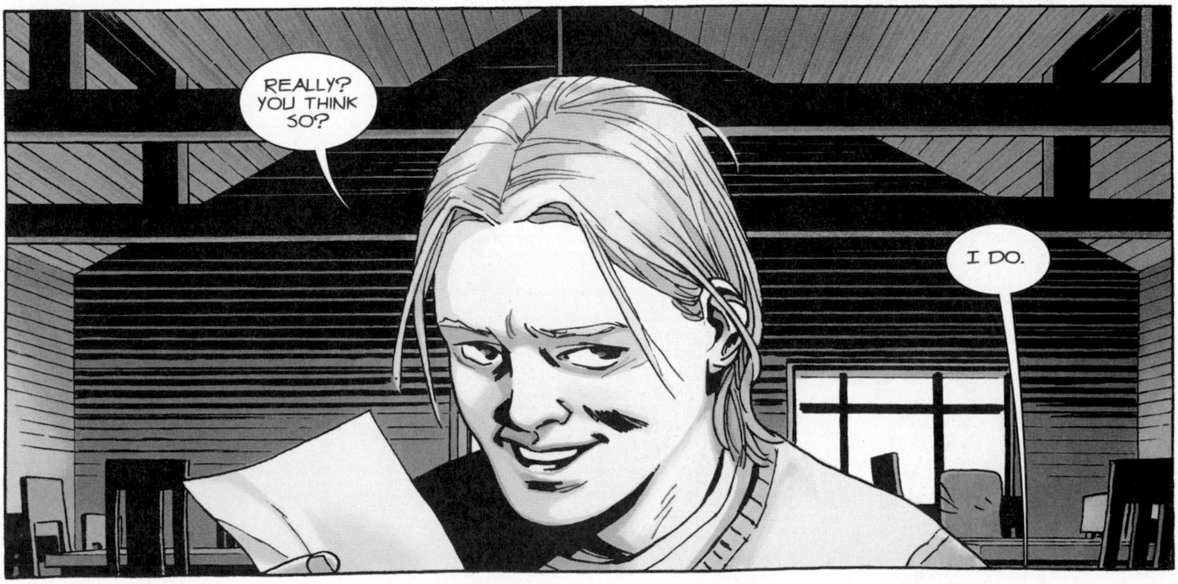
REALLY? YOU THINK SO?
I DO.

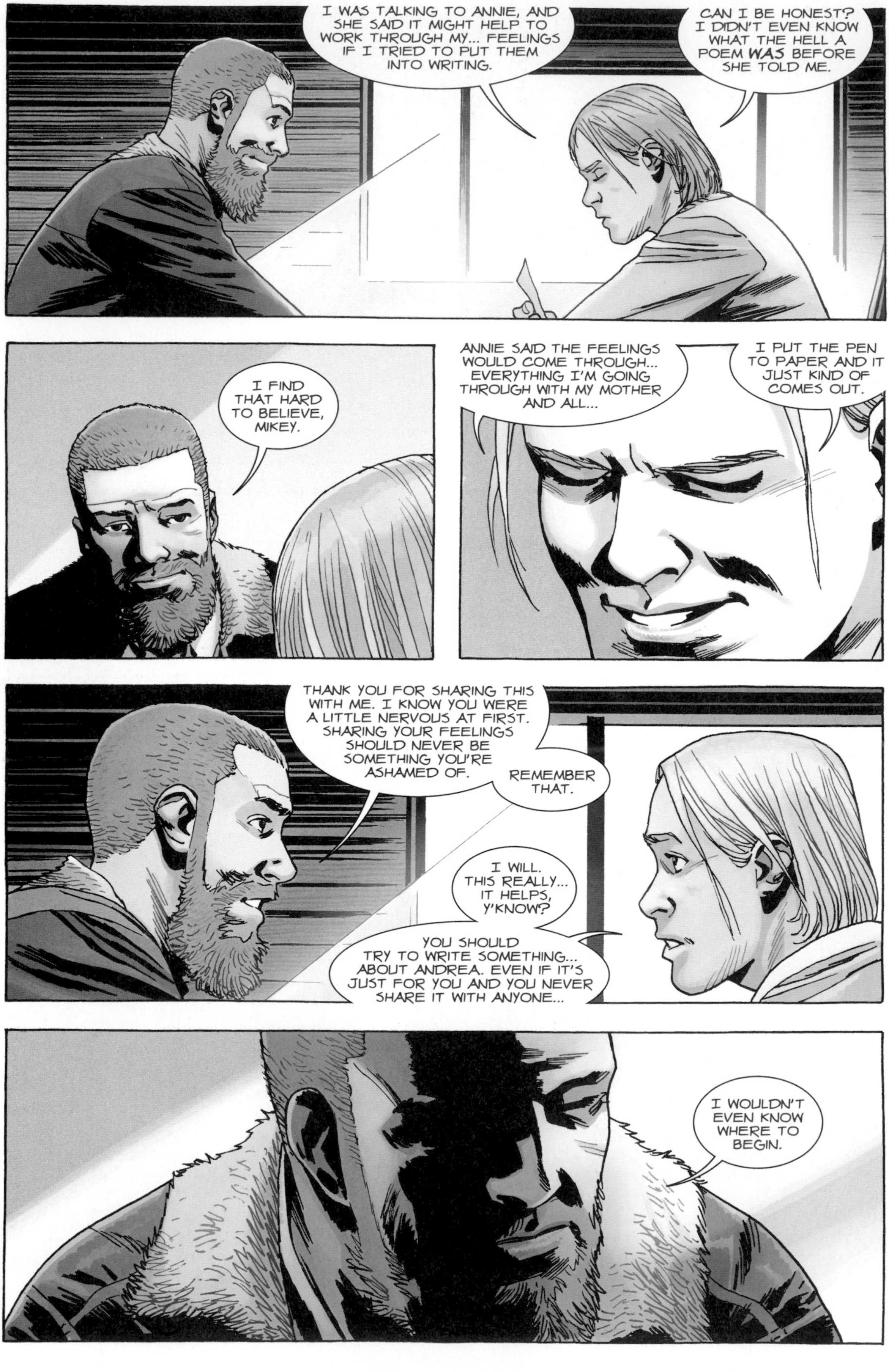
I WAS TALKING TO ANNIE, AND SHE SAID IT MIGHT HELP TO WORK THROUGH MY... FEELINGS IF I TRIED TO PUT THEM INTO WRITING.
CAN I BE HONEST? I DIDN'T EVEN KNOW WHAT THE HELL A POEM WAS BEFORE SHE TOLD ME.
I FIND THAT HARD TO BELIEVE, MIKEY.
ANNIE SAID THE FEELINGS WOULD COME THROUGH... EVERYTHING I'M GOING THROUGH WITH MY MOTHER AND ALL...
I PUT THE PEN TO PAPER AND IT JUST KIND OF COMES OUT.
THANK YOU FOR SHARING THIS WITH ME. I KNOW YOU WERE A LITTLE NERVOUS AT FIRST. SHARING YOUR FEELINGS SHOULD NEVER BE SOMETHING YOU'RE ASHAMED OF.
REMEMBER THAT.
I WILL. THIS REALLY... IT HELPS, Y'KNOW?
YOU SHOULD TRY TO WRITE SOMETHING... ABOUT ANDREA. EVEN IF IT'S JUST FOR YOU AND YOU NEVER SHARE IT WITH ANYONE...
I WOULDN'T EVEN KNOW WHERE TO BEGIN.

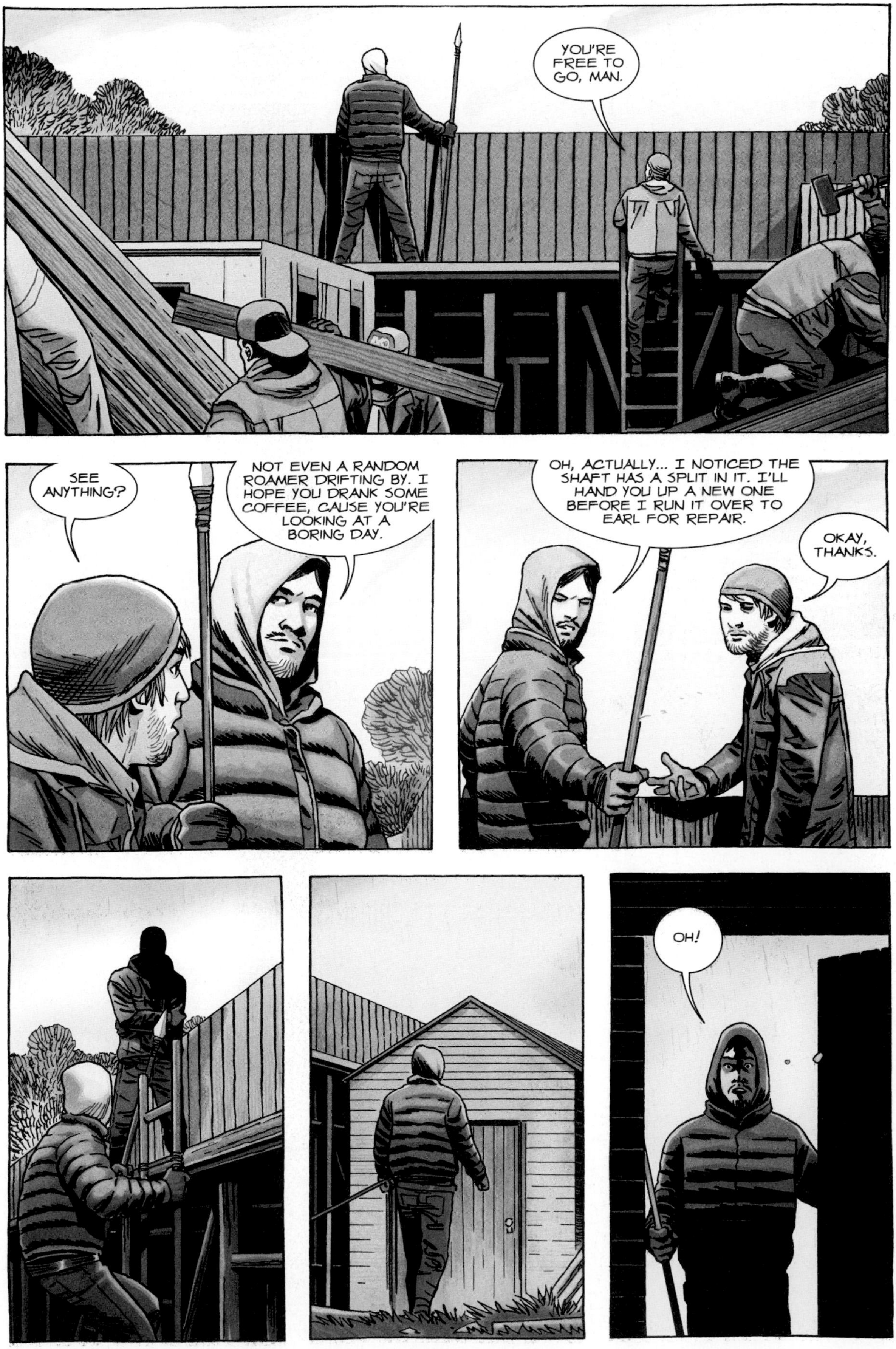
YOU'RE FREE TO GO, MAN.
SEE ANYTHING?
NOT EVEN A RANDOM ROAMER DRIFTING BY. I HOPE YOU DRANK SOME COFFEE, CAUSE YOU'RE LOOKING AT A BORING DAY.
OH, ACTUALLY... I NOTICED THE SHAFT HAS A SPLIT IN IT. I'LL HAND YOU UP A NEW ONE BEFORE I RUN IT OVER TO EARL FOR REPAIR.
OKAY, THANKS.
OH!

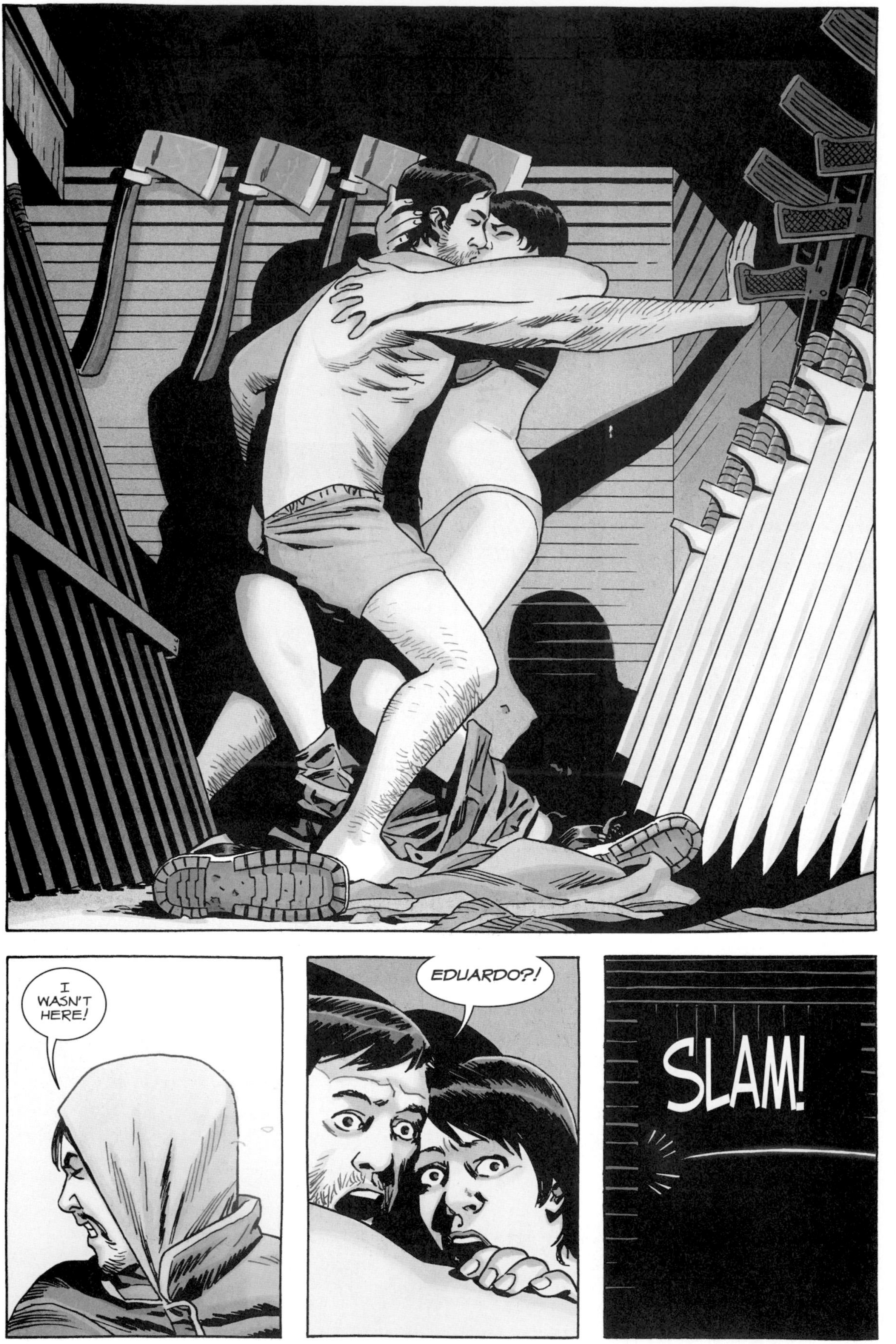
I WASN'T HERE!
EDUARDO?!
SLAM!

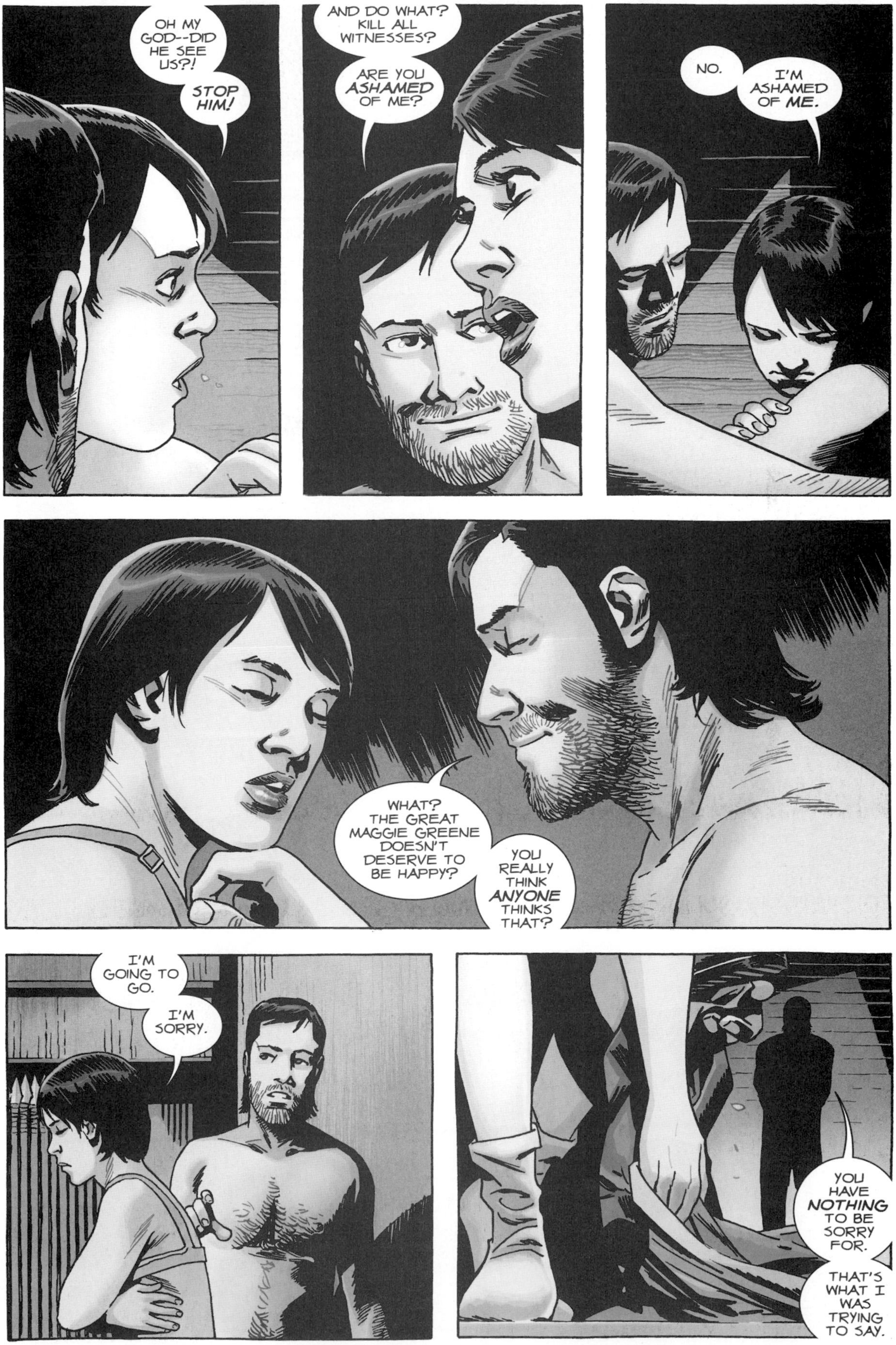
OH MY GOD--DID HE SEE US?!
STOP HIM!
AND DO WHAT? KILL ALL WITNESSES?
ARE YOU ASHAMED OF ME?
NO.
I'M ASHAMED OF ME.
WHAT? THE GREAT MAGGIE GREENE DOESN'T DESERVE TO BE HAPPY?
YOU REALLY THINK ANYONE THINKS THAT?
I'M GOING TO GO.
I'M SORRY.
YOU HAVE NOTHING TO BE SORRY FOR.
THAT'S WHAT I WAS TRYING TO SAY.

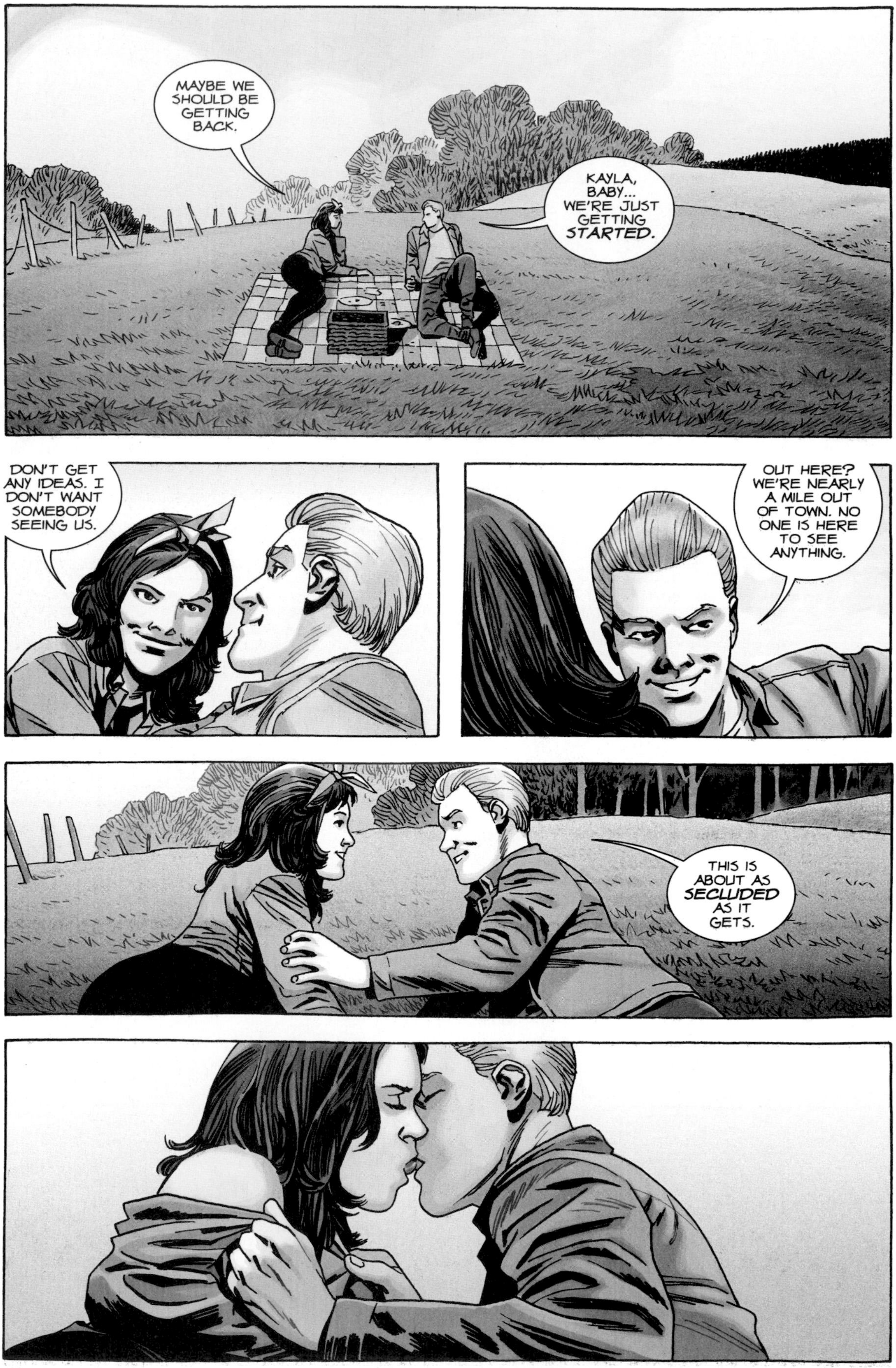
MAYBE WE SHOULD BE GETTING BACK.
KAYLA, BABY... WE'RE JUST GETTING STARTED.
DON'T GET ANY IDEAS. I DON'T WANT SOMEBODY SEEING US.
OUT HERE? WE'RE NEARLY A MILE OUT OF TOWN. NO ONE IS HERE TO SEE ANYTHING.
THIS IS ABOUT AS SECLUDED AS IT GETS.

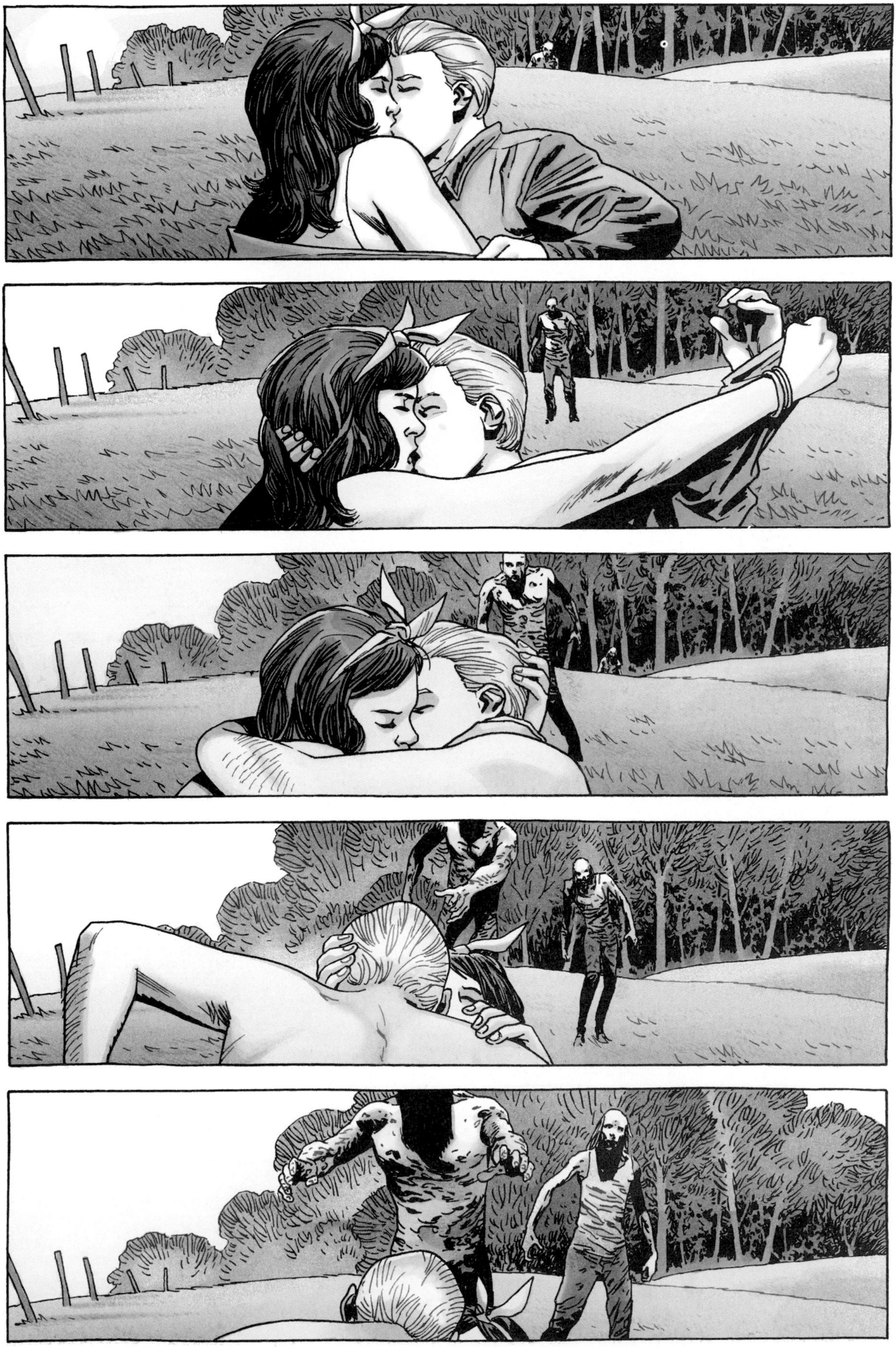

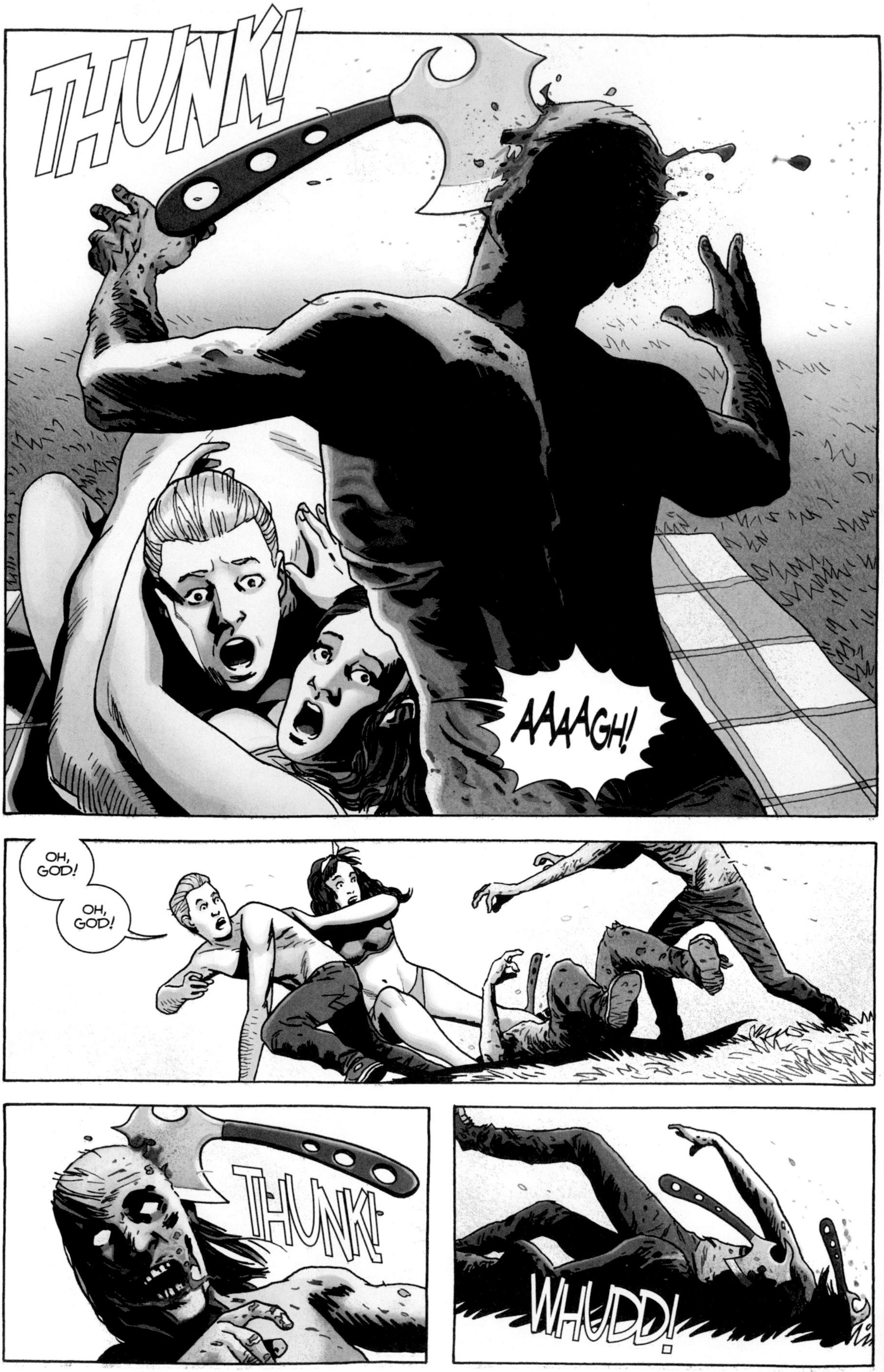
THUNK!
AAAAGH!
OH, GOD!
OH, GOD!
THUNK!
WHUDD!

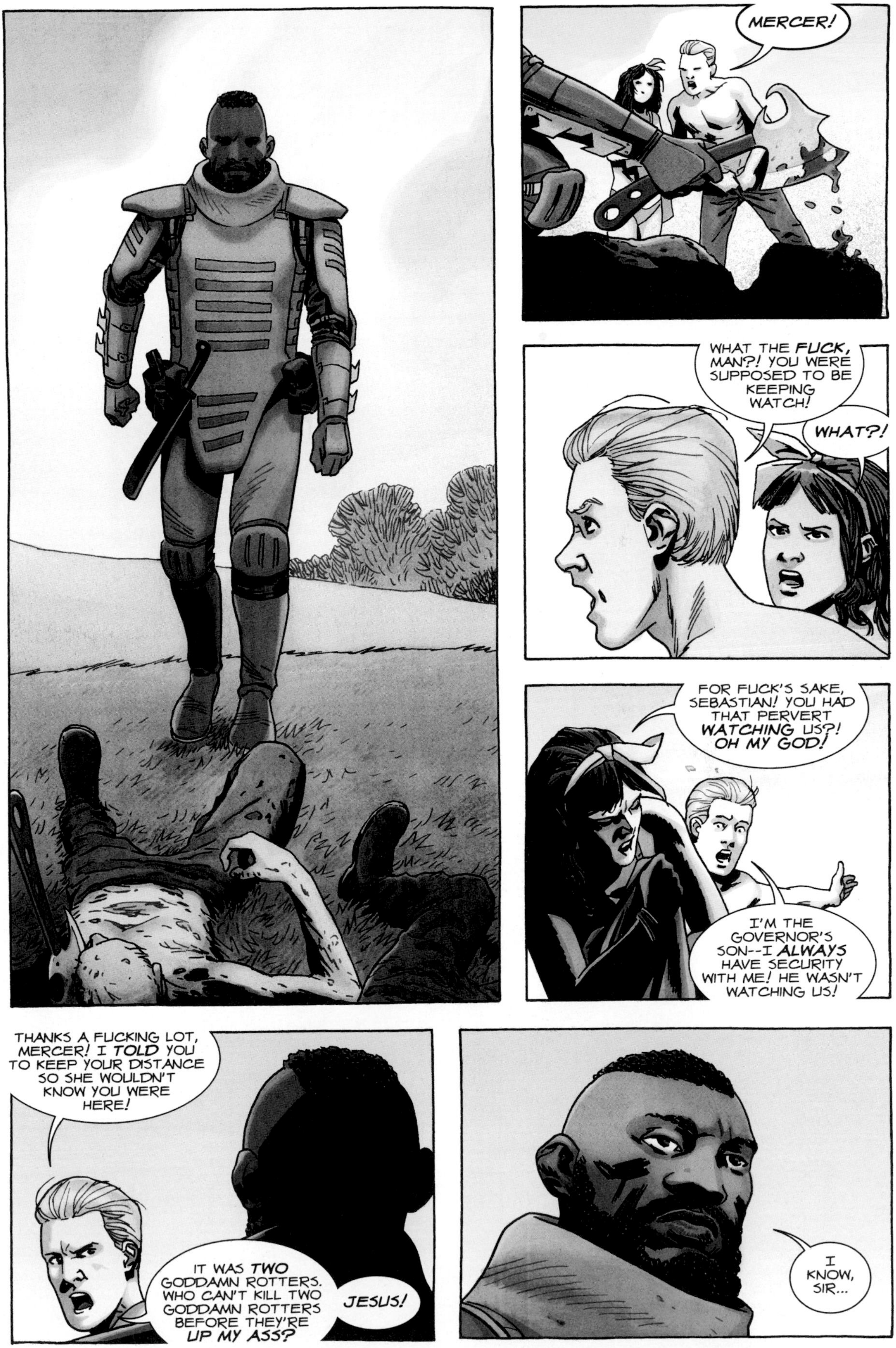

MERCER!
WHAT THE FUCK, MAN?! YOU WERE SUPPOSED TO BE KEEPING WATCH!
WHAT?!
FOR FUCK'S SAKE, SEBASTIAN! YOU HAD THAT PERVERT WATCHING US?! OH MY GOD!
I'M THE GOVERNOR'S SON--I ALWAYS HAVE SECURITY WITH ME! HE WASN'T WATCHING US!
THANKS A FUCKING LOT, MERCER! I TOLD YOU TO KEEP YOUR DISTANCE SO SHE WOULDN'T KNOW YOU WERE HERE!
IT WAS TWO GODDAMN ROTTERS. WHO CAN'T KILL TWO GODDAMN ROTTERS BEFORE THEY'RE UP MY ASS?
JESUS!
I KNOW, SIR...

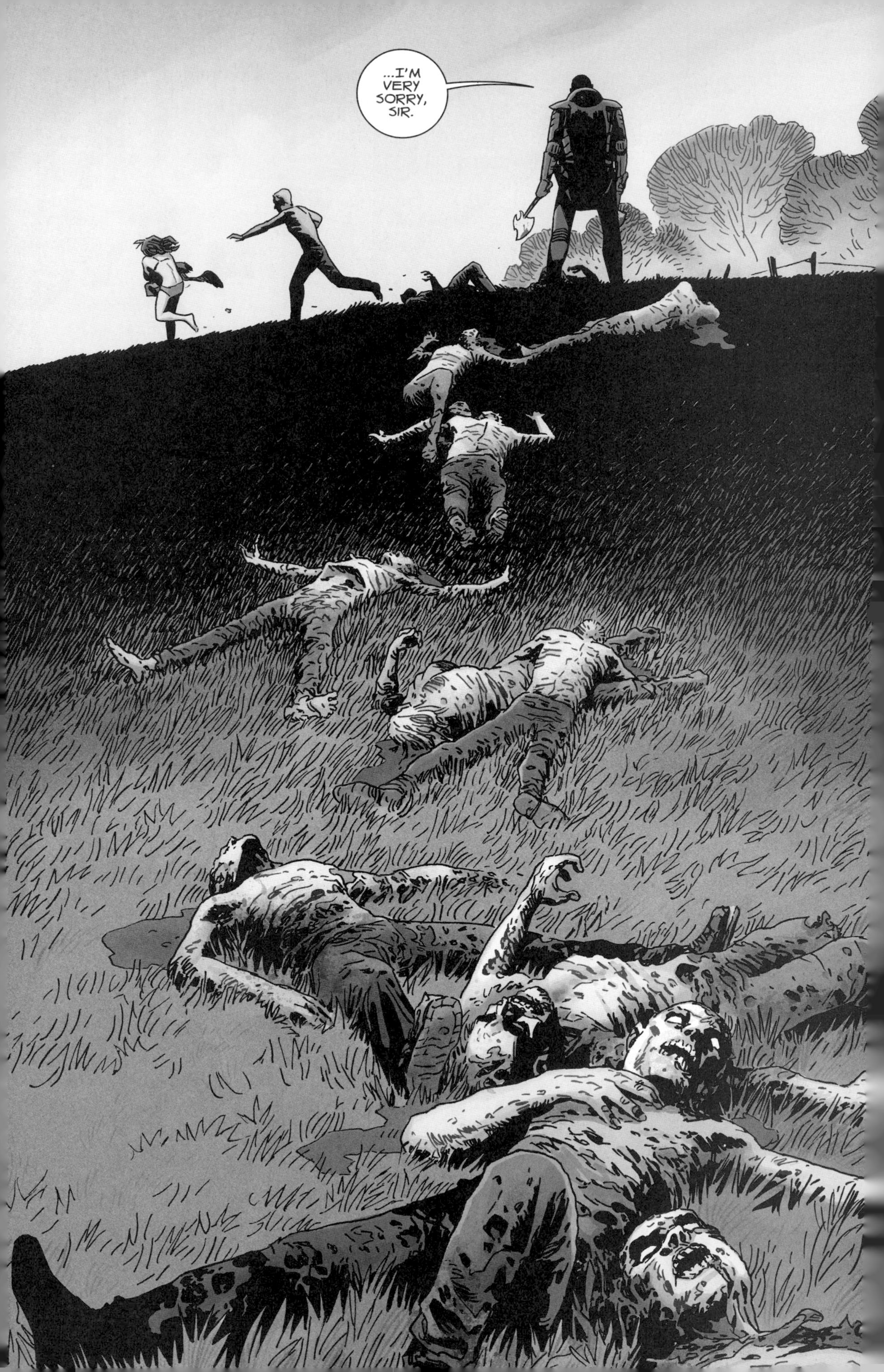
...I'M VERY SORRY, SIR.

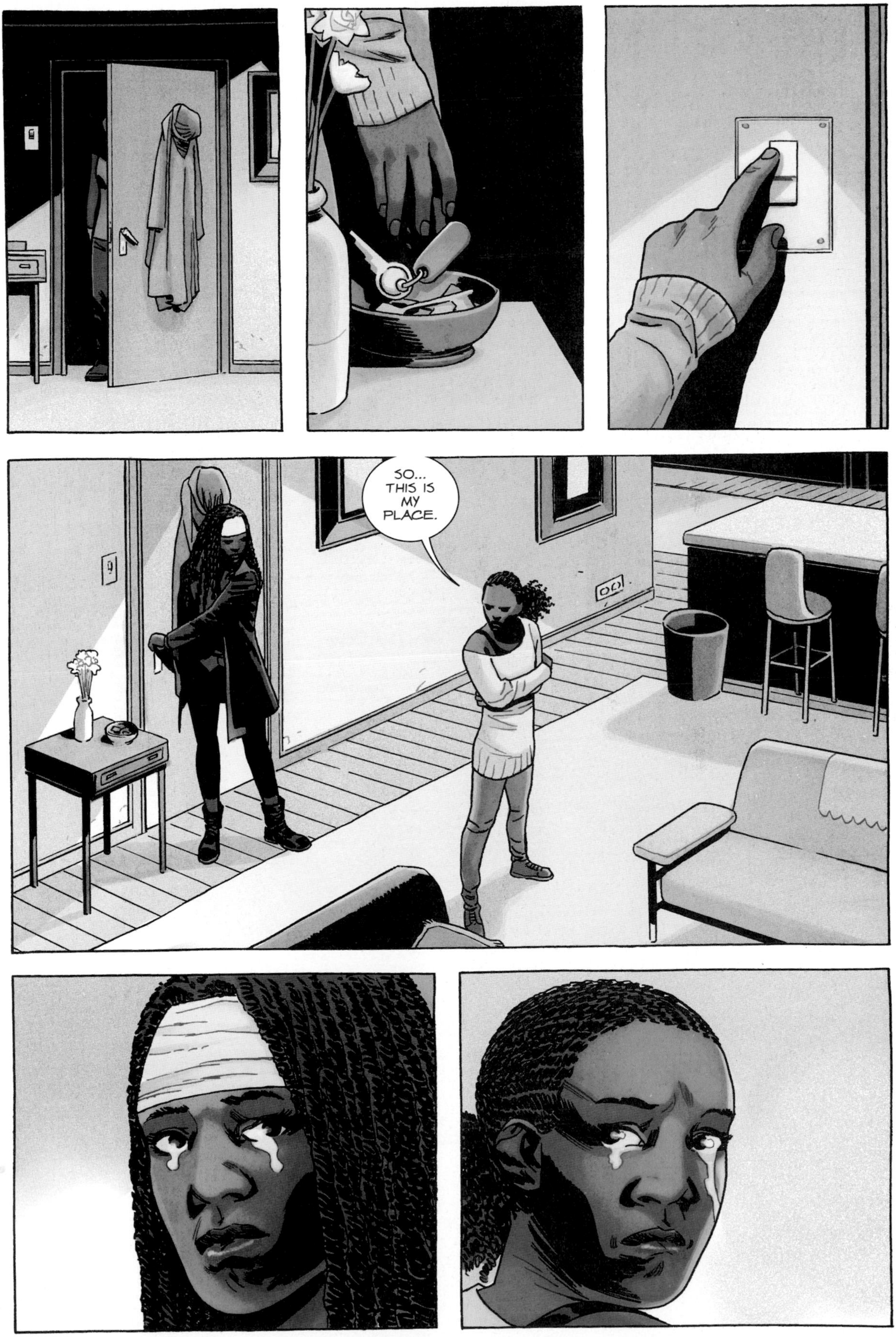
SO... THIS IS MY PLACE.

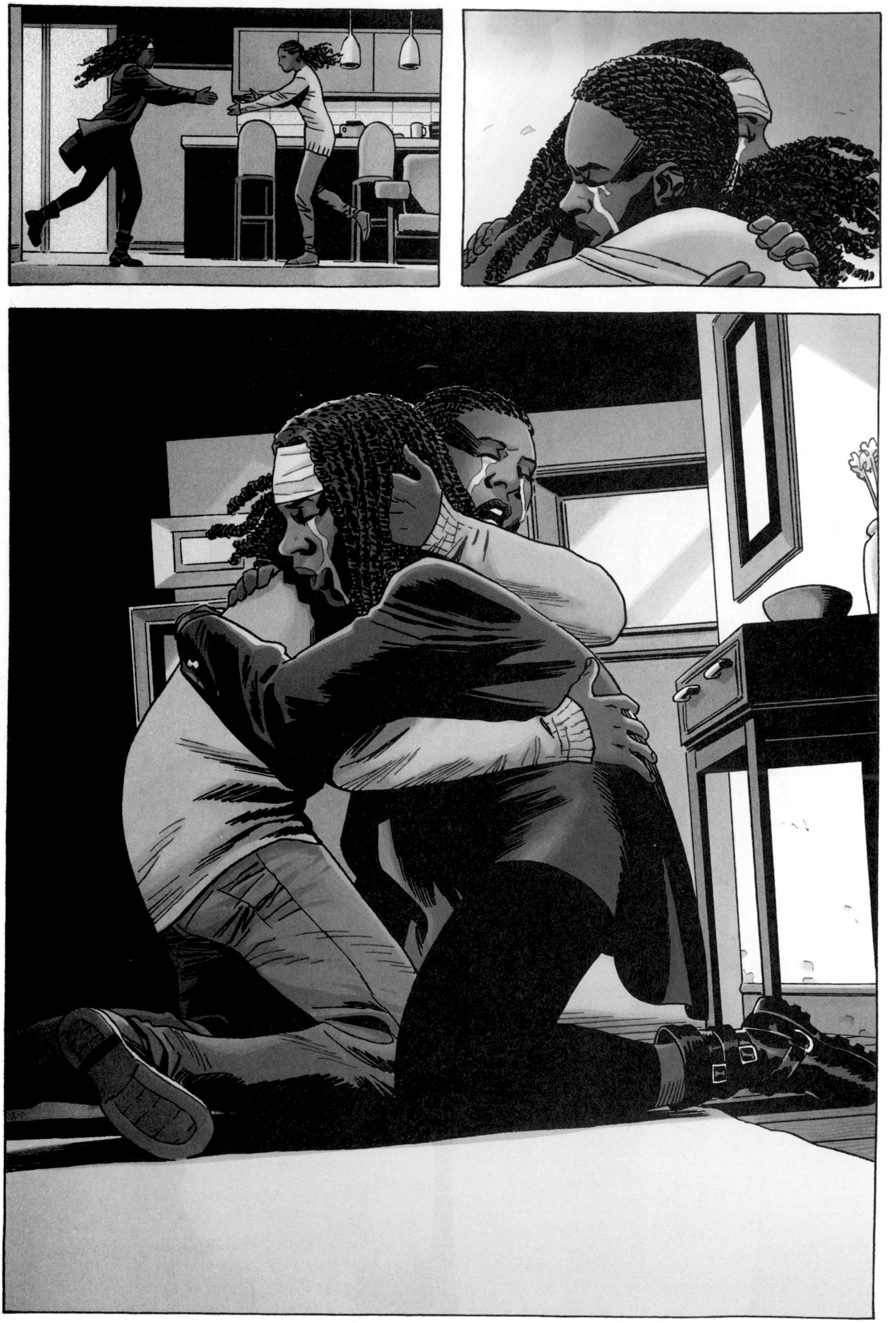

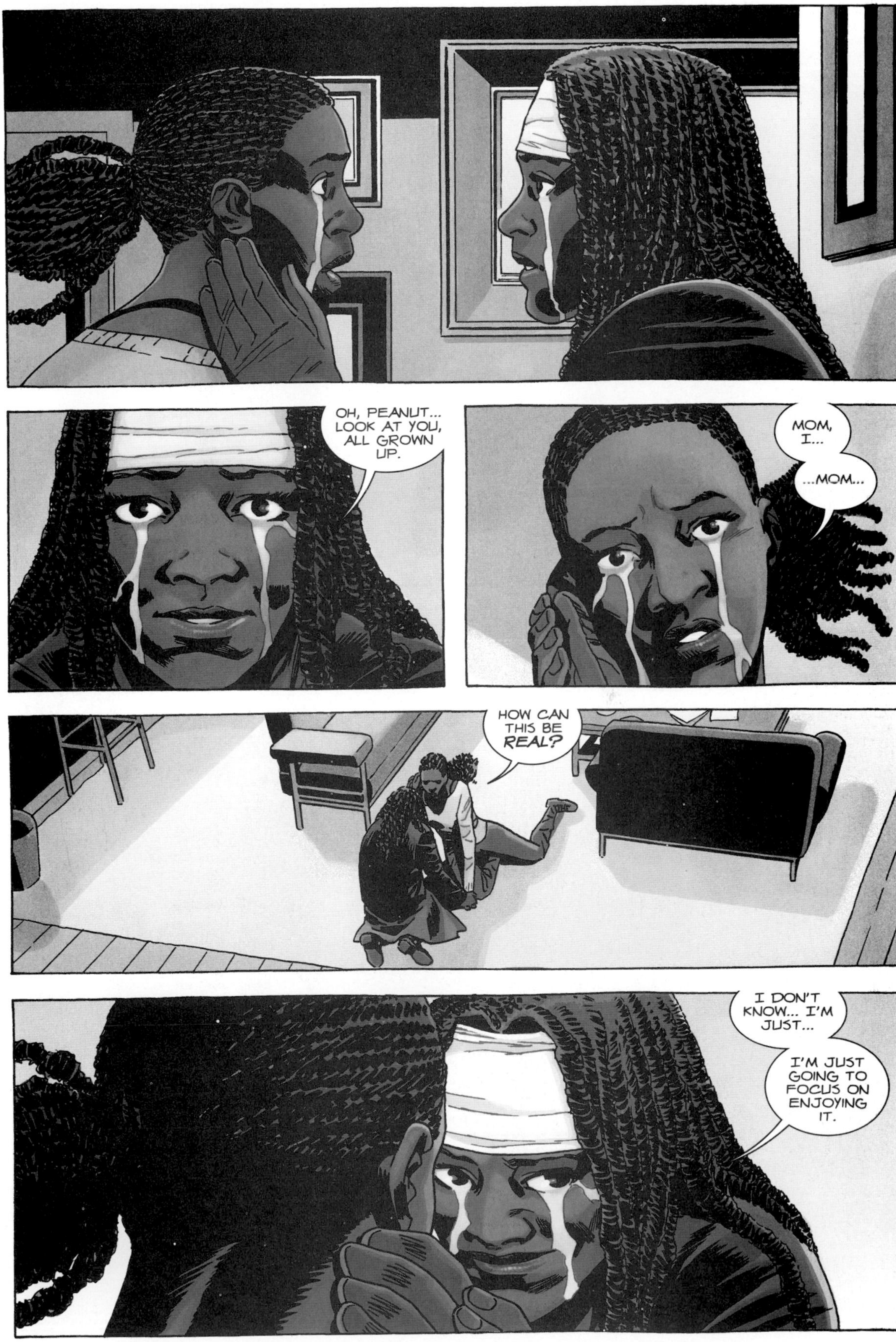
OH, PEANUT... LOOK AT YOU, ALL GROWN UP.
MOM, I...
...MOM...
HOW CAN THIS BE REAL?
I DON'T KNOW... I'M JUST...
I'M JUST GOING TO FOCUS ON ENJOYING IT.

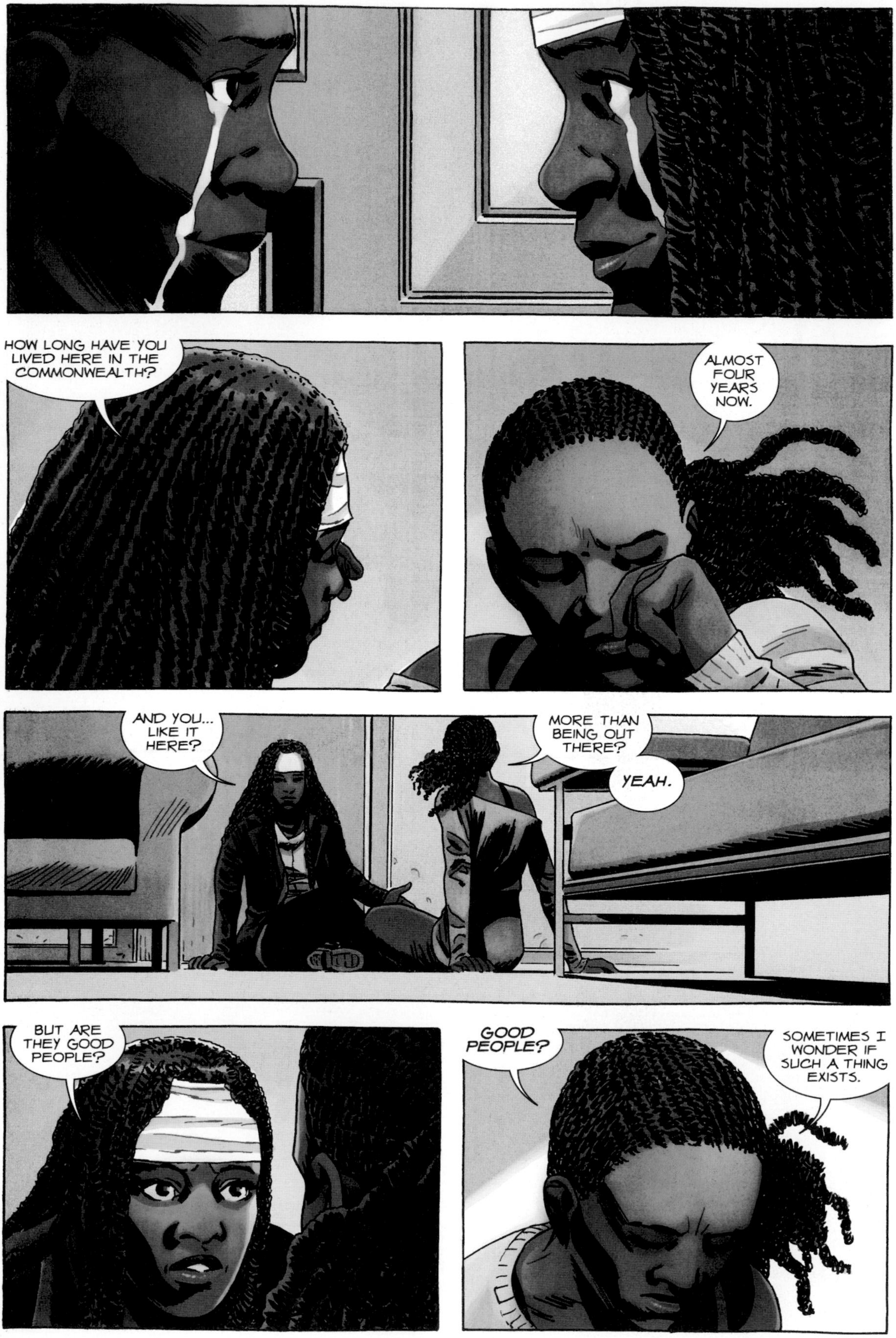
HOW LONG HAVE YOU LIVED HERE IN THE COMMONWEALTH?
ALMOST FOUR YEARS NOW.
AND YOU... LIKE IT HERE?
MORE THAN BEING OUT THERE?
YEAH.
BUT ARE THEY GOOD PEOPLE?
GOOD PEOPLE?
SOMETIMES I WONDER IF SUCH A THING EXISTS.

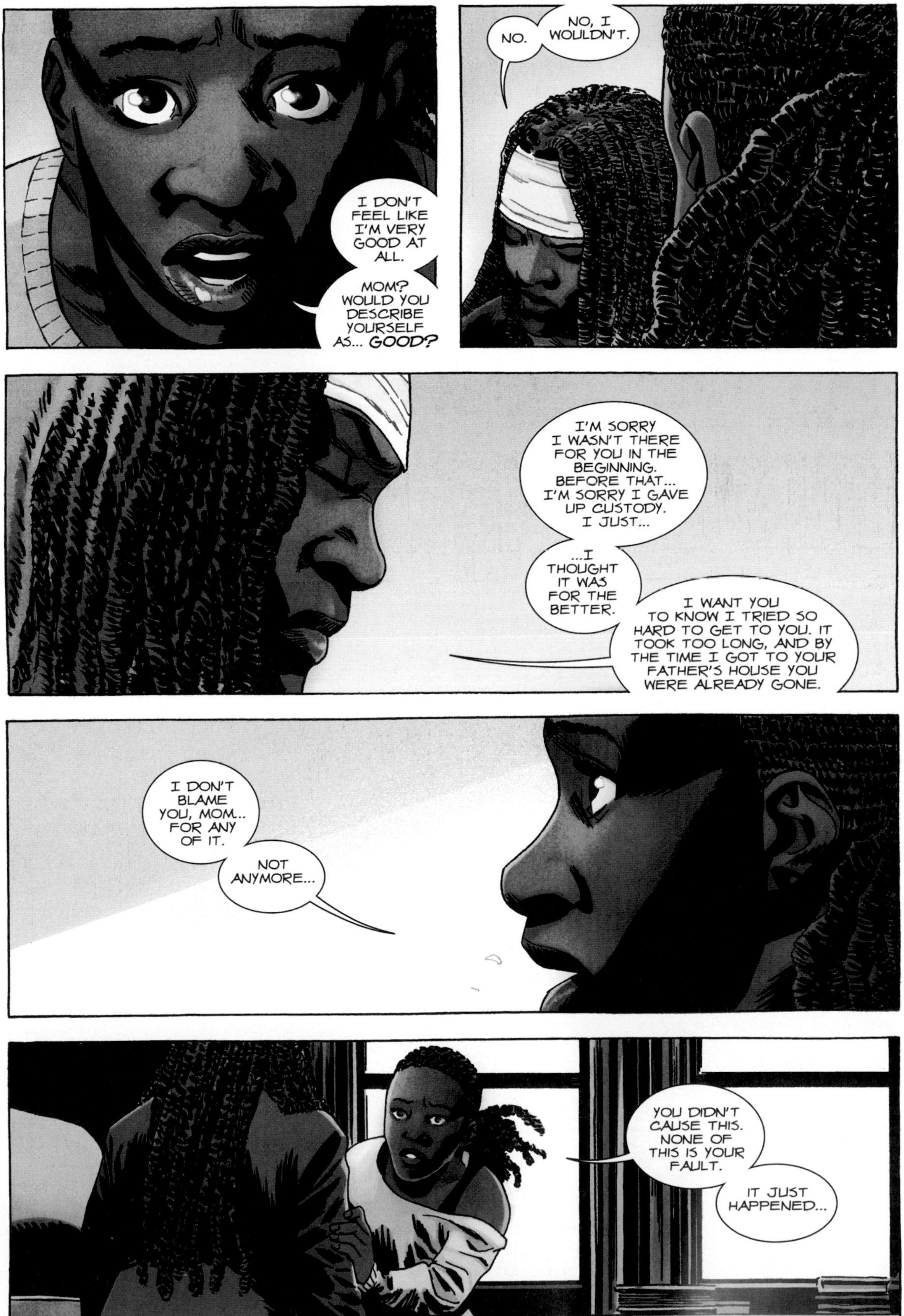
I DON'T FEEL LIKE I'M VERY GOOD AT ALL.
MOM? WOULD YOU DESCRIBE YOURSELF AS... GOOD?
NO.
NO, I WOULDN'T.
I'M SORRY I WASN'T THERE FOR YOU IN THE BEGINNING. BEFORE THAT... I'M SORRY I GAVE UP CUSTODY. I JUST...
...I THOUGHT IT WAS FOR THE BETTER.
I WANT YOU TO KNOW I TRIED SO HARD TO GET TO YOU. IT TOOK TOO LONG, AND BY THE TIME I GOT TO YOUR FATHER'S HOUSE YOU WERE ALREADY GONE.
I DON'T BLAME YOU, MOM.. FOR ANY OF IT.
NOT ANYMORE...
YOU DIDN'T CAUSE THIS. NONE OF THIS IS YOUR FAULT.
IT JUST HAPPENED...

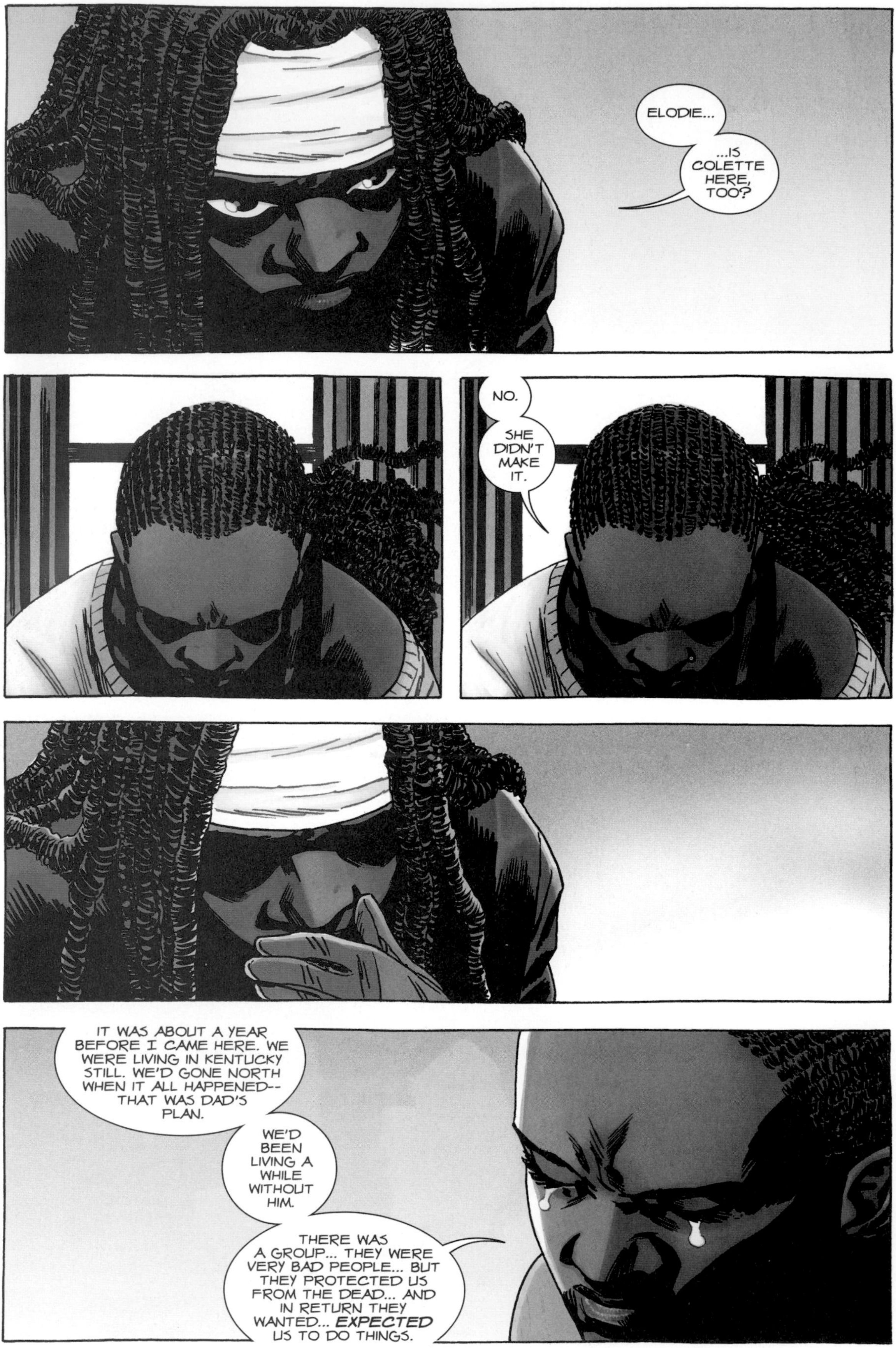
ELODIE...
...IS COLETTE HERE, TOO?
NO.
SHE DIDN'T MAKE IT.
IT WAS ABOUT A YEAR BEFORE I CAME HERE. WE WERE LIVING IN KENTUCKY STILL. WE'D GONE NORTH WHEN IT ALL HAPPENED-- THAT WAS DAD'S PLAN.
WE'D BEEN LIVING A WHILE WITHOUT HIM.
THERE WAS A GROUP... THEY WERE VERY BAD PEOPLE... BUT THEY PROTECTED US FROM THE DEAD... AND IN RETURN THEY WANTED... *EXPECTED* US TO DO THINGS.

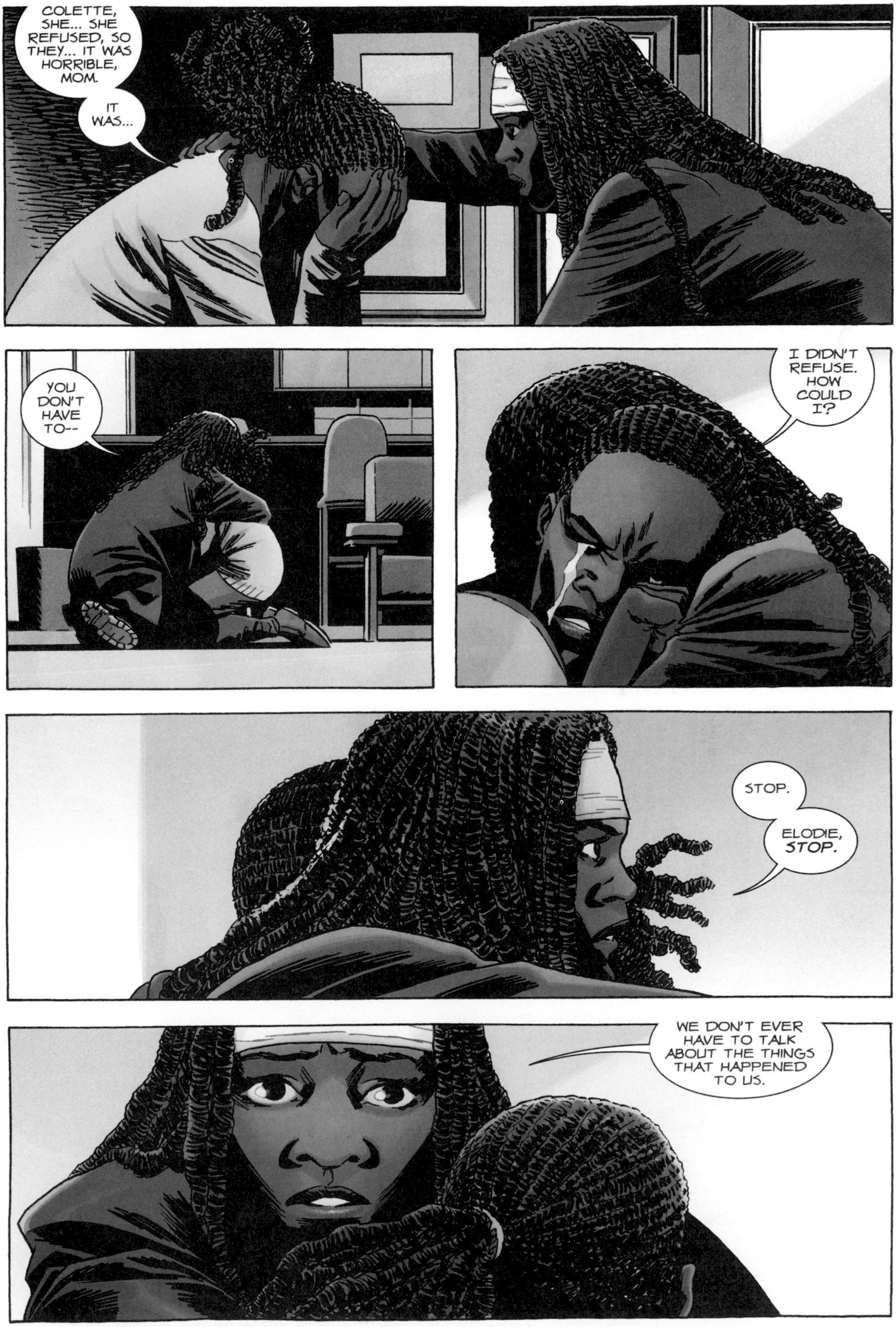
COLETTE, SHE... SHE REFUSED, SO THEY... IT WAS HORRIBLE, MOM.
IT WAS...
YOU DON'T HAVE TO--
I DIDN'T REFUSE. HOW COULD I?
STOP.
ELODIE, *STOP.*
WE DON'T EVER HAVE TO TALK ABOUT THE THINGS THAT HAPPENED TO US.

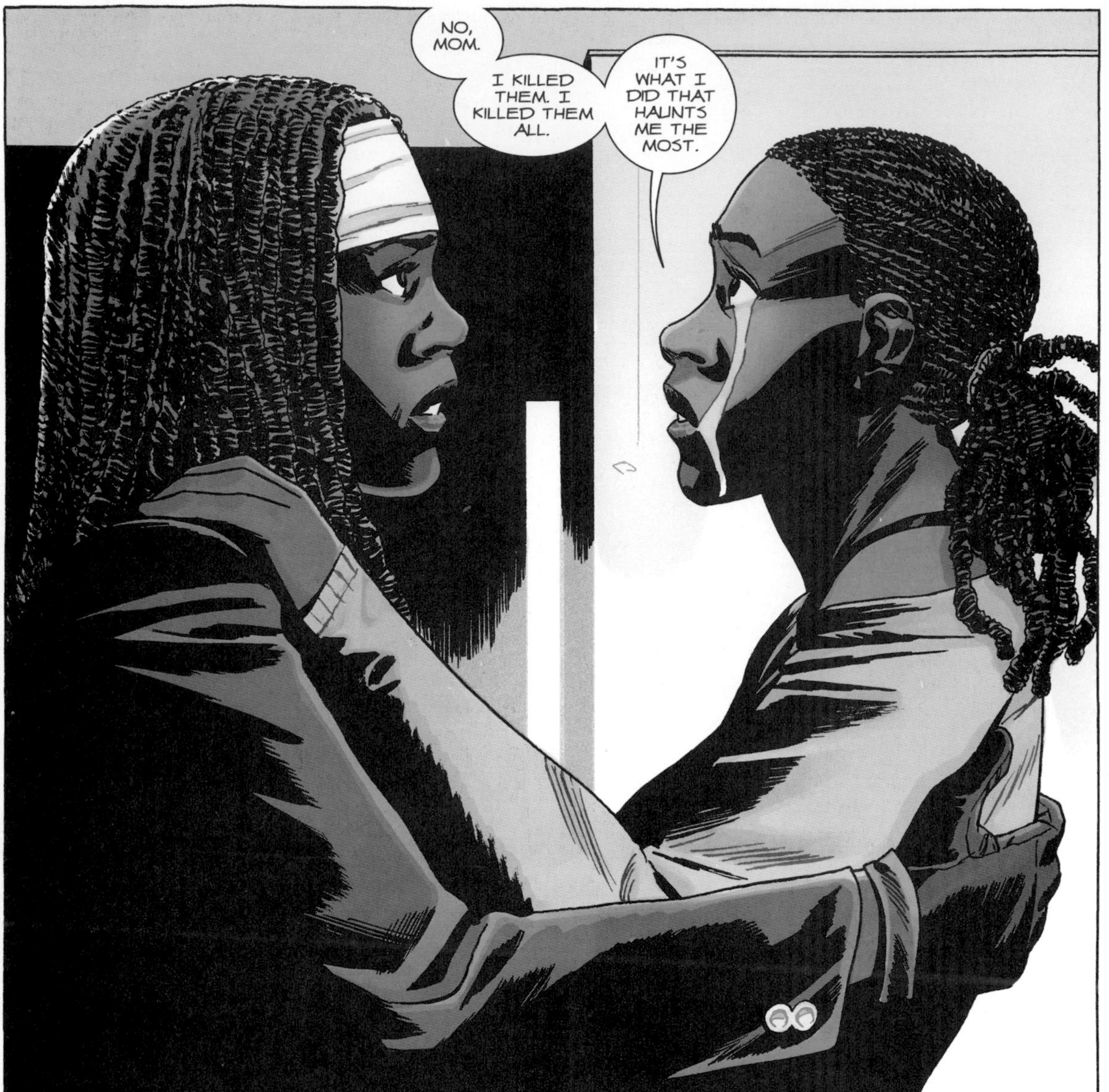
NO, MOM.
I KILLED THEM. I KILLED THEM ALL.
IT'S WHAT I DID THAT HAUNTS ME THE MOST.

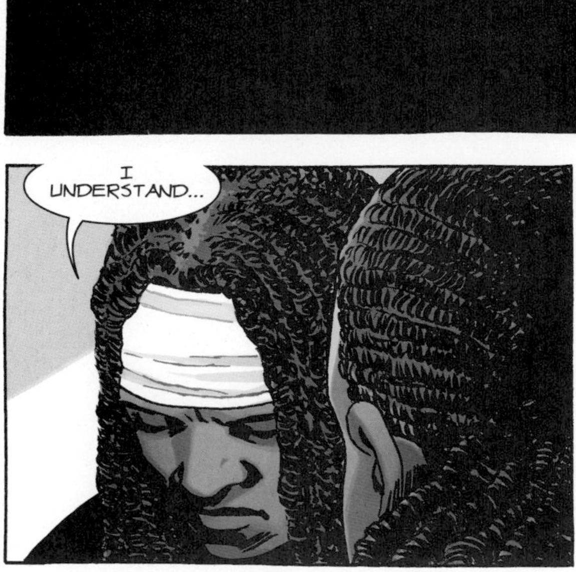
I UNDERSTAND...

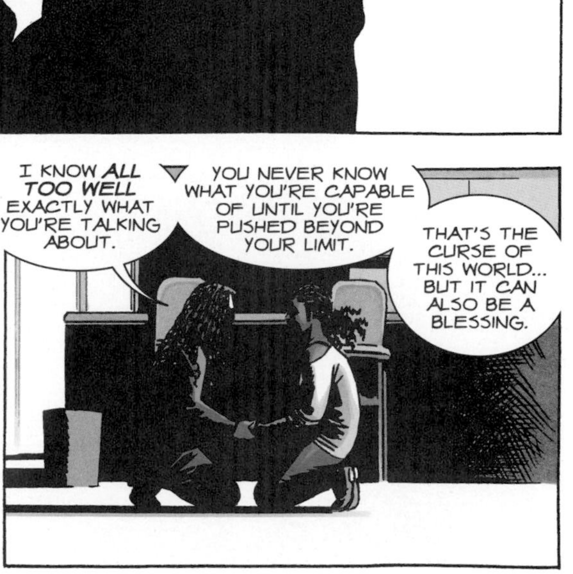
I KNOW ALL TOO WELL EXACTLY WHAT YOU'RE TALKING ABOUT.
YOU NEVER KNOW WHAT YOU'RE CAPABLE OF UNTIL YOU'RE PUSHED BEYOND YOUR LIMIT.
THAT'S THE CURSE OF THIS WORLD... BUT IT CAN ALSO BE A BLESSING.

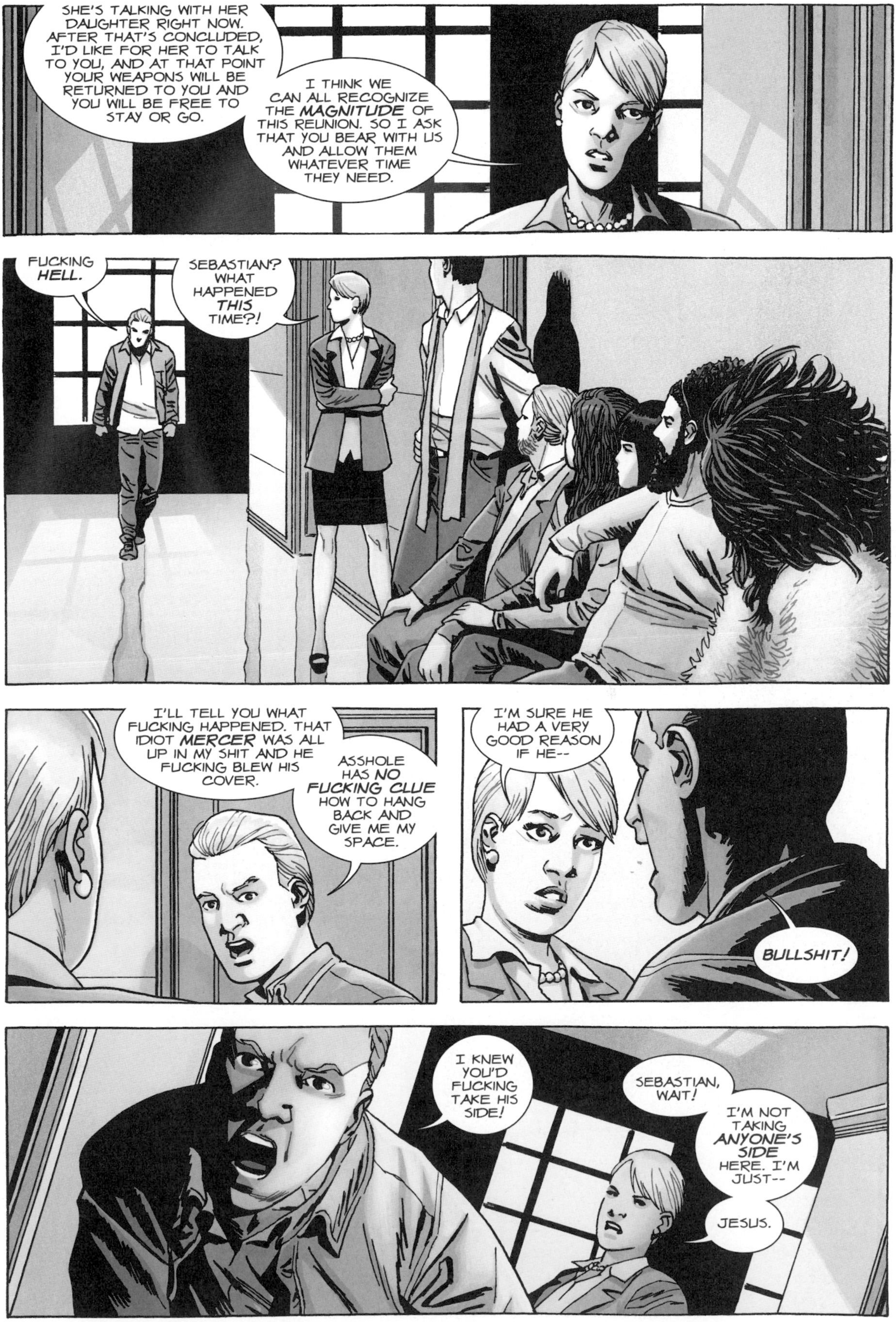
SHE'S TALKING WITH HER DAUGHTER RIGHT NOW. AFTER THAT'S CONCLUDED, I'D LIKE FOR HER TO TALK TO YOU, AND AT THAT POINT YOUR WEAPONS WILL BE RETURNED TO YOU AND YOU WILL BE FREE TO STAY OR GO.
I THINK WE CAN ALL RECOGNIZE THE MAGNITUDE OF THIS REUNION. SO I ASK THAT YOU BEAR WITH US AND ALLOW THEM WHATEVER TIME THEY NEED.
FUCKING HELL.
SEBASTIAN? WHAT HAPPENED THIS TIME?!
I'LL TELL YOU WHAT FUCKING HAPPENED. THAT IDIOT MERCER WAS ALL UP IN MY SHIT AND HE FUCKING BLEW HIS COVER.
ASSHOLE HAS NO FUCKING CLUE HOW TO HANG BACK AND GIVE ME MY SPACE.
I'M SURE HE HAD A VERY GOOD REASON IF HE--
BULLSHIT!
I KNEW YOU'D FUCKING TAKE HIS SIDE!
SEBASTIAN, WAIT!
I'M NOT TAKING ANYONE'S SIDE HERE. I'M JUST--
JESUS.

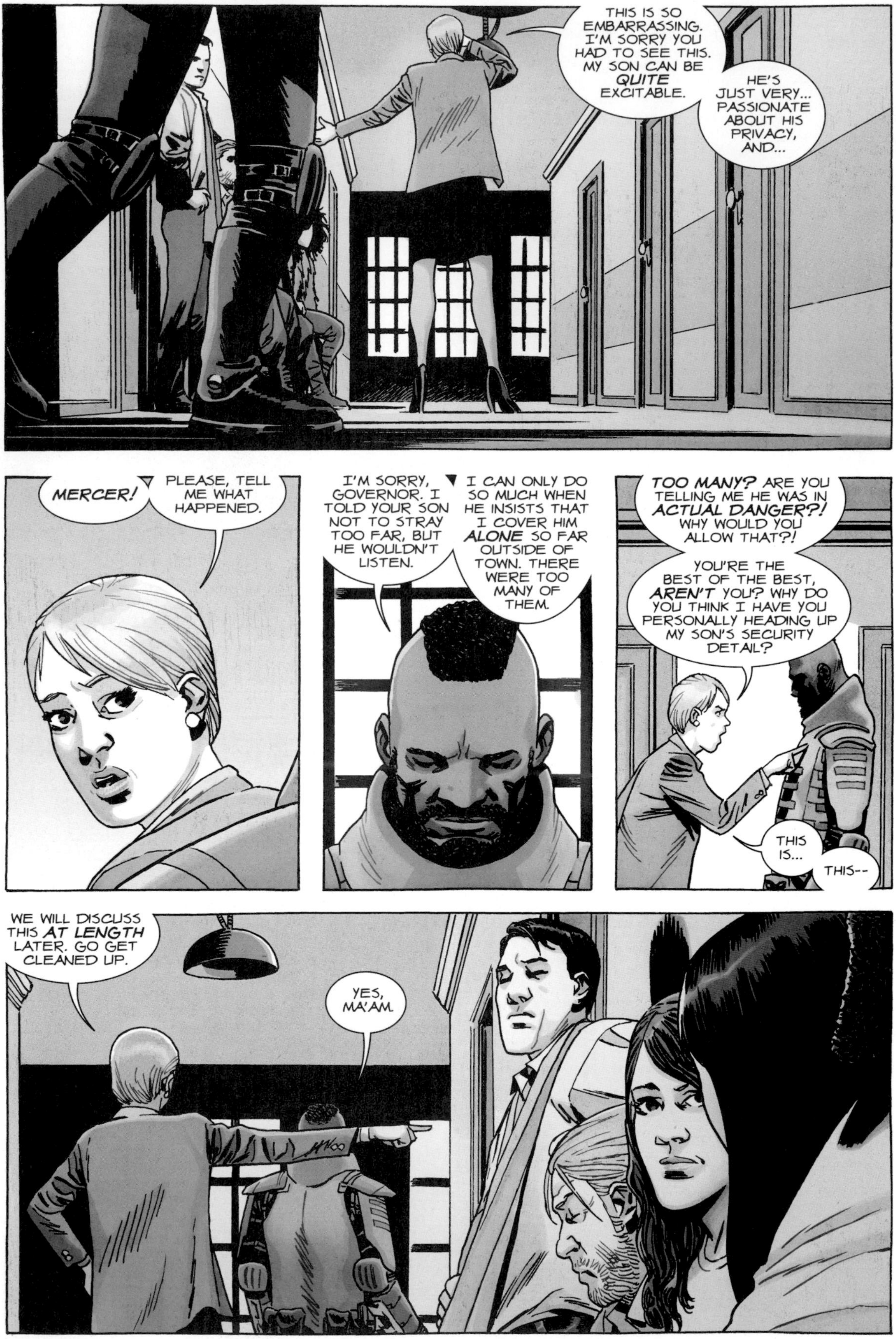
THIS IS SO EMBARRASSING. I'M SORRY YOU HAD TO SEE THIS. MY SON CAN BE QUITE EXCITABLE.
HE'S JUST VERY... PASSIONATE ABOUT HIS PRIVACY, AND...
MERCER!
PLEASE, TELL ME WHAT HAPPENED.
I'M SORRY, GOVERNOR. I TOLD YOUR SON NOT TO STRAY TOO FAR, BUT HE WOULDN'T LISTEN.
I CAN ONLY DO SO MUCH WHEN HE INSISTS THAT I COVER HIM ALONE SO FAR OUTSIDE OF TOWN. THERE WERE TOO MANY OF THEM.
TOO MANY? ARE YOU TELLING ME HE WAS IN ACTUAL DANGER?! WHY WOULD YOU ALLOW THAT?!
YOU'RE THE BEST OF THE BEST, AREN'T YOU? WHY DO YOU THINK I HAVE YOU PERSONALLY HEADING UP MY SON'S SECURITY DETAIL?
THIS IS...
THIS--
WE WILL DISCUSS THIS AT LENGTH LATER. GO GET CLEANED UP.
YES, MA'AM.

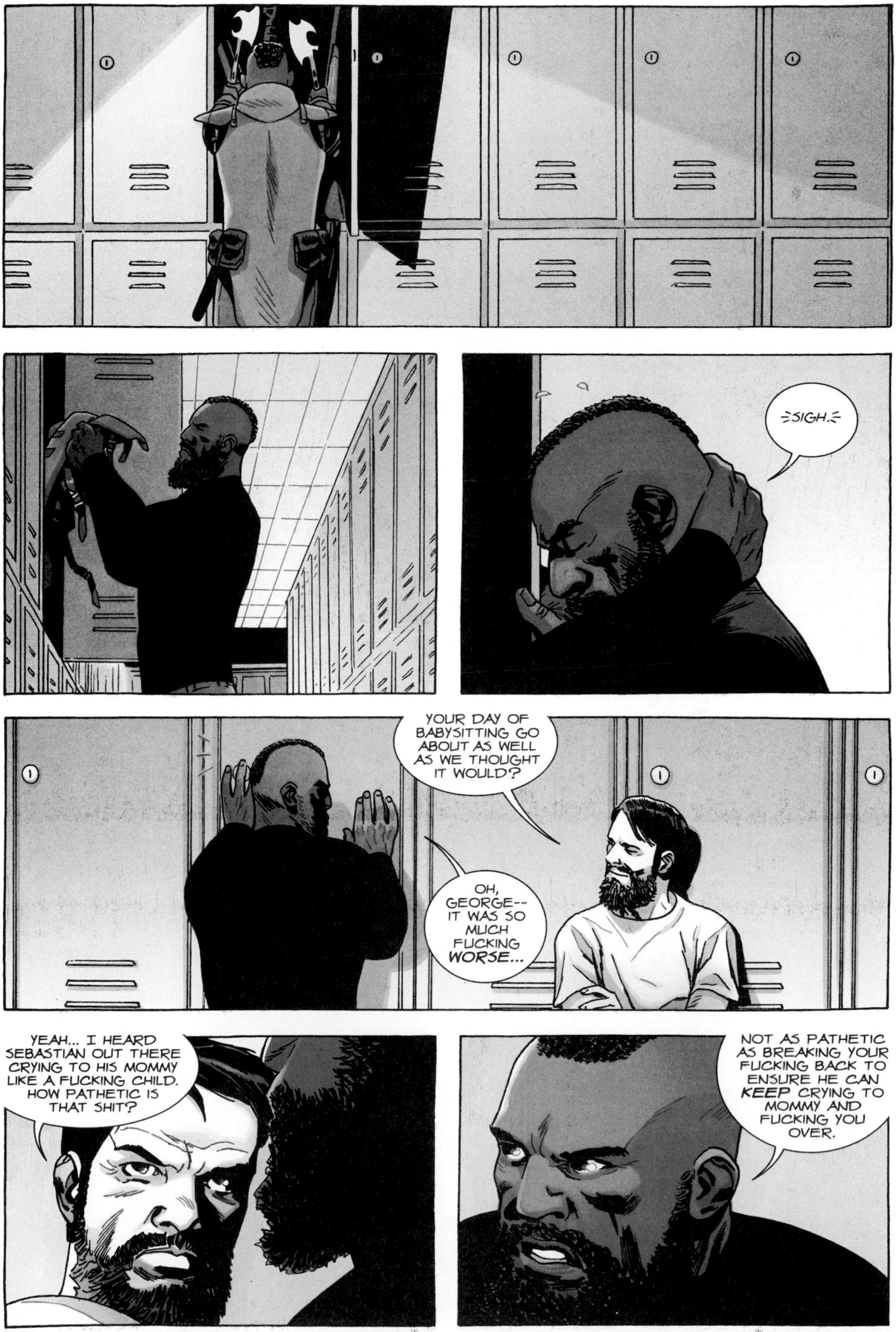

SIGH.
YOUR DAY OF BABYSITTING GO ABOUT AS WELL AS WE THOUGHT IT WOULD?
OH, GEORGE-- IT WAS SO MUCH FUCKING WORSE...
YEAH... I HEARD SEBASTIAN OUT THERE CRYING TO HIS MOMMY LIKE A FUCKING CHILD. HOW PATHETIC IS THAT SHIT?
NOT AS PATHETIC AS BREAKING YOUR FUCKING BACK TO ENSURE HE CAN KEEP CRYING TO MOMMY AND FUCKING YOU OVER.

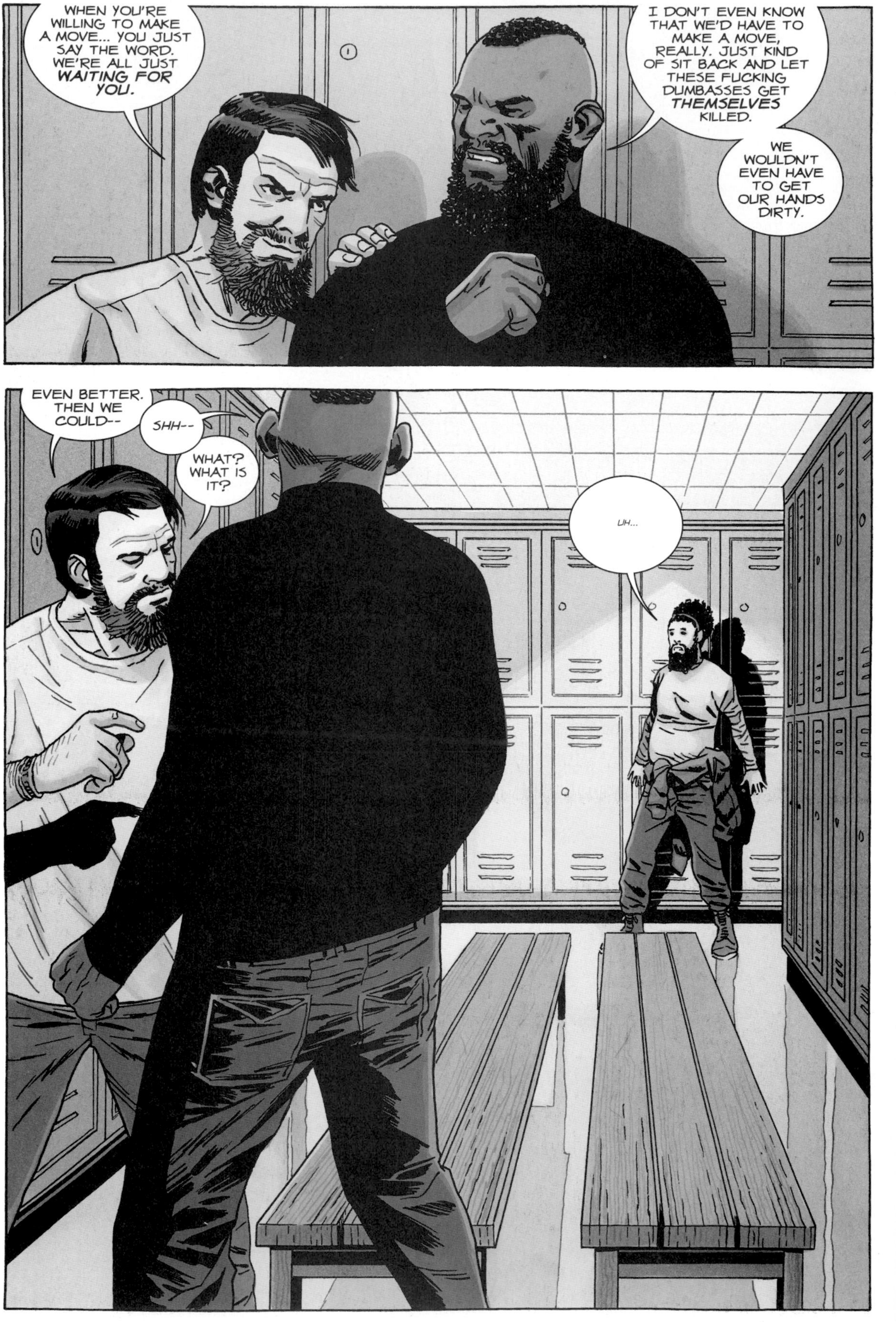
WHEN YOU'RE WILLING TO MAKE A MOVE... YOU JUST SAY THE WORD. WE'RE ALL JUST WAITING FOR YOU.
I DON'T EVEN KNOW THAT WE'D HAVE TO MAKE A MOVE, REALLY. JUST KIND OF SIT BACK AND LET THESE FUCKING DUMBASSES GET THEMSELVES KILLED.
WE WOULDN'T EVEN HAVE TO GET OUR HANDS DIRTY.
EVEN BETTER. THEN WE COULD--
SHH--
WHAT? WHAT IS IT?
UH...

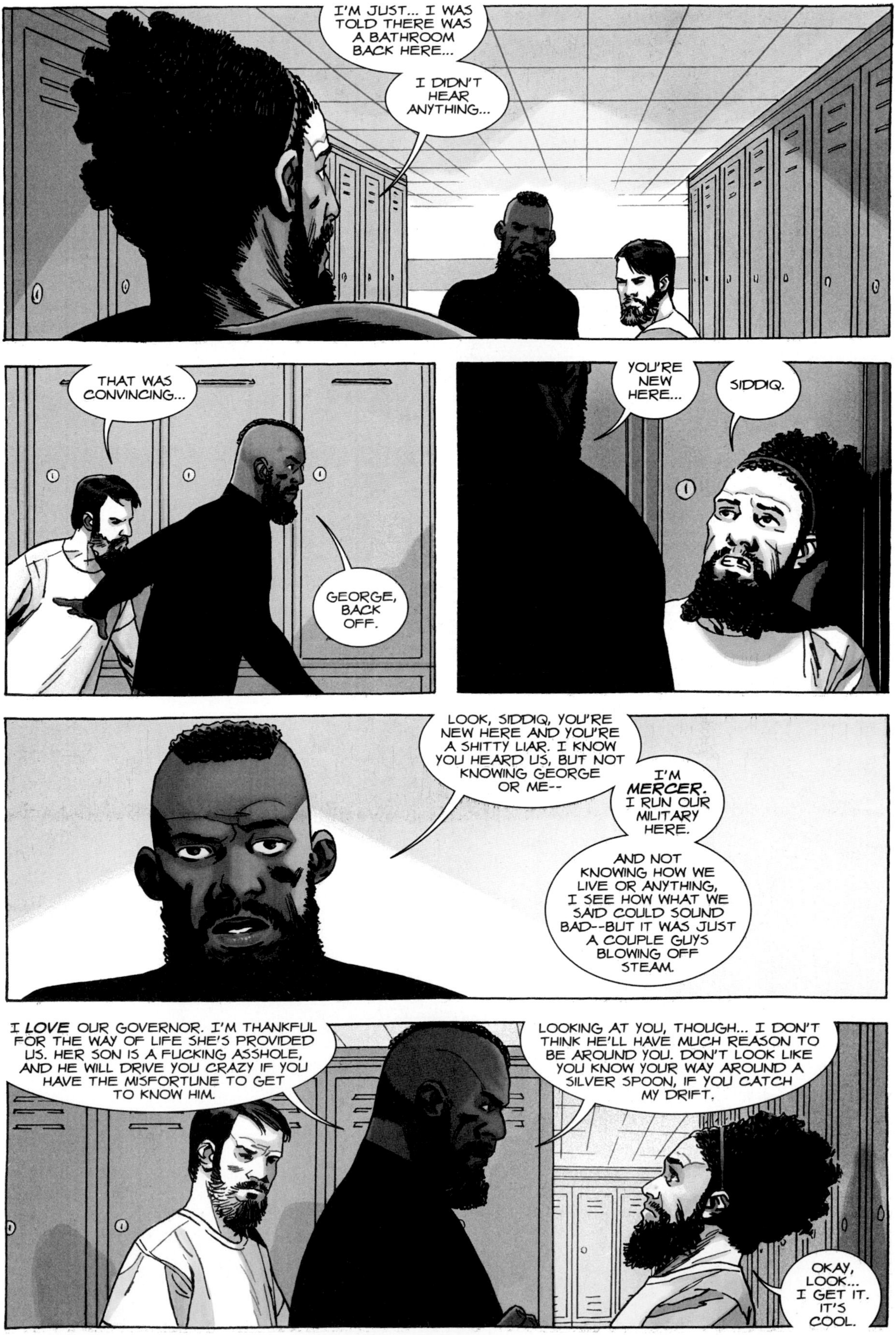
I'M JUST... I WAS TOLD THERE WAS A BATHROOM BACK HERE...
I DIDN'T HEAR ANYTHING...
THAT WAS CONVINCING...
GEORGE, BACK OFF.
YOU'RE NEW HERE...
SIDDIQ.
LOOK, SIDDIQ, YOU'RE NEW HERE AND YOU'RE A SHITTY LIAR. I KNOW YOU HEARD US, BUT NOT KNOWING GEORGE OR ME--
I'M MERCER. I RUN OUR MILITARY HERE.
AND NOT KNOWING HOW WE LIVE OR ANYTHING, I SEE HOW WHAT WE SAID COULD SOUND BAD--BUT IT WAS JUST A COUPLE GUYS BLOWING OFF STEAM.
I LOVE OUR GOVERNOR. I'M THANKFUL FOR THE WAY OF LIFE SHE'S PROVIDED US. HER SON IS A FUCKING ASSHOLE, AND HE WILL DRIVE YOU CRAZY IF YOU HAVE THE MISFORTUNE TO GET TO KNOW HIM.
LOOKING AT YOU, THOUGH... I DON'T THINK HE'LL HAVE MUCH REASON TO BE AROUND YOU. DON'T LOOK LIKE YOU KNOW YOUR WAY AROUND A SILVER SPOON, IF YOU CATCH MY DRIFT.
OKAY, LOOK... I GET IT. IT'S COOL.

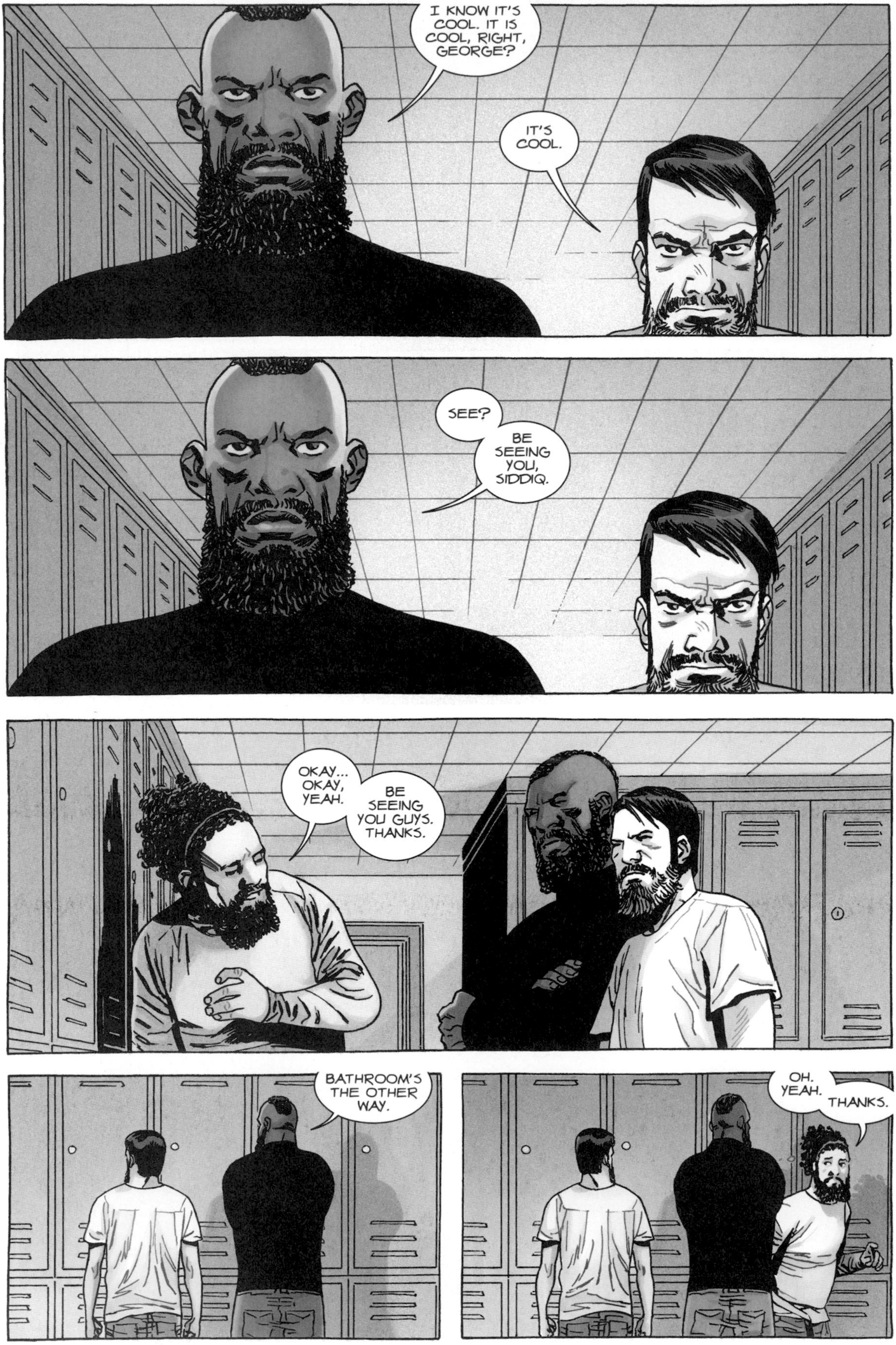
I KNOW IT'S COOL. IT IS COOL, RIGHT, GEORGE?
IT'S COOL.
SEE?
BE SEEING YOU, SIDDIQ.
OKAY... OKAY, YEAH.
BE SEEING YOU GUYS. THANKS.
BATHROOM'S THE OTHER WAY.
OH. YEAH.
THANKS.

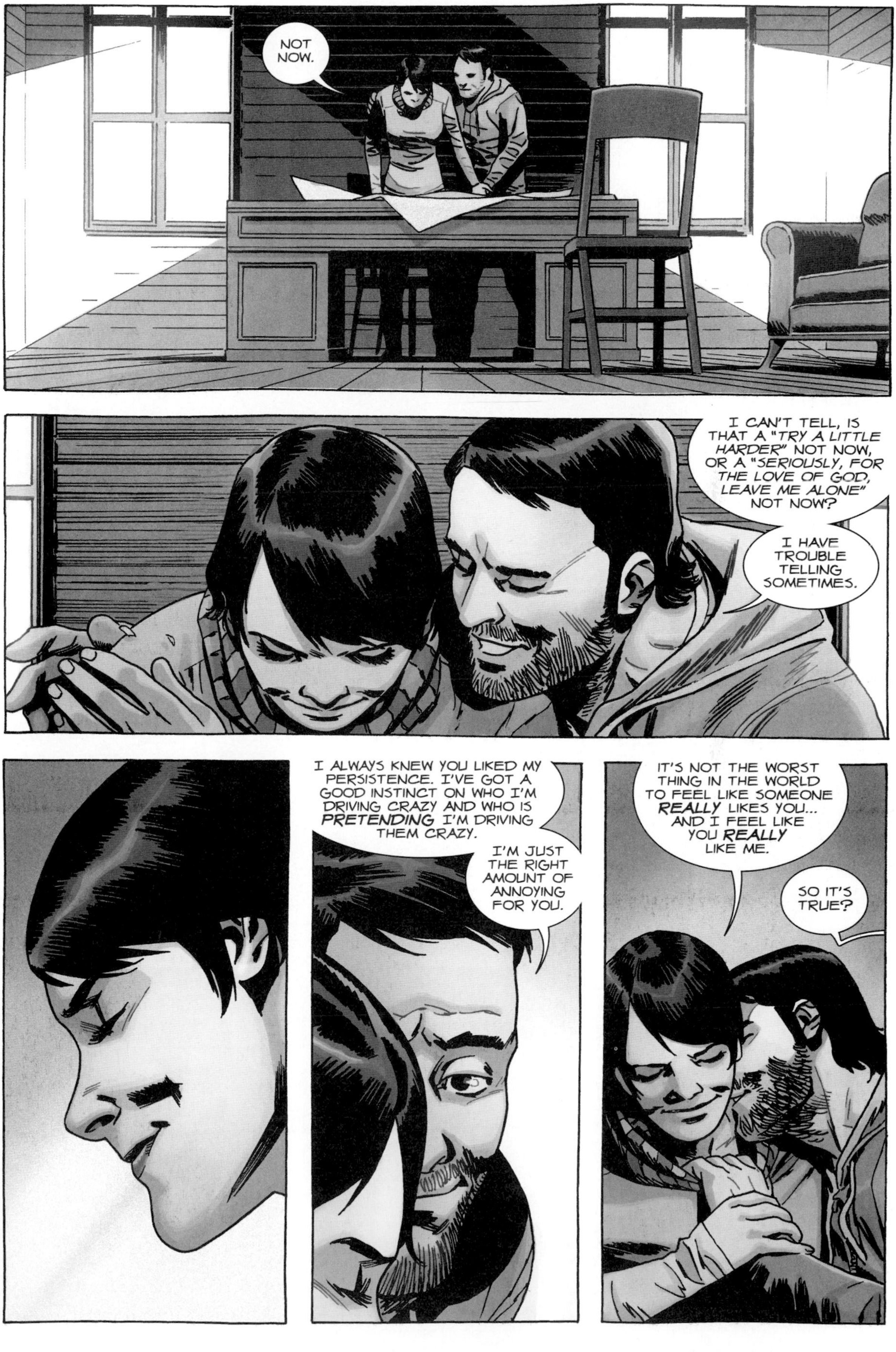
NOT NOW.
I CAN'T TELL, IS THAT A "TRY A LITTLE HARDER" NOT NOW, OR A "SERIOUSLY, FOR THE LOVE OF GOD, LEAVE ME ALONE" NOT NOW?
I HAVE TROUBLE TELLING SOMETIMES.
I ALWAYS KNEW YOU LIKED MY PERSISTENCE. I'VE GOT A GOOD INSTINCT ON WHO I'M DRIVING CRAZY AND WHO IS PRETENDING I'M DRIVING THEM CRAZY.
I'M JUST THE RIGHT AMOUNT OF ANNOYING FOR YOU.
IT'S NOT THE WORST THING IN THE WORLD TO FEEL LIKE SOMEONE REALLY LIKES YOU... AND I FEEL LIKE YOU REALLY LIKE ME.
SO IT'S TRUE?

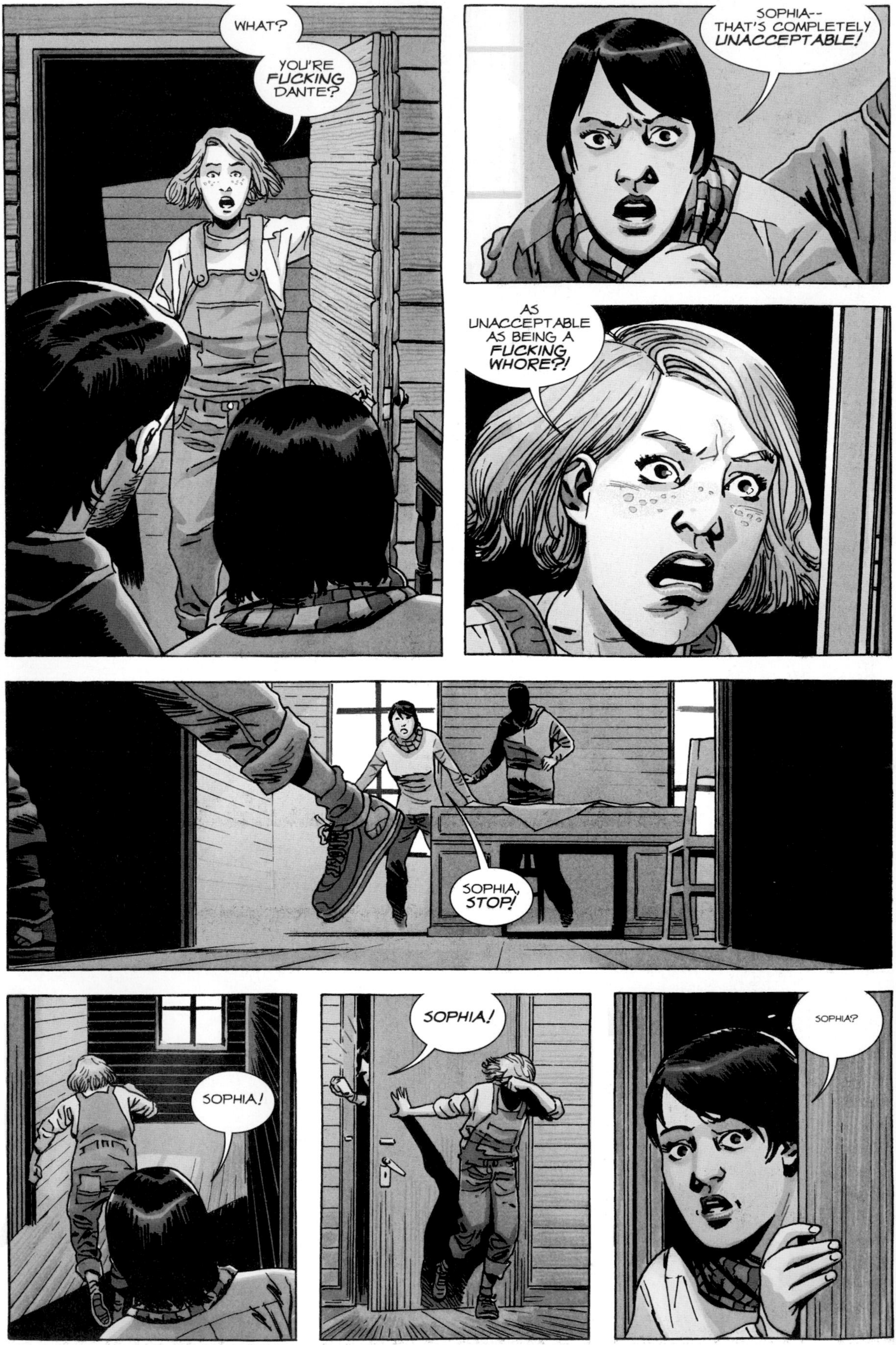
WHAT?
YOU'RE FUCKING DANTE?
SOPHIA-- THAT'S COMPLETELY UNACCEPTABLE!
AS UNACCEPTABLE AS BEING A FUCKING WHORE?!
SOPHIA, STOP!
SOPHIA!
SOPHIA!
SOPHIA?

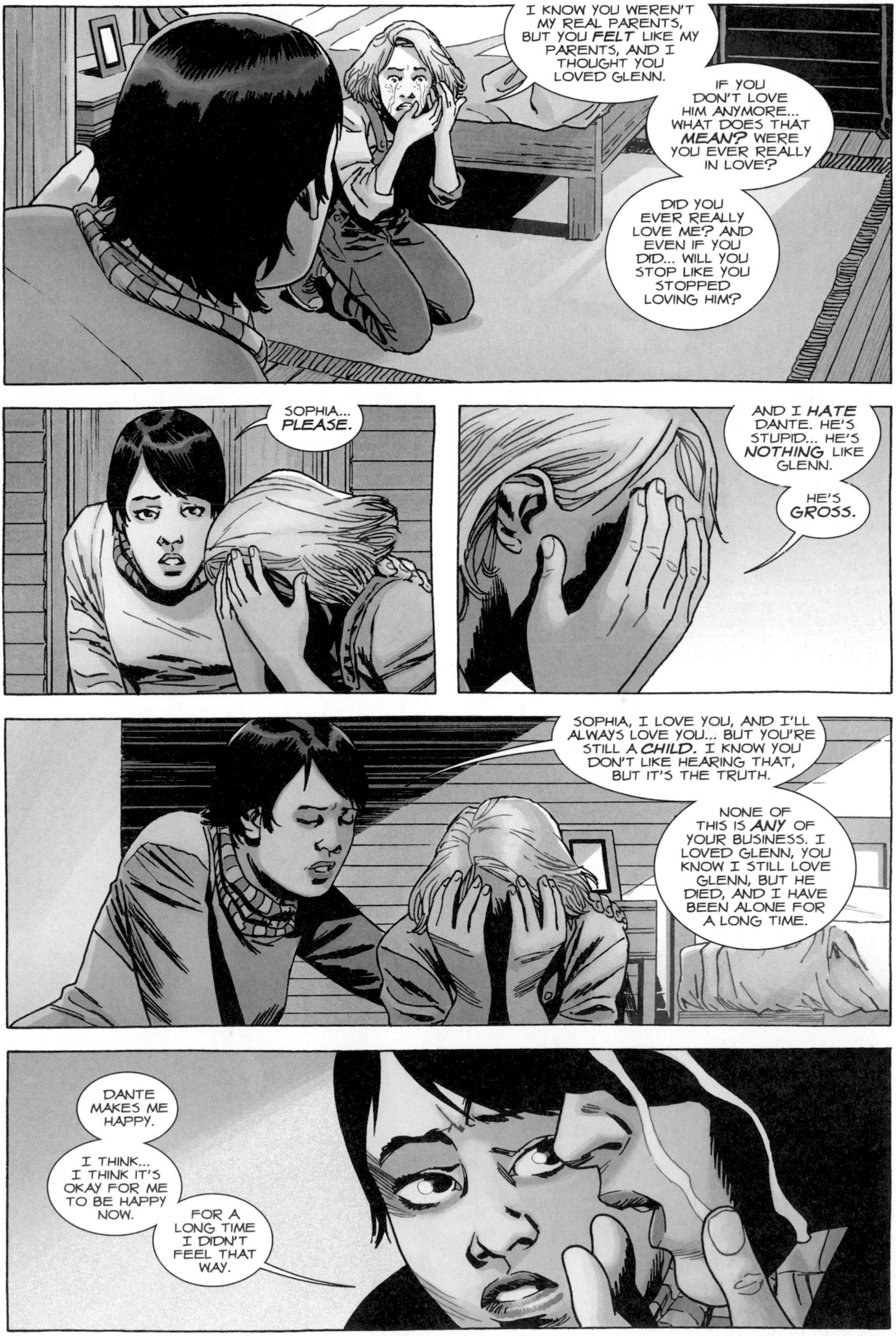
I KNOW YOU WEREN'T MY REAL PARENTS, BUT YOU FELT LIKE MY PARENTS, AND I THOUGHT YOU LOVED GLENN.
IF YOU DON'T LOVE HIM ANYMORE... WHAT DOES THAT MEAN? WERE YOU EVER REALLY IN LOVE?
DID YOU EVER REALLY LOVE ME? AND EVEN IF YOU DID... WILL YOU STOP LIKE YOU STOPPED LOVING HIM?
SOPHIA... PLEASE.
AND I HATE DANTE. HE'S STUPID... HE'S NOTHING LIKE GLENN.
HE'S GROSS.
SOPHIA, I LOVE YOU, AND I'LL ALWAYS LOVE YOU... BUT YOU'RE STILL A CHILD. I KNOW YOU DON'T LIKE HEARING THAT, BUT IT'S THE TRUTH.
NONE OF THIS IS ANY OF YOUR BUSINESS. I LOVED GLENN, YOU KNOW I STILL LOVE GLENN, BUT HE DIED, AND I HAVE BEEN ALONE FOR A LONG TIME.
DANTE MAKES ME HAPPY.
I THINK... I THINK IT'S OKAY FOR ME TO BE HAPPY NOW.
FOR A LONG TIME I DIDN'T FEEL THAT WAY.

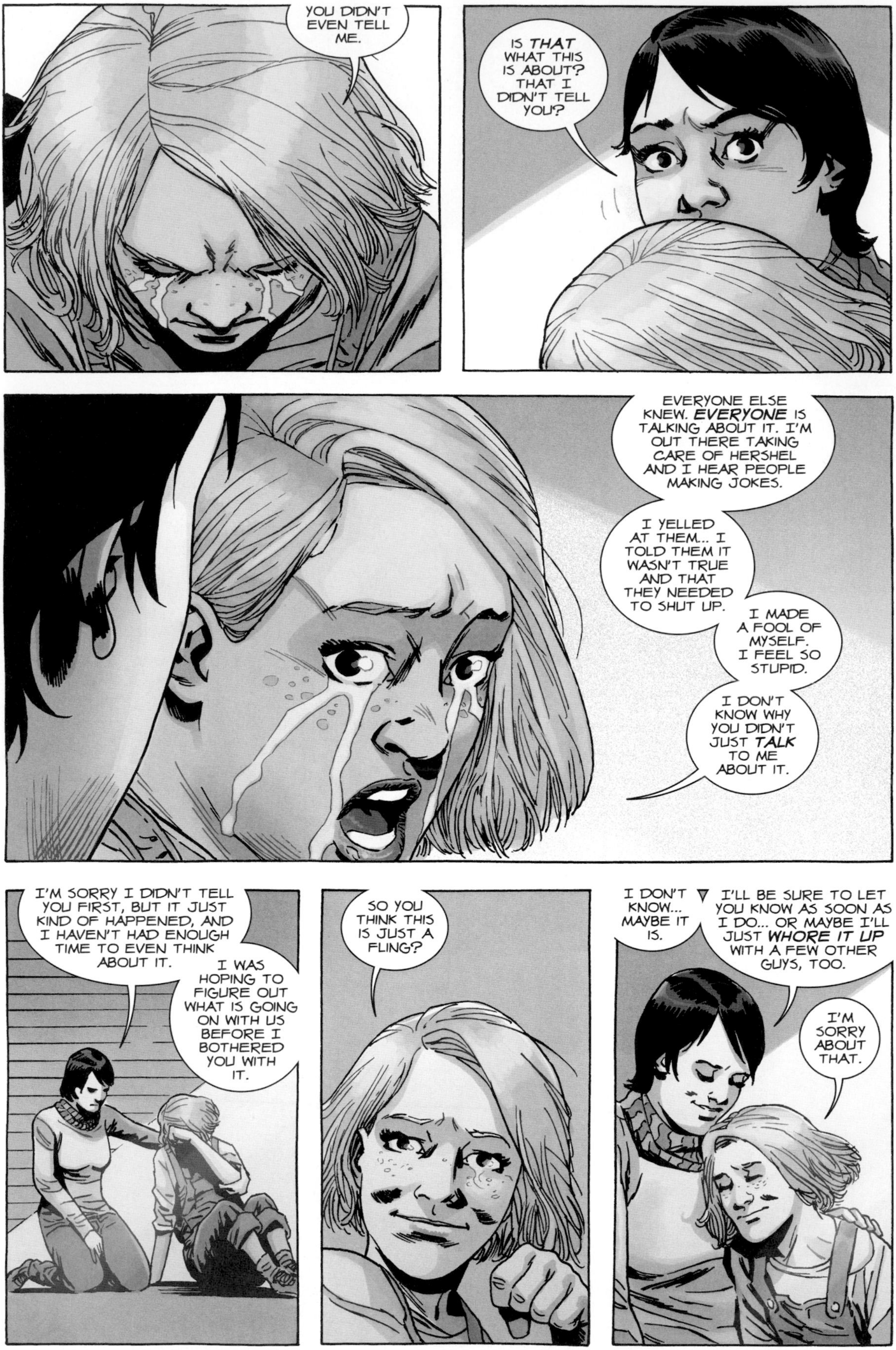
YOU DIDN'T EVEN TELL ME.
IS *THAT* WHAT THIS IS ABOUT? THAT I DIDN'T TELL YOU?
EVERYONE ELSE KNEW. *EVERYONE* IS TALKING ABOUT IT. I'M OUT THERE TAKING CARE OF HERSHEL AND I HEAR PEOPLE MAKING JOKES.
I YELLED AT THEM... I TOLD THEM IT WASN'T TRUE AND THAT THEY NEEDED TO SHUT UP.
I MADE A FOOL OF MYSELF. I FEEL SO STUPID.
I DON'T KNOW WHY YOU DIDN'T JUST *TALK* TO ME ABOUT IT.
I'M SORRY I DIDN'T TELL YOU FIRST, BUT IT JUST KIND OF HAPPENED, AND I HAVEN'T HAD ENOUGH TIME TO EVEN THINK ABOUT IT.
I WAS HOPING TO FIGURE OUT WHAT IS GOING ON WITH US BEFORE I BOTHERED YOU WITH IT.
SO YOU THINK THIS IS JUST A FLING?
I DON'T KNOW... MAYBE IT IS.
I'LL BE SURE TO LET YOU KNOW AS SOON AS I DO... OR MAYBE I'LL JUST *WHORE IT UP* WITH A FEW OTHER GUYS, TOO.
I'M SORRY ABOUT THAT.

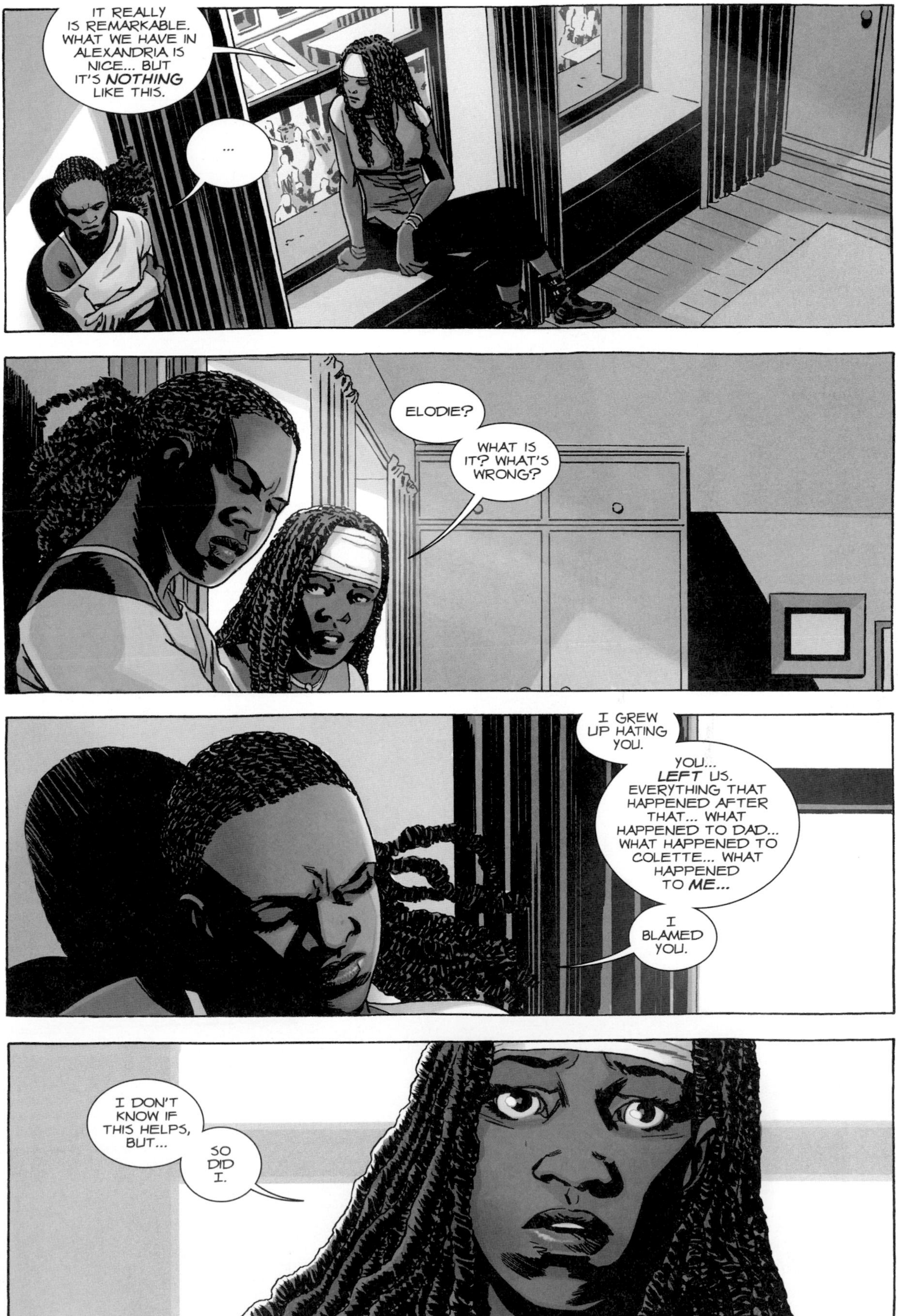
IT REALLY IS REMARKABLE. WHAT WE HAVE IN ALEXANDRIA IS NICE... BUT IT'S **NOTHING** LIKE THIS.
...
ELODIE?
WHAT IS IT? WHAT'S WRONG?
I GREW UP HATING YOU.
YOU... **LEFT** US. EVERYTHING THAT HAPPENED AFTER THAT... WHAT HAPPENED TO DAD... WHAT HAPPENED TO COLETTE... WHAT HAPPENED TO **ME...**
I BLAMED YOU.
I DON'T KNOW IF THIS HELPS, BUT...
SO DID I.

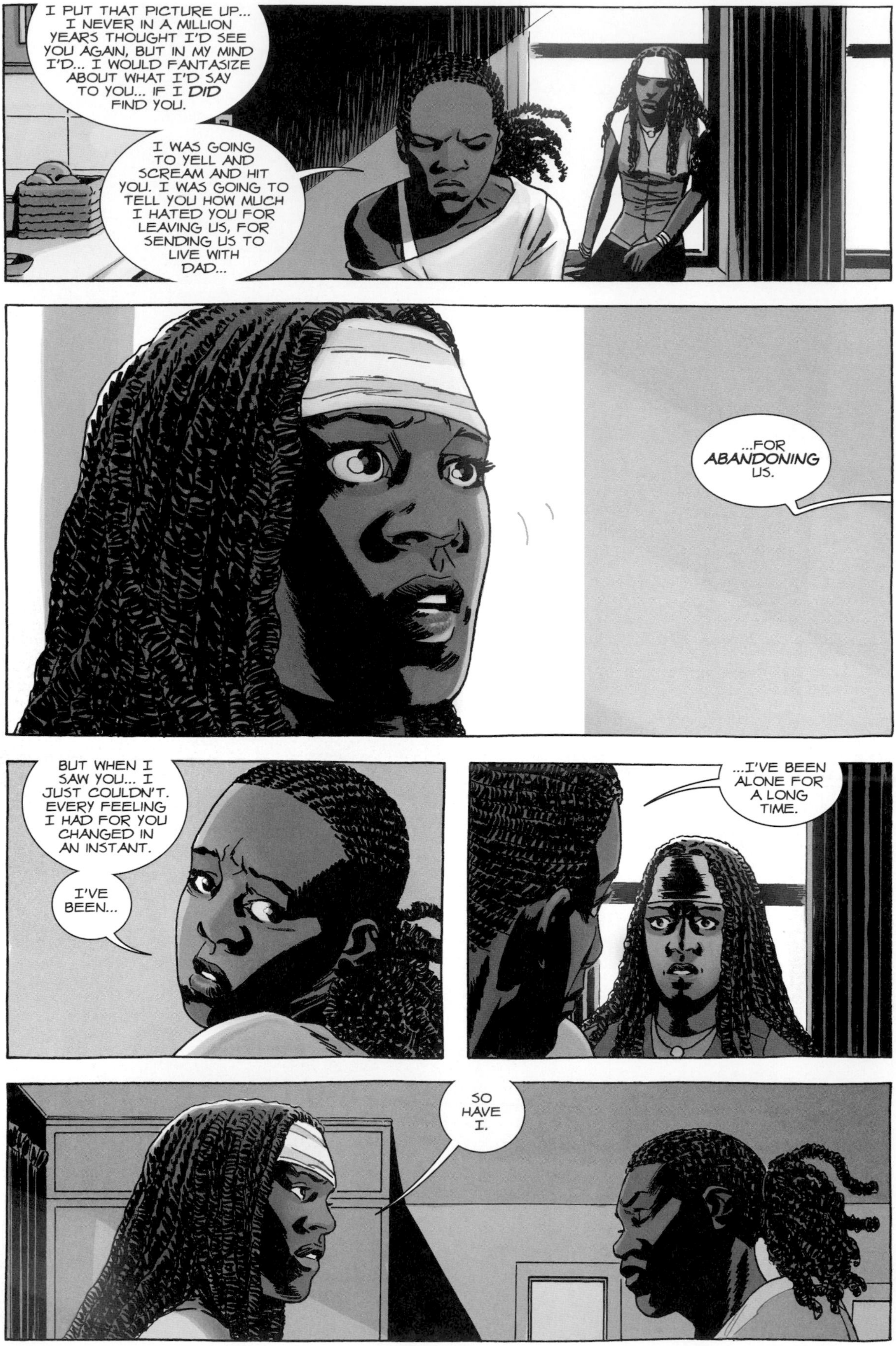

I PUT THAT PICTURE UP... I NEVER IN A MILLION YEARS THOUGHT I'D SEE YOU AGAIN, BUT IN MY MIND I'D... I WOULD FANTASIZE ABOUT WHAT I'D SAY TO YOU... IF I DID FIND YOU.
I WAS GOING TO YELL AND SCREAM AND HIT YOU. I WAS GOING TO TELL YOU HOW MUCH I HATED YOU FOR LEAVING US, FOR SENDING US TO LIVE WITH DAD...
...FOR ABANDONING US.
BUT WHEN I SAW YOU... I JUST COULDN'T. EVERY FEELING I HAD FOR YOU CHANGED IN AN INSTANT.
I'VE BEEN...
...I'VE BEEN ALONE FOR A LONG TIME.
SO HAVE I.

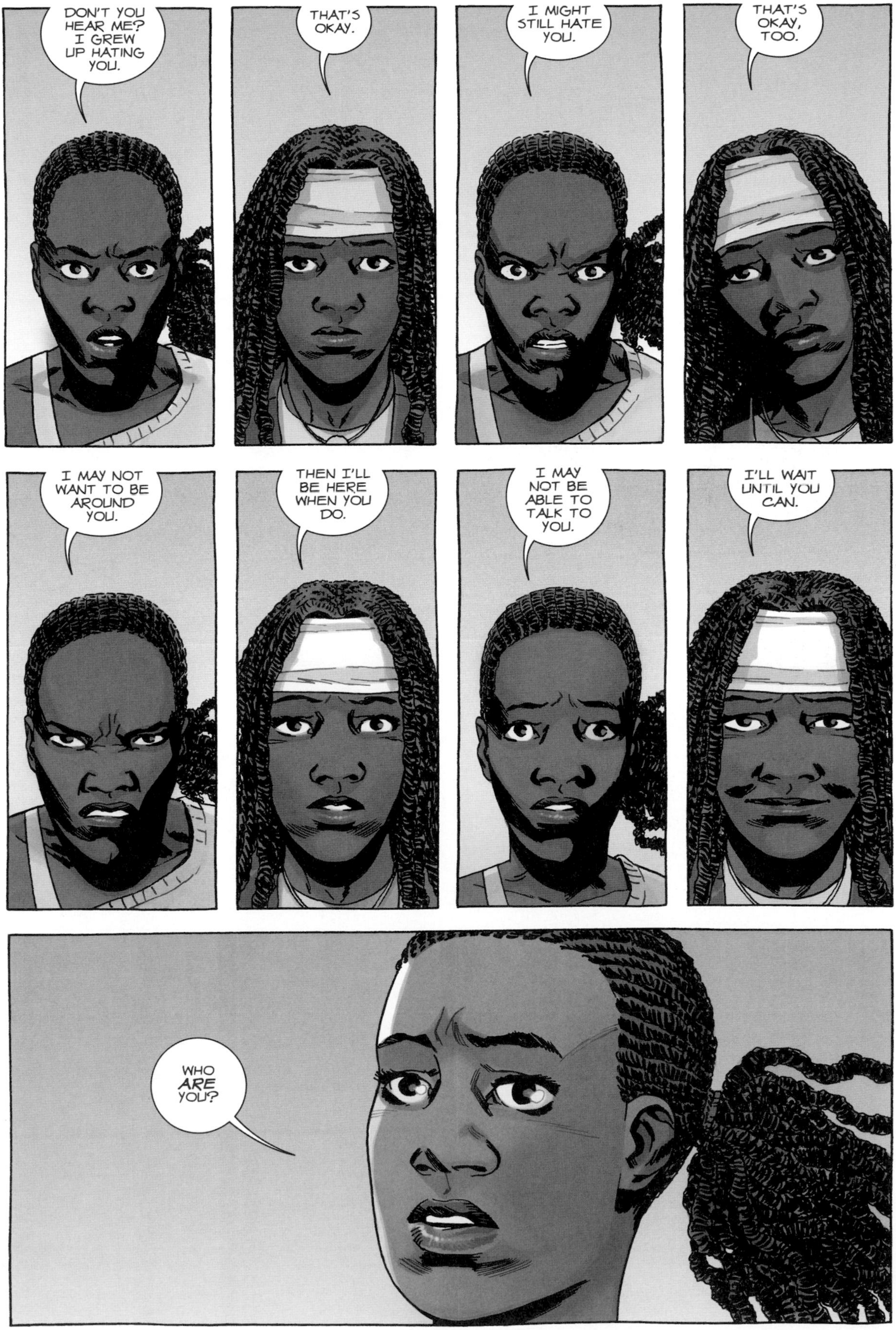
DON'T YOU HEAR ME? I GREW UP HATING YOU.
THAT'S OKAY.
I MIGHT STILL HATE YOU.
THAT'S OKAY, TOO.
I MAY NOT WANT TO BE AROUND YOU.
THEN I'LL BE HERE WHEN YOU DO.
I MAY NOT BE ABLE TO TALK TO YOU.
I'LL WAIT UNTIL YOU CAN.
WHO *ARE* YOU?

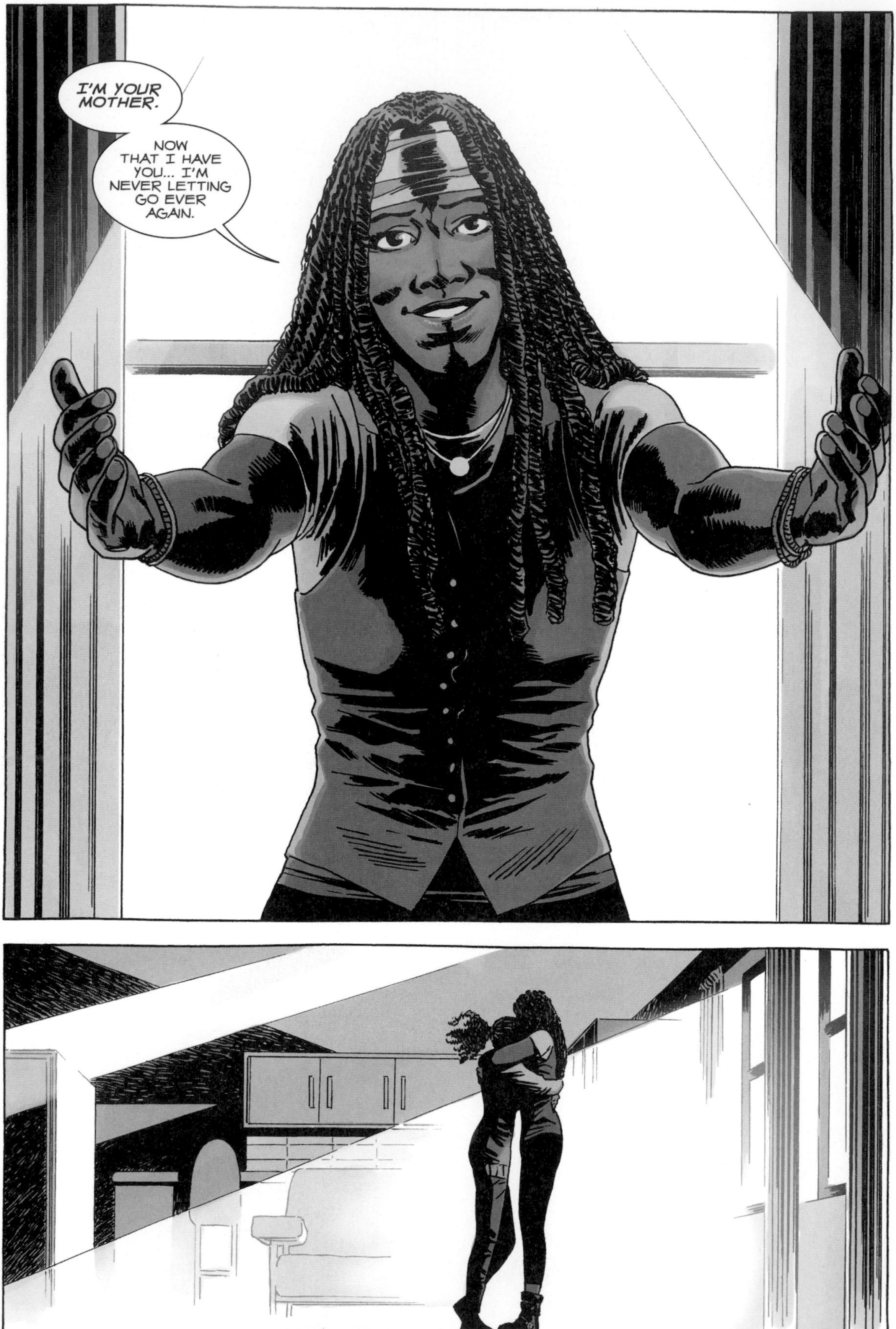
I'M YOUR MOTHER.
NOW THAT I HAVE YOU... I'M NEVER LETTING GO EVER AGAIN.

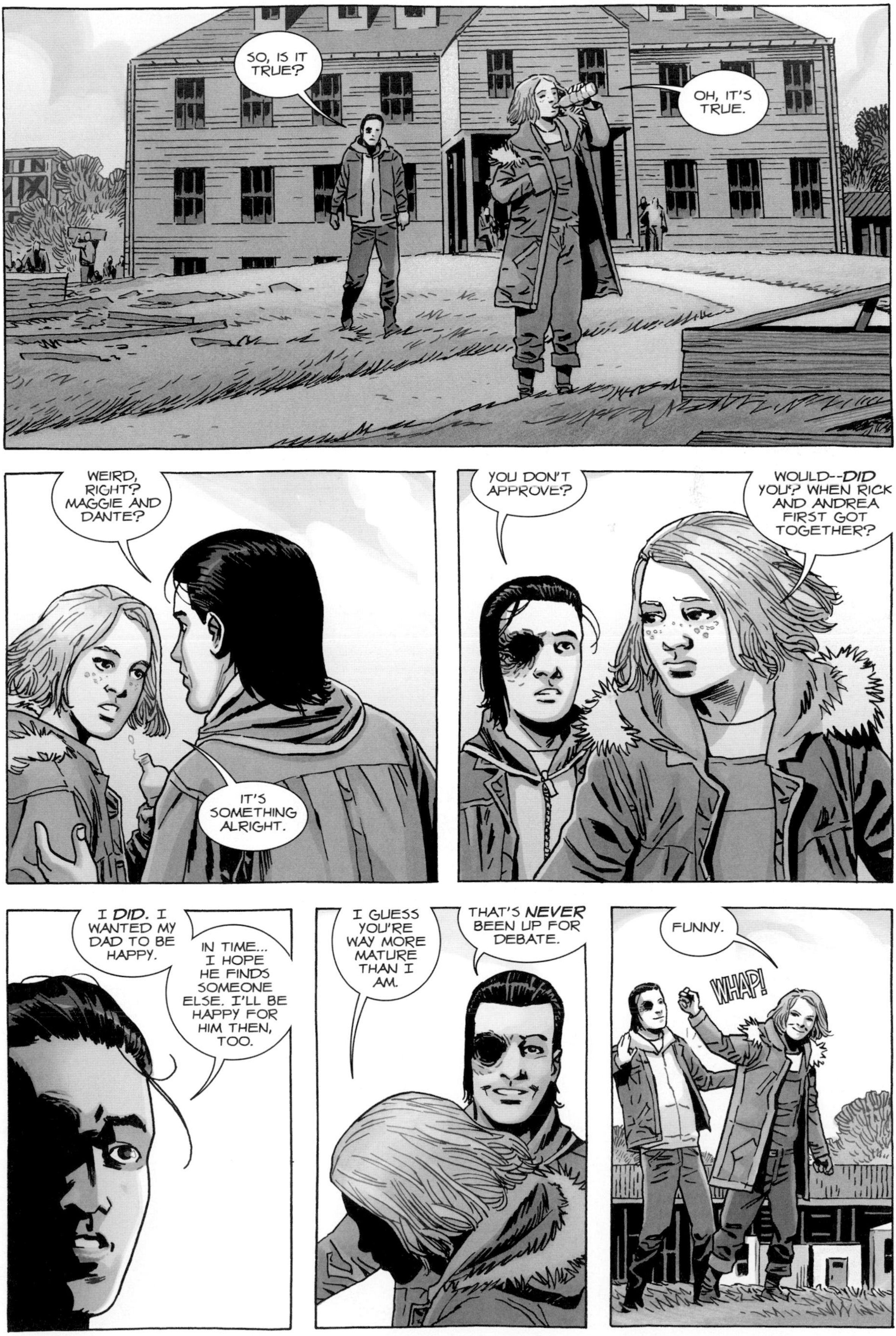
SO, IS IT TRUE?
OH, IT'S TRUE.
WEIRD, RIGHT? MAGGIE AND DANTE?
IT'S SOMETHING ALRIGHT.
YOU DON'T APPROVE?
WOULD--*DID* YOU? WHEN RICK AND ANDREA FIRST GOT TOGETHER?
I *DID*. I WANTED MY DAD TO BE HAPPY.
IN TIME... I HOPE HE FINDS SOMEONE ELSE. I'LL BE HAPPY FOR HIM THEN, TOO.
I GUESS YOU'RE WAY MORE MATURE THAN I AM.
THAT'S *NEVER* BEEN UP FOR DEBATE.
FUNNY.
WHAP!

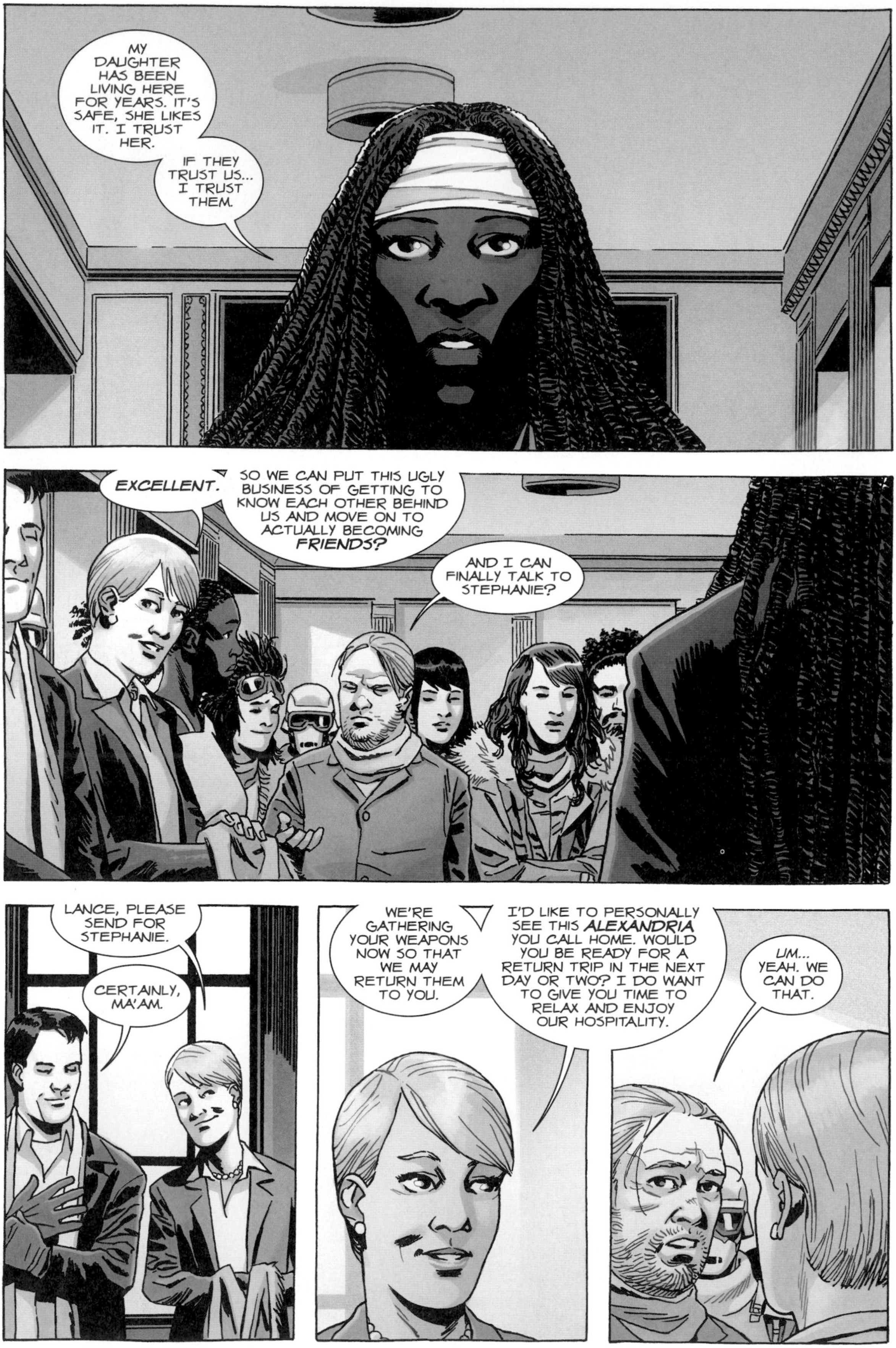

MY DAUGHTER HAS BEEN LIVING HERE FOR YEARS. IT'S SAFE, SHE LIKES IT. I TRUST HER.
IF THEY TRUST US... I TRUST THEM.
EXCELLENT.
SO WE CAN PUT THIS UGLY BUSINESS OF GETTING TO KNOW EACH OTHER BEHIND US AND MOVE ON TO ACTUALLY BECOMING FRIENDS?
AND I CAN FINALLY TALK TO STEPHANIE?
LANCE, PLEASE SEND FOR STEPHANIE.
CERTAINLY, MA'AM.
WE'RE GATHERING YOUR WEAPONS NOW SO THAT WE MAY RETURN THEM TO YOU.
I'D LIKE TO PERSONALLY SEE THIS ALEXANDRIA YOU CALL HOME. WOULD YOU BE READY FOR A RETURN TRIP IN THE NEXT DAY OR TWO? I DO WANT TO GIVE YOU TIME TO RELAX AND ENJOY OUR HOSPITALITY.
UM... YEAH. WE CAN DO THAT.

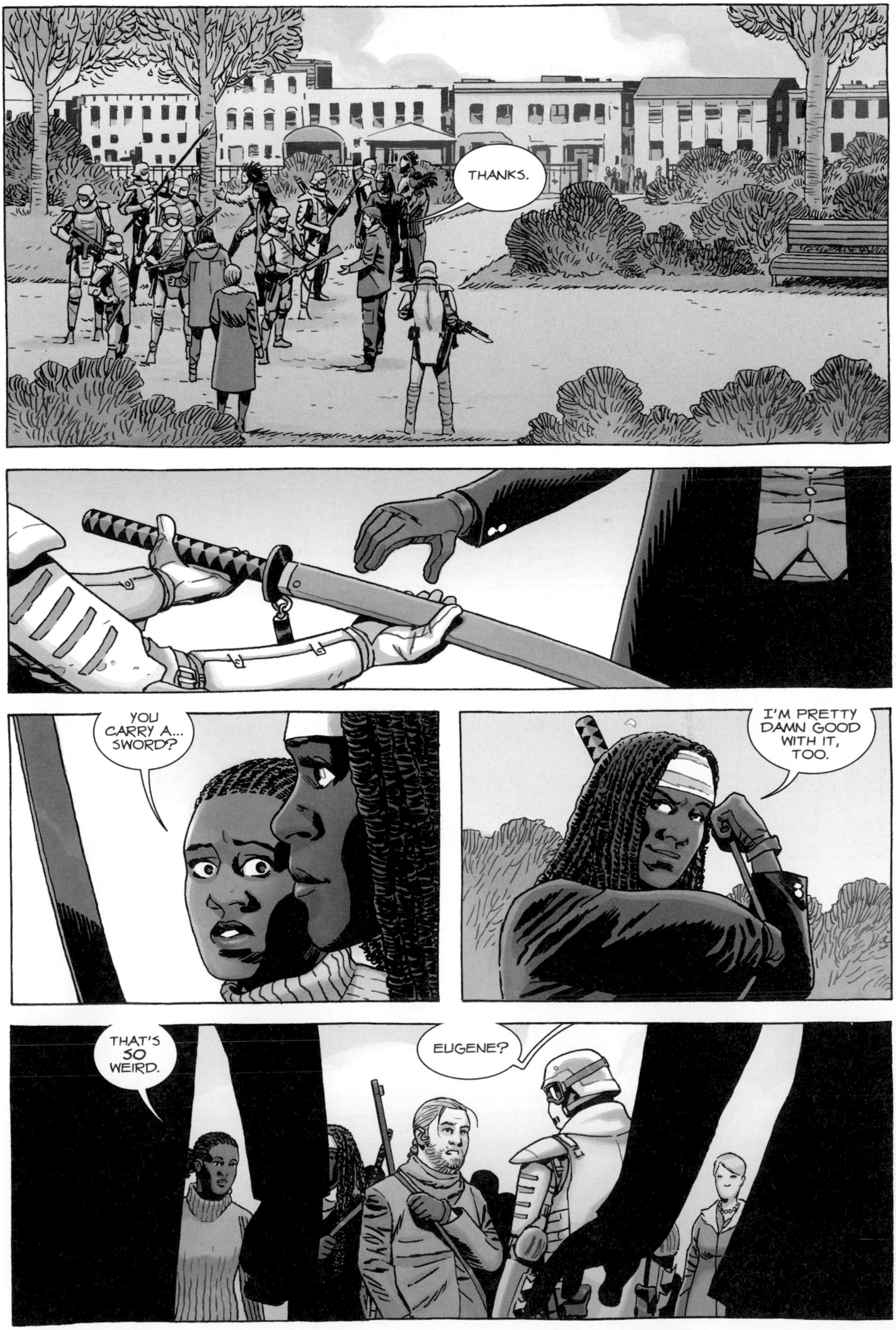
THANKS.
YOU CARRY A... SWORD?
I'M PRETTY DAMN GOOD WITH IT, TOO.
THAT'S SO WEIRD.
EUGENE?

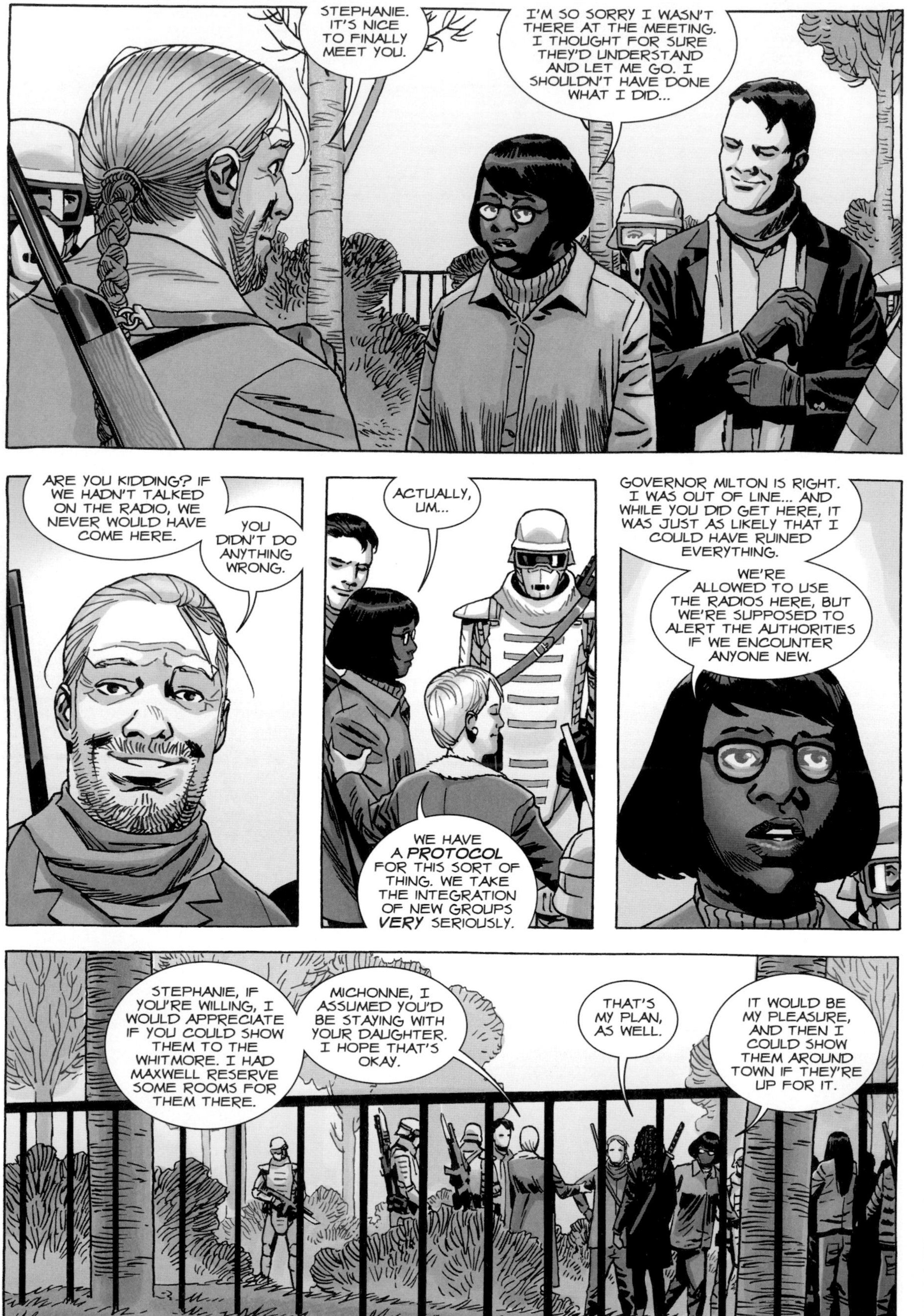
STEPHANIE. IT'S NICE TO FINALLY MEET YOU.
I'M SO SORRY I WASN'T THERE AT THE MEETING. I THOUGHT FOR SURE THEY'D UNDERSTAND AND LET ME GO. I SHOULDN'T HAVE DONE WHAT I DID...
ARE YOU KIDDING? IF WE HADN'T TALKED ON THE RADIO, WE NEVER WOULD HAVE COME HERE.
YOU DIDN'T DO ANYTHING WRONG.
ACTUALLY, UM...
WE HAVE A **PROTOCOL** FOR THIS SORT OF THING. WE TAKE THE INTEGRATION OF NEW GROUPS **VERY** SERIOUSLY.
GOVERNOR MILTON IS RIGHT. I WAS OUT OF LINE... AND WHILE YOU DID GET HERE, IT WAS JUST AS LIKELY THAT I COULD HAVE RUINED EVERYTHING.
WE'RE ALLOWED TO USE THE RADIOS HERE, BUT WE'RE SUPPOSED TO ALERT THE AUTHORITIES IF WE ENCOUNTER ANYONE NEW.
STEPHANIE, IF YOU'RE WILLING, I WOULD APPRECIATE IF YOU COULD SHOW THEM TO THE WHITMORE. I HAD MAXWELL RESERVE SOME ROOMS FOR THEM THERE.
MICHONNE, I ASSUMED YOU'D BE STAYING WITH YOUR DAUGHTER. I HOPE THAT'S OKAY.
THAT'S MY PLAN, AS WELL.
IT WOULD BE MY PLEASURE, AND THEN I COULD SHOW THEM AROUND TOWN IF THEY'RE UP FOR IT.

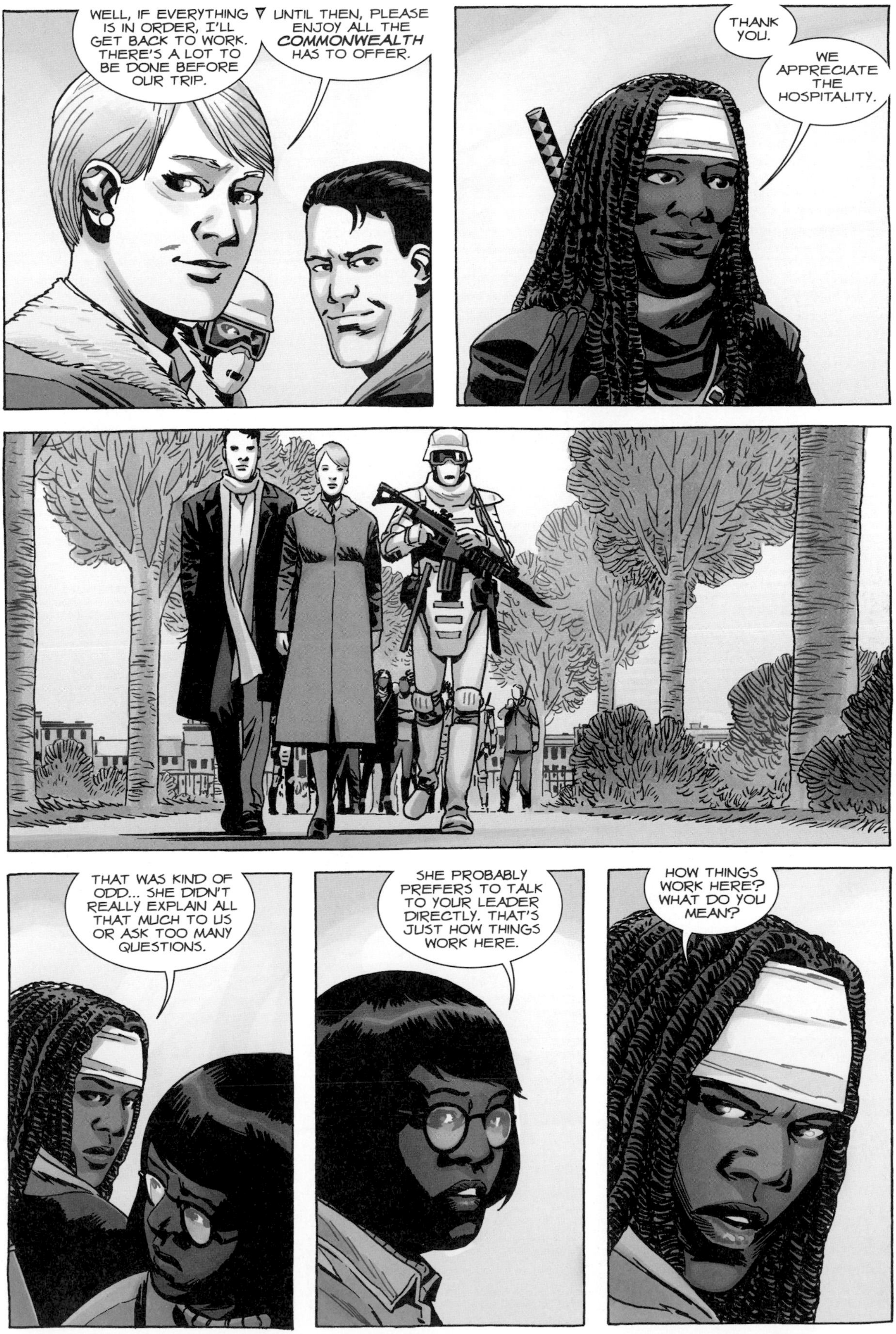
WELL, IF EVERYTHING IS IN ORDER, I'LL GET BACK TO WORK. THERE'S A LOT TO BE DONE BEFORE OUR TRIP.
UNTIL THEN, PLEASE ENJOY ALL THE COMMONWEALTH HAS TO OFFER.
THANK YOU.
WE APPRECIATE THE HOSPITALITY.
THAT WAS KIND OF ODD... SHE DIDN'T REALLY EXPLAIN ALL THAT MUCH TO US OR ASK TOO MANY QUESTIONS.
SHE PROBABLY PREFERS TO TALK TO YOUR LEADER DIRECTLY. THAT'S JUST HOW THINGS WORK HERE.
HOW THINGS WORK HERE? WHAT DO YOU MEAN?

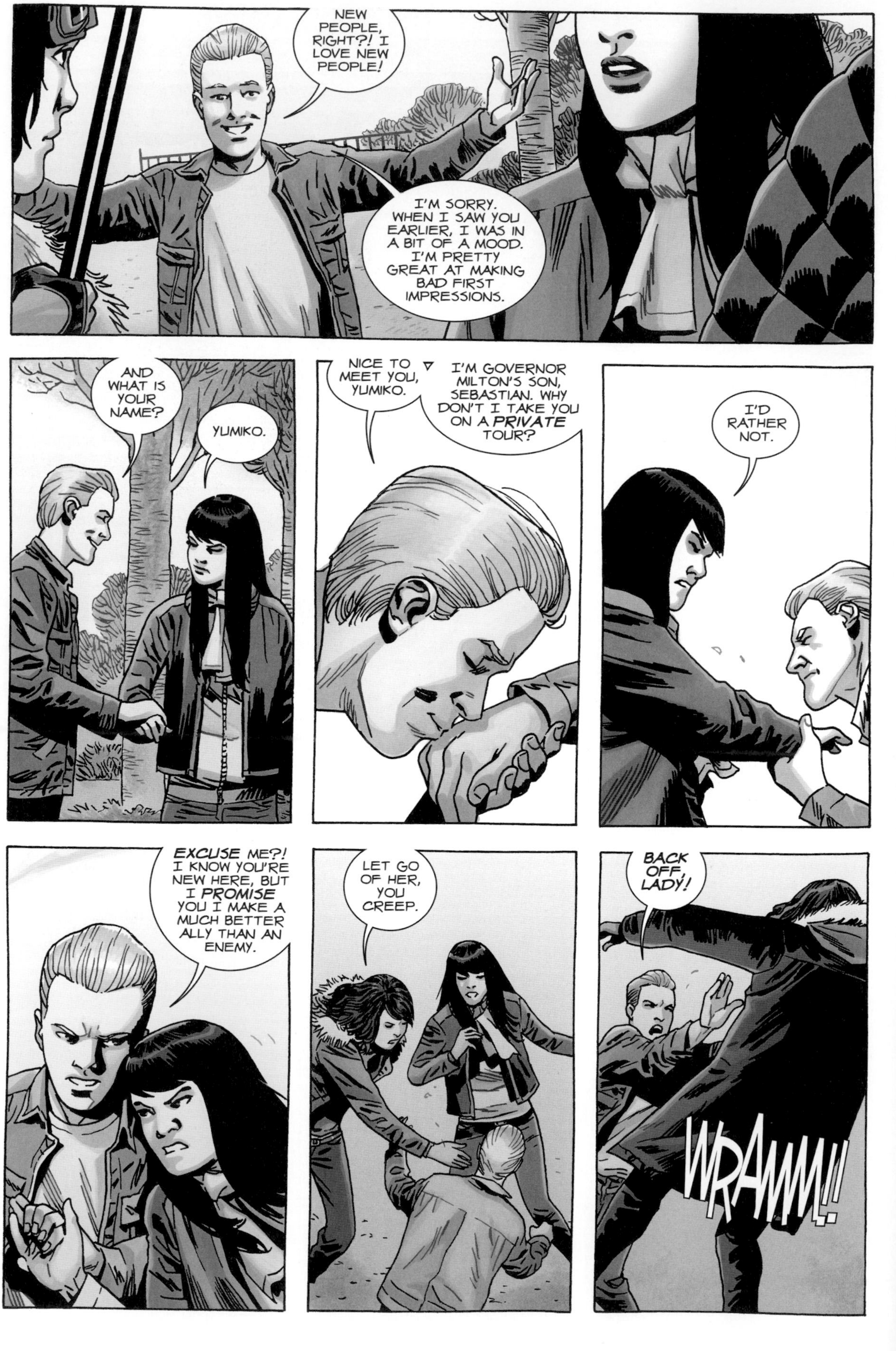

NEW PEOPLE, RIGHT?! I LOVE NEW PEOPLE!
I'M SORRY. WHEN I SAW YOU EARLIER, I WAS IN A BIT OF A MOOD. I'M PRETTY GREAT AT MAKING BAD FIRST IMPRESSIONS.
AND WHAT IS YOUR NAME?
YUMIKO.
NICE TO MEET YOU, YUMIKO.
I'M GOVERNOR MILTON'S SON, SEBASTIAN. WHY DON'T I TAKE YOU ON A PRIVATE TOUR?
I'D RATHER NOT.
EXCUSE ME?! I KNOW YOU'RE NEW HERE, BUT I PROMISE YOU I MAKE A MUCH BETTER ALLY THAN AN ENEMY.
LET GO OF HER, YOU CREEP.
BACK OFF, LADY!
WRAMM!!

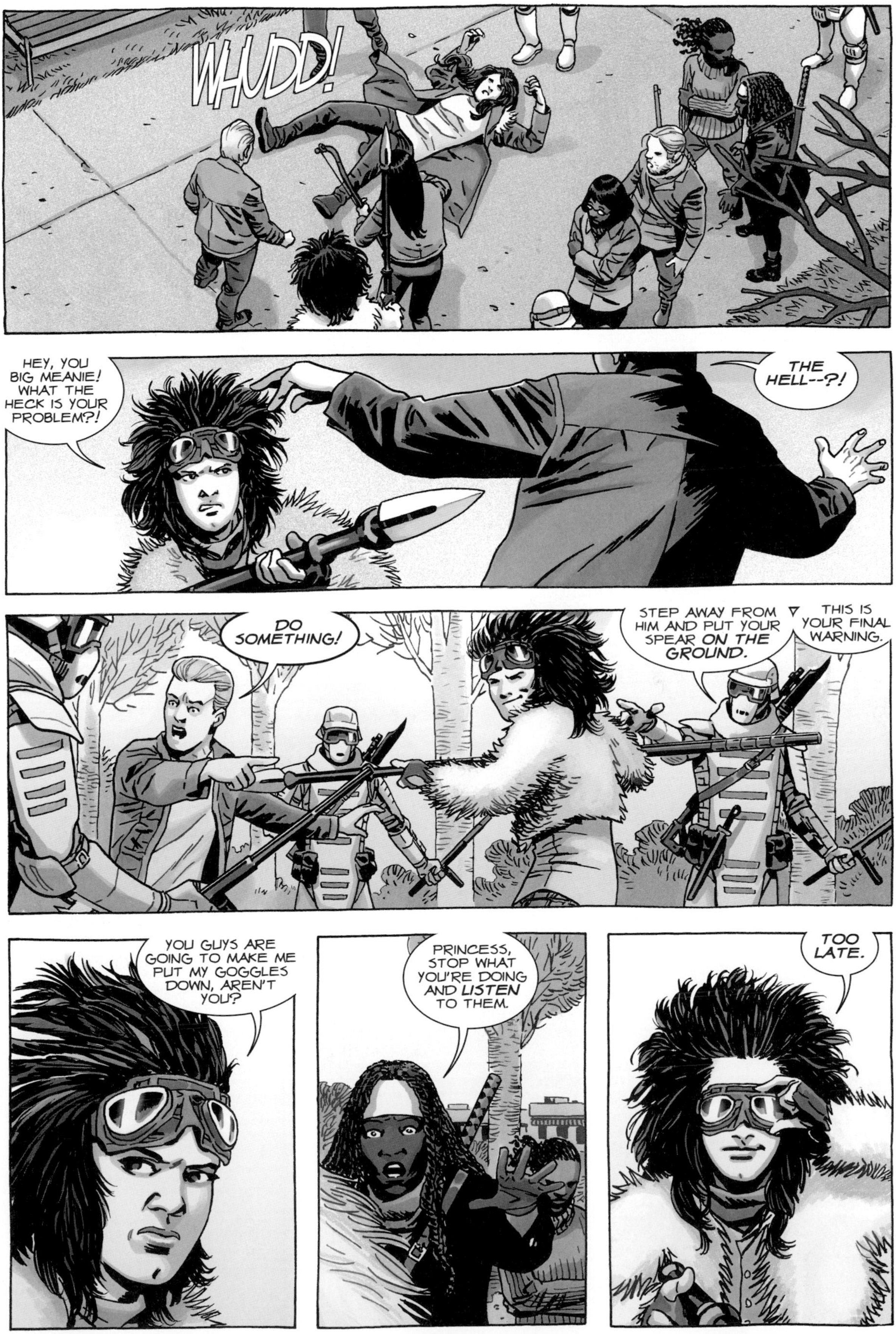
WHUDD!
HEY, YOU BIG MEANIE! WHAT THE HECK IS YOUR PROBLEM?!
THE HELL--?!
DO SOMETHING!
STEP AWAY FROM HIM AND PUT YOUR SPEAR ON THE GROUND.
THIS IS YOUR FINAL WARNING.
YOU GUYS ARE GOING TO MAKE ME PUT MY GOGGLES DOWN, AREN'T YOU?
PRINCESS, STOP WHAT YOU'RE DOING AND LISTEN TO THEM.
TOO LATE.

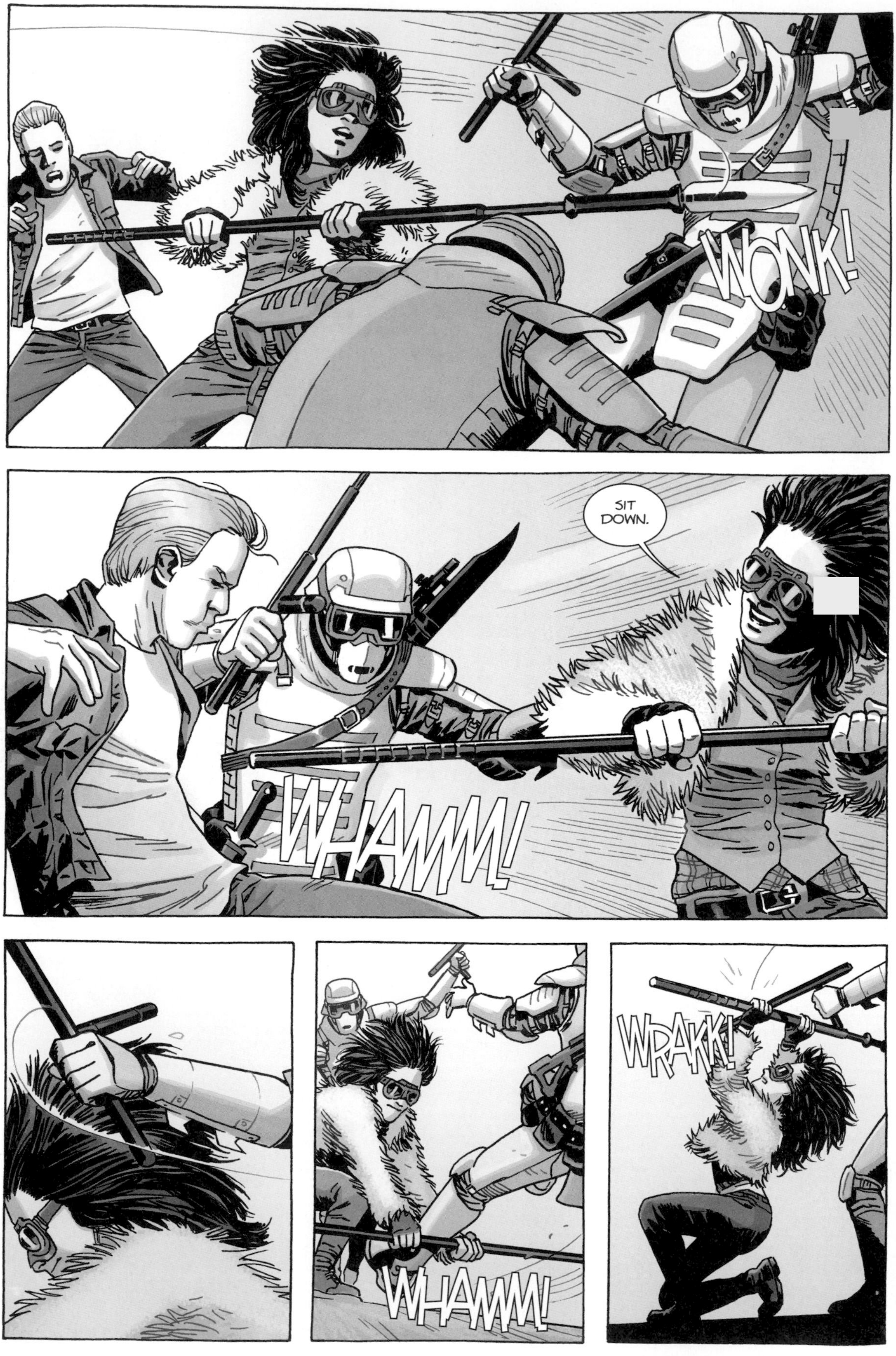
WONK!
SIT DOWN.
WHAMM!
WHAMM!
WRAKK!

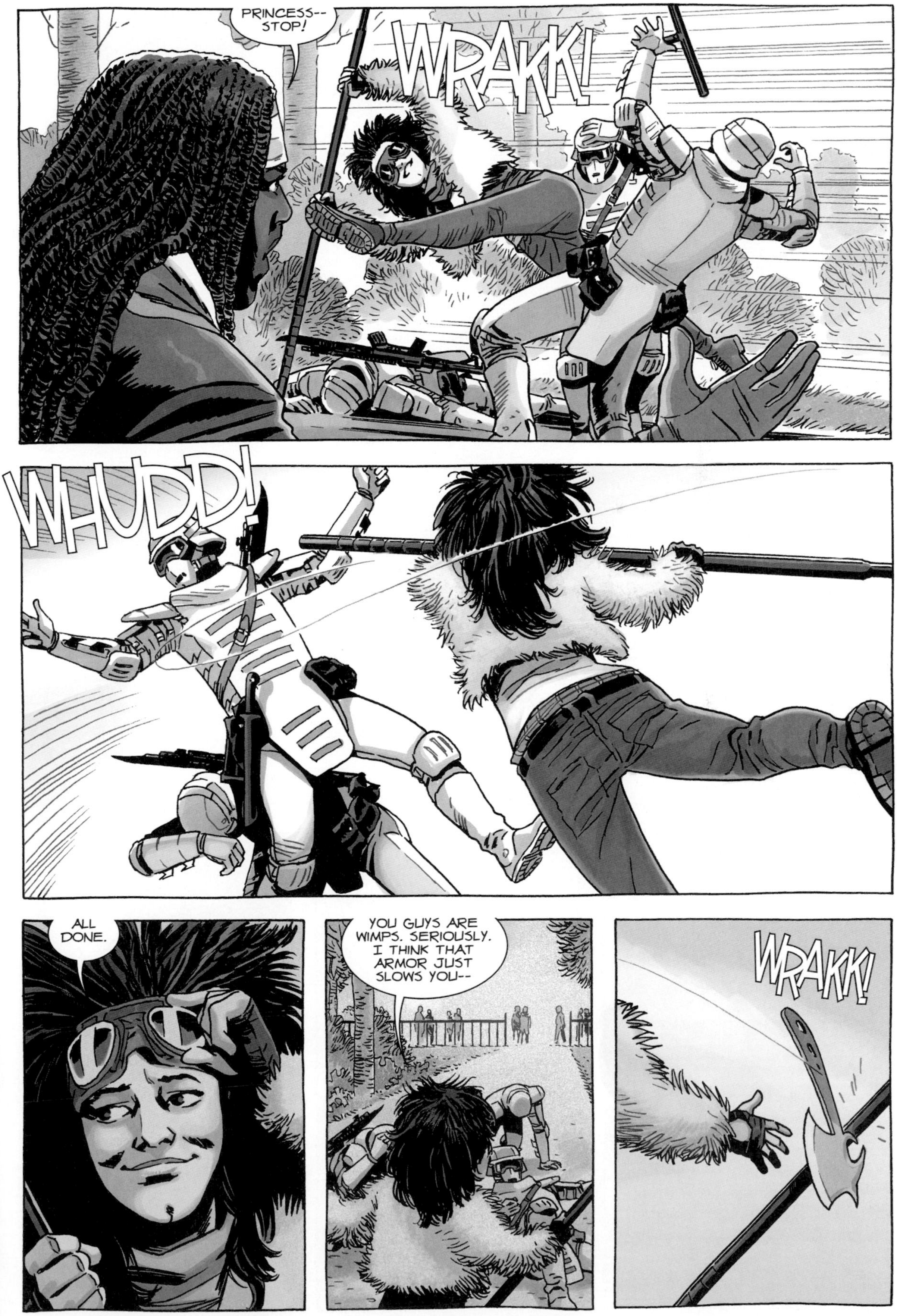
PRINCESS--
STOP!
WRAKK!
WHUDD!
ALL DONE.
YOU GUYS ARE WIMPS. SERIOUSLY. I THINK THAT ARMOR JUST SLOWS YOU--
WRAKK!

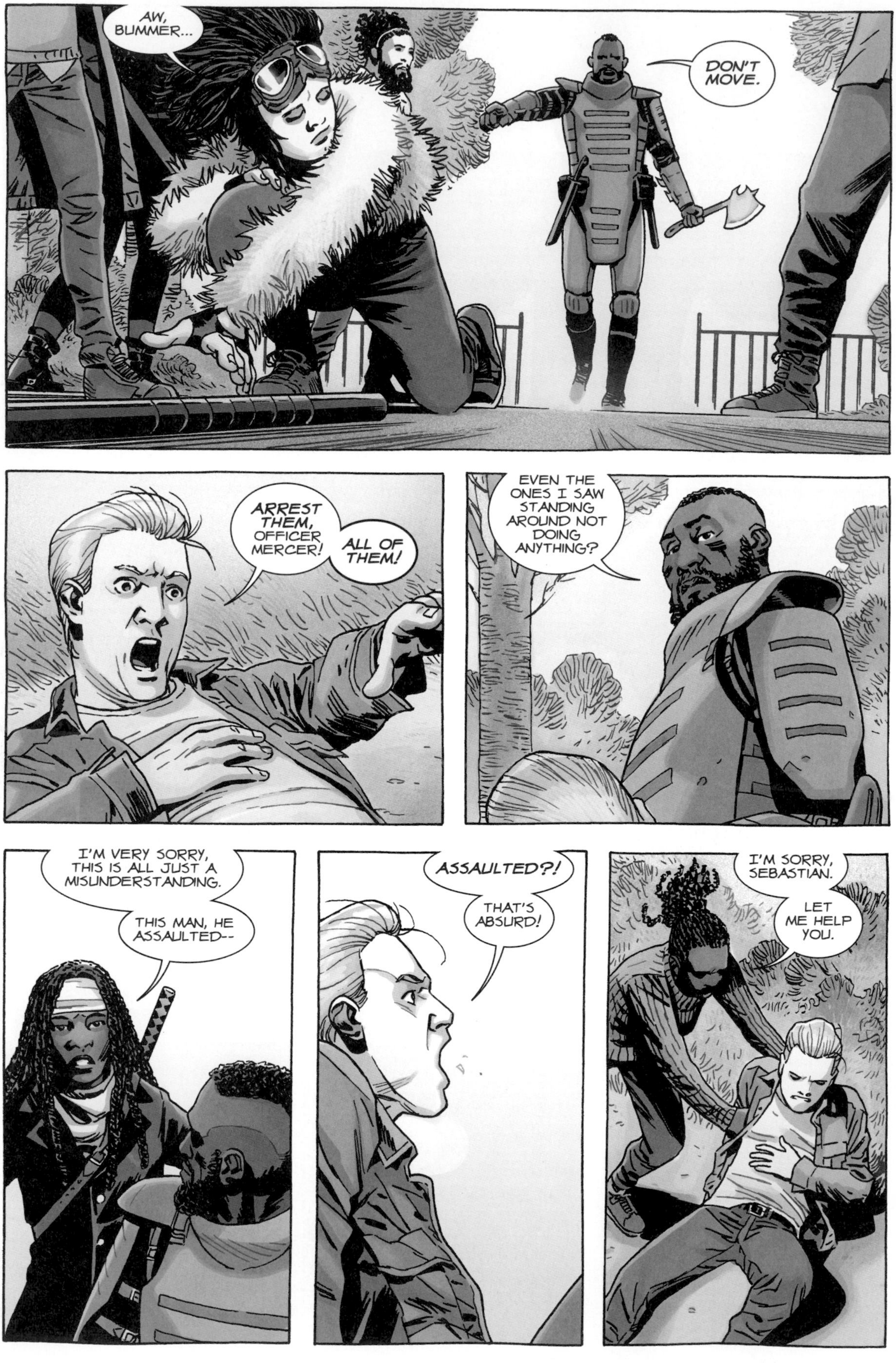

AW, BUMMER...
DON'T MOVE.
ARREST THEM, OFFICER MERCER!
ALL OF THEM!
EVEN THE ONES I SAW STANDING AROUND NOT DOING ANYTHING?
I'M VERY SORRY, THIS IS ALL JUST A MISUNDERSTANDING.
THIS MAN, HE ASSAULTED--
ASSAULTED?!
THAT'S ABSURD!
I'M SORRY, SEBASTIAN.
LET ME HELP YOU.

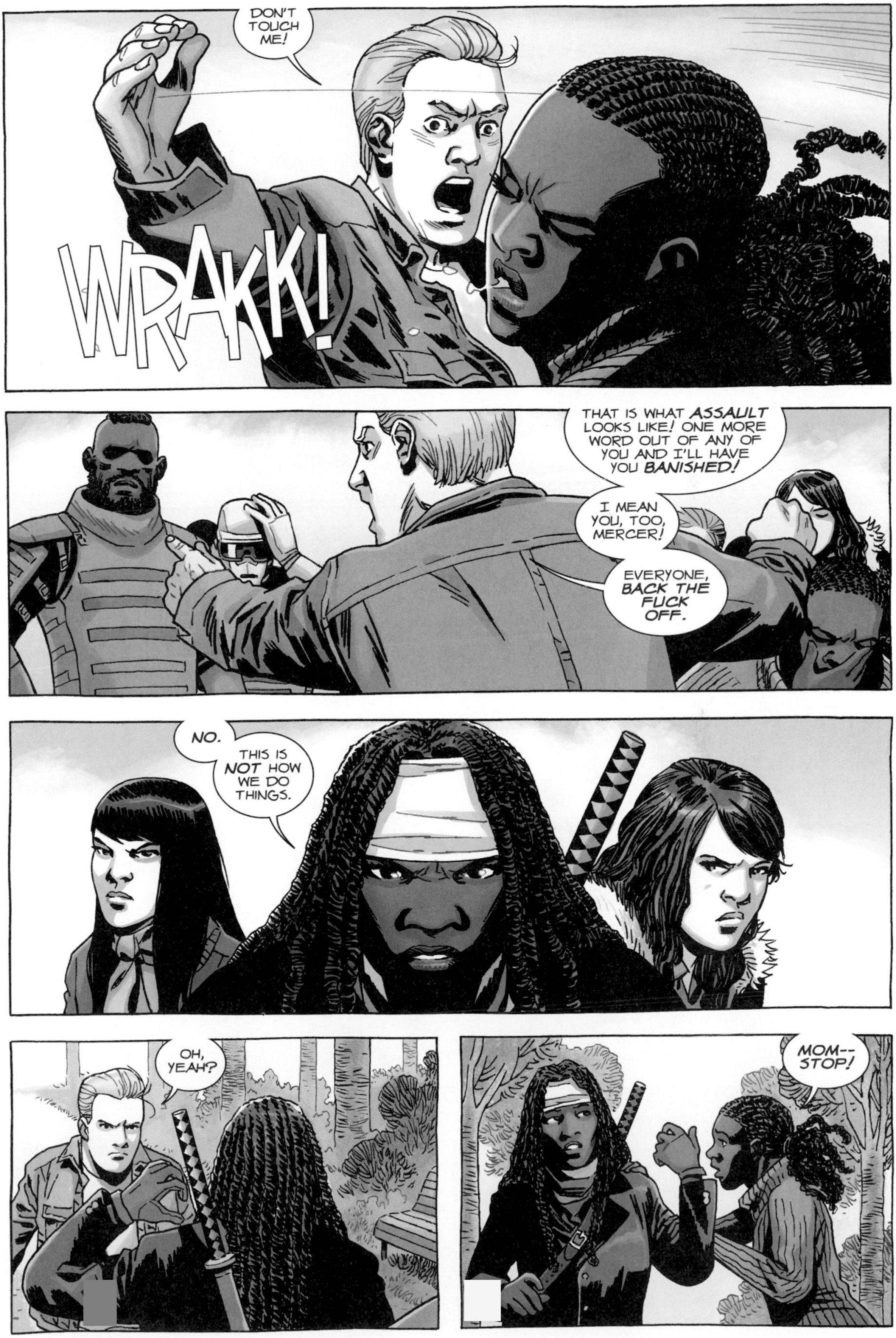
DON'T TOUCH ME!
WRAKK!
THAT IS WHAT ASSAULT LOOKS LIKE! ONE MORE WORD OUT OF ANY OF YOU AND I'LL HAVE YOU BANISHED!
I MEAN YOU, TOO, MERCER!
EVERYONE, BACK THE FUCK OFF.
NO.
THIS IS NOT HOW WE DO THINGS.
OH, YEAH?
MOM-- STOP!

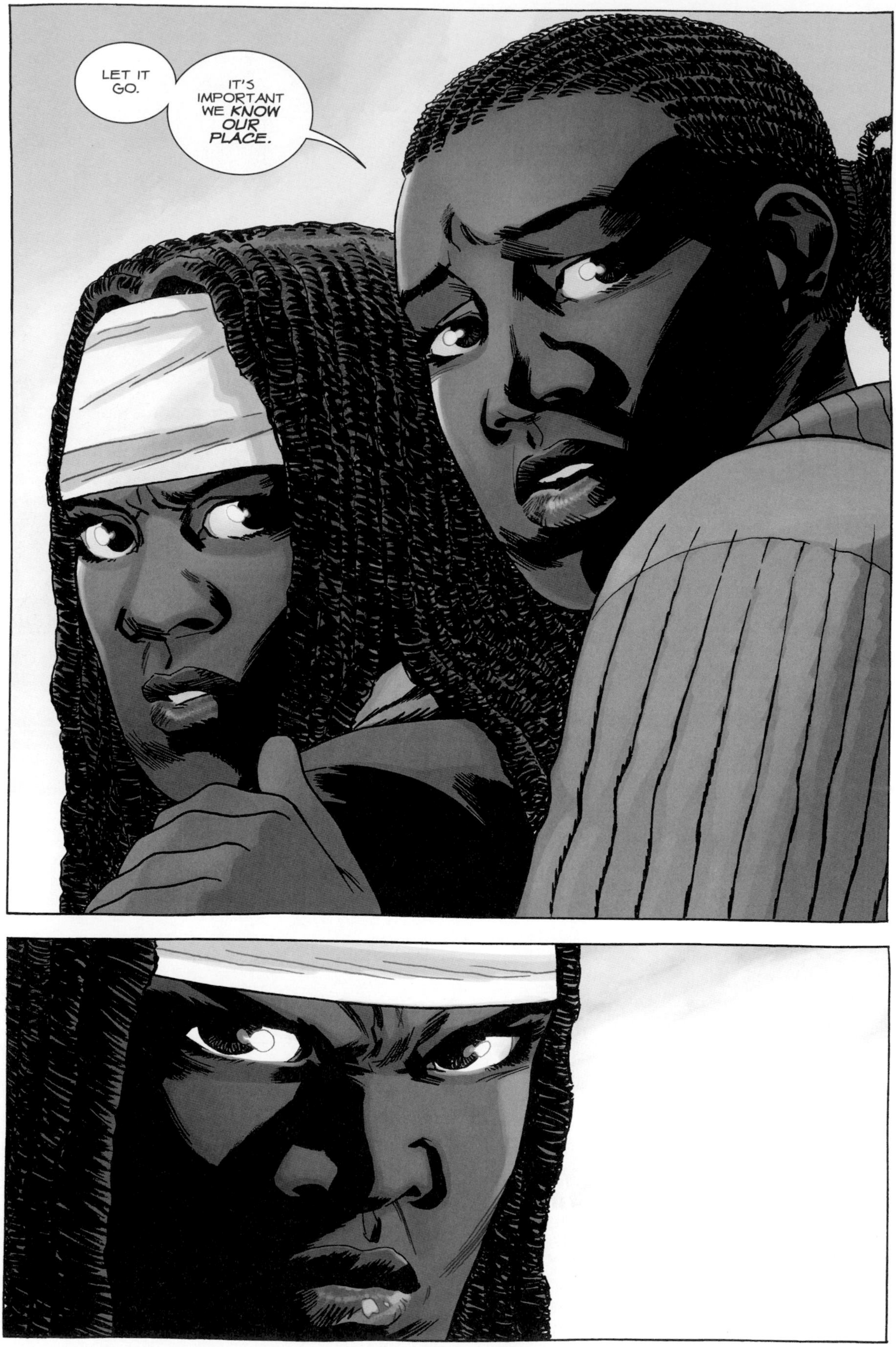
LET IT GO.
IT'S IMPORTANT WE KNOW OUR PLACE.

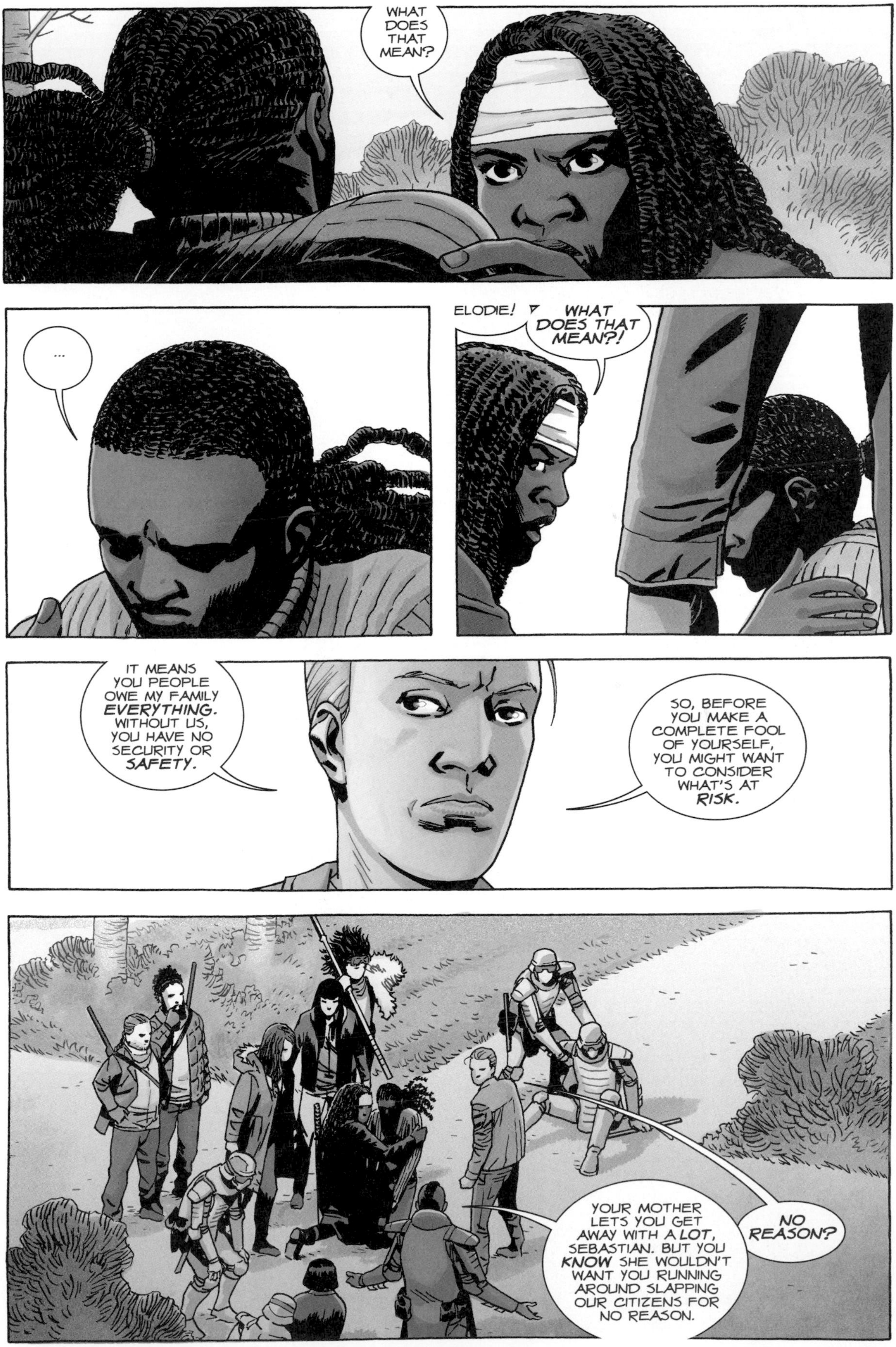
WHAT DOES THAT MEAN?
...
ELODIE!
WHAT DOES THAT MEAN?!
IT MEANS YOU PEOPLE OWE MY FAMILY EVERYTHING. WITHOUT US, YOU HAVE NO SECURITY OR SAFETY.
SO, BEFORE YOU MAKE A COMPLETE FOOL OF YOURSELF, YOU MIGHT WANT TO CONSIDER WHAT'S AT RISK.
NO REASON?
YOUR MOTHER LETS YOU GET AWAY WITH A LOT, SEBASTIAN. BUT YOU KNOW SHE WOULDN'T WANT YOU RUNNING AROUND SLAPPING OUR CITIZENS FOR NO REASON.

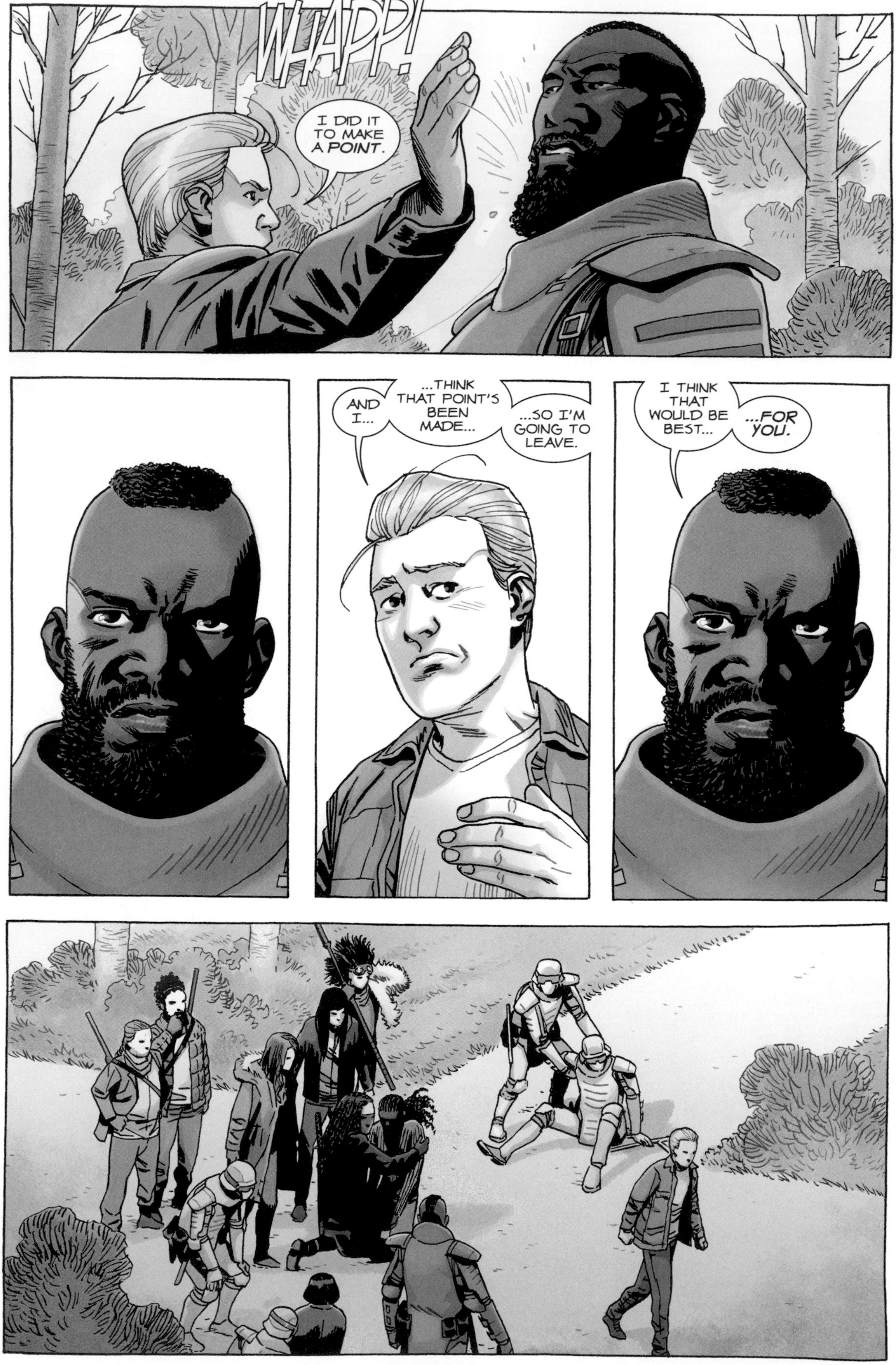
WHAPP!
I DID IT TO MAKE A POINT.
AND I...
...THINK THAT POINT'S BEEN MADE...
...SO I'M GOING TO LEAVE.
I THINK THAT WOULD BE BEST...
...FOR YOU.

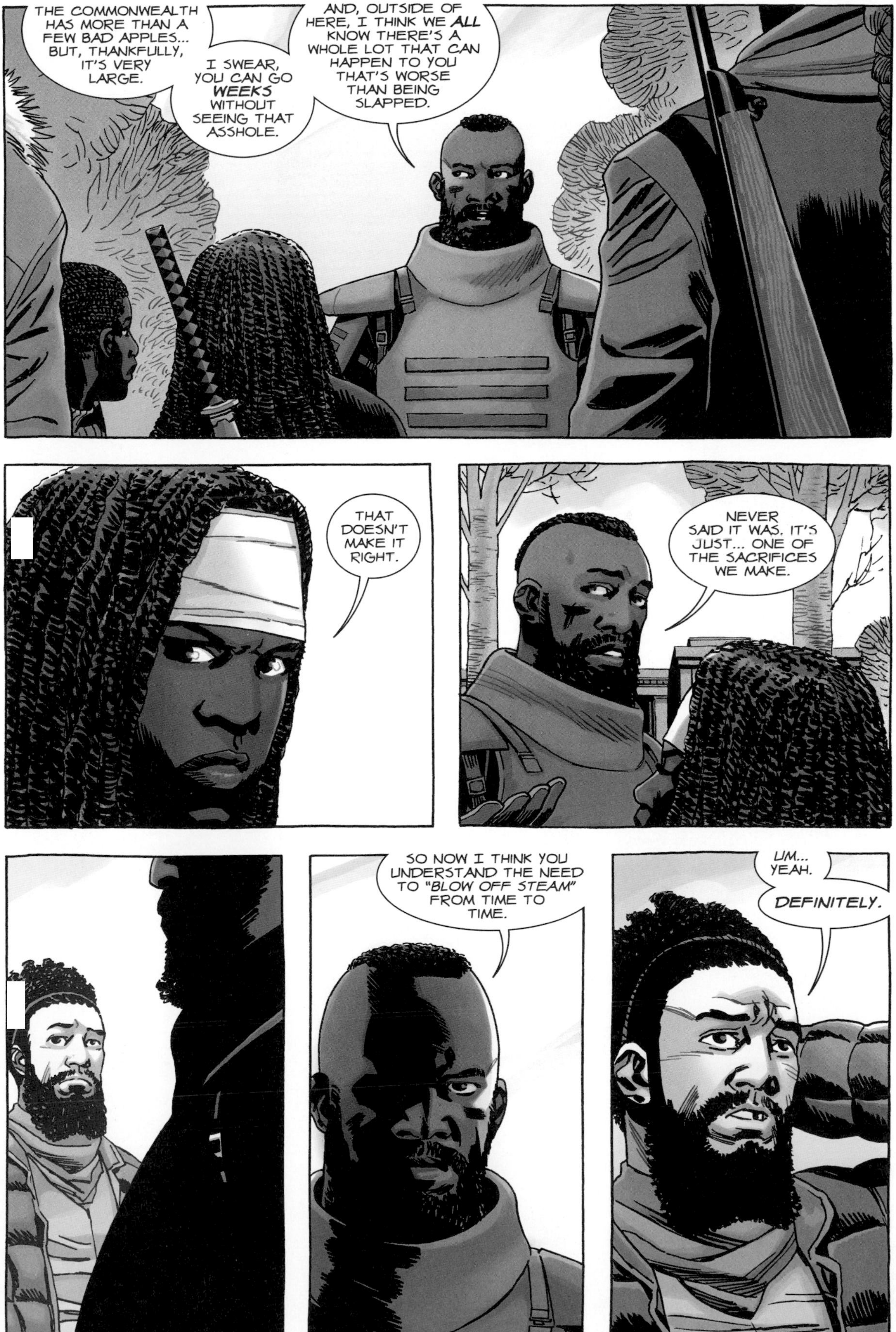
THE COMMONWEALTH HAS MORE THAN A FEW BAD APPLES... BUT, THANKFULLY, IT'S VERY LARGE.
I SWEAR, YOU CAN GO WEEKS WITHOUT SEEING THAT ASSHOLE.
AND, OUTSIDE OF HERE, I THINK WE ALL KNOW THERE'S A WHOLE LOT THAT CAN HAPPEN TO YOU THAT'S WORSE THAN BEING SLAPPED.
THAT DOESN'T MAKE IT RIGHT.
NEVER SAID IT WAS. IT'S JUST... ONE OF THE SACRIFICES WE MAKE.
SO NOW I THINK YOU UNDERSTAND THE NEED TO "BLOW OFF STEAM" FROM TIME TO TIME.
UM... YEAH.
DEFINITELY.

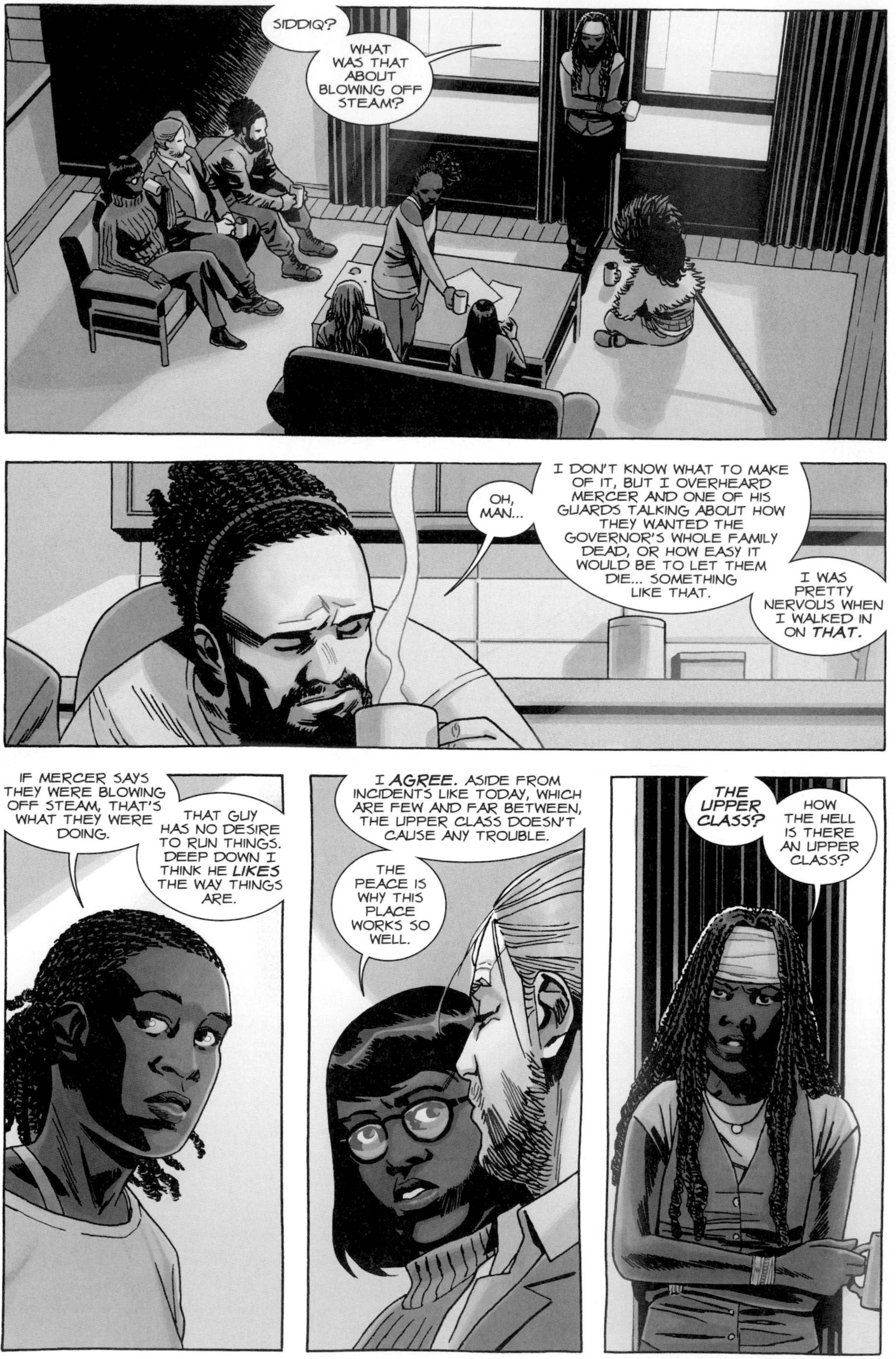
SIDDIQ?
WHAT WAS THAT ABOUT BLOWING OFF STEAM?
OH, MAN...
I DON'T KNOW WHAT TO MAKE OF IT, BUT I OVERHEARD MERCER AND ONE OF HIS GUARDS TALKING ABOUT HOW THEY WANTED THE GOVERNOR'S WHOLE FAMILY DEAD, OR HOW EASY IT WOULD BE TO LET THEM DIE... SOMETHING LIKE THAT.
I WAS PRETTY NERVOUS WHEN I WALKED IN ON *THAT.*
IF MERCER SAYS THEY WERE BLOWING OFF STEAM, THAT'S WHAT THEY WERE DOING.
THAT GUY HAS NO DESIRE TO RUN THINGS. DEEP DOWN I THINK HE *LIKES* THE WAY THINGS ARE.
I *AGREE.* ASIDE FROM INCIDENTS LIKE TODAY, WHICH ARE FEW AND FAR BETWEEN, THE UPPER CLASS DOESN'T CAUSE ANY TROUBLE.
THE PEACE IS WHY THIS PLACE WORKS SO WELL.
THE UPPER CLASS?
HOW THE HELL IS THERE AN UPPER CLASS?

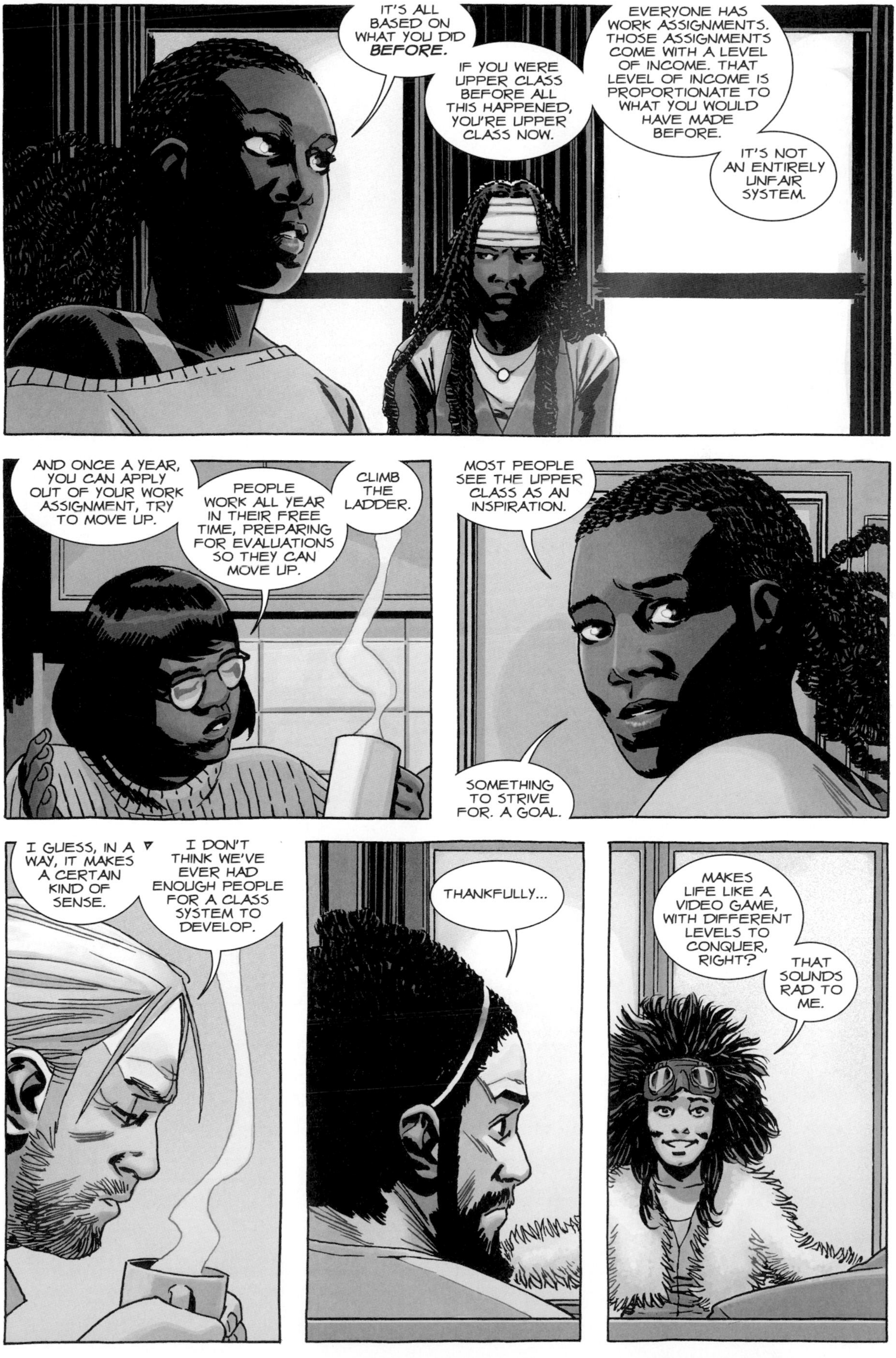
IT'S ALL BASED ON WHAT YOU DID *BEFORE.*
IF YOU WERE UPPER CLASS BEFORE ALL THIS HAPPENED, YOU'RE UPPER CLASS NOW.
EVERYONE HAS WORK ASSIGNMENTS. THOSE ASSIGNMENTS COME WITH A LEVEL OF INCOME. THAT LEVEL OF INCOME IS PROPORTIONATE TO WHAT YOU WOULD HAVE MADE BEFORE.
IT'S NOT AN ENTIRELY UNFAIR SYSTEM.
AND ONCE A YEAR, YOU CAN APPLY OUT OF YOUR WORK ASSIGNMENT, TRY TO MOVE UP.
PEOPLE WORK ALL YEAR IN THEIR FREE TIME, PREPARING FOR EVALUATIONS SO THEY CAN MOVE UP.
CLIMB THE LADDER.
MOST PEOPLE SEE THE UPPER CLASS AS AN INSPIRATION.
SOMETHING TO STRIVE FOR. A GOAL.
I GUESS, IN A WAY, IT MAKES A CERTAIN KIND OF SENSE.
I DON'T THINK WE'VE EVER HAD ENOUGH PEOPLE FOR A CLASS SYSTEM TO DEVELOP.
THANKFULLY...
MAKES LIFE LIKE A VIDEO GAME, WITH DIFFERENT LEVELS TO CONQUER, RIGHT?
THAT SOUNDS RAD TO ME.

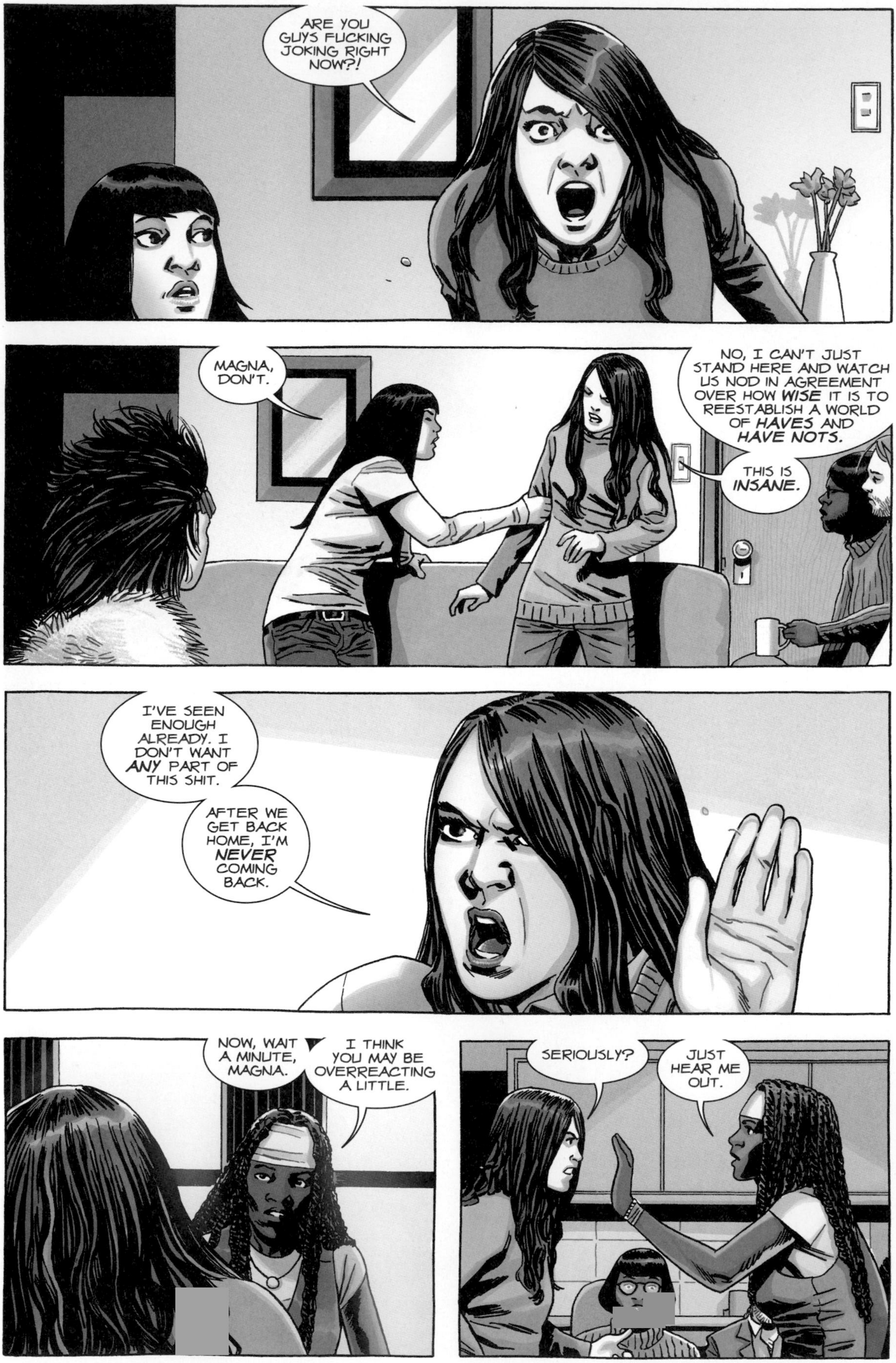
ARE YOU GUYS FUCKING JOKING RIGHT NOW?!
MAGNA, DON'T.
NO, I CAN'T JUST STAND HERE AND WATCH US NOD IN AGREEMENT OVER HOW WISE IT IS TO REESTABLISH A WORLD OF HAVES AND HAVE NOTS.
THIS IS INSANE.
I'VE SEEN ENOUGH ALREADY. I DON'T WANT ANY PART OF THIS SHIT.
AFTER WE GET BACK HOME, I'M NEVER COMING BACK.
NOW, WAIT A MINUTE, MAGNA.
I THINK YOU MAY BE OVERREACTING A LITTLE.
SERIOUSLY?
JUST HEAR ME OUT.

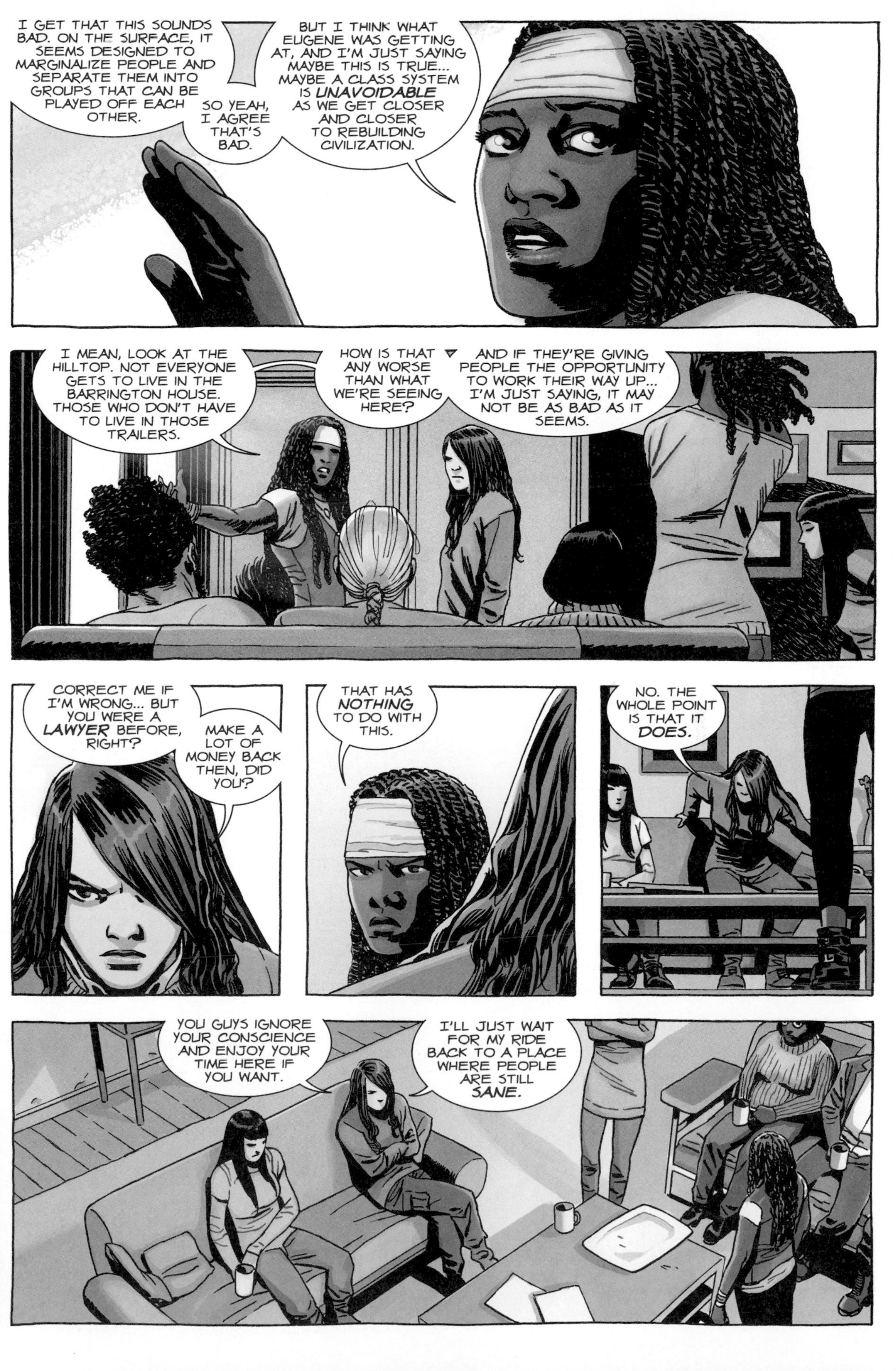
I GET THAT THIS SOUNDS BAD. ON THE SURFACE, IT SEEMS DESIGNED TO MARGINALIZE PEOPLE AND SEPARATE THEM INTO GROUPS THAT CAN BE PLAYED OFF EACH OTHER.
SO YEAH, I AGREE THAT'S BAD.
BUT I THINK WHAT EUGENE WAS GETTING AT, AND I'M JUST SAYING MAYBE THIS IS TRUE... MAYBE A CLASS SYSTEM IS UNAVOIDABLE AS WE GET CLOSER AND CLOSER TO REBUILDING CIVILIZATION.
I MEAN, LOOK AT THE HILLTOP. NOT EVERYONE GETS TO LIVE IN THE BARRINGTON HOUSE. THOSE WHO DON'T HAVE TO LIVE IN THOSE TRAILERS.
HOW IS THAT ANY WORSE THAN WHAT WE'RE SEEING HERE?
AND IF THEY'RE GIVING PEOPLE THE OPPORTUNITY TO WORK THEIR WAY UP... I'M JUST SAYING, IT MAY NOT BE AS BAD AS IT SEEMS.
CORRECT ME IF I'M WRONG... BUT YOU WERE A LAWYER BEFORE, RIGHT?
MAKE A LOT OF MONEY BACK THEN, DID YOU?
THAT HAS NOTHING TO DO WITH THIS.
NO. THE WHOLE POINT IS THAT IT DOES.
YOU GUYS IGNORE YOUR CONSCIENCE AND ENJOY YOUR TIME HERE IF YOU WANT.
I'LL JUST WAIT FOR MY RIDE BACK TO A PLACE WHERE PEOPLE ARE STILL SANE.

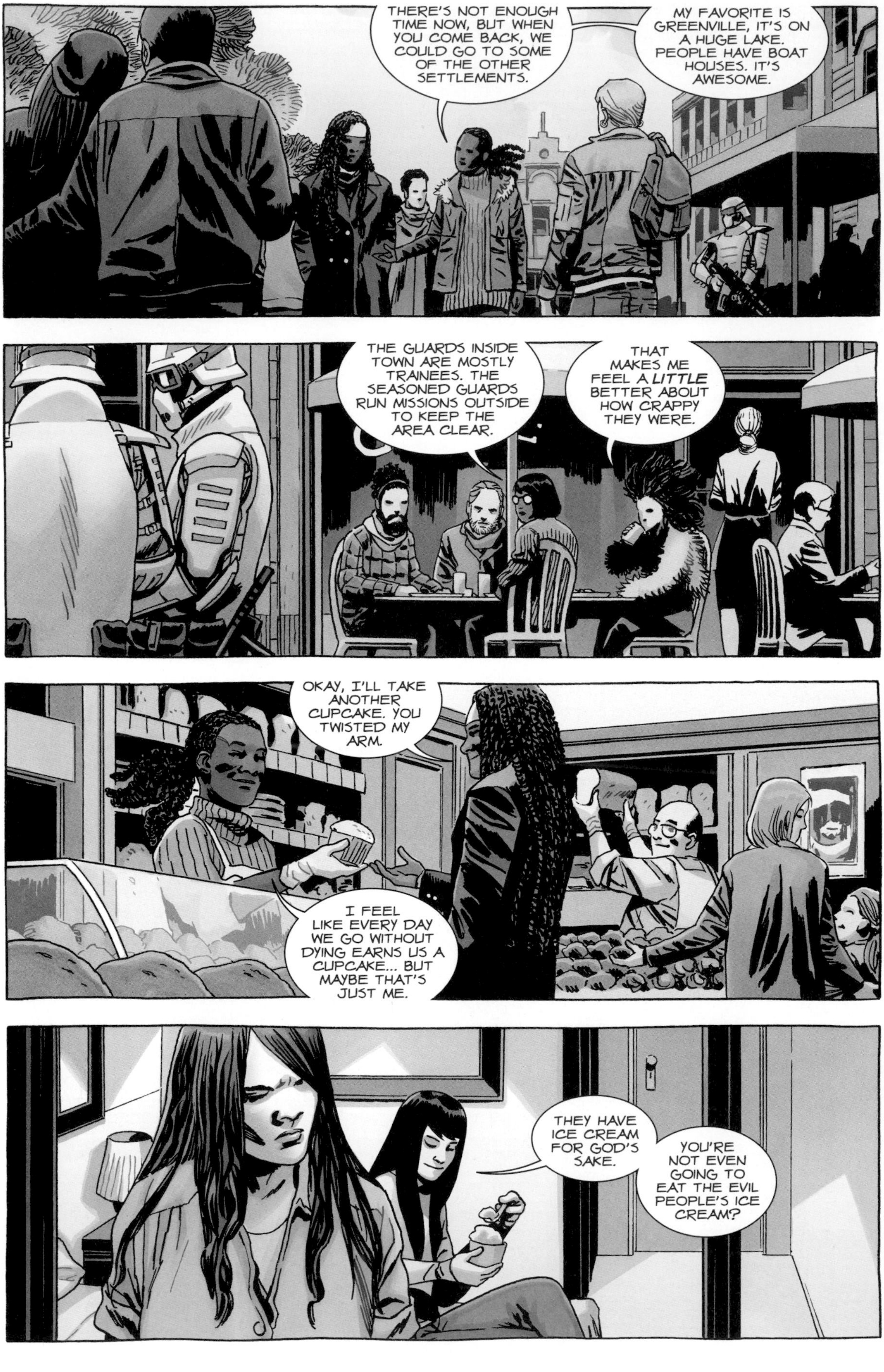
THERE'S NOT ENOUGH TIME NOW, BUT WHEN YOU COME BACK, WE COULD GO TO SOME OF THE OTHER SETTLEMENTS.
MY FAVORITE IS GREENVILLE, IT'S ON A HUGE LAKE. PEOPLE HAVE BOAT HOUSES. IT'S AWESOME.
THE GUARDS INSIDE TOWN ARE MOSTLY TRAINEES. THE SEASONED GUARDS RUN MISSIONS OUTSIDE TO KEEP THE AREA CLEAR.
THAT MAKES ME FEEL A *LITTLE* BETTER ABOUT HOW CRAPPY THEY WERE.
OKAY, I'LL TAKE ANOTHER CUPCAKE. YOU TWISTED MY ARM.
I FEEL LIKE EVERY DAY WE GO WITHOUT DYING EARNS US A CUPCAKE... BUT MAYBE THAT'S JUST ME.
THEY HAVE ICE CREAM FOR GOD'S SAKE.
YOU'RE NOT EVEN GOING TO EAT THE EVIL PEOPLE'S ICE CREAM?

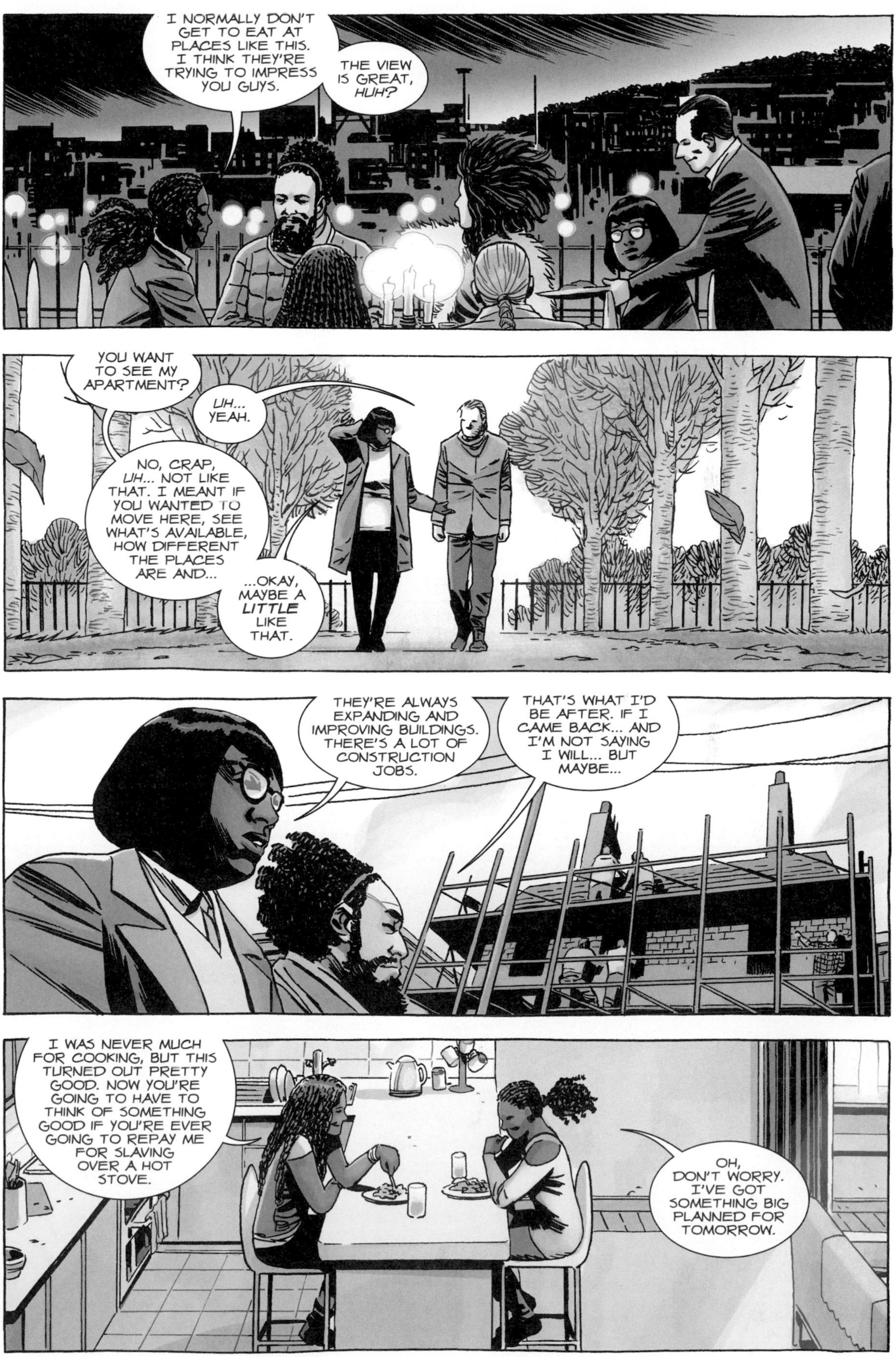
I NORMALLY DON'T GET TO EAT AT PLACES LIKE THIS. I THINK THEY'RE TRYING TO IMPRESS YOU GUYS.
THE VIEW IS GREAT, HUH?
YOU WANT TO SEE MY APARTMENT?
UH... YEAH.
NO, CRAP, UH... NOT LIKE THAT. I MEANT IF YOU WANTED TO MOVE HERE, SEE WHAT'S AVAILABLE, HOW DIFFERENT THE PLACES ARE AND...
...OKAY, MAYBE A LITTLE LIKE THAT.
THEY'RE ALWAYS EXPANDING AND IMPROVING BUILDINGS. THERE'S A LOT OF CONSTRUCTION JOBS.
THAT'S WHAT I'D BE AFTER. IF I CAME BACK... AND I'M NOT SAYING I WILL... BUT MAYBE...
I WAS NEVER MUCH FOR COOKING, BUT THIS TURNED OUT PRETTY GOOD. NOW YOU'RE GOING TO HAVE TO THINK OF SOMETHING GOOD IF YOU'RE EVER GOING TO REPAY ME FOR SLAVING OVER A HOT STOVE.
OH, DON'T WORRY. I'VE GOT SOMETHING BIG PLANNED FOR TOMORROW.

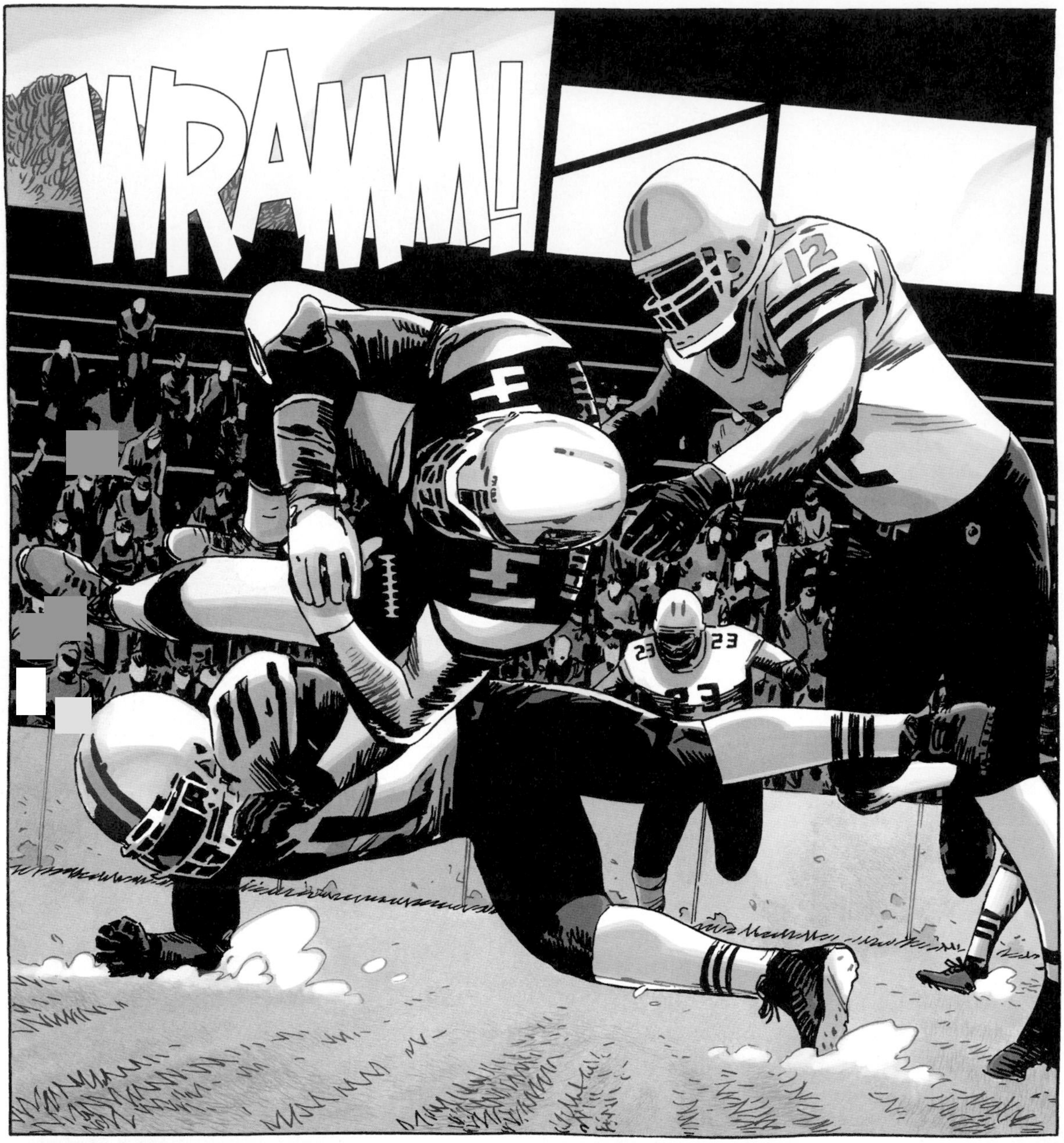
WRAMM!

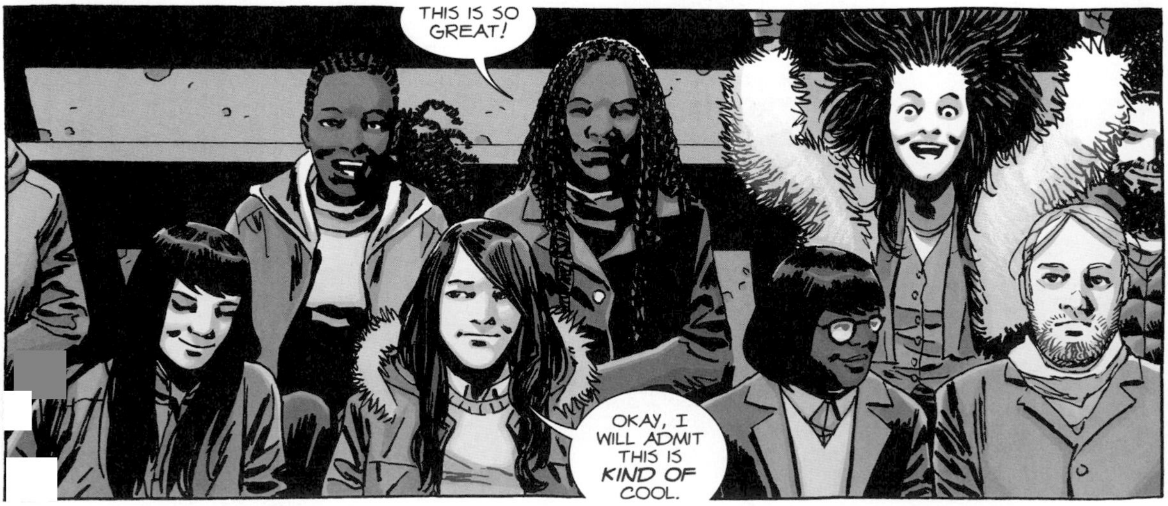
THIS IS SO GREAT!
OKAY, I WILL ADMIT THIS IS *KIND OF* COOL.

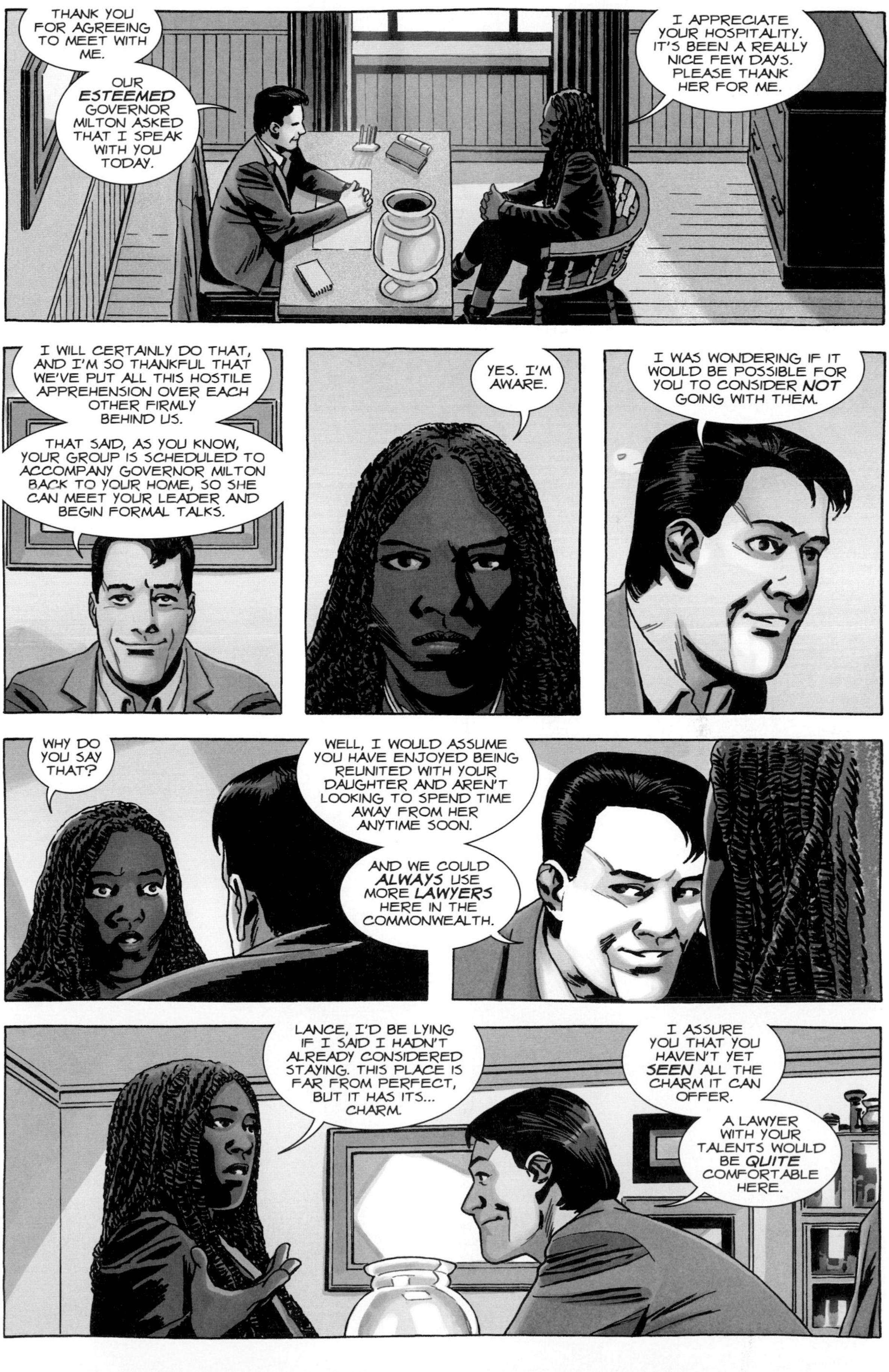
THANK YOU FOR AGREEING TO MEET WITH ME.
OUR ESTEEMED GOVERNOR MILTON ASKED THAT I SPEAK WITH YOU TODAY.
I APPRECIATE YOUR HOSPITALITY. IT'S BEEN A REALLY NICE FEW DAYS. PLEASE THANK HER FOR ME.
I WILL CERTAINLY DO THAT, AND I'M SO THANKFUL THAT WE'VE PUT ALL THIS HOSTILE APPREHENSION OVER EACH OTHER FIRMLY BEHIND US.
THAT SAID, AS YOU KNOW, YOUR GROUP IS SCHEDULED TO ACCOMPANY GOVERNOR MILTON BACK TO YOUR HOME, SO SHE CAN MEET YOUR LEADER AND BEGIN FORMAL TALKS.
YES. I'M AWARE.
I WAS WONDERING IF IT WOULD BE POSSIBLE FOR YOU TO CONSIDER NOT GOING WITH THEM.
WHY DO YOU SAY THAT?
WELL, I WOULD ASSUME YOU HAVE ENJOYED BEING REUNITED WITH YOUR DAUGHTER AND AREN'T LOOKING TO SPEND TIME AWAY FROM HER ANYTIME SOON.
AND WE COULD ALWAYS USE MORE LAWYERS HERE IN THE COMMONWEALTH.
LANCE, I'D BE LYING IF I SAID I HADN'T ALREADY CONSIDERED STAYING. THIS PLACE IS FAR FROM PERFECT, BUT IT HAS ITS... CHARM.
I ASSURE YOU THAT YOU HAVEN'T YET SEEN ALL THE CHARM IT CAN OFFER.
A LAWYER WITH YOUR TALENTS WOULD BE QUITE COMFORTABLE HERE.

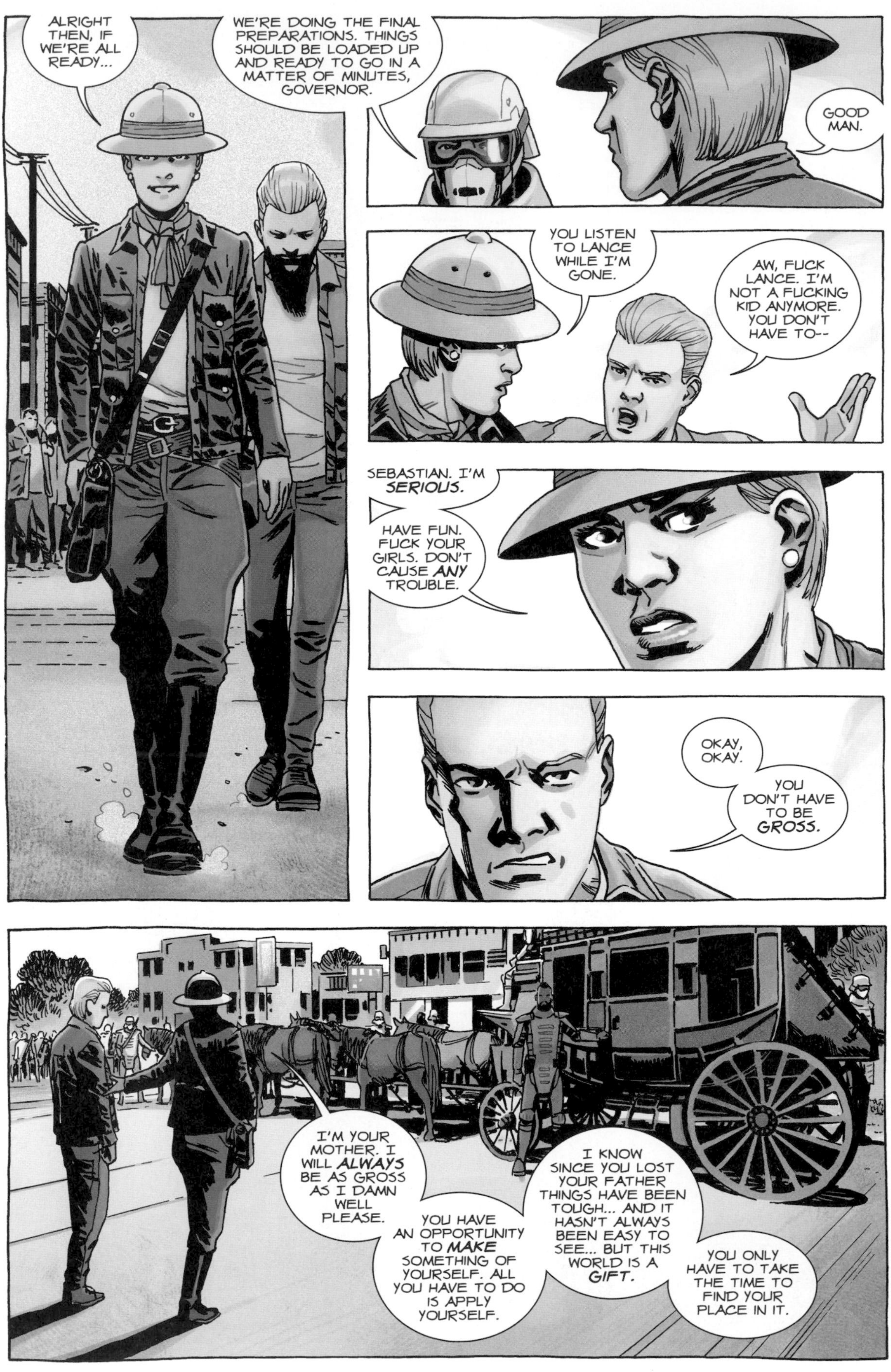
ALRIGHT THEN, IF WE'RE ALL READY...
WE'RE DOING THE FINAL PREPARATIONS. THINGS SHOULD BE LOADED UP AND READY TO GO IN A MATTER OF MINUTES, GOVERNOR.
GOOD MAN.
YOU LISTEN TO LANCE WHILE I'M GONE.
AW, FUCK LANCE. I'M NOT A FUCKING KID ANYMORE. YOU DON'T HAVE TO--
SEBASTIAN. I'M SERIOUS.
HAVE FUN. FUCK YOUR GIRLS. DON'T CAUSE ANY TROUBLE.
OKAY, OKAY.
YOU DON'T HAVE TO BE GROSS.
I'M YOUR MOTHER. I WILL ALWAYS BE AS GROSS AS I DAMN WELL PLEASE.
YOU HAVE AN OPPORTUNITY TO MAKE SOMETHING OF YOURSELF. ALL YOU HAVE TO DO IS APPLY YOURSELF.
I KNOW SINCE YOU LOST YOUR FATHER THINGS HAVE BEEN TOUGH... AND IT HASN'T ALWAYS BEEN EASY TO SEE... BUT THIS WORLD IS A GIFT.
YOU ONLY HAVE TO TAKE THE TIME TO FIND YOUR PLACE IN IT.

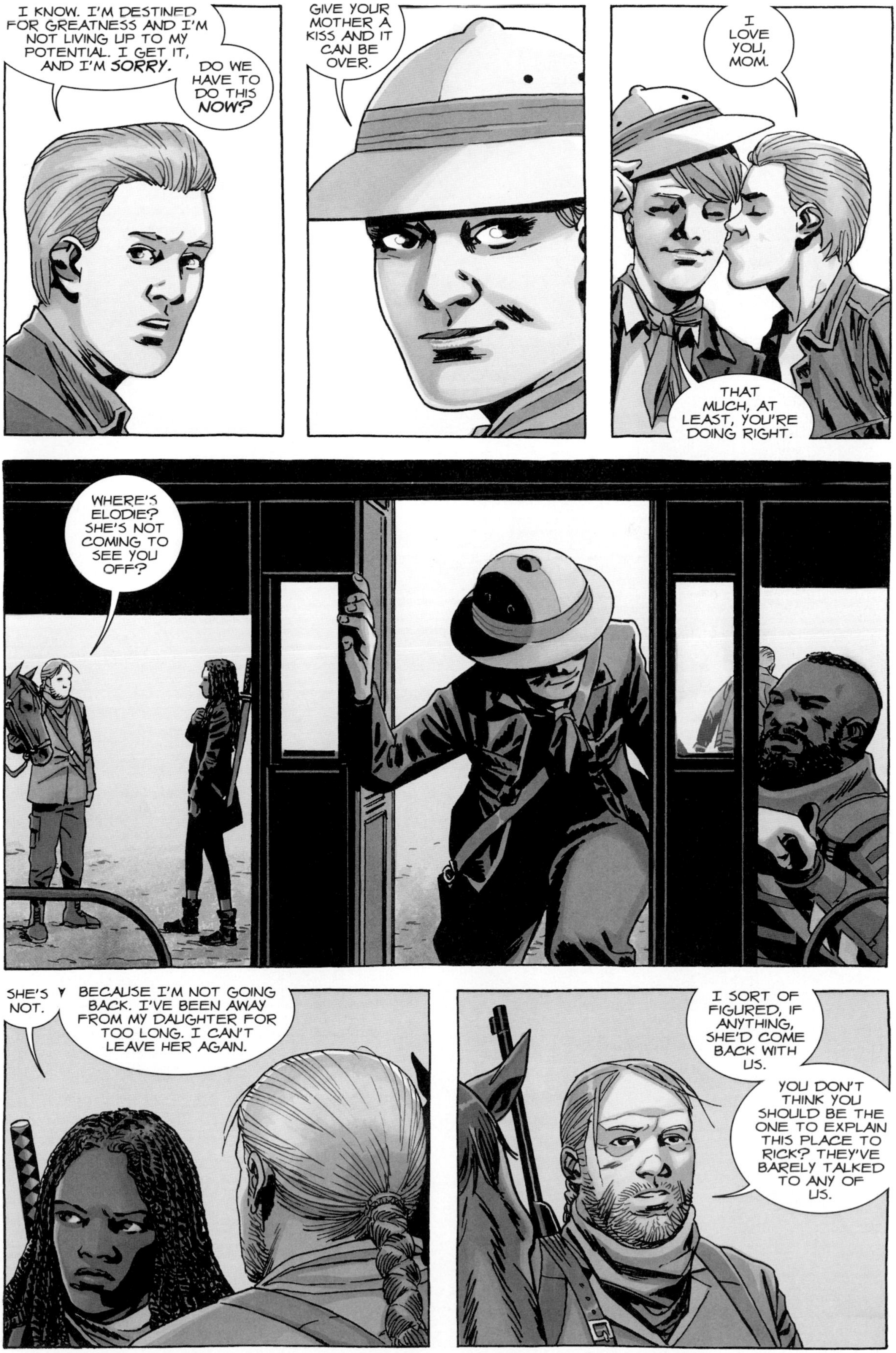
I KNOW. I'M DESTINED FOR GREATNESS AND I'M NOT LIVING UP TO MY POTENTIAL. I GET IT, AND I'M SORRY.
DO WE HAVE TO DO THIS NOW?
GIVE YOUR MOTHER A KISS AND IT CAN BE OVER.
I LOVE YOU, MOM.
THAT MUCH, AT LEAST, YOU'RE DOING RIGHT.
WHERE'S ELODIE? SHE'S NOT COMING TO SEE YOU OFF?
SHE'S NOT.
BECAUSE I'M NOT GOING BACK. I'VE BEEN AWAY FROM MY DAUGHTER FOR TOO LONG. I CAN'T LEAVE HER AGAIN.
I SORT OF FIGURED, IF ANYTHING, SHE'D COME BACK WITH US.
YOU DON'T THINK YOU SHOULD BE THE ONE TO EXPLAIN THIS PLACE TO RICK? THEY'VE BARELY TALKED TO ANY OF US.

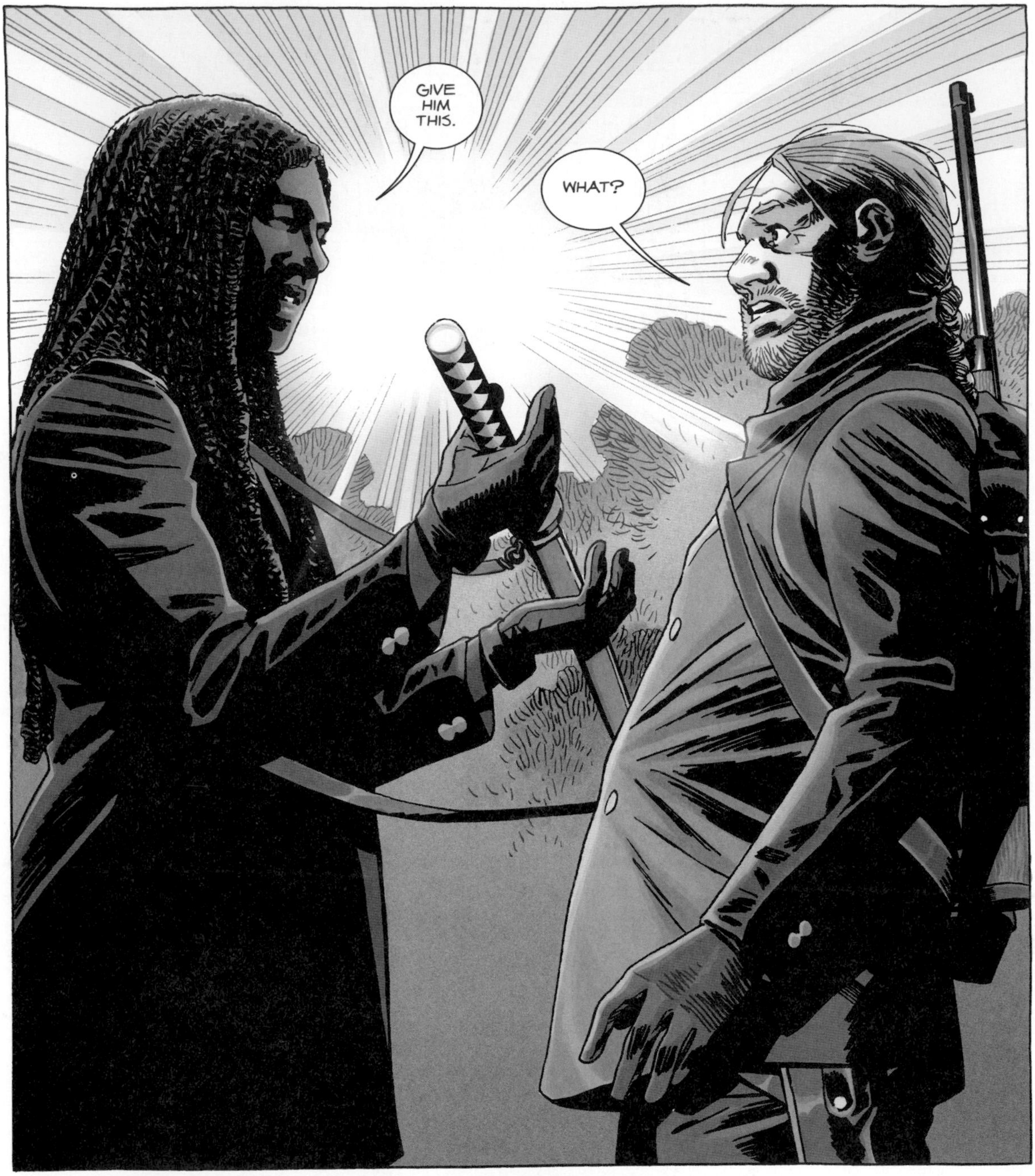
GIVE HIM THIS.
WHAT?

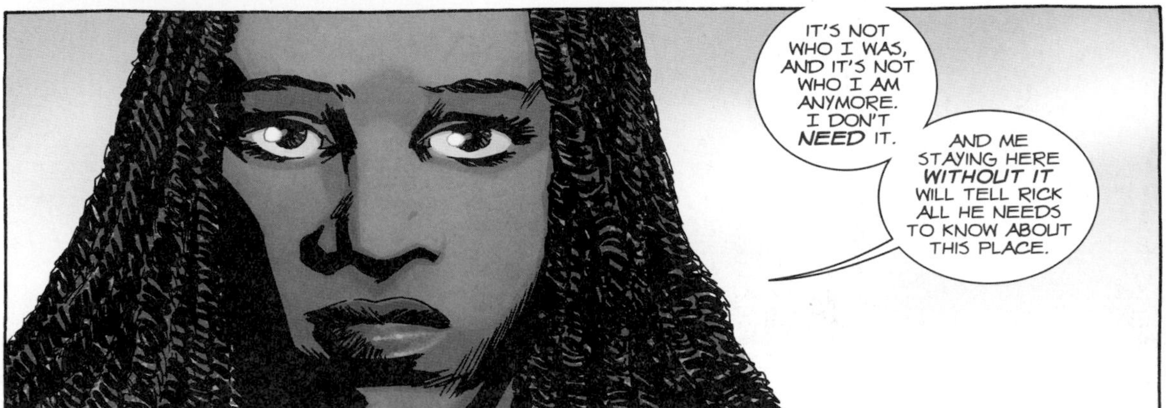
IT'S NOT WHO I WAS, AND IT'S NOT WHO I AM ANYMORE. I DON'T NEED IT.
AND ME STAYING HERE WITHOUT IT WILL TELL RICK ALL HE NEEDS TO KNOW ABOUT THIS PLACE.

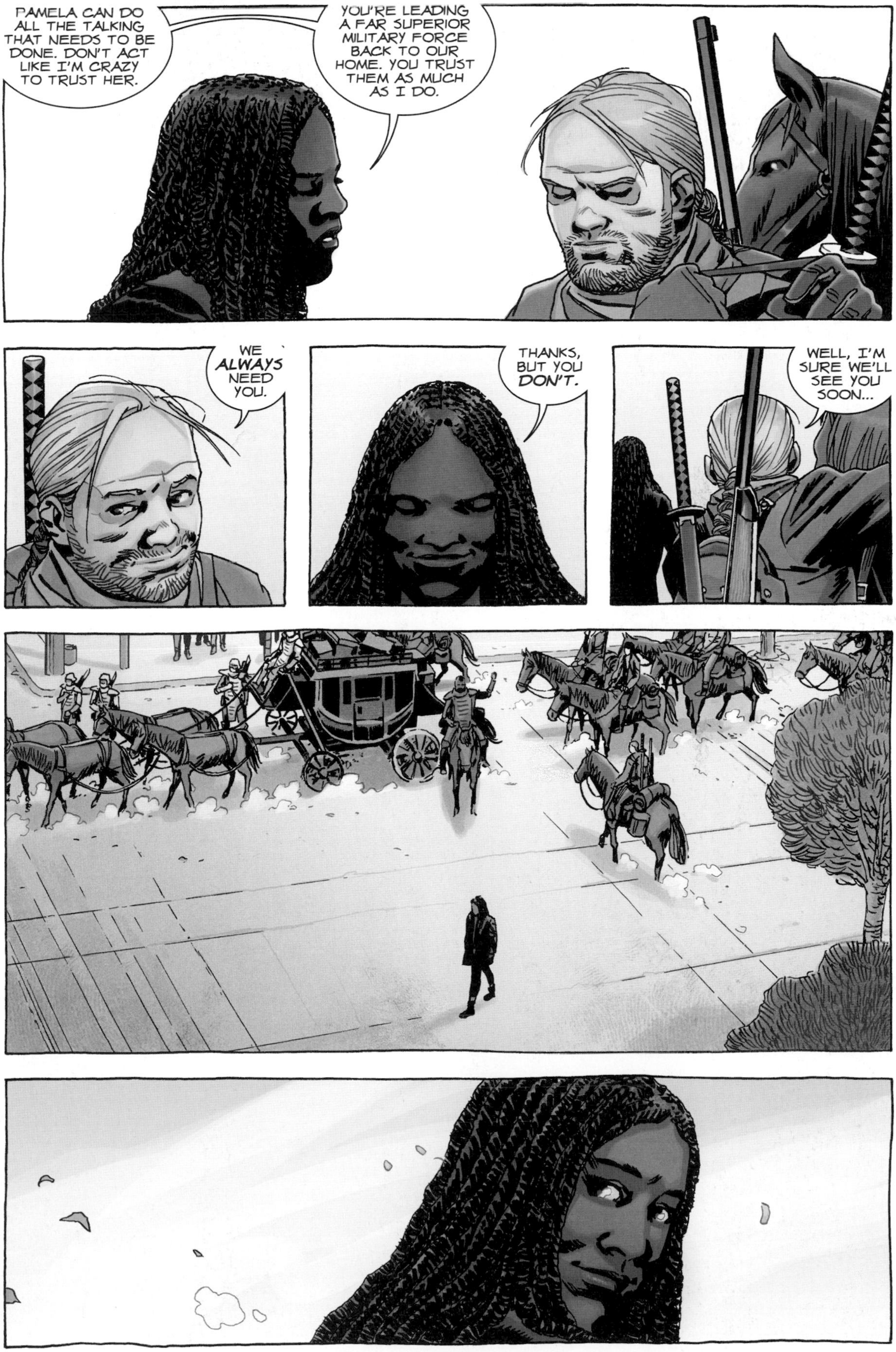
PAMELA CAN DO ALL THE TALKING THAT NEEDS TO BE DONE. DON'T ACT LIKE I'M CRAZY TO TRUST HER.
YOU'RE LEADING A FAR SUPERIOR MILITARY FORCE BACK TO OUR HOME. YOU TRUST THEM AS MUCH AS I DO.
WE *ALWAYS* NEED YOU.
THANKS, BUT YOU *DON'T.*
WELL, I'M SURE WE'LL SEE YOU SOON...

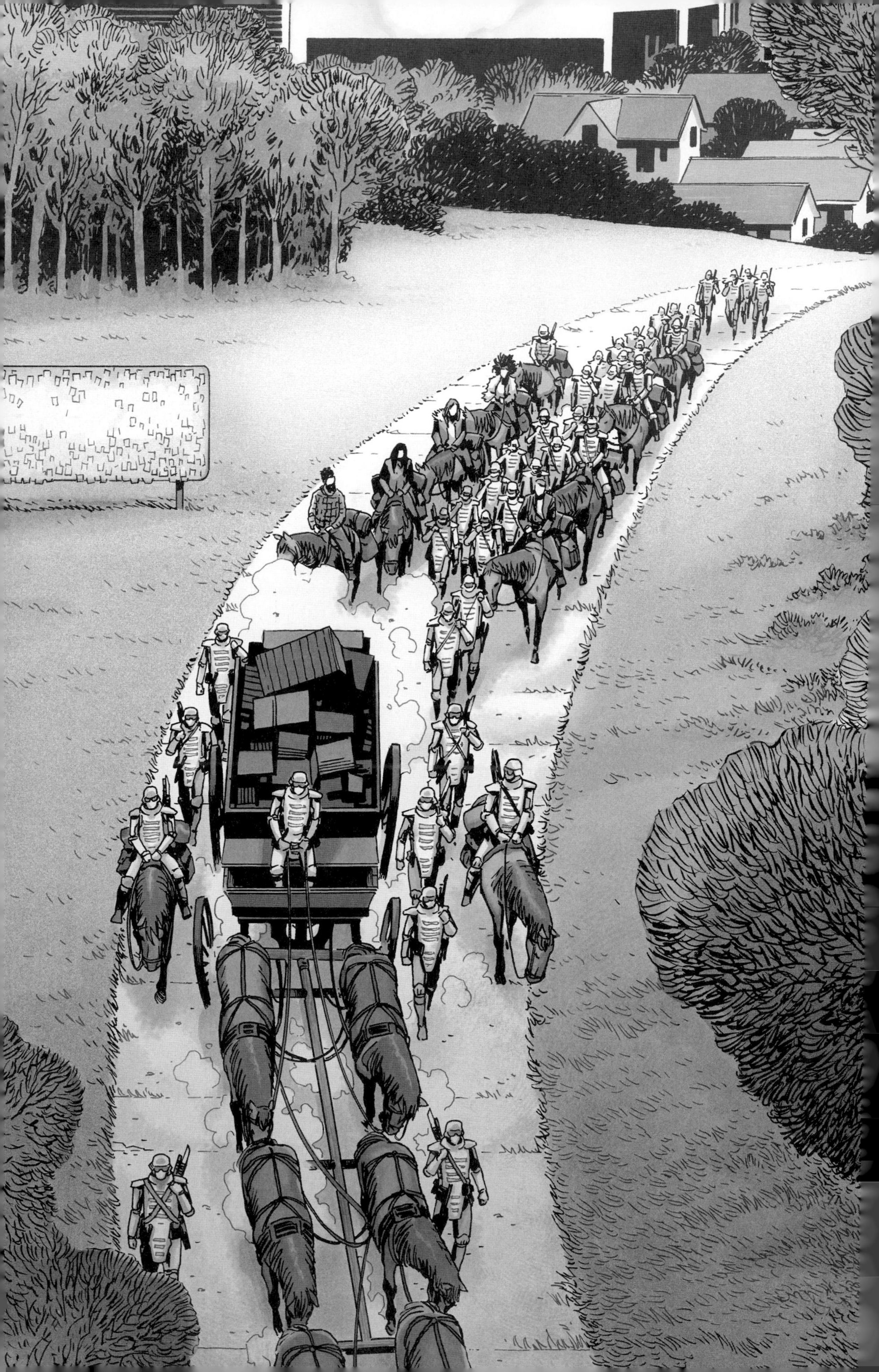

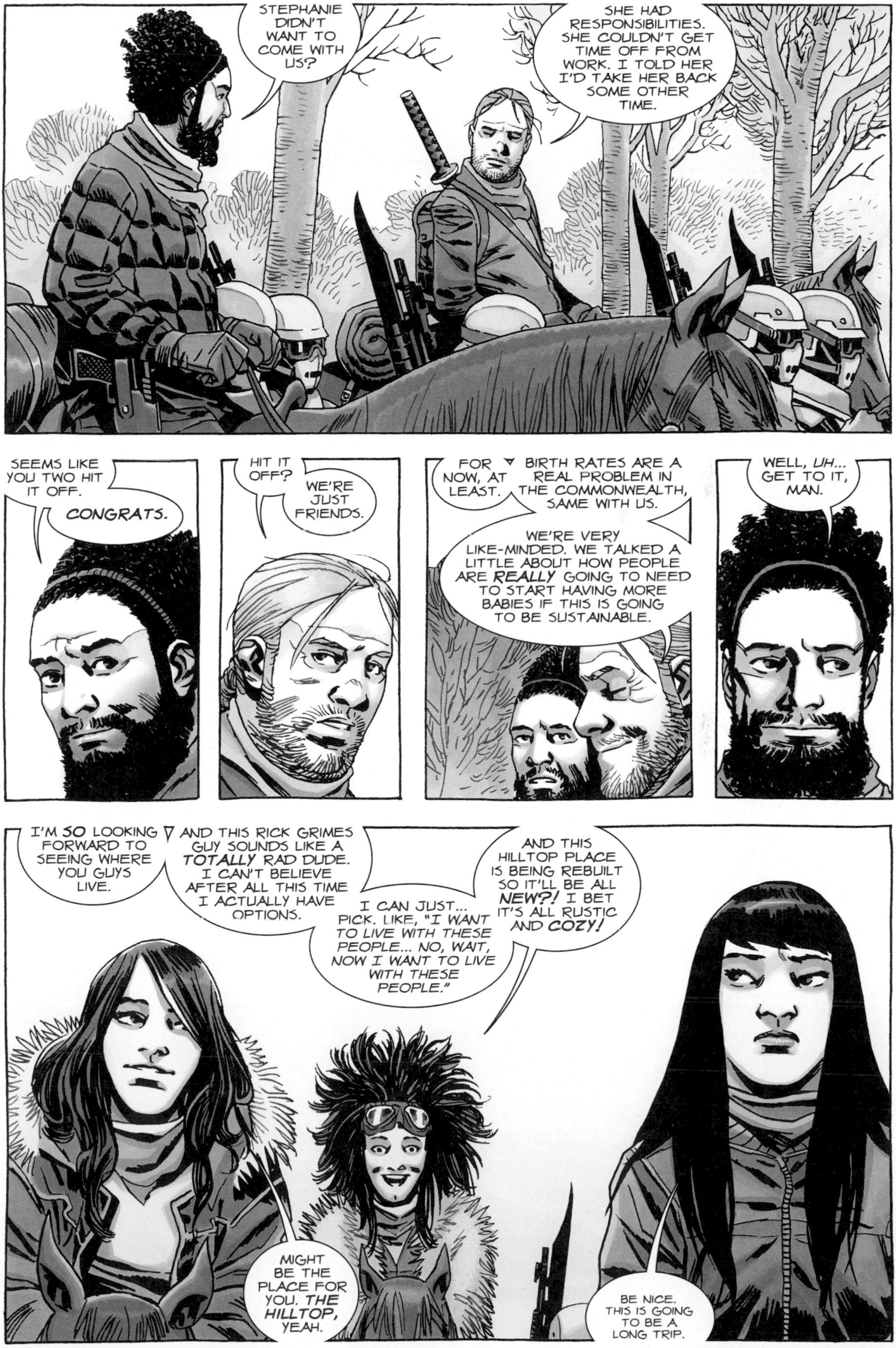

STEPHANIE DIDN'T WANT TO COME WITH US?
SHE HAD RESPONSIBILITIES. SHE COULDN'T GET TIME OFF FROM WORK. I TOLD HER I'D TAKE HER BACK SOME OTHER TIME.
SEEMS LIKE YOU TWO HIT IT OFF.
CONGRATS.
HIT IT OFF?
WE'RE JUST FRIENDS.
FOR NOW, AT LEAST.
BIRTH RATES ARE A REAL PROBLEM IN THE COMMONWEALTH, SAME WITH US.
WE'RE VERY LIKE-MINDED. WE TALKED A LITTLE ABOUT HOW PEOPLE ARE REALLY GOING TO NEED TO START HAVING MORE BABIES IF THIS IS GOING TO BE SUSTAINABLE.
WELL, UH... GET TO IT, MAN.
I'M SO LOOKING FORWARD TO SEEING WHERE YOU GUYS LIVE.
AND THIS RICK GRIMES GUY SOUNDS LIKE A TOTALLY RAD DUDE. I CAN'T BELIEVE AFTER ALL THIS TIME I ACTUALLY HAVE OPTIONS.
I CAN JUST... PICK. LIKE, "I WANT TO LIVE WITH THESE PEOPLE... NO, WAIT, NOW I WANT TO LIVE WITH THESE PEOPLE."
AND THIS HILLTOP PLACE IS BEING REBUILT SO IT'LL BE ALL NEW?! I BET IT'S ALL RUSTIC AND COZY!
MIGHT BE THE PLACE FOR YOU. THE HILLTOP, YEAH.
BE NICE. THIS IS GOING TO BE A LONG TRIP.

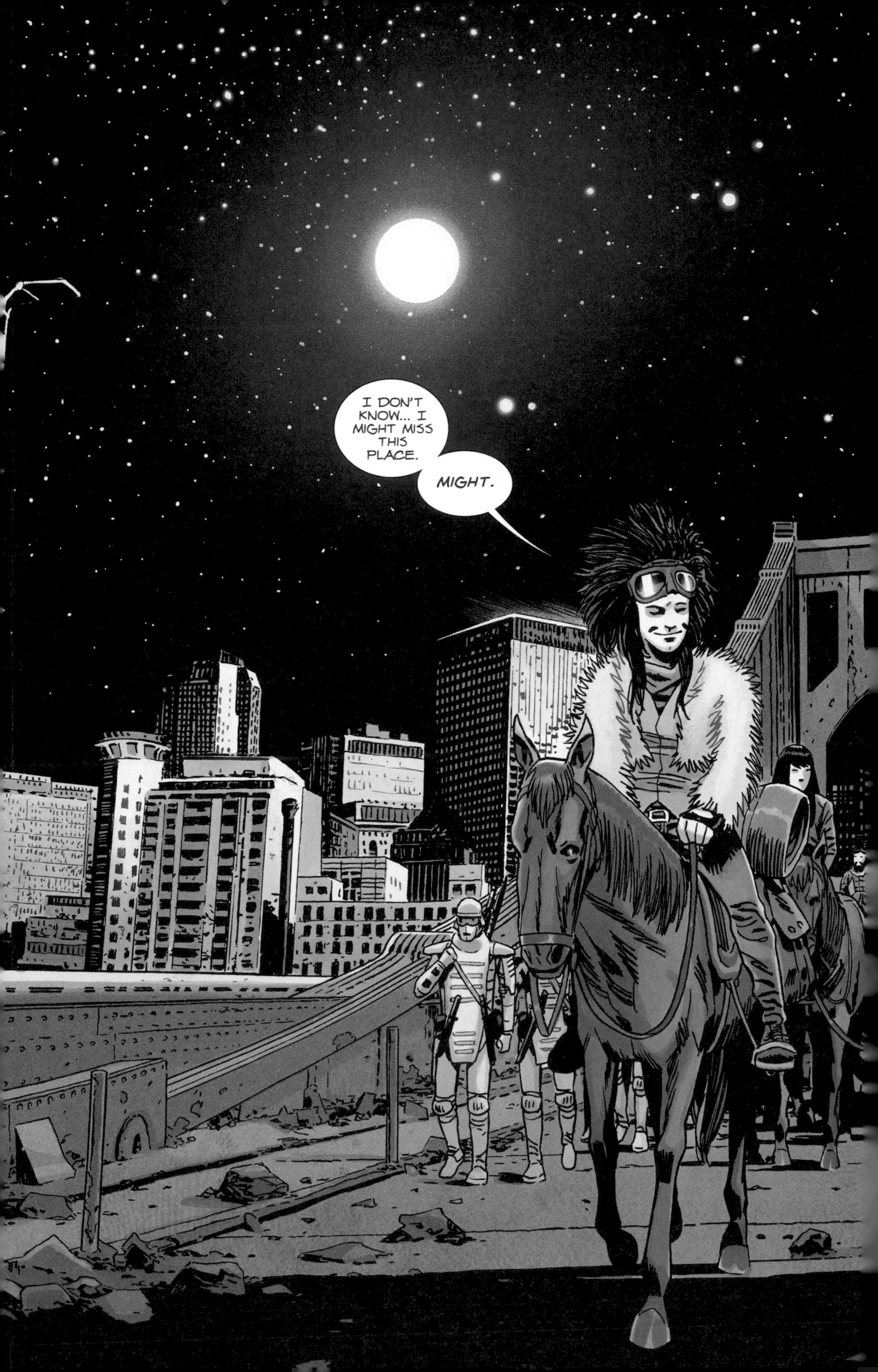
I DON'T KNOW... I MIGHT MISS THIS PLACE.
MIGHT.

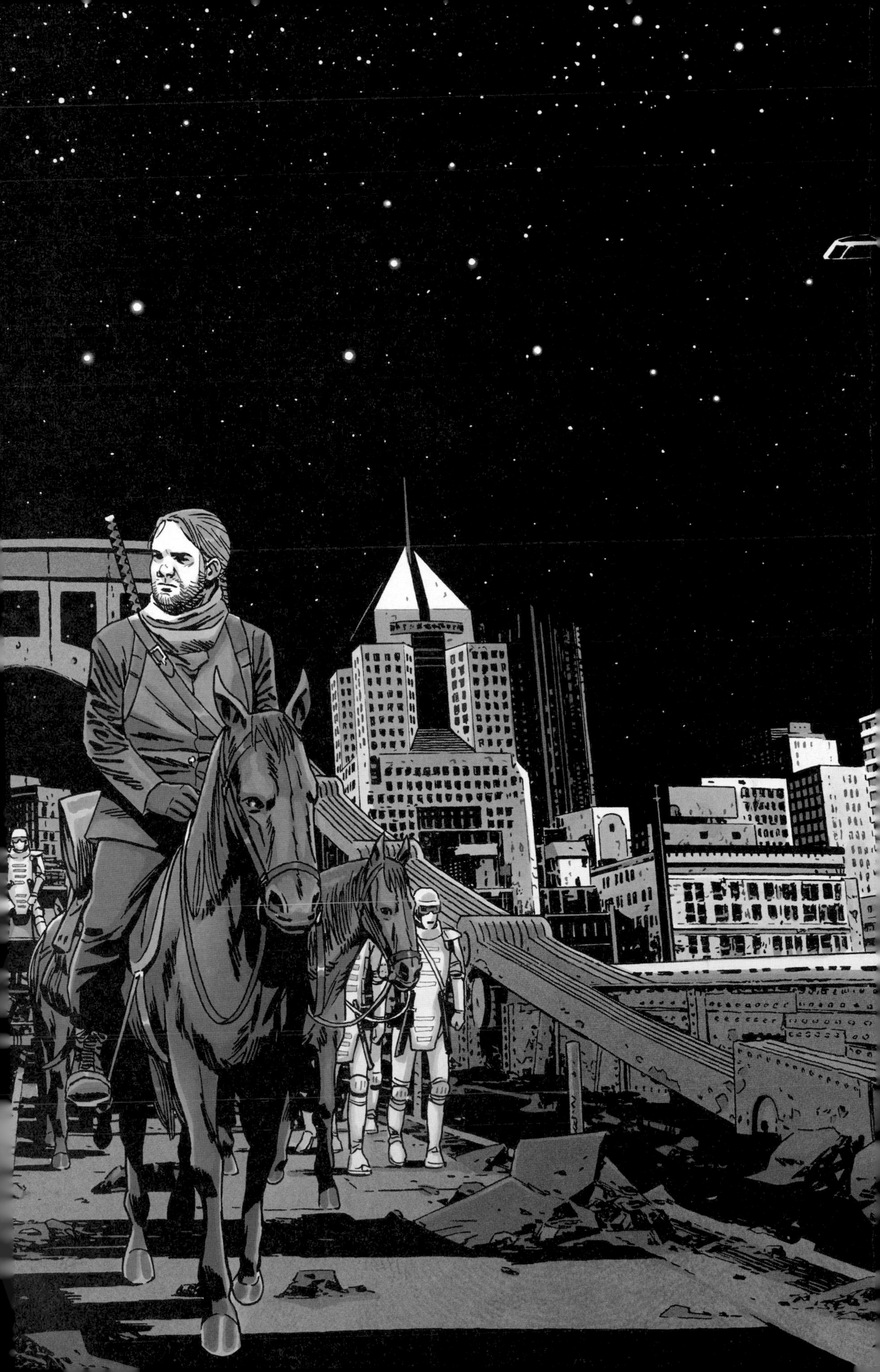

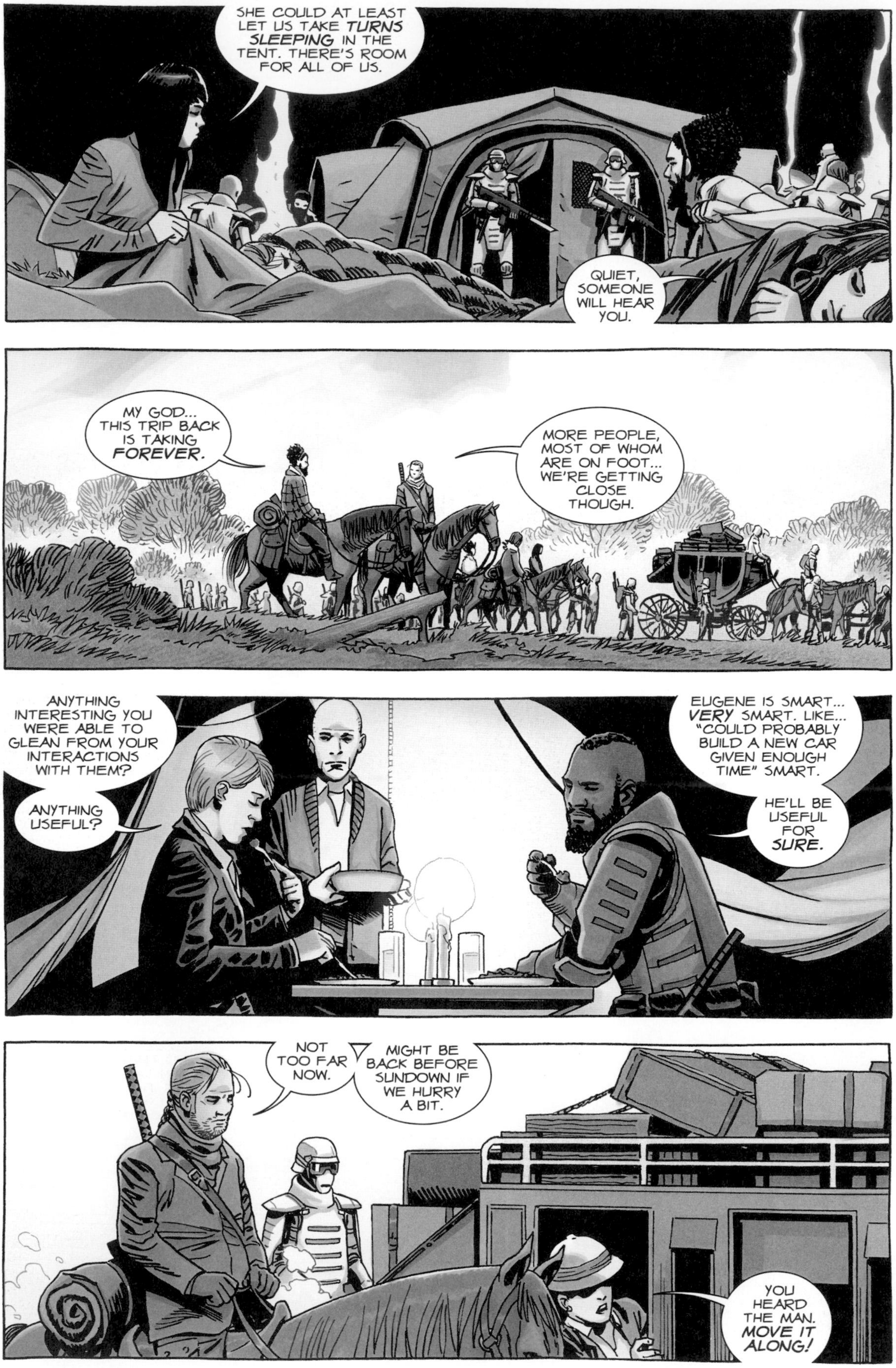
SHE COULD AT LEAST LET US TAKE TURNS SLEEPING IN THE TENT. THERE'S ROOM FOR ALL OF US.
QUIET, SOMEONE WILL HEAR YOU.
MY GOD... THIS TRIP BACK IS TAKING FOREVER.
MORE PEOPLE, MOST OF WHOM ARE ON FOOT... WE'RE GETTING CLOSE THOUGH.
ANYTHING INTERESTING YOU WERE ABLE TO GLEAN FROM YOUR INTERACTIONS WITH THEM?
ANYTHING USEFUL?
EUGENE IS SMART... VERY SMART. LIKE... "COULD PROBABLY BUILD A NEW CAR GIVEN ENOUGH TIME" SMART.
HE'LL BE USEFUL FOR SURE.
NOT TOO FAR NOW.
MIGHT BE BACK BEFORE SUNDOWN IF WE HURRY A BIT.
YOU HEARD THE MAN. MOVE IT ALONG!

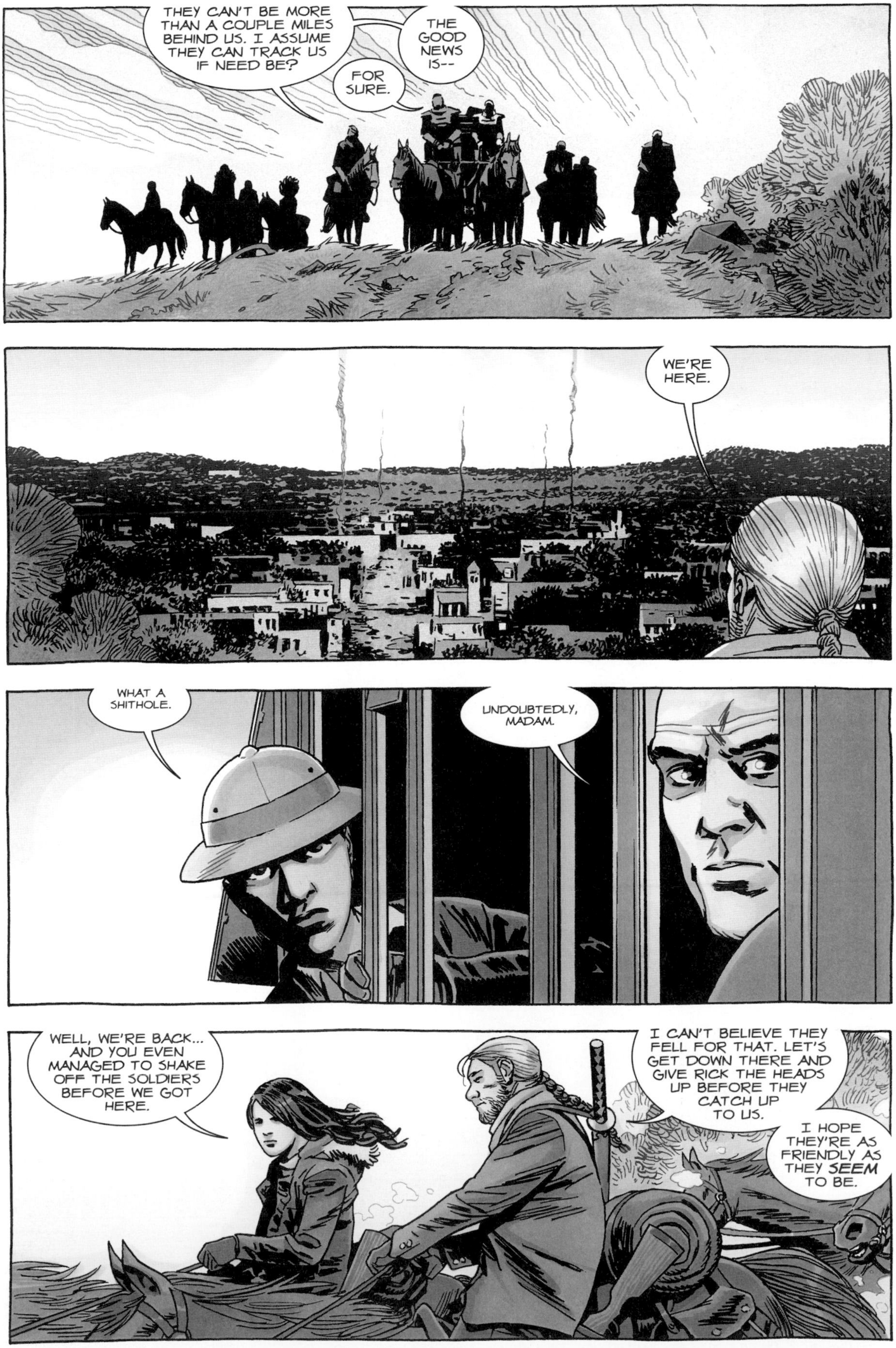
THEY CAN'T BE MORE THAN A COUPLE MILES BEHIND US. I ASSUME THEY CAN TRACK US IF NEED BE?
FOR SURE.
THE GOOD NEWS IS--
WE'RE HERE.
WHAT A SHITHOLE.
UNDOUBTEDLY, MADAM.
WELL, WE'RE BACK... AND YOU EVEN MANAGED TO SHAKE OFF THE SOLDIERS BEFORE WE GOT HERE.
I CAN'T BELIEVE THEY FELL FOR THAT. LET'S GET DOWN THERE AND GIVE RICK THE HEADS UP BEFORE THEY CATCH UP TO US.
I HOPE THEY'RE AS FRIENDLY AS THEY *SEEM* TO BE.

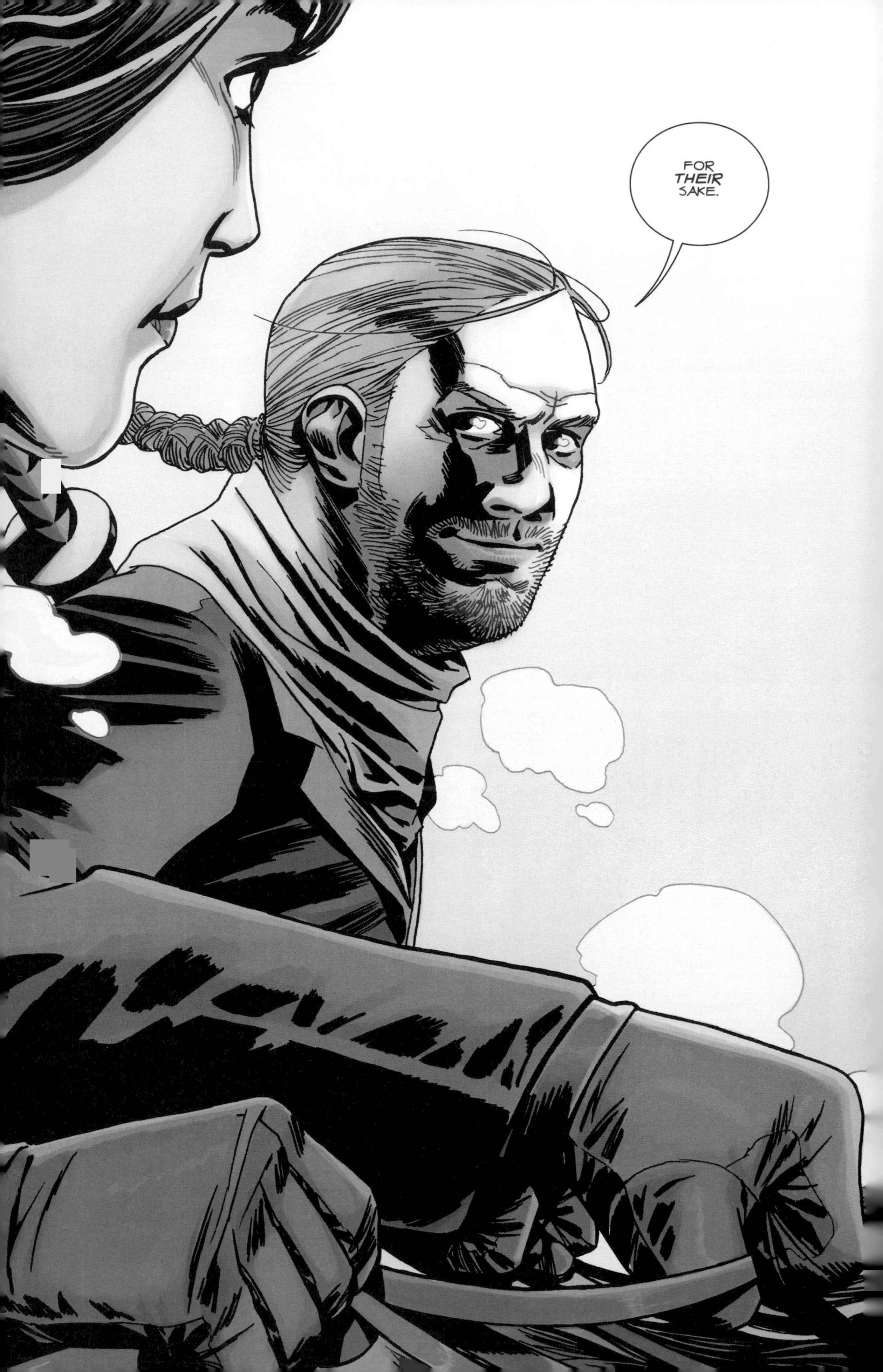
FOR THEIR SAKE.

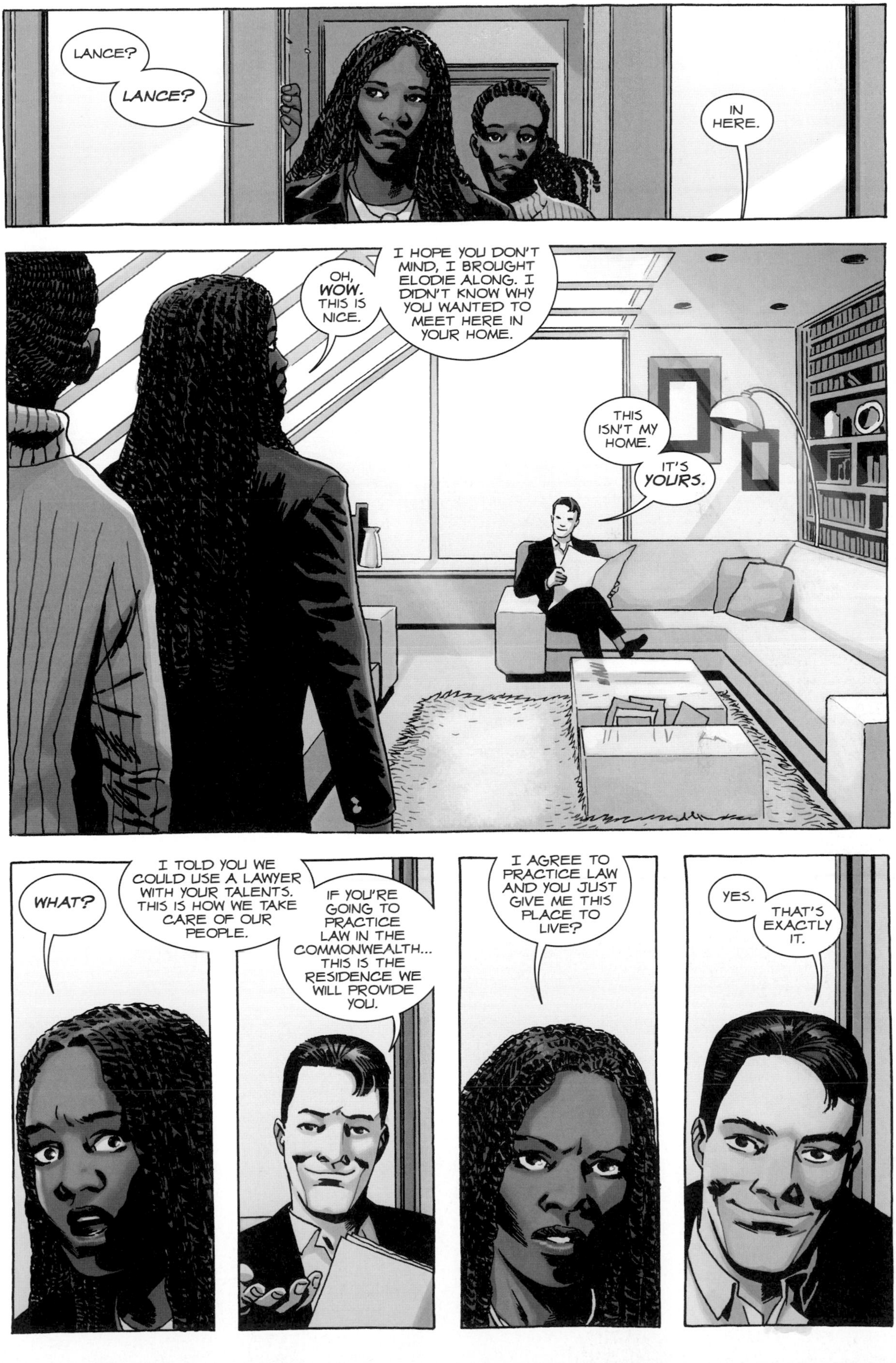
LANCE?
LANCE?
IN HERE.
OH, WOW. THIS IS NICE.
I HOPE YOU DON'T MIND, I BROUGHT ELODIE ALONG. I DIDN'T KNOW WHY YOU WANTED TO MEET HERE IN YOUR HOME.
THIS ISN'T MY HOME.
IT'S YOURS.
WHAT?
I TOLD YOU WE COULD USE A LAWYER WITH YOUR TALENTS. THIS IS HOW WE TAKE CARE OF OUR PEOPLE.
IF YOU'RE GOING TO PRACTICE LAW IN THE COMMONWEALTH... THIS IS THE RESIDENCE WE WILL PROVIDE YOU.
I AGREE TO PRACTICE LAW AND YOU JUST GIVE ME THIS PLACE TO LIVE?
YES.
THAT'S EXACTLY IT.

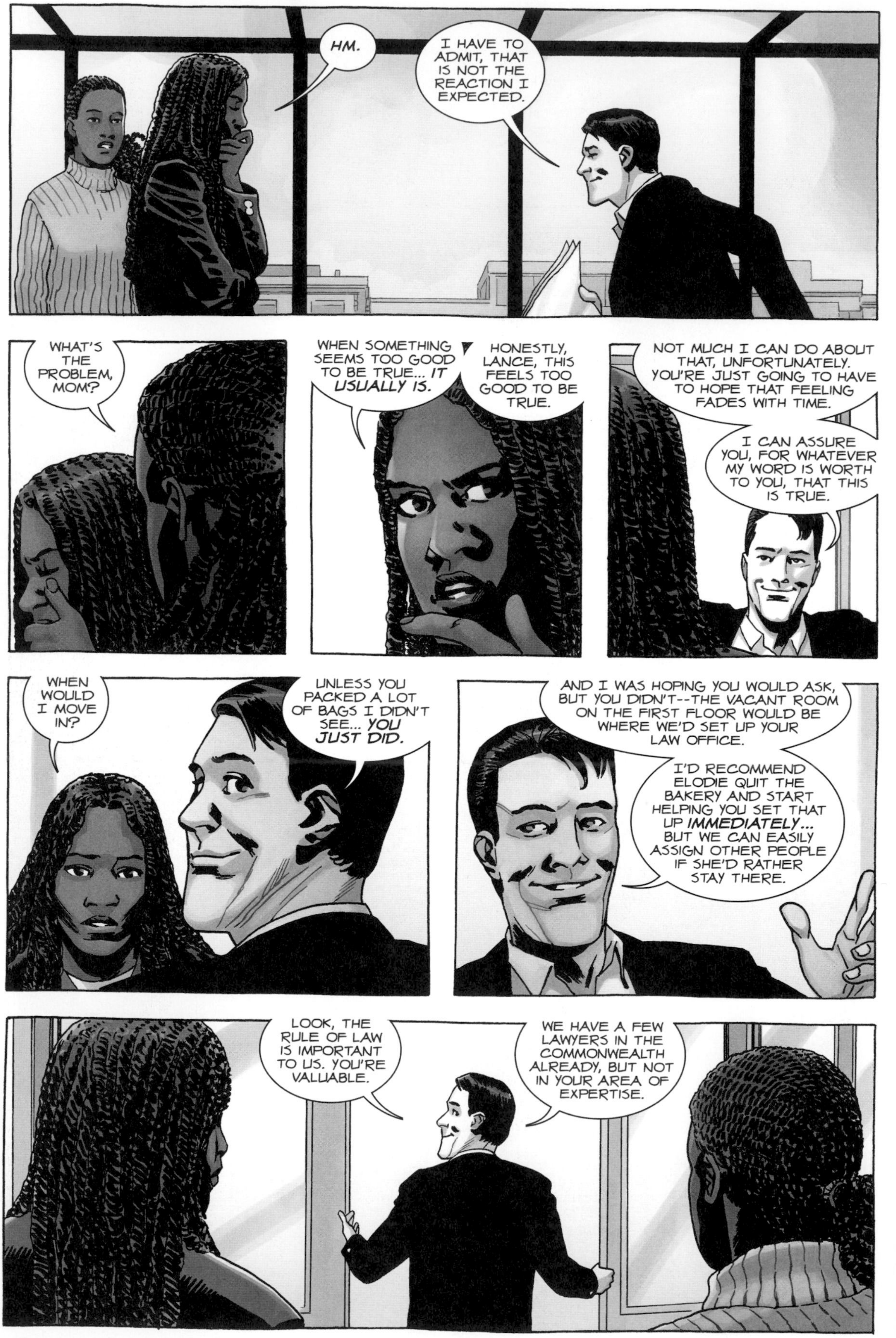
HM.
I HAVE TO ADMIT, THAT IS NOT THE REACTION I EXPECTED.
WHAT'S THE PROBLEM, MOM?
WHEN SOMETHING SEEMS TOO GOOD TO BE TRUE... IT USUALLY IS.
HONESTLY, LANCE, THIS FEELS TOO GOOD TO BE TRUE.
NOT MUCH I CAN DO ABOUT THAT, UNFORTUNATELY. YOU'RE JUST GOING TO HAVE TO HOPE THAT FEELING FADES WITH TIME.
I CAN ASSURE YOU, FOR WHATEVER MY WORD IS WORTH TO YOU, THAT THIS IS TRUE.
WHEN WOULD I MOVE IN?
UNLESS YOU PACKED A LOT OF BAGS I DIDN'T SEE... YOU JUST DID.
AND I WAS HOPING YOU WOULD ASK, BUT YOU DIDN'T--THE VACANT ROOM ON THE FIRST FLOOR WOULD BE WHERE WE'D SET UP YOUR LAW OFFICE.
I'D RECOMMEND ELODIE QUIT THE BAKERY AND START HELPING YOU SET THAT UP IMMEDIATELY... BUT WE CAN EASILY ASSIGN OTHER PEOPLE IF SHE'D RATHER STAY THERE.
LOOK, THE RULE OF LAW IS IMPORTANT TO US. YOU'RE VALUABLE.
WE HAVE A FEW LAWYERS IN THE COMMONWEALTH ALREADY, BUT NOT IN YOUR AREA OF EXPERTISE.

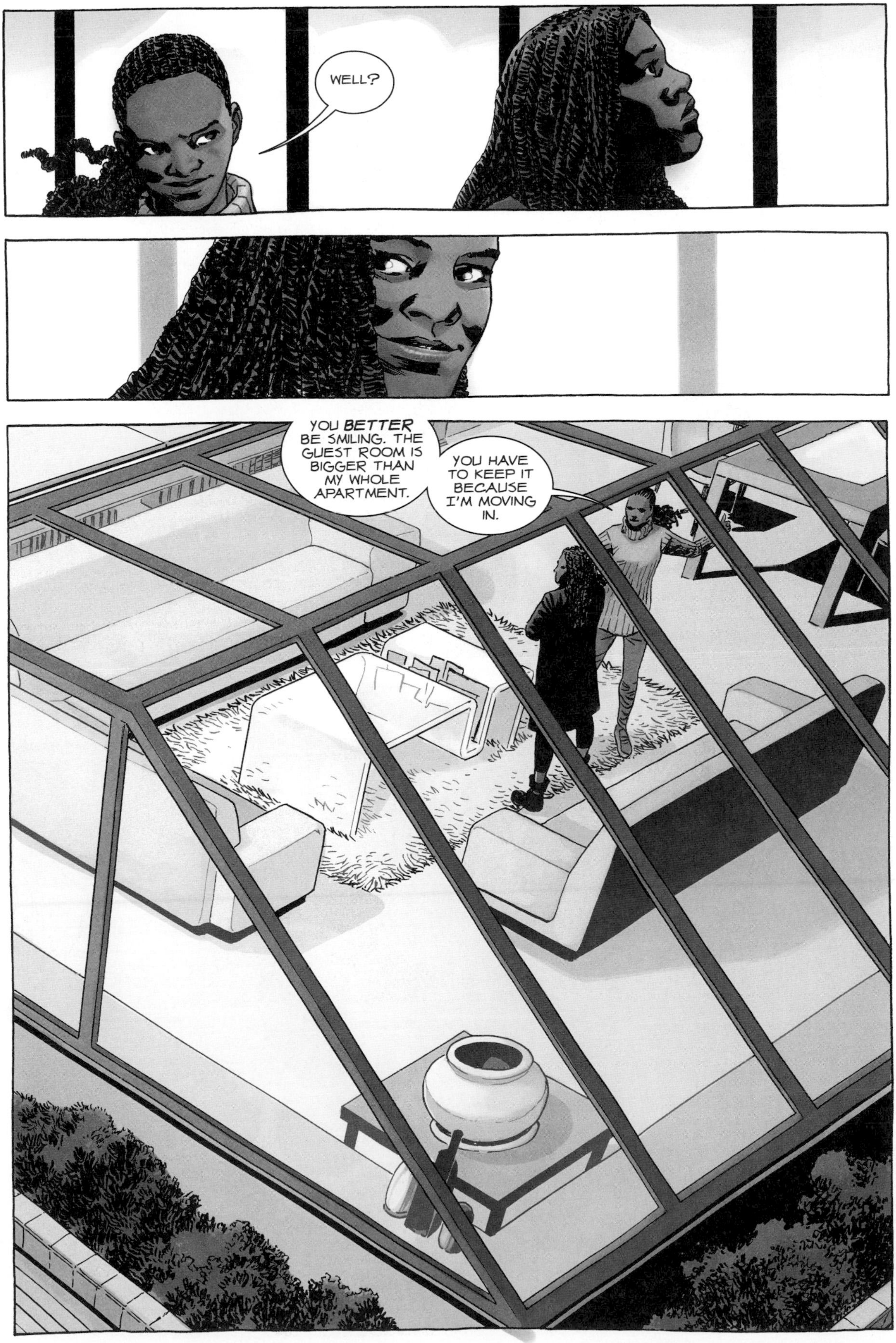
WELL?
YOU BETTER BE SMILING. THE GUEST ROOM IS BIGGER THAN MY WHOLE APARTMENT.
YOU HAVE TO KEEP IT BECAUSE I'M MOVING IN.

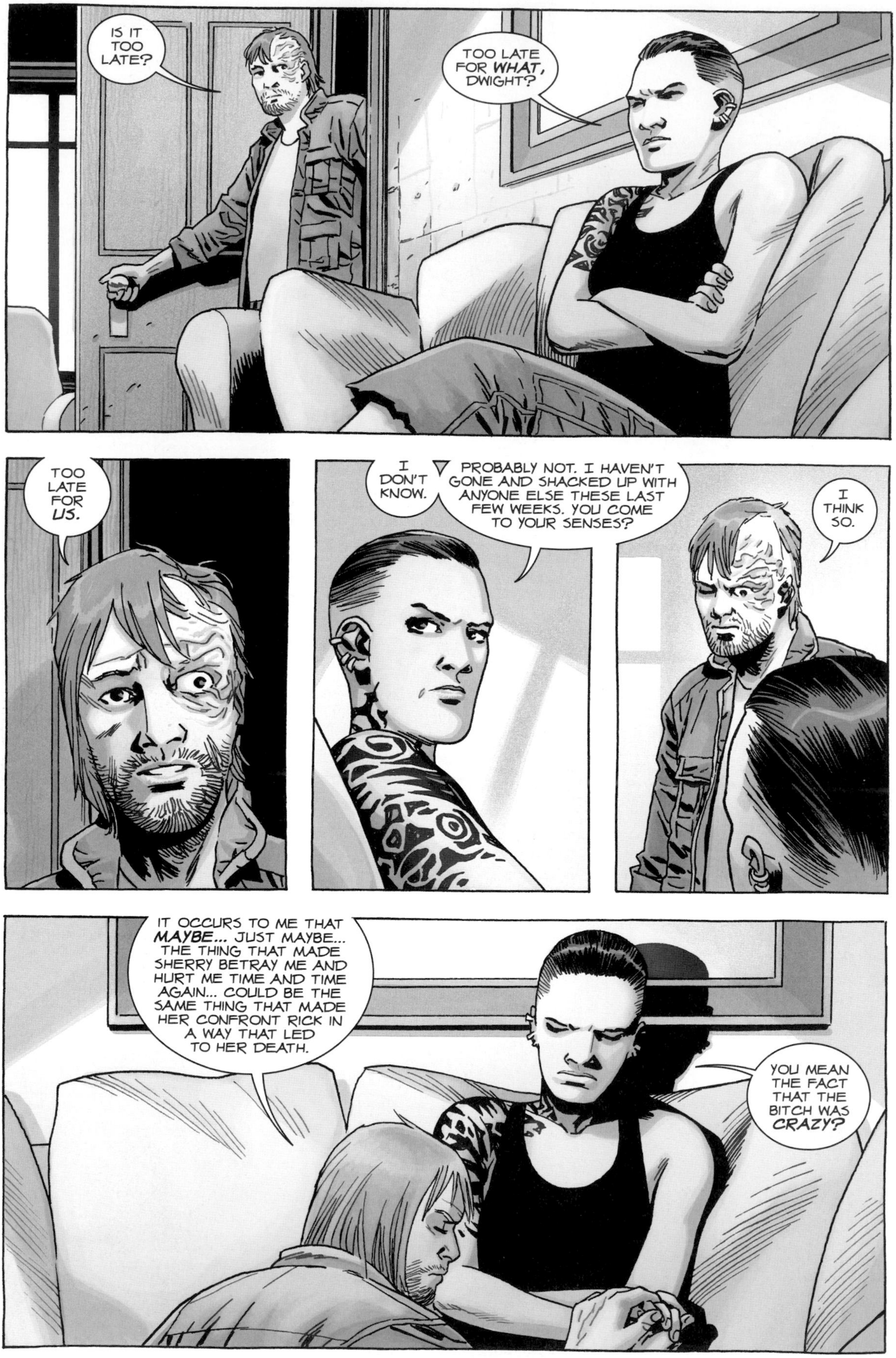
IS IT TOO LATE?
TOO LATE FOR WHAT, DWIGHT?
TOO LATE FOR US.
I DON'T KNOW.
PROBABLY NOT. I HAVEN'T GONE AND SHACKED UP WITH ANYONE ELSE THESE LAST FEW WEEKS. YOU COME TO YOUR SENSES?
I THINK SO.
IT OCCURS TO ME THAT MAYBE... JUST MAYBE... THE THING THAT MADE SHERRY BETRAY ME AND HURT ME TIME AND TIME AGAIN... COULD BE THE SAME THING THAT MADE HER CONFRONT RICK IN A WAY THAT LED TO HER DEATH.
YOU MEAN THE FACT THAT THE BITCH WAS CRAZY?

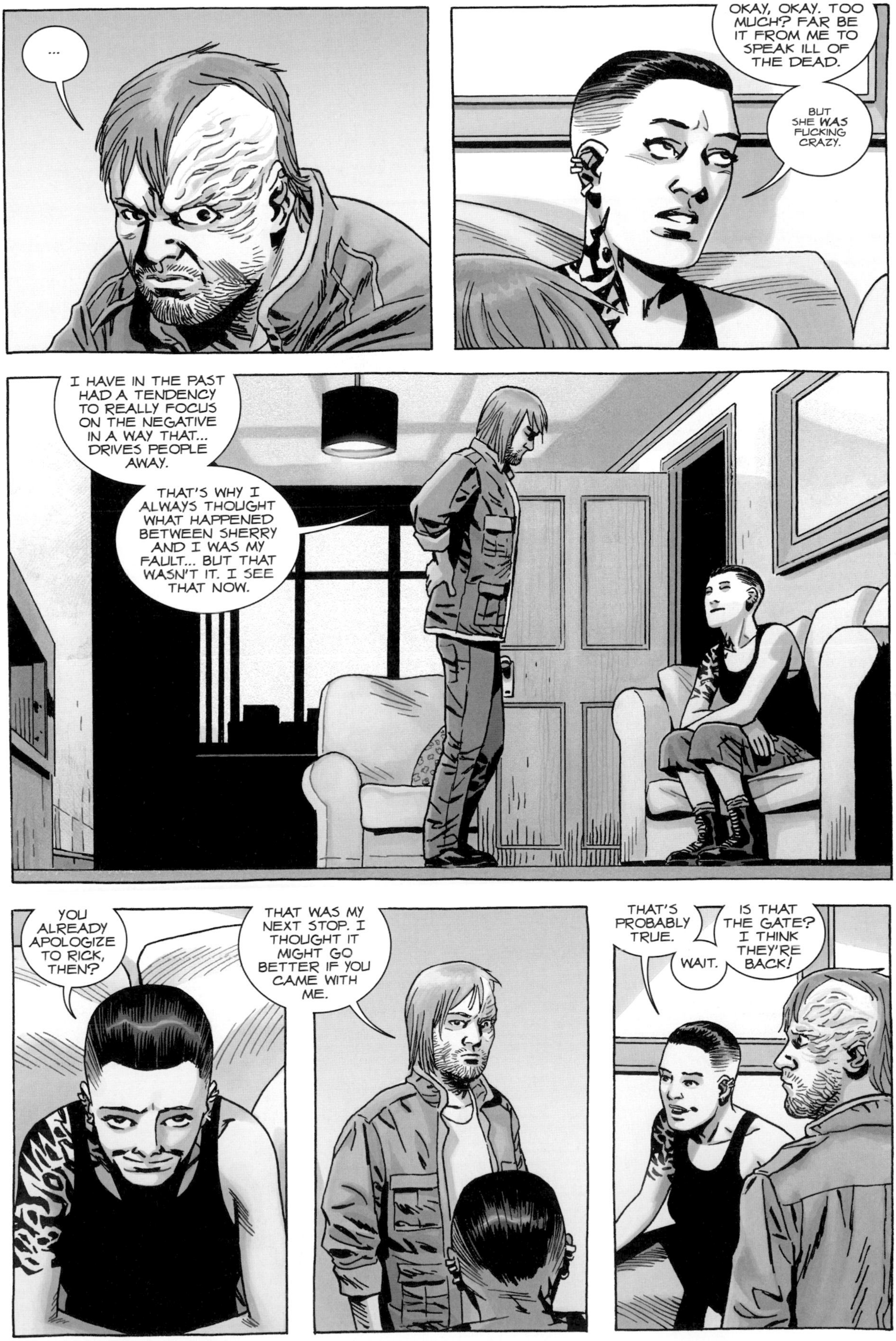
...
OKAY, OKAY. TOO MUCH? FAR BE IT FROM ME TO SPEAK ILL OF THE DEAD.
BUT SHE WAS FUCKING CRAZY.
I HAVE IN THE PAST HAD A TENDENCY TO REALLY FOCUS ON THE NEGATIVE IN A WAY THAT... DRIVES PEOPLE AWAY.
THAT'S WHY I ALWAYS THOUGHT WHAT HAPPENED BETWEEN SHERRY AND I WAS MY FAULT... BUT THAT WASN'T IT. I SEE THAT NOW.
YOU ALREADY APOLOGIZE TO RICK, THEN?
THAT WAS MY NEXT STOP. I THOUGHT IT MIGHT GO BETTER IF YOU CAME WITH ME.
THAT'S PROBABLY TRUE.
WAIT.
IS THAT THE GATE? I THINK THEY'RE BACK!

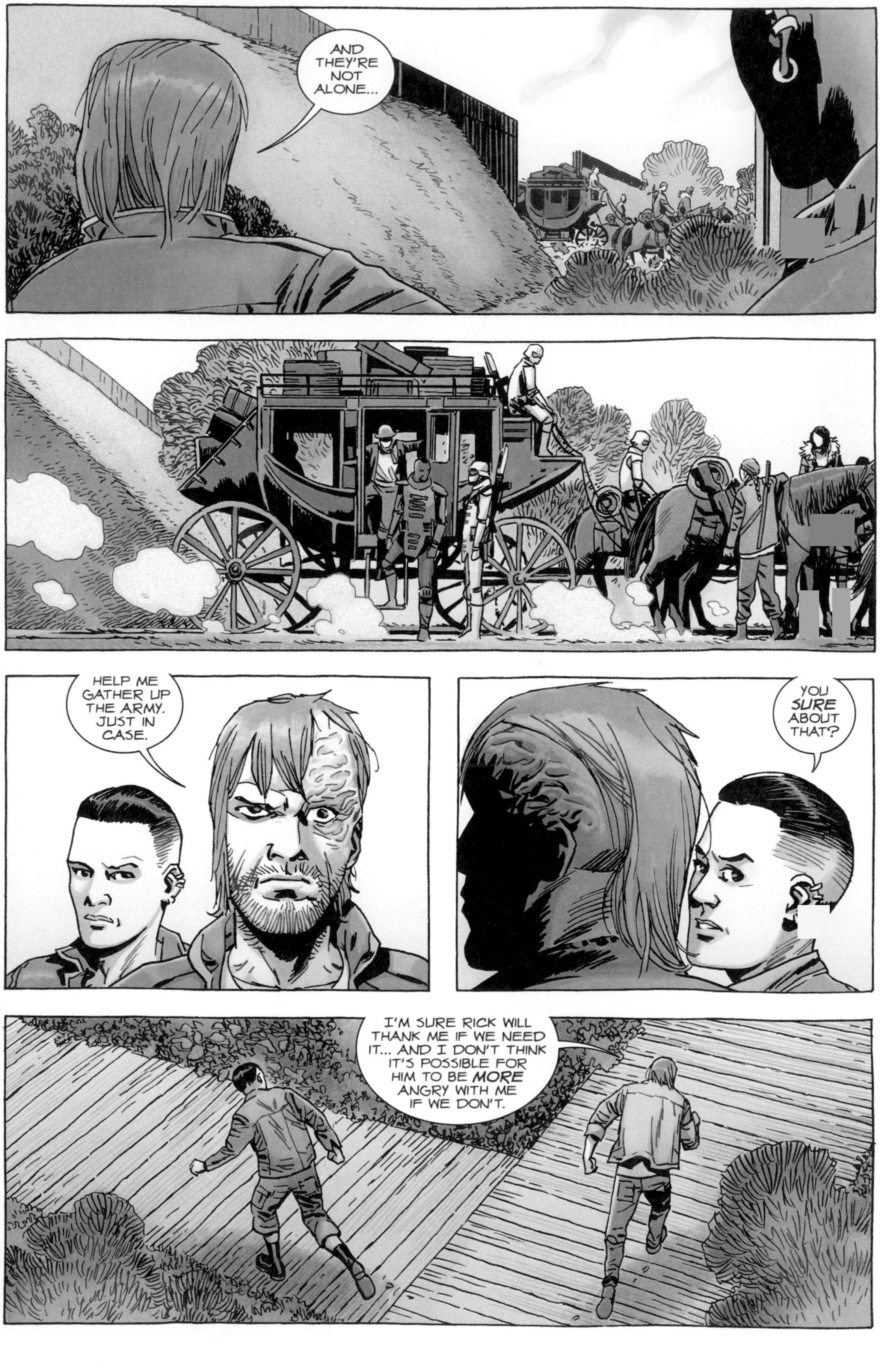
AND THEY'RE NOT ALONE...
HELP ME GATHER UP THE ARMY. JUST IN CASE.
YOU SURE ABOUT THAT?
I'M SURE RICK WILL THANK ME IF WE NEED IT... AND I DON'T THINK IT'S POSSIBLE FOR HIM TO BE MORE ANGRY WITH ME IF WE DON'T.

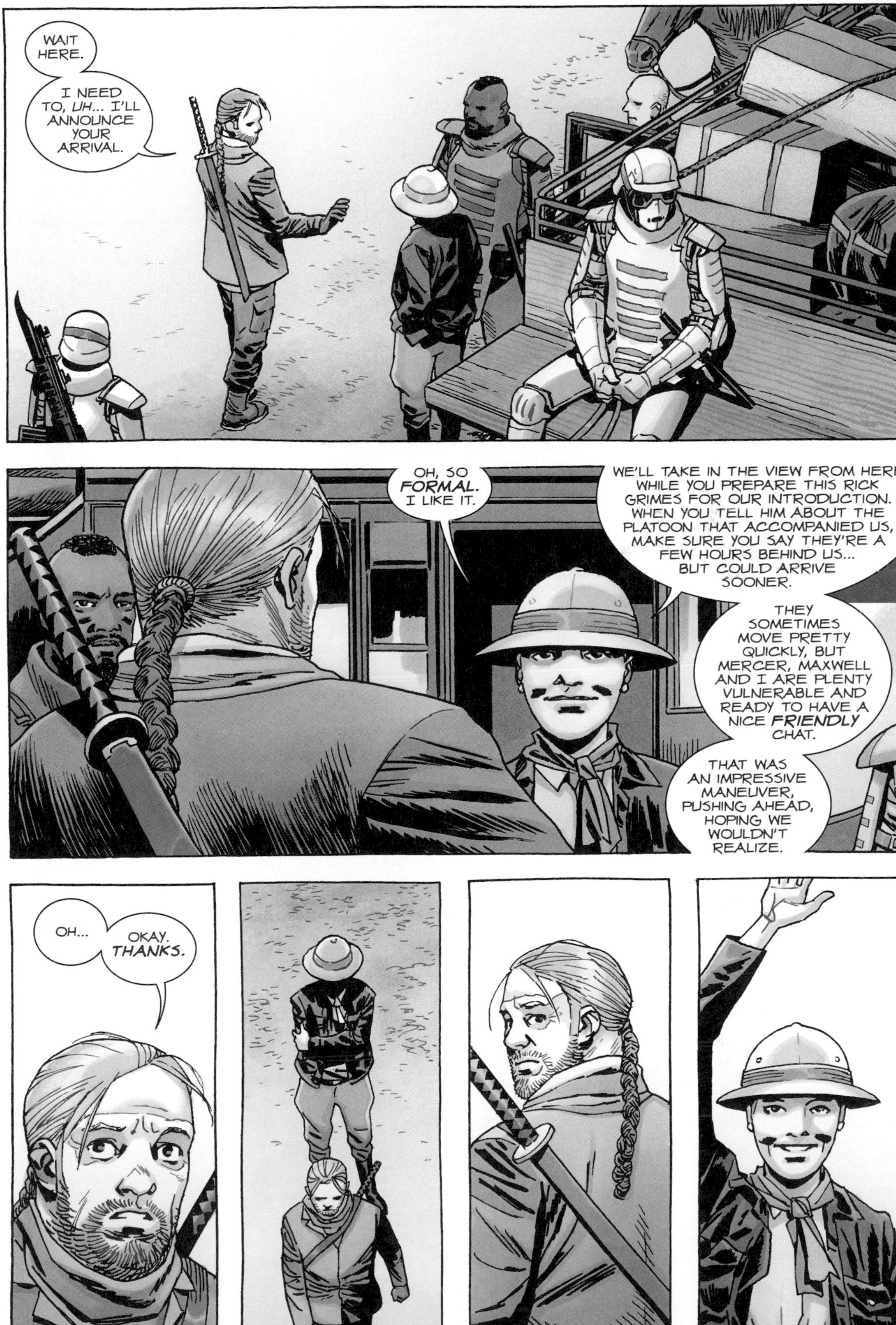
WAIT HERE.
I NEED TO, *UH*... I'LL ANNOUNCE YOUR ARRIVAL.
OH, SO ***FORMAL.*** I LIKE IT.
WE'LL TAKE IN THE VIEW FROM HERE WHILE YOU PREPARE THIS RICK GRIMES FOR OUR INTRODUCTION. WHEN YOU TELL HIM ABOUT THE PLATOON THAT ACCOMPANIED US, MAKE SURE YOU SAY THEY'RE A FEW HOURS BEHIND US... BUT COULD ARRIVE SOONER.
THEY SOMETIMES MOVE PRETTY QUICKLY, BUT MERCER, MAXWELL AND I ARE PLENTY VULNERABLE AND READY TO HAVE A NICE ***FRIENDLY*** CHAT.
THAT WAS AN IMPRESSIVE MANEUVER, PUSHING AHEAD, HOPING WE WOULDN'T REALIZE.
OH...
OKAY. ***THANKS.***

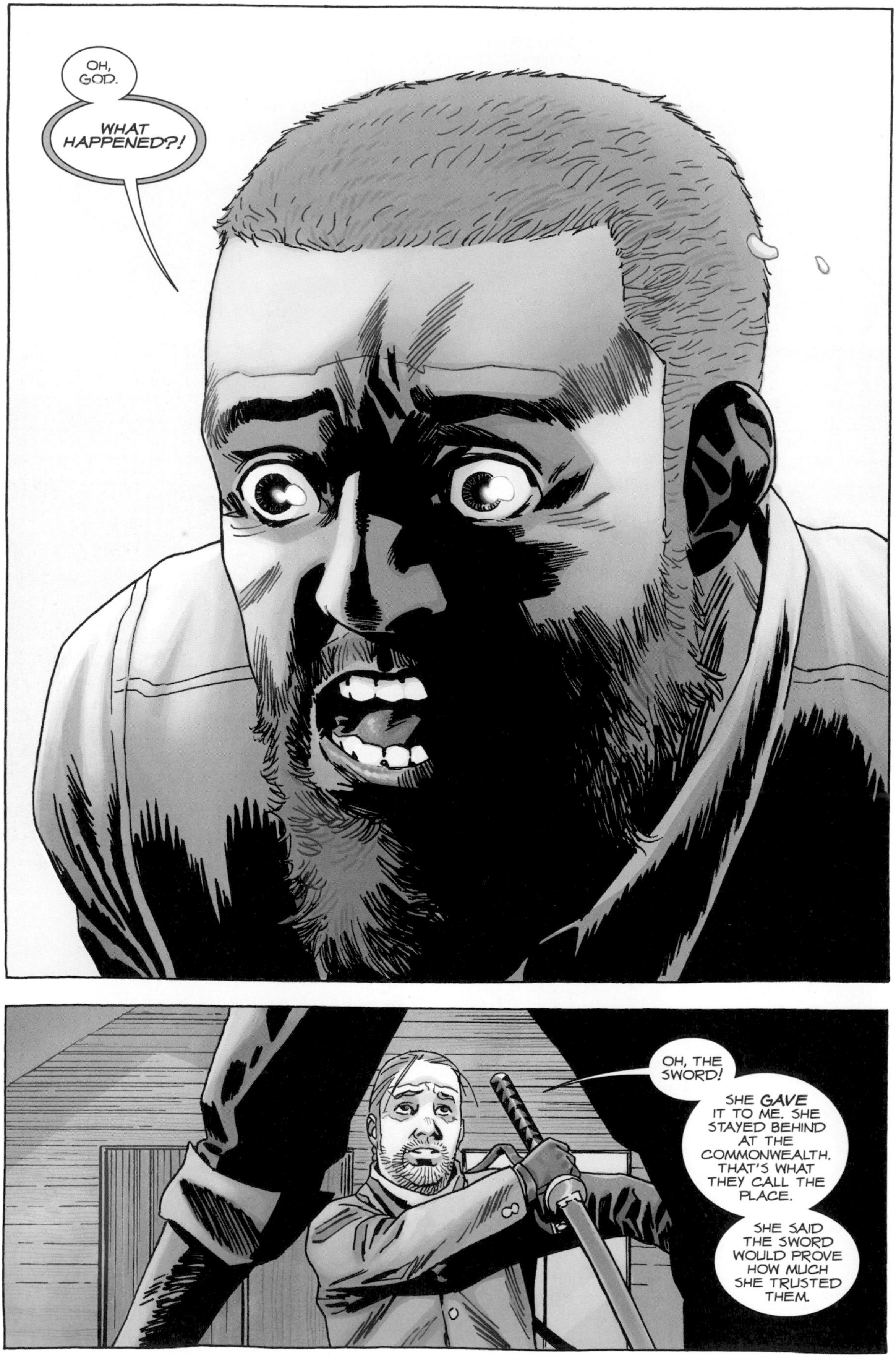
OH, GOD.
WHAT HAPPENED?!
OH, THE SWORD!
SHE GAVE IT TO ME. SHE STAYED BEHIND AT THE COMMONWEALTH. THAT'S WHAT THEY CALL THE PLACE.
SHE SAID THE SWORD WOULD PROVE HOW MUCH SHE TRUSTED THEM.

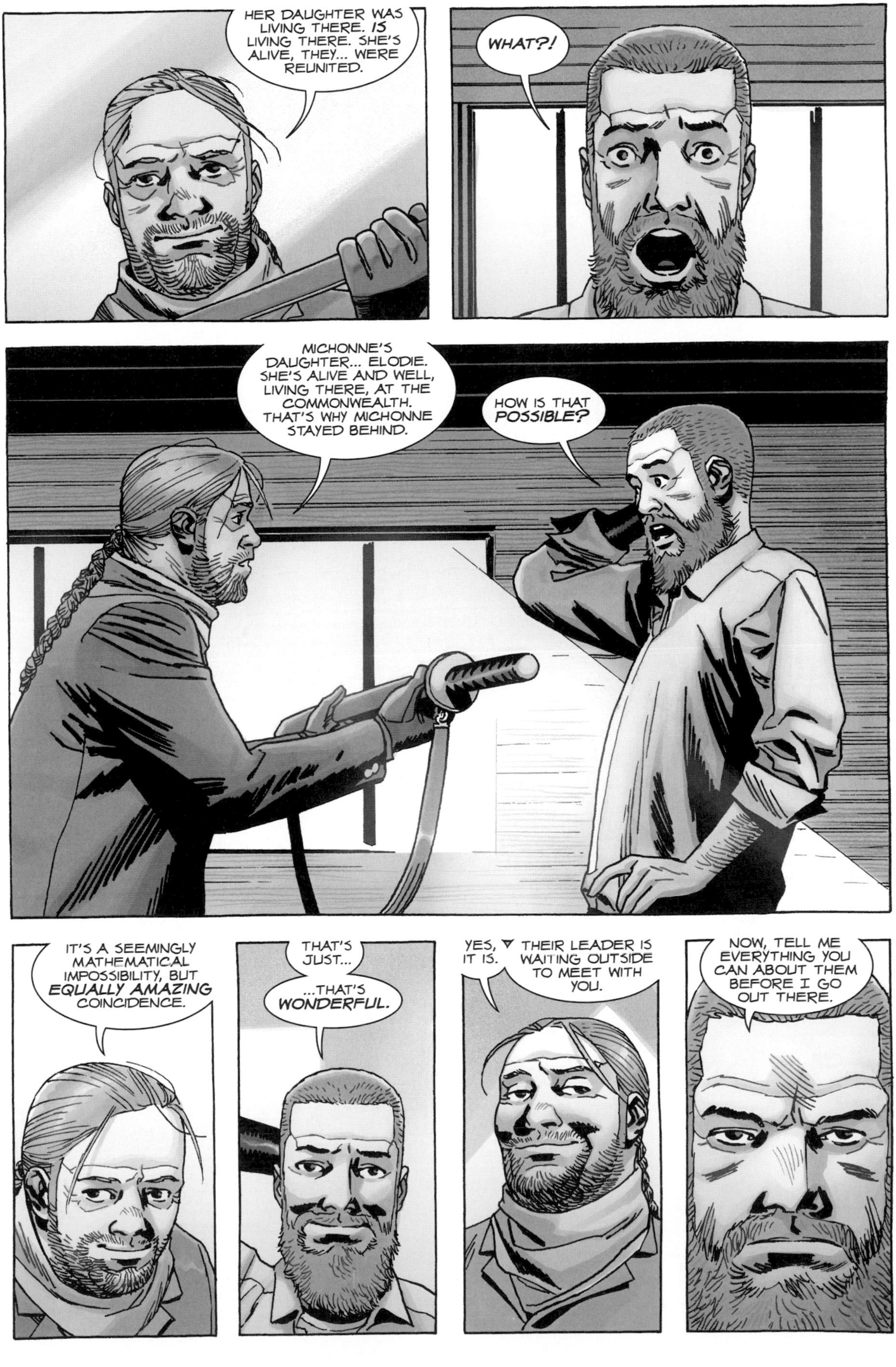
HER DAUGHTER WAS LIVING THERE. *IS* LIVING THERE. SHE'S ALIVE, THEY... WERE REUNITED.
WHAT?!
MICHONNE'S DAUGHTER... ELODIE. SHE'S ALIVE AND WELL, LIVING THERE, AT THE COMMONWEALTH. THAT'S WHY MICHONNE STAYED BEHIND.
HOW IS THAT ***POSSIBLE?***
IT'S A SEEMINGLY MATHEMATICAL IMPOSSIBILITY, BUT ***EQUALLY AMAZING*** COINCIDENCE.
THAT'S JUST...
...THAT'S ***WONDERFUL.***
YES, IT IS.
THEIR LEADER IS WAITING OUTSIDE TO MEET WITH YOU.
NOW, TELL ME EVERYTHING YOU CAN ABOUT THEM BEFORE I GO OUT THERE.

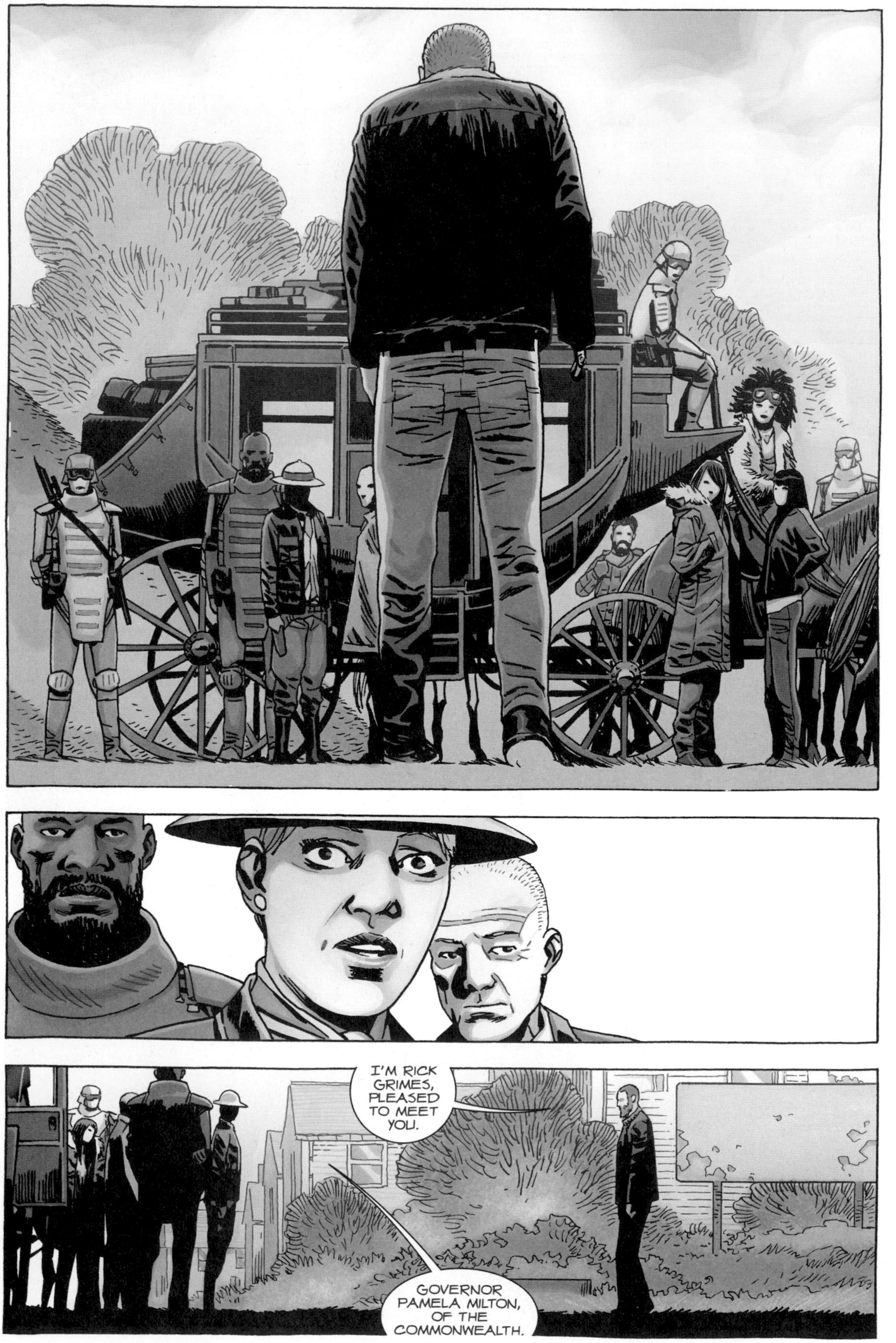
I'M RICK GRIMES, PLEASED TO MEET YOU.
GOVERNOR PAMELA MILTON, OF THE COMMONWEALTH.

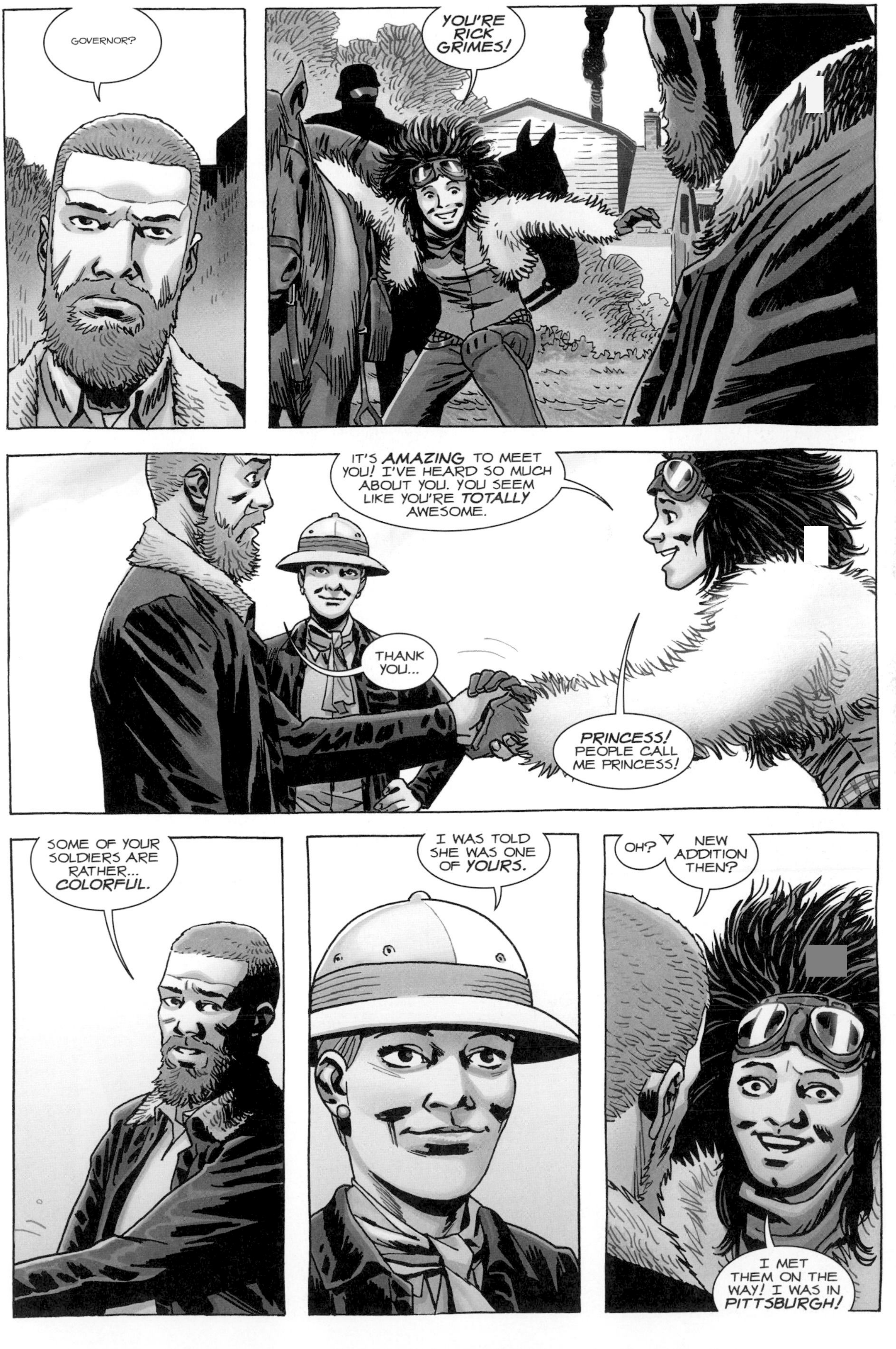
GOVERNOR?
YOU'RE RICK GRIMES!
IT'S AMAZING TO MEET YOU! I'VE HEARD SO MUCH ABOUT YOU. YOU SEEM LIKE YOU'RE TOTALLY AWESOME.
THANK YOU...
PRINCESS! PEOPLE CALL ME PRINCESS!
SOME OF YOUR SOLDIERS ARE RATHER... COLORFUL.
I WAS TOLD SHE WAS ONE OF YOURS.
OH?
NEW ADDITION THEN?
I MET THEM ON THE WAY! I WAS IN PITTSBURGH!

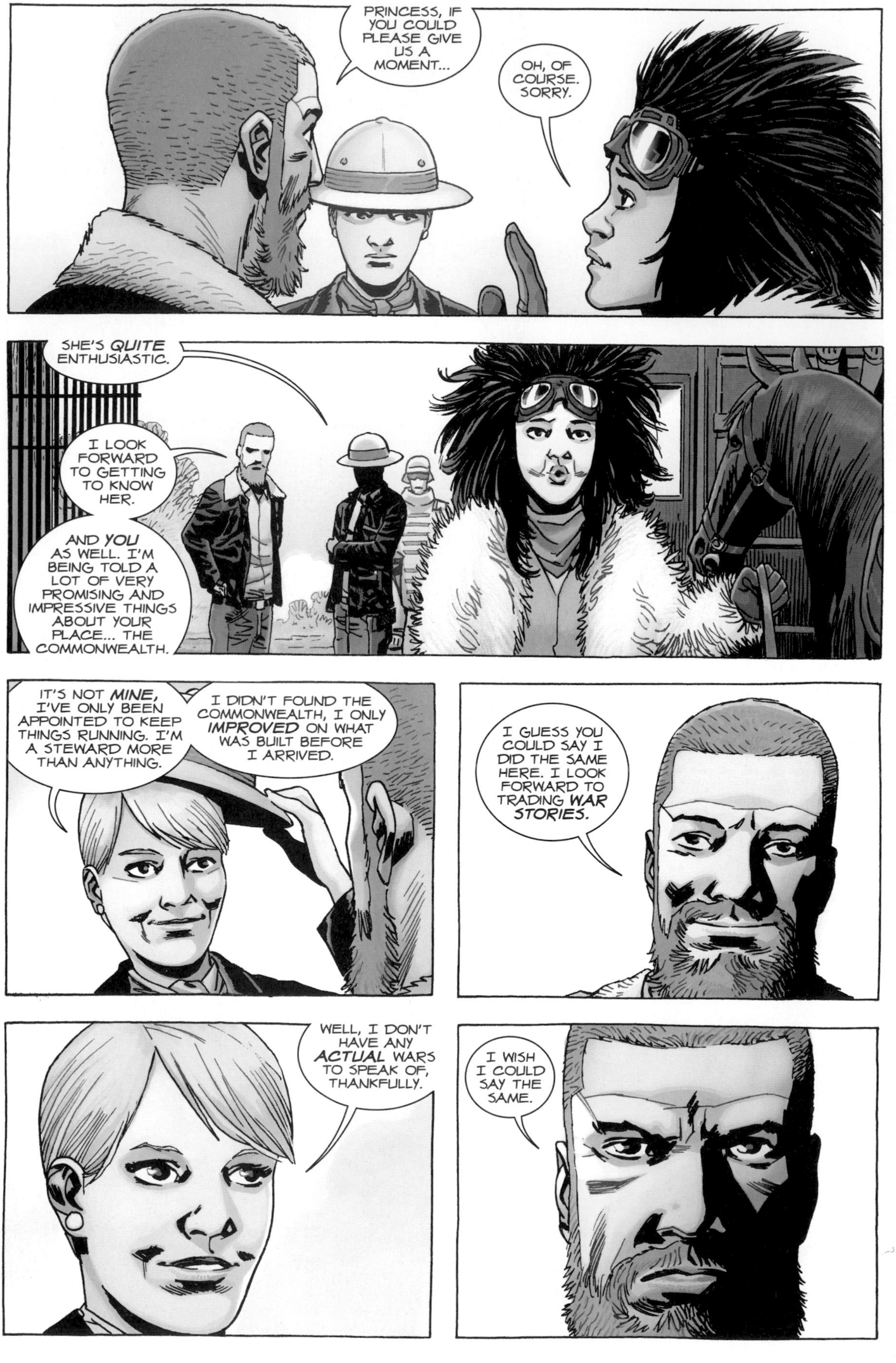
PRINCESS, IF YOU COULD PLEASE GIVE US A MOMENT...
OH, OF COURSE. SORRY.
SHE'S QUITE ENTHUSIASTIC.
I LOOK FORWARD TO GETTING TO KNOW HER.
AND YOU AS WELL. I'M BEING TOLD A LOT OF VERY PROMISING AND IMPRESSIVE THINGS ABOUT YOUR PLACE... THE COMMONWEALTH.
IT'S NOT MINE, I'VE ONLY BEEN APPOINTED TO KEEP THINGS RUNNING. I'M A STEWARD MORE THAN ANYTHING.
I DIDN'T FOUND THE COMMONWEALTH, I ONLY IMPROVED ON WHAT WAS BUILT BEFORE I ARRIVED.
I GUESS YOU COULD SAY I DID THE SAME HERE. I LOOK FORWARD TO TRADING WAR STORIES.
WELL, I DON'T HAVE ANY ACTUAL WARS TO SPEAK OF, THANKFULLY.
I WISH I COULD SAY THE SAME.

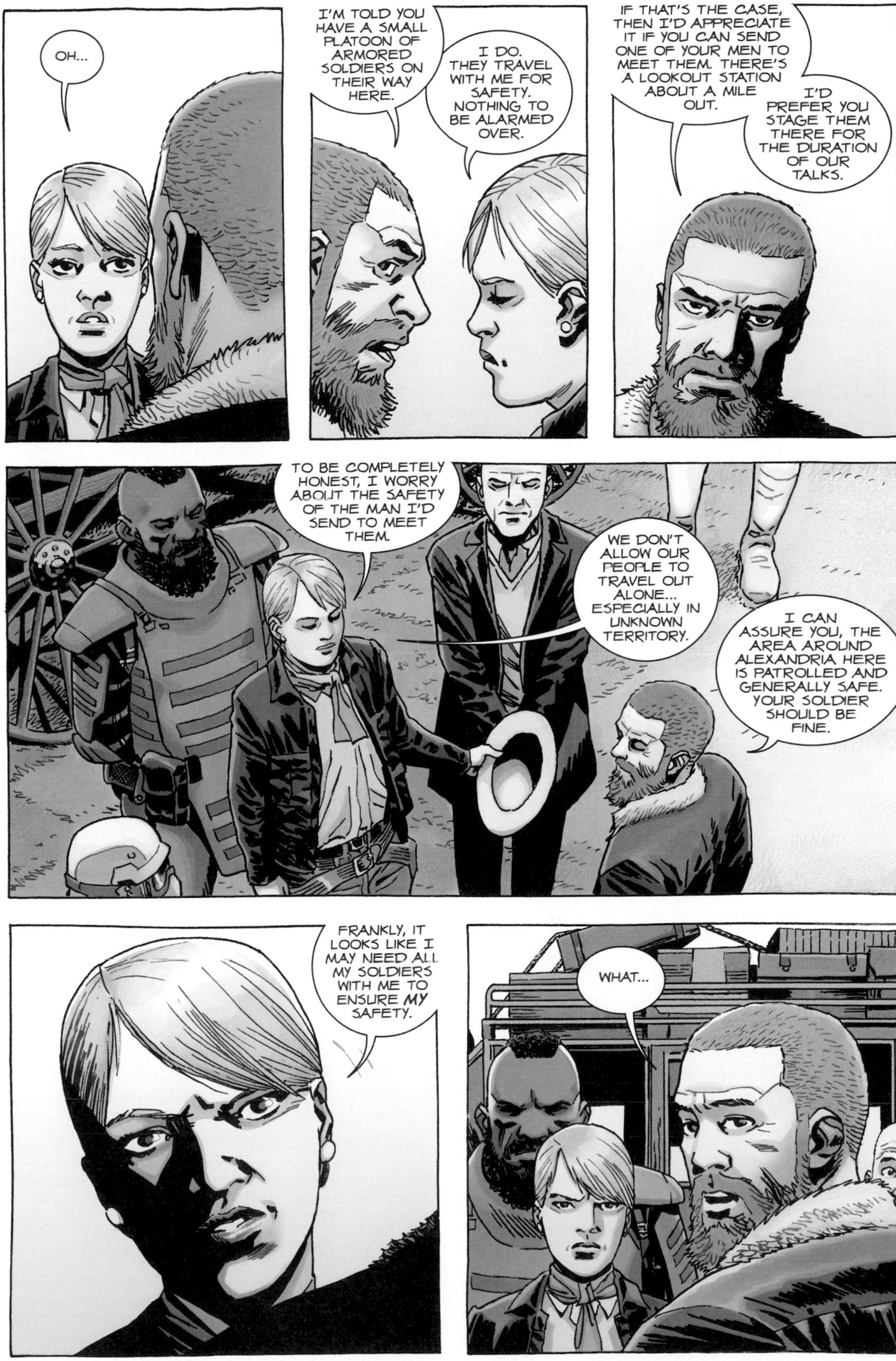
OH...
I'M TOLD YOU HAVE A SMALL PLATOON OF ARMORED SOLDIERS ON THEIR WAY HERE.
I DO. THEY TRAVEL WITH ME FOR SAFETY. NOTHING TO BE ALARMED OVER.
IF THAT'S THE CASE, THEN I'D APPRECIATE IT IF YOU CAN SEND ONE OF YOUR MEN TO MEET THEM. THERE'S A LOOKOUT STATION ABOUT A MILE OUT.
I'D PREFER YOU STAGE THEM THERE FOR THE DURATION OF OUR TALKS.
TO BE COMPLETELY HONEST, I WORRY ABOUT THE SAFETY OF THE MAN I'D SEND TO MEET THEM.
WE DON'T ALLOW OUR PEOPLE TO TRAVEL OUT ALONE... ESPECIALLY IN UNKNOWN TERRITORY.
I CAN ASSURE YOU, THE AREA AROUND ALEXANDRIA HERE IS PATROLLED AND GENERALLY SAFE. YOUR SOLDIER SHOULD BE FINE.
FRANKLY, IT LOOKS LIKE I MAY NEED ALL MY SOLDIERS WITH ME TO ENSURE MY SAFETY.
WHAT...

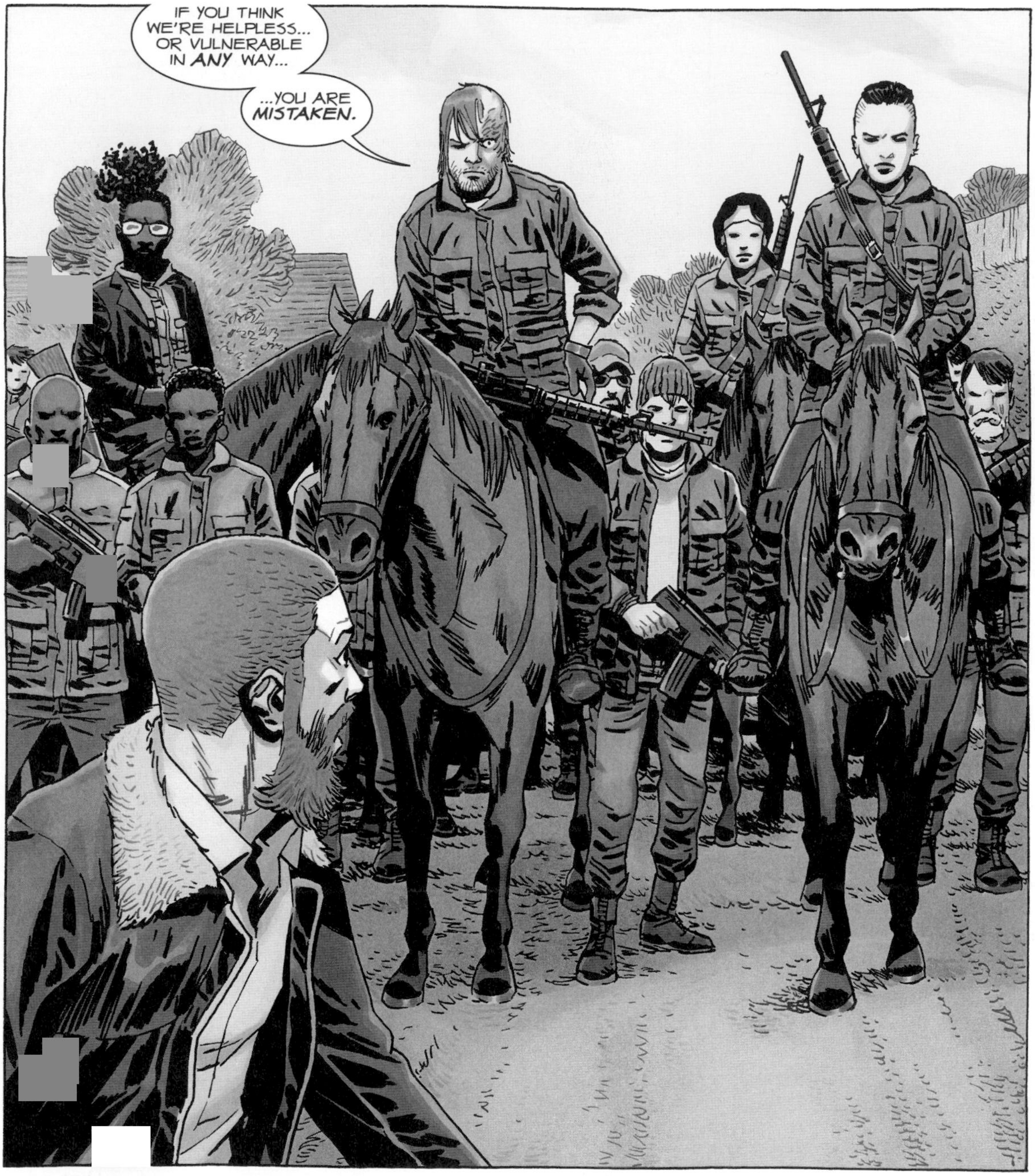
IF YOU THINK WE'RE HELPLESS... OR VULNERABLE IN *ANY* WAY...
...YOU ARE *MISTAKEN.*

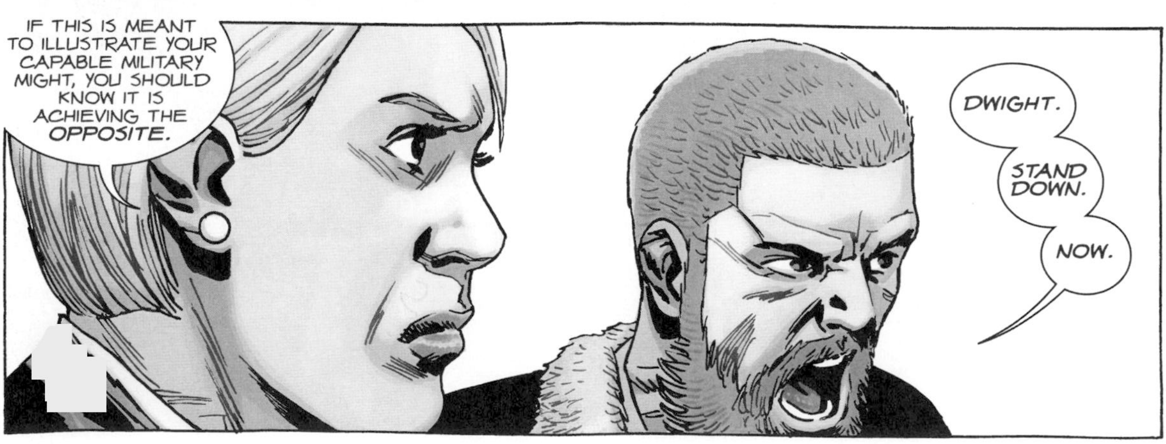
IF THIS IS MEANT TO ILLUSTRATE YOUR CAPABLE MILITARY MIGHT, YOU SHOULD KNOW IT IS ACHIEVING THE *OPPOSITE.*
DWIGHT.
STAND DOWN.
NOW.

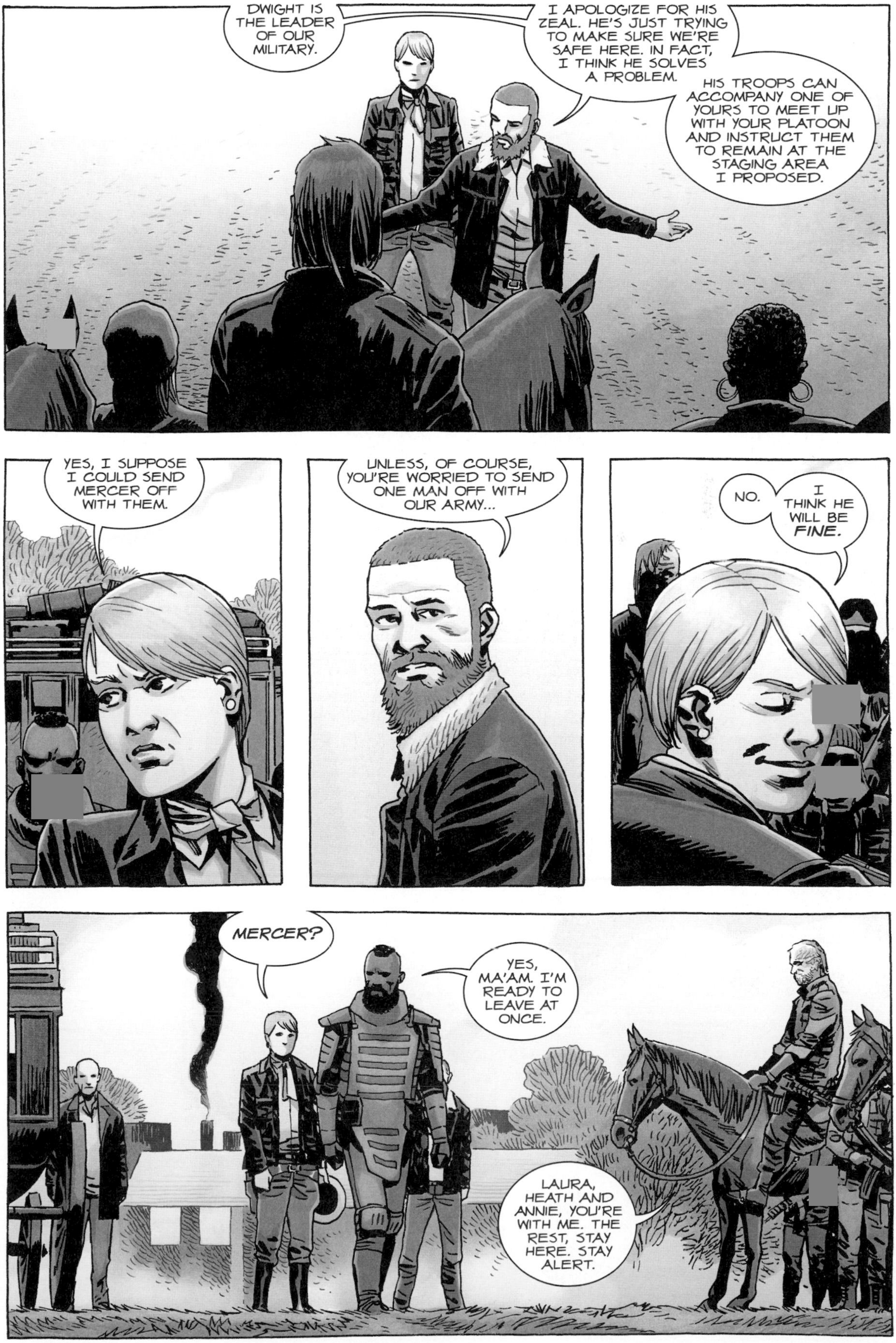
DWIGHT IS THE LEADER OF OUR MILITARY.
I APOLOGIZE FOR HIS ZEAL. HE'S JUST TRYING TO MAKE SURE WE'RE SAFE HERE. IN FACT, I THINK HE SOLVES A PROBLEM.
HIS TROOPS CAN ACCOMPANY ONE OF YOURS TO MEET UP WITH YOUR PLATOON AND INSTRUCT THEM TO REMAIN AT THE STAGING AREA I PROPOSED.
YES, I SUPPOSE I COULD SEND MERCER OFF WITH THEM.
UNLESS, OF COURSE, YOU'RE WORRIED TO SEND ONE MAN OFF WITH OUR ARMY...
NO.
I THINK HE WILL BE *FINE.*
MERCER?
YES, MA'AM. I'M READY TO LEAVE AT ONCE.
LAURA, HEATH AND ANNIE, YOU'RE WITH ME. THE REST, STAY HERE. STAY ALERT.

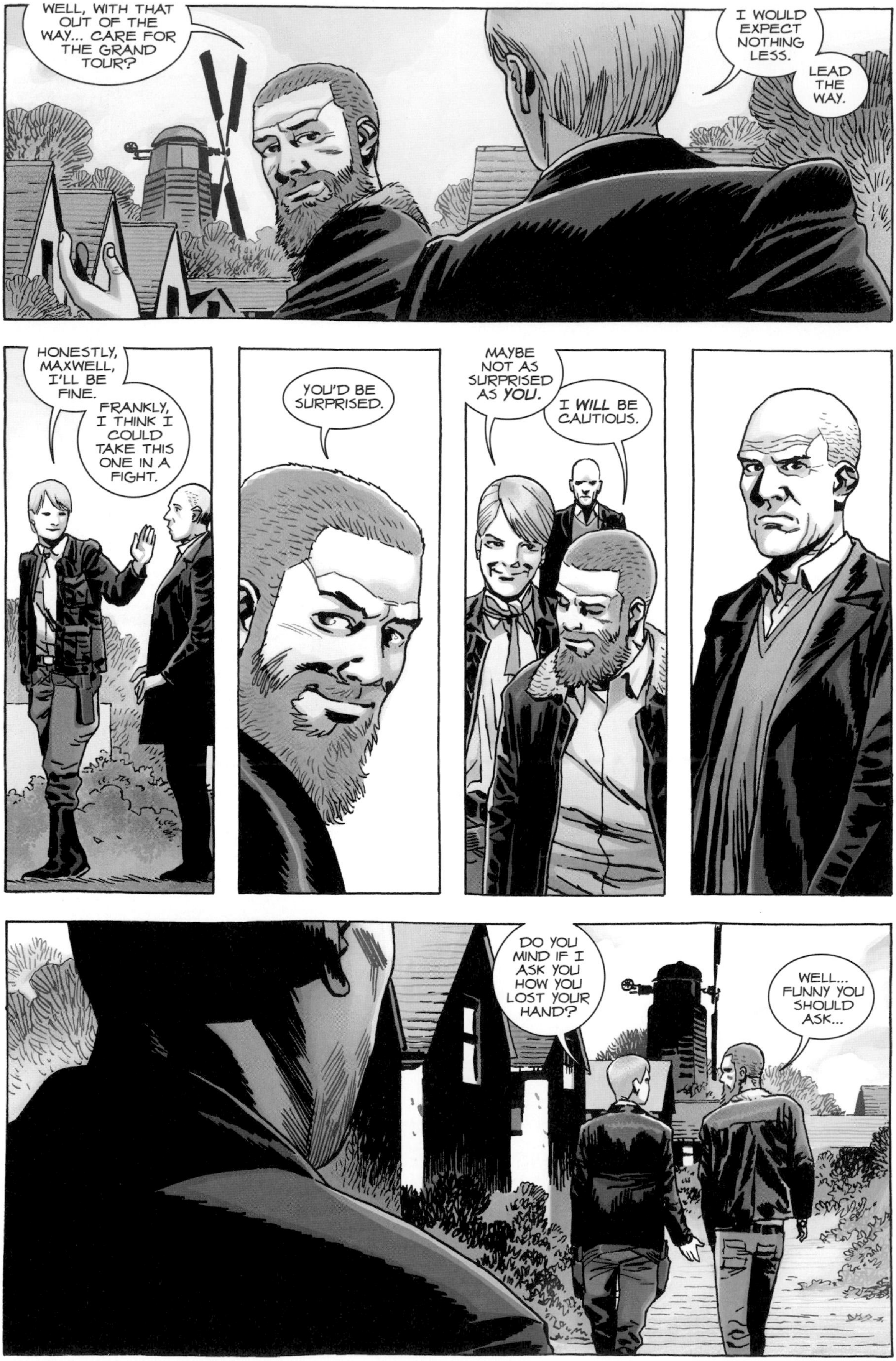
WELL, WITH THAT OUT OF THE WAY... CARE FOR THE GRAND TOUR?
I WOULD EXPECT NOTHING LESS.
LEAD THE WAY.
HONESTLY, MAXWELL, I'LL BE FINE.
FRANKLY, I THINK I COULD TAKE THIS ONE IN A FIGHT.
YOU'D BE SURPRISED.
MAYBE NOT AS SURPRISED AS *YOU*.
I *WILL* BE CAUTIOUS.
DO YOU MIND IF I ASK YOU HOW YOU LOST YOUR HAND?
WELL... FUNNY YOU SHOULD ASK...

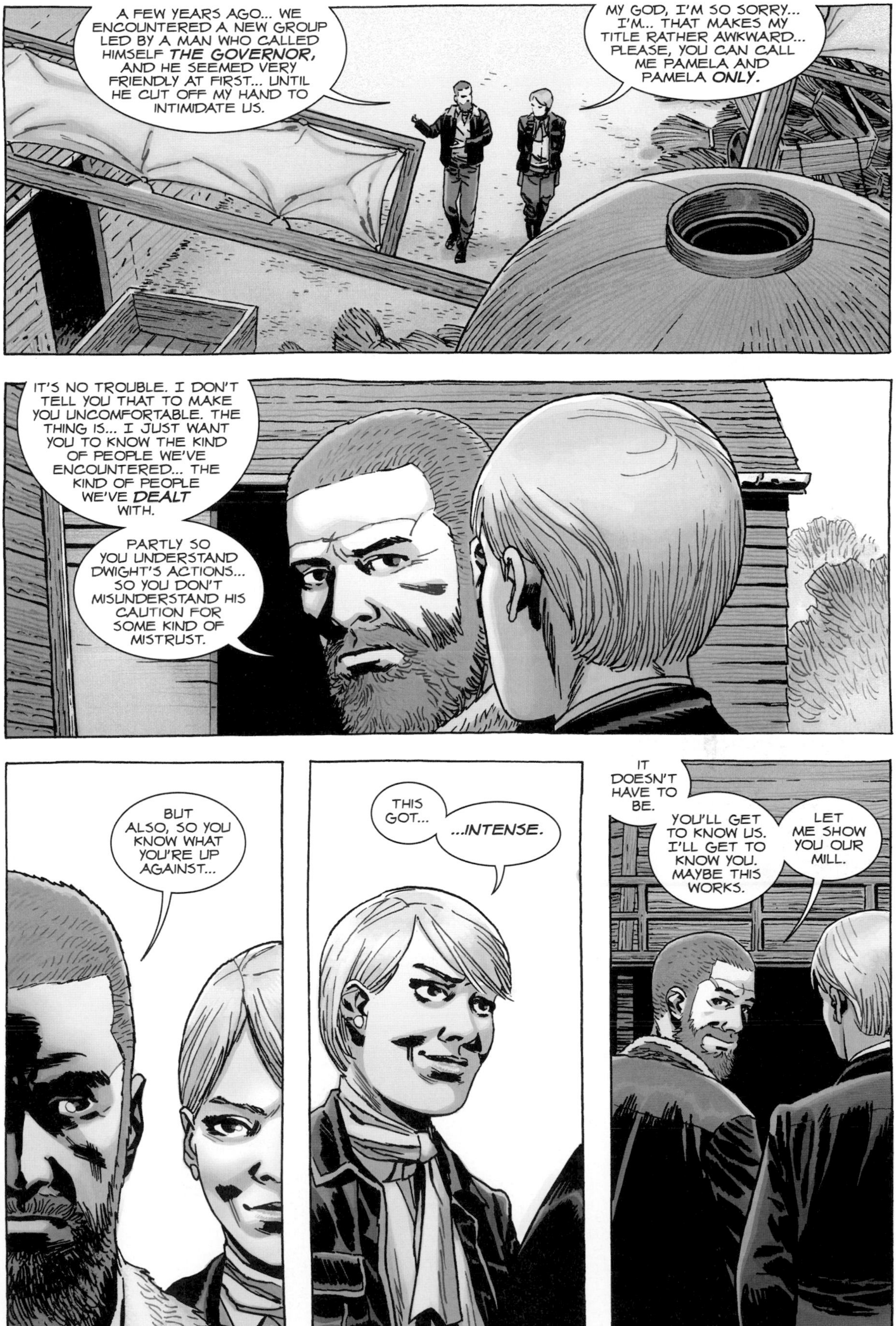
A FEW YEARS AGO... WE ENCOUNTERED A NEW GROUP LED BY A MAN WHO CALLED HIMSELF *THE GOVERNOR,* AND HE SEEMED VERY FRIENDLY AT FIRST... UNTIL HE CUT OFF MY HAND TO INTIMIDATE US.
MY GOD, I'M SO SORRY... I'M... THAT MAKES MY TITLE RATHER AWKWARD... PLEASE, YOU CAN CALL ME PAMELA AND PAMELA *ONLY.*
IT'S NO TROUBLE. I DON'T TELL YOU THAT TO MAKE YOU UNCOMFORTABLE. THE THING IS... I JUST WANT YOU TO KNOW THE KIND OF PEOPLE WE'VE ENCOUNTERED... THE KIND OF PEOPLE WE'VE *DEALT* WITH.
PARTLY SO YOU UNDERSTAND DWIGHT'S ACTIONS... SO YOU DON'T MISUNDERSTAND HIS CAUTION FOR SOME KIND OF MISTRUST.
BUT ALSO, SO YOU KNOW WHAT YOU'RE UP AGAINST...
THIS GOT...
...INTENSE.
IT DOESN'T HAVE TO BE.
YOU'LL GET TO KNOW US. I'LL GET TO KNOW YOU. MAYBE THIS WORKS.
LET ME SHOW YOU OUR MILL.

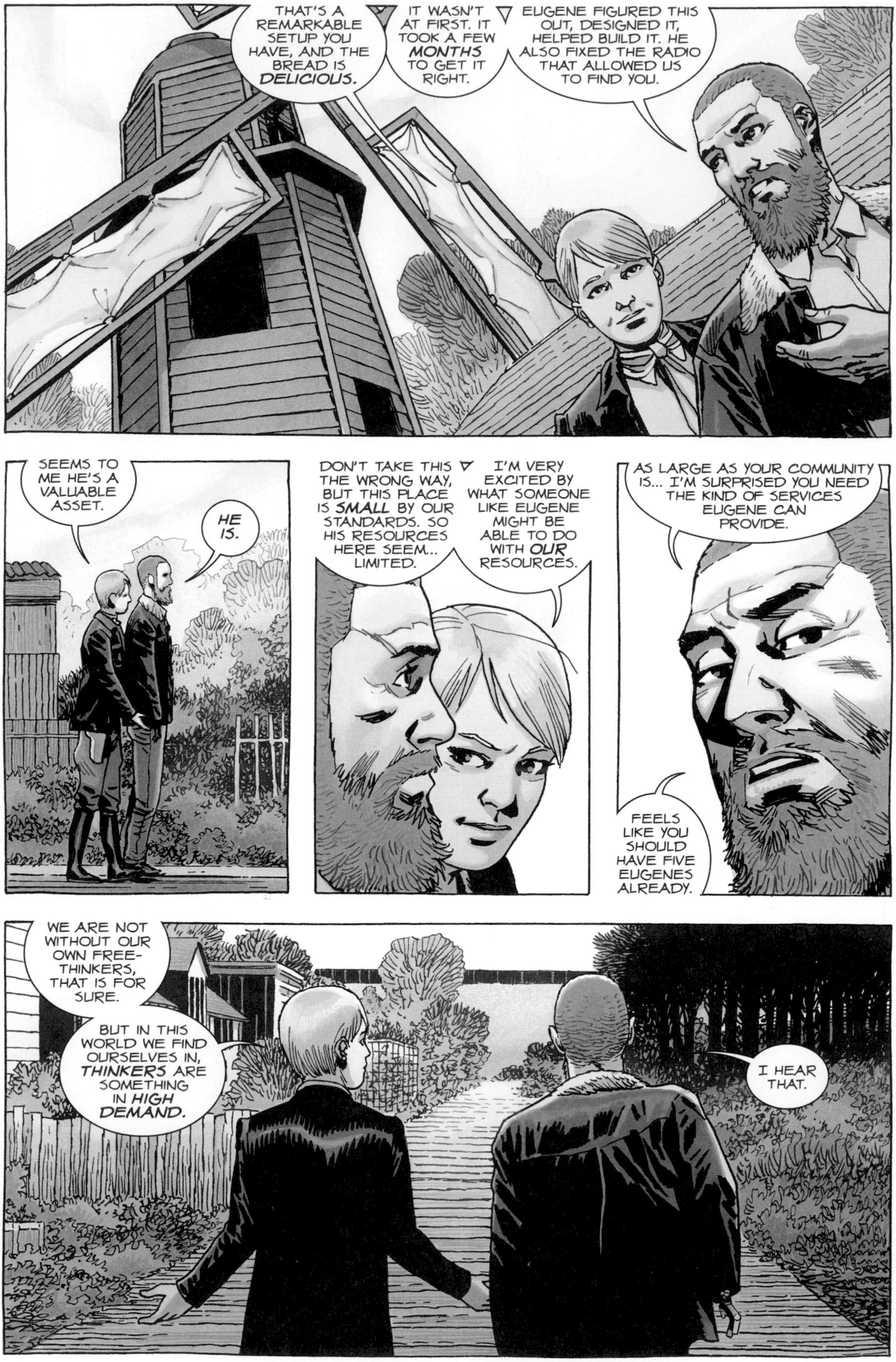
THAT'S A REMARKABLE SETUP YOU HAVE, AND THE BREAD IS DELICIOUS.
IT WASN'T AT FIRST. IT TOOK A FEW MONTHS TO GET IT RIGHT.
EUGENE FIGURED THIS OUT, DESIGNED IT, HELPED BUILD IT. HE ALSO FIXED THE RADIO THAT ALLOWED US TO FIND YOU.
SEEMS TO ME HE'S A VALUABLE ASSET.
HE IS.
DON'T TAKE THIS THE WRONG WAY, BUT THIS PLACE IS SMALL BY OUR STANDARDS. SO HIS RESOURCES HERE SEEM... LIMITED.
I'M VERY EXCITED BY WHAT SOMEONE LIKE EUGENE MIGHT BE ABLE TO DO WITH OUR RESOURCES.
AS LARGE AS YOUR COMMUNITY IS... I'M SURPRISED YOU NEED THE KIND OF SERVICES EUGENE CAN PROVIDE.
FEELS LIKE YOU SHOULD HAVE FIVE EUGENES ALREADY.
WE ARE NOT WITHOUT OUR OWN FREE-THINKERS, THAT IS FOR SURE.
BUT IN THIS WORLD WE FIND OURSELVES IN, THINKERS ARE SOMETHING IN HIGH DEMAND.
I HEAR THAT.

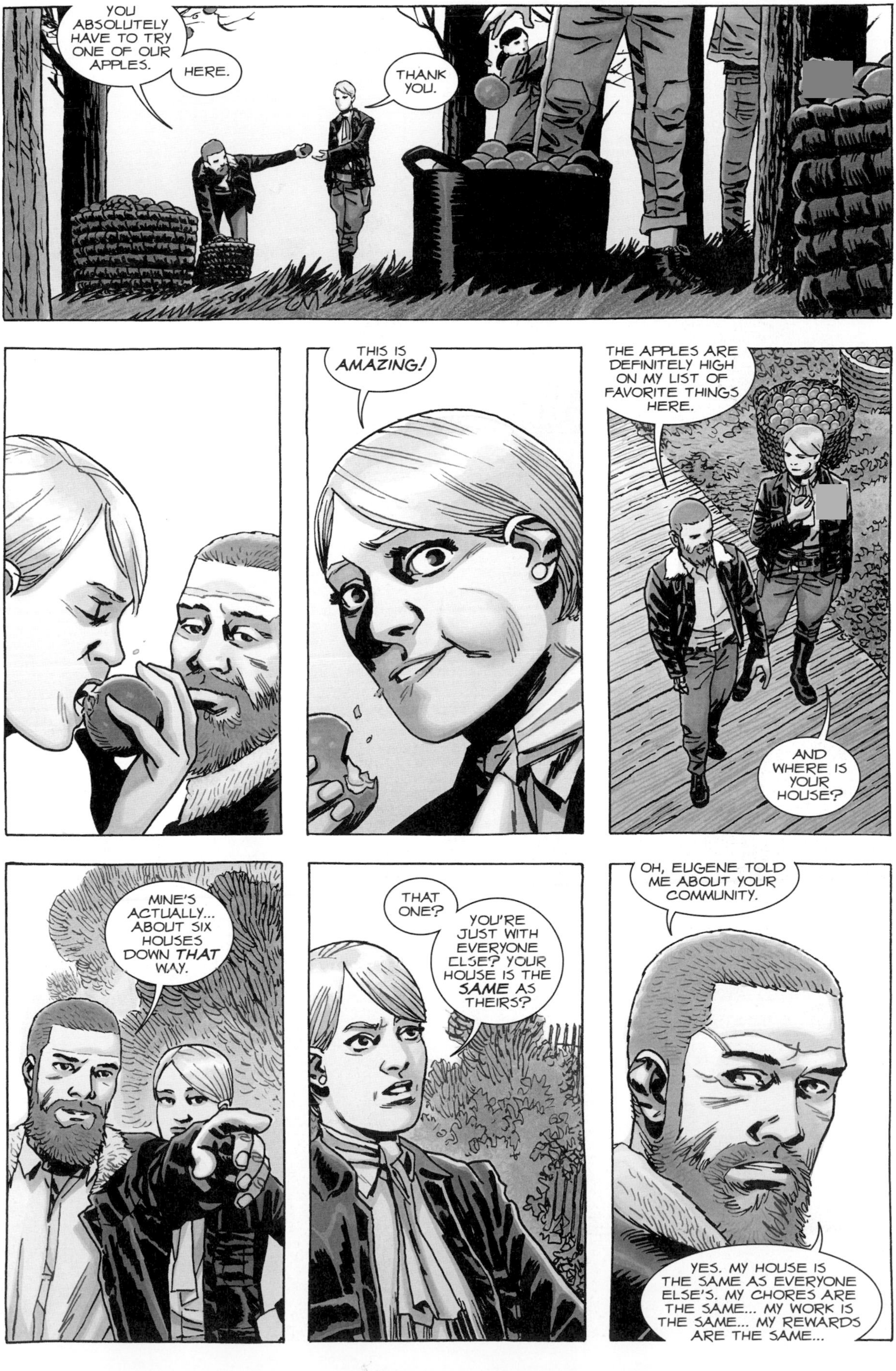
YOU ABSOLUTELY HAVE TO TRY ONE OF OUR APPLES.
HERE.
THANK YOU.
THIS IS AMAZING!
THE APPLES ARE DEFINITELY HIGH ON MY LIST OF FAVORITE THINGS HERE.
AND WHERE IS YOUR HOUSE?
MINE'S ACTUALLY... ABOUT SIX HOUSES DOWN THAT WAY.
THAT ONE?
YOU'RE JUST WITH EVERYONE ELSE? YOUR HOUSE IS THE SAME AS THEIRS?
OH, EUGENE TOLD ME ABOUT YOUR COMMUNITY.
YES. MY HOUSE IS THE SAME AS EVERYONE ELSE'S. MY CHORES ARE THE SAME... MY WORK IS THE SAME... MY REWARDS ARE THE SAME...

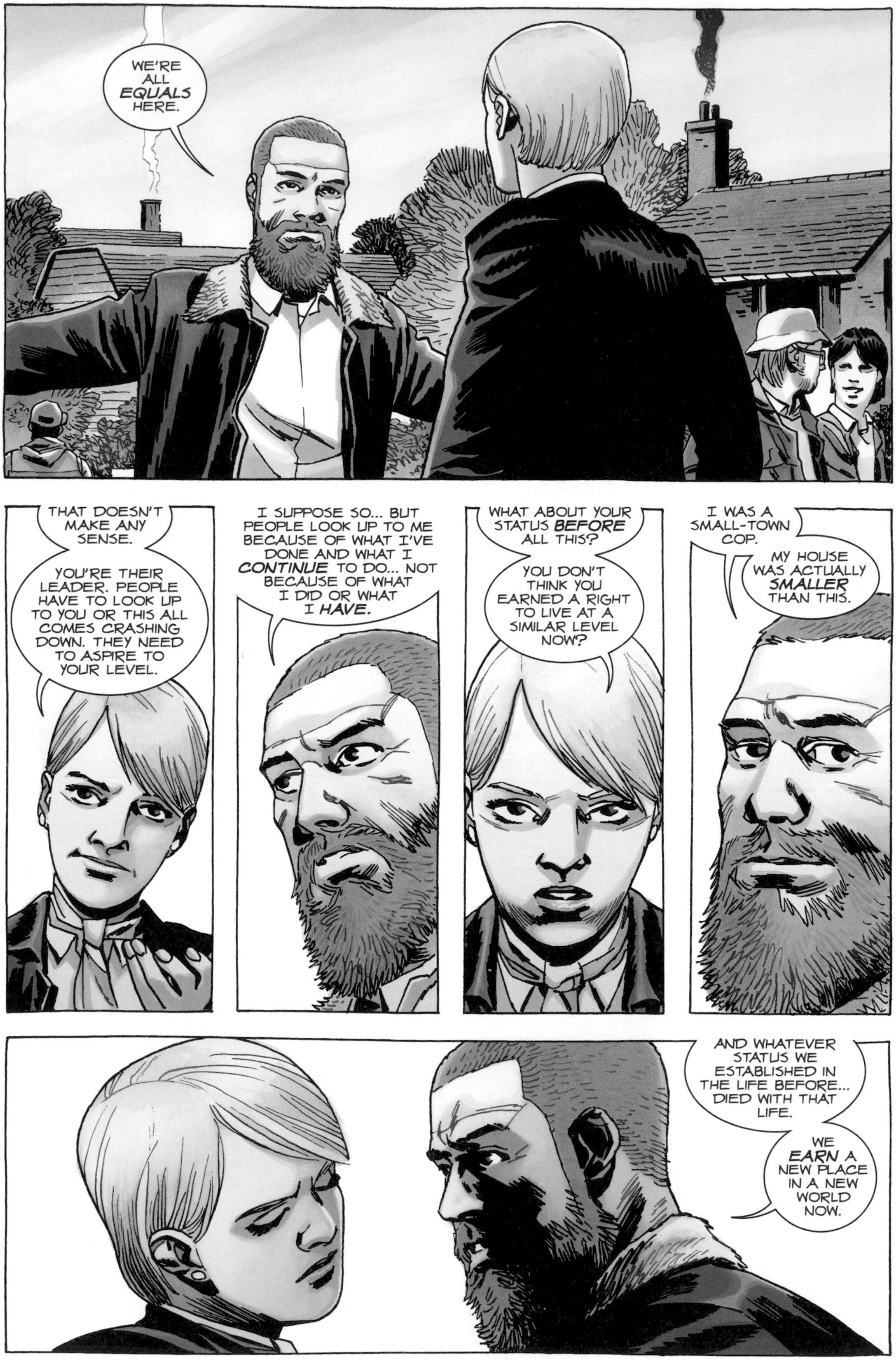
WE'RE ALL EQUALS HERE.
THAT DOESN'T MAKE ANY SENSE.
YOU'RE THEIR LEADER. PEOPLE HAVE TO LOOK UP TO YOU OR THIS ALL COMES CRASHING DOWN. THEY NEED TO ASPIRE TO YOUR LEVEL.
I SUPPOSE SO... BUT PEOPLE LOOK UP TO ME BECAUSE OF WHAT I'VE DONE AND WHAT I CONTINUE TO DO... NOT BECAUSE OF WHAT I DID OR WHAT I HAVE.
WHAT ABOUT YOUR STATUS BEFORE ALL THIS?
YOU DON'T THINK YOU EARNED A RIGHT TO LIVE AT A SIMILAR LEVEL NOW?
I WAS A SMALL-TOWN COP.
MY HOUSE WAS ACTUALLY SMALLER THAN THIS.
AND WHATEVER STATUS WE ESTABLISHED IN THE LIFE BEFORE... DIED WITH THAT LIFE.
WE EARN A NEW PLACE IN A NEW WORLD NOW.

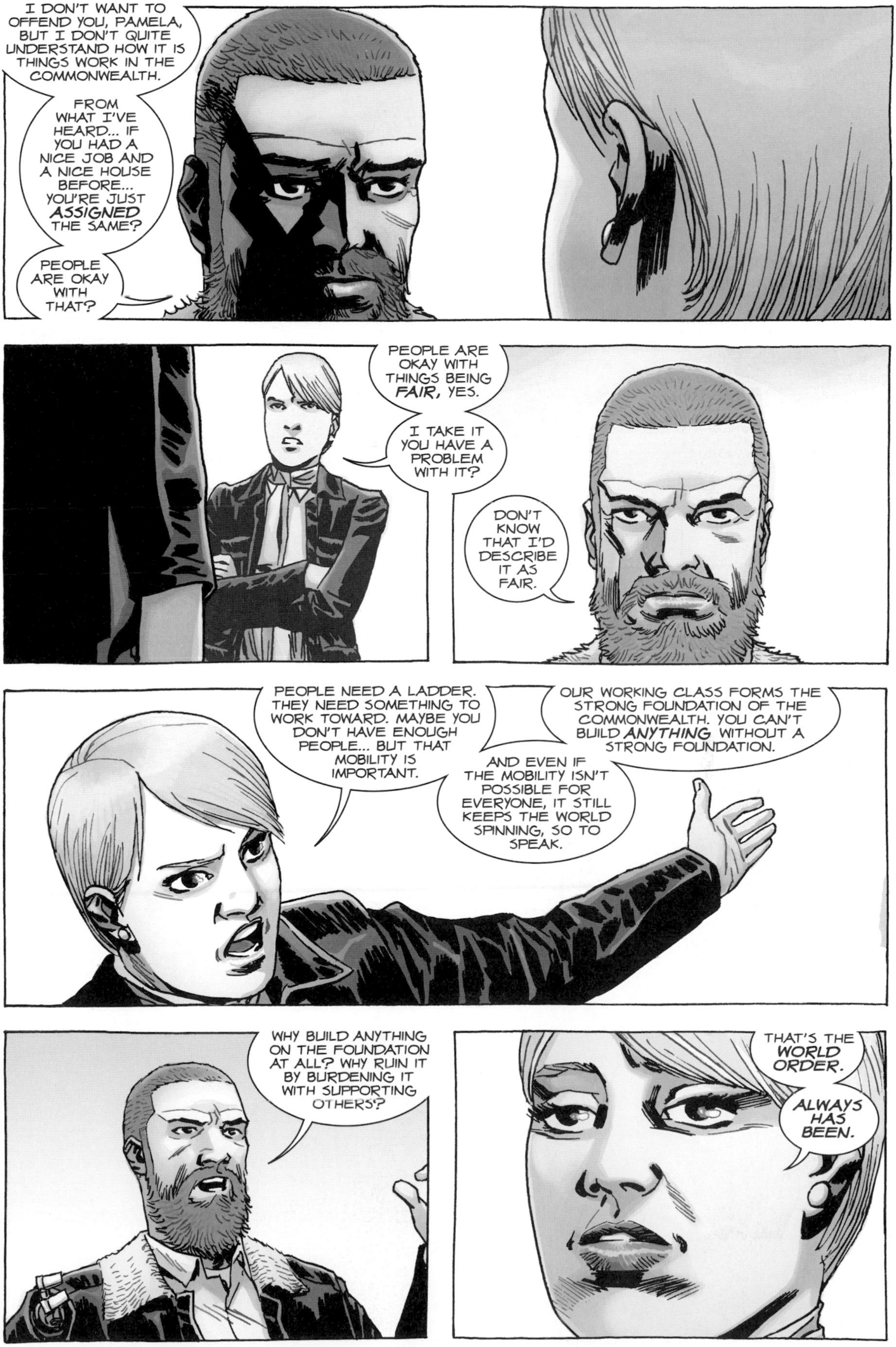

I DON'T WANT TO OFFEND YOU, PAMELA, BUT I DON'T QUITE UNDERSTAND HOW IT IS THINGS WORK IN THE COMMONWEALTH.
FROM WHAT I'VE HEARD... IF YOU HAD A NICE JOB AND A NICE HOUSE BEFORE... YOU'RE JUST ASSIGNED THE SAME?
PEOPLE ARE OKAY WITH THAT?
PEOPLE ARE OKAY WITH THINGS BEING FAIR, YES.
I TAKE IT YOU HAVE A PROBLEM WITH IT?
DON'T KNOW THAT I'D DESCRIBE IT AS FAIR.
PEOPLE NEED A LADDER. THEY NEED SOMETHING TO WORK TOWARD. MAYBE YOU DON'T HAVE ENOUGH PEOPLE... BUT THAT MOBILITY IS IMPORTANT.
AND EVEN IF THE MOBILITY ISN'T POSSIBLE FOR EVERYONE, IT STILL KEEPS THE WORLD SPINNING, SO TO SPEAK.
OUR WORKING CLASS FORMS THE STRONG FOUNDATION OF THE COMMONWEALTH. YOU CAN'T BUILD ANYTHING WITHOUT A STRONG FOUNDATION.
WHY BUILD ANYTHING ON THE FOUNDATION AT ALL? WHY RUIN IT BY BURDENING IT WITH SUPPORTING OTHERS?
THAT'S THE WORLD ORDER.
ALWAYS HAS BEEN.

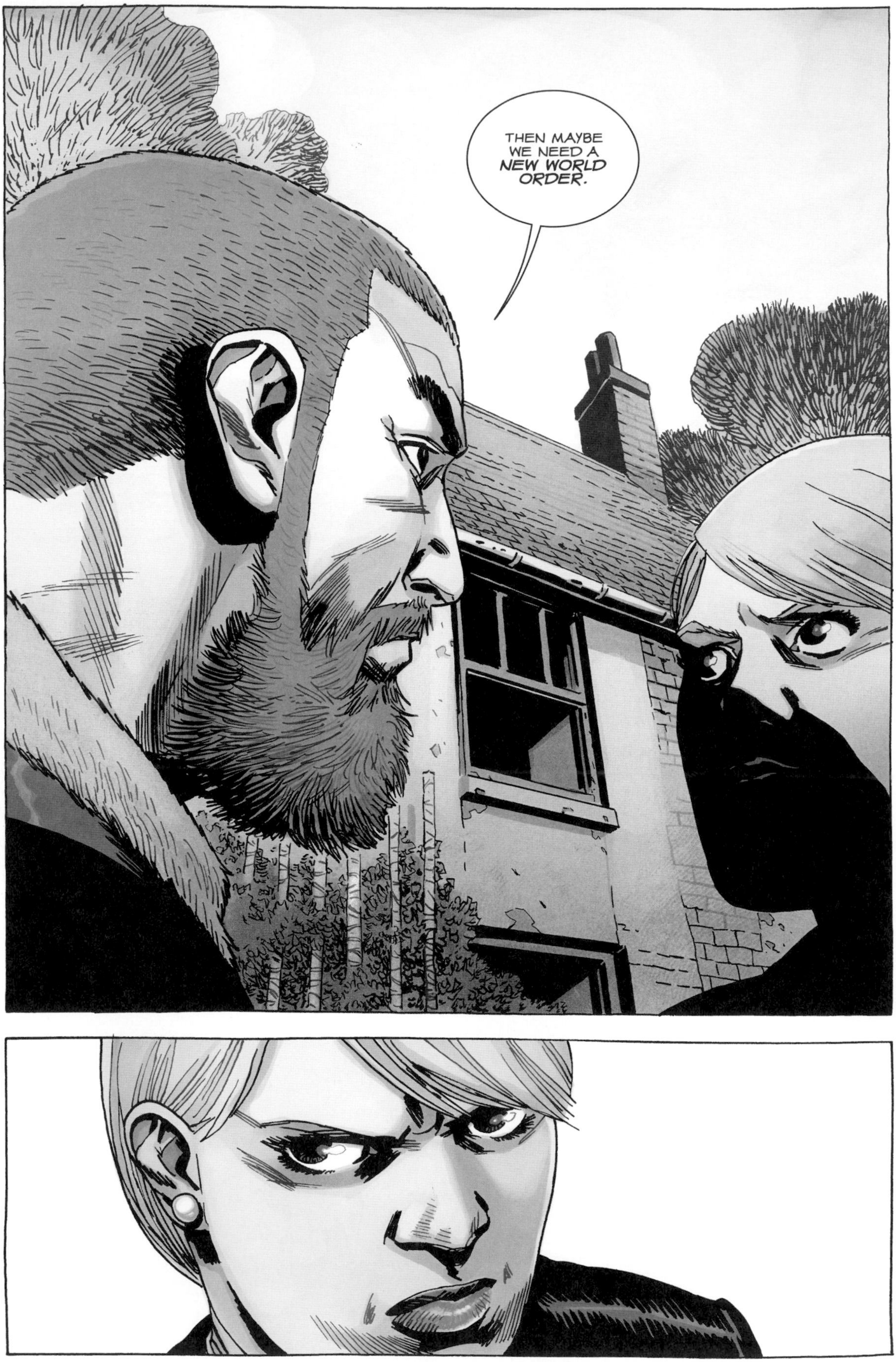
THEN MAYBE WE NEED A NEW WORLD ORDER.

TO BE CONTINUED...

FOR MORE OF THE WALKING DEAD

TRADE PAPERBACKS

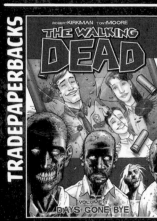

ROBERT KIRKMAN TONY MOORE

THE WALKING DEAD

VOLUME 1
DAYS GONE BYE

VOL. 1: DAYS GONE BYE TP
ISBN: 978-1-58240-672-5
$14.99
VOL. 2: MILES BEHIND US TP
ISBN: 978-1-58240-775-3
$14.99
VOL. 3: SAFETY BEHIND BARS TP
ISBN: 978-1-58240-805-7
$14.99
VOL. 4: THE HEART'S DESIRE TP
ISBN: 978-1-58240-530-8
$14.99
VOL. 5: THE BEST DEFENSE TP
ISBN: 978-1-58240-612-1
$14.99
VOL. 6: THIS SORROWFUL LIFE TP
ISBN: 978-1-58240-684-8
$14.99
VOL. 7: THE CALM BEFORE TP
ISBN: 978-1-58240-828-6
$14.99
VOL. 8: MADE TO SUFFER TP
ISBN: 978-1-58240-883-5
$14.99
VOL. 9: HERE WE REMAIN TP
ISBN: 978-1-60706-022-2
$14.99

VOL. 10: WHAT WE BECOME TP
ISBN: 978-1-60706-075-8
$14.99
VOL. 11: FEAR THE HUNTERS TP
ISBN: 978-1-60706-181-6
$14.99
VOL. 12: LIFE AMONG THEM TP
ISBN: 978-1-60706-254-7
$14.99
VOL. 13: TOO FAR GONE TP
ISBN: 978-1-60706-329-2
$14.99
VOL. 14: NO WAY OUT TP
ISBN: 978-1-60706-392-6
$14.99
VOL. 15: WE FIND OURSELVES TP
ISBN: 978-1-60706-440-4
$14.99
VOL. 16: A LARGER WORLD TP
ISBN: 978-1-60706-559-3
$14.99
VOL. 17: SOMETHING TO FEAR TP
ISBN: 978-1-60706-615-6
$14.99
VOL. 18: WHAT COMES AFTER TP
ISBN: 978-1-60706-687-3
$14.99

VOL. 19: MARCH TO WAR TP
ISBN: 978-1-60706-818-1
$14.99
VOL. 20: ALL OUT WAR PART ONE TP
ISBN: 978-1-60706-882-2
$14.99
VOL. 21: ALL OUT WAR PART TWO TP
ISBN: 978-1-63215-030-1
$14.99
VOL. 22: A NEW BEGINNING TP
ISBN: 978-1-63215-041-7
$14.99
VOL. 23: WHISPERS INTO SCREAMS TP
ISBN: 978-1-63215-258-9
$14.99
VOL. 24: LIFE AND DEATH TP
ISBN: 978-1-63215-402-6
$14.99
VOL. 25: NO TURNING BACK TP
ISBN: 978-1-63215-612-9
$14.99
VOL. 26: CALL TO ARMS TP
ISBN: 978-1-63215-917-5
$14.99
VOL. 27: THE WHISPERER WAR TP
ISBN: 978-1-5343-0052-1
$14.99

VOL. 28: A CERTAIN DOOM TP
ISBN: 978-1-5343-0244-0
$16.99
VOL. 29: LINES WE CROSS TP
ISBN: 978-1-5343-0497-0
$16.99
VOL. 30: NEW WORLD ORDER TP
ISBN: 978-1-5343-0884-8
$16.99
VOL. 1: SPANISH EDITION TP
ISBN: 978-1-60706-797-9
$14.99
VOL. 2: SPANISH EDITION TP
ISBN: 978-1-60706-845-7
$14.99
VOL. 3: SPANISH EDITION TP
ISBN: 978-1-60706-883-9
$14.99
VOL. 4: SPANISH EDITION TP
ISBN: 978-1-63215-035-6
$14.99

HARDCOVERS

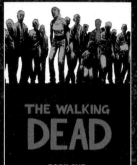

THE WALKING DEAD

BOOK ONE
a continuing story of survival horror.

BOOK ONE HC
ISBN: 978-1-58240-619-0
$34.99
BOOK TWO HC
ISBN: 978-1-58240-698-5
$34.99
BOOK THREE HC
ISBN: 978-1-58240-825-5
$34.99
BOOK FOUR HC
ISBN: 978-1-60706-000-0
$34.99
BOOK FIVE HC
ISBN: 978-1-60706-171-7
$34.99
BOOK SIX HC
ISBN: 978-1-60706-327-8
$34.99
BOOK SEVEN HC
ISBN: 978-1-60706-439-8
$34.99
BOOK EIGHT HC
ISBN: 978-1-60706-593-7
$34.99
BOOK NINE HC
ISBN: 978-1-60706-798-6
$34.99
BOOK TEN HC
ISBN: 978-1-63215-034-9
$34.99
BOOK ELEVEN HC
ISBN: 978-1-63215-271-8
$34.99
BOOK TWELVE HC
ISBN: 978-1-63215-451-4
$34.99
BOOK THIRTEEN HC
ISBN: 978-1-63215-916-8
$34.99
BOOK FOURTEEN HC
ISBN: 978-1-5343-0329-4
$34.99

COMPENDIUMS

The ultimate edition of The New York Times bestseller!

THE WALKING DEAD
COMPENDIUM ONE

Robert Kirkman · Charlie Adlard · Tony Moore · Cliff Rathburn

COMPENDIUM TP, VOL. 1
ISBN: 978-1-60706-076-5
$59.99
COMPENDIUM TP, VOL. 2
ISBN: 978-1-60706-596-8
$59.99
COMPENDIUM TP, VOL. 3
ISBN: 978-1-63215-456-9
$59.99

SPECIALTY BOOKS

THE WALKING DEAD

THE COVERS

THE WALKING DEAD: THE COVERS, VOL. 1 HC
ISBN: 978-1-60706-002-4
$24.99
THE WALKING DEAD: ALL OUT WAR HC
ISBN: 978-1-63215-038-7
$34.99
THE WALKING DEAD COLORING BOOK
ISBN: 978-1-63215-774-4
$14.99
THE WALKING DEAD RICK GRIMES COLORING BOOK
ISBN: 978-1-5343-0003-3
$14.99

OMNIBUS

THE WALKING DEAD

OMNIBUS, VOL. 1
ISBN: 978-1-60706-503-6
$100.00
OMNIBUS, VOL. 2
ISBN: 978-1-60706-515-9
$100.00
OMNIBUS, VOL. 3
ISBN: 978-1-60706-330-8
$100.00
OMNIBUS, VOL. 4
ISBN: 978-1-60706-616-3
$100.00
OMNIBUS, VOL. 5
ISBN: 978-1-63215-042-4
$100.00
OMNIBUS, VOL. 6
ISBN: 978-1-63215-521-4
$100.00
OMNIBUS, VOL. 7
ISBN: 978-1-5343-0335-5
$100.00